James Craig has worked as a journalist and consultant for more than thirty years. He lives in London with his family. His previous Inspector Carlyle novels, *London Calling; Never Apologise, Never Explain; Buckingham Palac**ie; A Man of Sorrows; Shoot to* *y's Hero; Acts of Violence; All* *ay Goodbye; Dying Days; Into th* *so* available from Constable.

Also by James Craig

Novels
London Calling
Never Apologise, Never Explain
Buckingham Palace Blues
The Circus
Then We Die
A Man of Sorrows
Shoot to Kill
Sins of the Fathers
Nobody's Hero
Acts of Violence
All Kinds of Dead
This is Where I Say Goodbye
Dying Days
Into the Valley
Circus Games

Short Stories
The Enemy Within
What Dies Inside
The Hand of God

The Taste of Blood

James Craig

CONSTABLE

CONSTABLE

First published in Great Britain in 2022 by Constable

Copyright © James Craig, 2022

1 3 5 7 9 10 8 6 4 2

A CIP catalogue record for this book is available from the British Library.

ISBN: 978-1-47213-277-2

Typeset in Times New Roman by Initial Typesetting Services, Edinburgh
Printed and bound in Great Britain by Clays Ltd, Elcograf S.p.A.

Papers used by Constable are from well-managed forests and other responsible sources.

MIX
Paper from
responsible sources
FSC® C104740

Constable
An imprint of
Little, Brown Book Group
Carmelite House
50 Victoria Embankment
London EC4Y 0DZ

An Hachette UK Company
www.hachette.co.uk

www.littlebrown.co.uk

For Catherine and Cate

*This is the sixteenth Carlyle novel.
Thanks for getting it done go to
Michael Doggart, Krystyna Green,
Rebecca Sheppard, Zoe Carroll
and Hazel Orme.*

'Life is first boredom, then fear.'

Philip Larkin

ONE

'I'm very sorry.'

'Hm.'

'I've been doing this a long time now. I've never seen anything like it happen before.'

'No.'

'It's very . . . unfortunate.'

'I can imagine.' What did the doctor expect her to say? Charlotte Monkseaton squirmed in her seat, wanting the conversation to end as quickly as possible. A young male nurse walked slowly down the corridor, carrying a bedpan as if it was an unexploded bomb. Grimacing, he nodded at them before ducking into a disabled toilet. There were some unpleasantly loud sounds, followed by a cistern flushing. She scrutinised the medic, who was avoiding eye contact. 'Was my father asleep the whole time?'

'Your father didn't notice a thing,' he insisted. 'Didn't even stir. The nurses cleaned him up in no time.'

Charlotte liked to think she was not the type of person to make too much of a fuss about things. Plus, all these NHS people were heroes and you shouldn't have a go at heroes. 'I suppose it could've been worse,' she said.

'It definitely could've been a lot worse.' Running a hand over the stubble on his chin, Dr Declan Brady bit his lower lip so hard it

1

started to bleed. The poor woman was taking the news with an almost unnatural calm and Brady didn't want to blow his grovelling apology by bursting into gales of hysterical, sleep-deprived laughter. 'That's certainly true.'

Brady was surprised she hadn't called PALS already. Patient Advice and Liaison Services liked nothing better than kicking the shit out of junior doctors at every opportunity. And this was certainly an opportunity. He tasted the blood in his mouth. 'It was all sorted out very quickly.'

In all honesty, the doctor didn't see how he could be deemed personally at fault for the assault on the woman's hapless father. Apart from anything else, he hadn't even been on the ward at the time. But Philip Monkseaton was his patient, as was Mr Monkseaton's attacker, one Samuel Fisher. Should PALS get involved, Brady would be the obvious scapegoat. 'We've moved Mr Fisher away from your father, put him in another ward, so there's no chance of it, erm, happening again.' Another bubble of nervous laughter bloomed in his throat and he had to fake a minor coughing fit to keep the giggles at bay.

'Are you all right?' The woman offered him a small plastic bottle of water from her bag.

'I'm good.' Brady waved a finger in the air. 'Just a frog in my throat, so to speak.'

She put the bottle back into her bag. 'Must be tough doing your job. Working all hours. The lack of resources. The pressure.'

'We just have to get on with it, but it has its moments, right enough.' Like now, for example. 'I knew what I was signing up for.' More or less. 'And I knew what I was getting myself into.' Up to a point. 'There's lots of medical experience in my family. My mum's a GP and I have a cousin who's a consultant at Guy's.'

'Still, it must be hard.'

Her feeble smile prompted him to agree. 'This is my third night shift on the trot. I reckon I've had about four hours' sleep this week, in total.' A minute ago, he was explaining how her vulnerable, elderly father had been assaulted in his hospital bed and now he was angling for sympathy. You bad lad, Declan. He bit his lip harder.

'You guys do such an amazing job. If it wasn't for all your hard work and dedication, the NHS would probably collapse.'

Look around you, love. The NHS collapsed a long time ago. 'Very kind of you to say so.' Brady felt the pager on his hip start to buzz. 'Sorry.' The doctor was on the move before he'd even checked the message. 'Don't worry, I'll be back to check in on your father, later on.'

By the time he found a moment to slip outside for a fag and a can of Red Bull, the misfortunes of Philip Monkseaton were but a distant memory. A bunch of drunken yobs had landed in A and E; it had taken the best part of three hours to attend to their injuries, while trying to avoid the impressive array of bodily secretions decanted at his feet. By four in the morning, Brady had entered a kind of dreamlike state, which made him wonder if what he was experiencing was real or just the figment of his imagination.

Philip Monkseaton was real enough. The eighty-nine-year-old had been the victim of a bizarre assault by the man in the next bed. Samuel Fisher, ninety-four, suffering from severe dementia, had mistaken Monkseaton for his late wife, Agnes. Showing impressive agility, not to mention a healthy sex drive, the nonagenarian had clambered onto Monkseaton in search of his conjugals. By the time Brady and two of the nurses had managed to pull him off, Fisher had ejaculated over the poor bastard's face.

Brady waited for the uproar to ebb. 'Who'd have imagined the poor man had so much juice in him?'

'Tsk.' A no-nonsense Polish nurse called Anna quickly

3

cleaned up the mess. 'It's not a joke, Declan. We could all get into big trouble for this.'

'You've gotta laugh, Anna,' the doctor counselled, 'or you're gonna cry.'

'Big, big trouble.' Anna quickly removed all traces of the assault from the victim's face. Amazingly, Mr Monkseaton had slept through the whole thing. Then again, the guy was currently so heavily medicated he was sleeping about twenty-two hours a day.

'There's nothing good or bad but thinking makes it so.'

'Why do you always talk such nonsense?'

'It's not nonsense,' Brady insisted. 'It's the Bard.' Going to university, it had been a toss-up between medicine and English literature. Much to his parents' delight, he'd given medicine the nod. 'Literature may be good for the soul,' as his father liked to put it, 'but it won't pay the bills.'

You were right there, Da. Then again, the NHS's largesse didn't exactly stretch far.

'All done.' Anna dropped a handful of sterilised wipes into a clinical waste bag and peeled off her latex gloves. 'Have you spoken to the next of kin?'

'I was thinking,' Brady looked around conspiratorially, 'we could forget this happened.'

'You can't do that.' Anna seemed genuinely outraged.

'Why not?' Brady lowered his voice. They were the only two people on the ward who were (a) below eighty, (b) awake and (c) compos mentis, but why take the risk of being overheard proposing a cover-up? 'What they don't know can't hurt them.'

Anna watched the victim, snoring peacefully in his bed. 'What happens if *he* complains?'

'The man can't even remember his own name,' Brady reasoned. 'Doesn't know what year it is. He's sound asleep. Worst-case scenario, he thinks he had a bad dream.' He watched a range of competing thoughts scroll across Anna's face. The nurse would want the unfortunate incident to be forgotten, but her dark Catholic soul would refuse to believe they could possibly get away with it. And they both knew the penalties for an unsuccessful cover-up could be far more severe than for the original offence.

'What happens if Mr Fisher does it again?'

Now *that* is a very good question, Brady conceded. No immediate answer came to mind.

The debate was ended by the reappearance of the second nurse, a big-boned Geordie girl called Laura.

'I've put Mr Fisher in one of the empty beds in the Wenger Ward and given him another sleeping pill.'

Brady approved of this course of action.

'And Mr Monkseaton's daughter's on the way,' Laura announced cheerily. 'You'd better get your story straight.'

Brady intercepted the daughter before she reached the ward. Visiting hours were long since over but, under the circumstances, he wasn't going to show her the door. The woman looked almost as tired as he felt. She apologised for being late and gave him a story about one of her kids being sick. Brady dialled up the sympathy and found her a seat. Taking a deep breath, he offered the most colourless account possible of the incident.

For several moments, Charlotte Monkseaton stared off into the middle distance, as if struggling to process the information. 'I suppose it could've been worse.'

What a great woman.

What a great line.

I must write that one down, Brady thought. Like a lot of junior doctors, he fancied he had a book in him, if not multiple books. And a comedy tour. Maybe a TV show. Definitely a podcast. Hospitals were a great place for drama, and who better to chronicle the toxic brew of hope and despair than a dashing young doctor on the front line?

As well as a notebook half filled with anecdotes, he had a title for his proposed page-turner: *Pills, Thrills and Bellyaches.* It was a shameless lift from the Happy Mondays – an eighties Manchester band he'd discovered through raiding the CD collection of his elder brother, Brian – but imitation was the highest form of flattery, right?

The original title for his memoir had been *This Is Going to Hurt.* Unfortunately, another scrubs-wearing scribe had nicked it, an English doctor who'd packed in medicine after losing a patient and gone off to work in television.

Despite his literary aspirations, however, Brady had no plans to quit. Forget the insane hours, the crap pay, the stupid punters, the lazy consultants and the nurses who wouldn't even consent to a quick hand job in a quiet moment on shift, being a doctor rocked. It was all he had ever wanted and more. Nothing could beat playing God, day in, day out. It was like being a stand-up comedian, but with the power of life and death over the audience.

Even God, however, couldn't survive on nothing but tobacco and energy drinks. Listening to his stomach rumble, Brady calculated that the last time he'd had a proper meal – which he defined as something hot, served on a plate – was five days ago. He'd gone round to see Ellen, his girlfriend's mother, and she'd microwaved him a chicken pie and chips. Suzie, the girlfriend, was currently in Madrid, on a four-month secondment for her employer, one of the 'big four' accountancy firms. Ellen, a single mum with only the one kid, wasn't very happy about the situation, but Brady was philosophical. Their long-distance relationship basically boiled down to a random selection of text messages and the occasional FaceTime call. Once you got your head round that, it had its advantages. At a distance of a thousand miles, it was almost impossible to fuck things up. You couldn't miss a dinner date if you were in a different country.

What was he rambling on about? Brady recognised the point in a shift where his brain was shutting down, going off on tangents and generally refusing to work normally. Flicking the stub of his cigarette into the gutter, he breathed in deeply, pulling the chill night air down into his lungs as he readied himself for one final push. Six more hours, then breakfast, then bed. It was almost like a half-day.

Heading back inside, Brady registered movement at the edge of his field of vision. Squinting past the glare of the car park's sodium lights, he watched a figure coming towards him. It was a woman, head bowed, arms folded. As she came closer, he saw she was wearing only a T-shirt and a pair of knickers.

Unusual, but doubtless capable of explanation.

The woman passed within ten feet of him, without acknowledging his presence. At this distance, it registered that her face was caked with blood and she had large bruises on both legs.

'Excuse me,' Brady called out to her, 'are you okay?'

The woman spat a gobbet of blood onto the tarmac before disappearing through the automatic doors.

It was turning into one of those nights. A battered woman emerging out of the darkness wasn't quite up there with Philip Monkseaton being sexually assaulted by a ninety-four-year-old sex pest, but it had potential. Finishing his Red Bull, Brady followed his latest patient inside to see what he could do to help.

TWO

The downstairs neighbours were arguing again. Yawning, Bruno Soutine shuffled into his kitchen, opened a cupboard above his head and pulled out a box of breakfast cereal. Filling a plastic bowl with muesli, he added flaxseed, a handful of blueberries, a chopped-up banana and some soya milk. Moving to the postage-stamp-sized kitchen table, he began methodically eating while checking his phone messages. Of the four clients booked in for this morning, one had cancelled, and another was looking to reschedule. Bruno texted the latter with a couple of possible slots later in the day and dropped the phone on top of a pristine copy of yesterday's *Standard*, which he hadn't got around to reading.

The argument under his feet died away, lost beneath the hum of the traffic outside. Bruno finished his food and made himself a cup of instant coffee. Black, no sugar.

His first mouthful was interrupted by the sound of the doorbell, harsh, flat and insistent. Resting his backside against the oven, Bruno made no move to answer it. Must be a delivery for the couple next door, he thought. It was annoying that they were forever using him as a free concierge service.

What to do with the time released by his unreliable clients? The temptation to go back to bed was considerable. On the other hand, his cleaning lady would be here in an hour. All in all, it would be best if he vacated the premises.

The bell went again, a series of short staccato bursts, which translated as *Answer the damn door. I'm not going to take no for an answer.*

Grumbling to himself, Bruno placed the mug on the draining board. 'All right, all right, I'm coming. Calm down.' As he entered the hallway, the doorbell went again, louder and longer than ever. '*Merde.*' He unhooked the chain and pulled open the door to find no one there. 'Hello?' He looked down to see a brown envelope sitting on the doormat on the landing. 'What's wrong with using the letterbox?' As he bent down to pick it up, a sharp blow behind his ear brought stars to his eyes. He pitched forward, and a second blow sent him down and out.

'This is a nasty one.' Sergeant Laura Nixon kept one eye on the young Irish doctor as she scribbled her notes. 'Not good.'

'Sexual violence is always nasty,' Declan Brady said earnestly. His shift should have ended more than an hour ago, he was starving and he could barely keep his eyes open. However, neither hunger nor tiredness stopped him noticing just how attractive the cop was. Tall, slim, blue eyes, blonde hair, the whole caboodle. And no sign of a wedding band either.

'Presumably you want to keep her here for a few days, for observation?'

'Definitely.' Brady stared at the cop, grinning like an eejit. His brain started playing tricks on him again, flooding his mind with images of Sergeant Nixon in his bed, naked as Nature intended. He tried to replace her with Suzie but his subconscious wasn't playing ball. 'For Christ's sake, man,' he hissed, 'get a grip of yersel'.'

'What?'

'Nothing.' Looking up from her notes, the cop blushed slightly. Oh, feck, she can see I fancy her rotten. 'Been a long night,' Brady offered lamely. 'Sometimes you start losing it. Talking to yourself and stuff.'

'Tell me about it.' Nixon's smile made him go weak at the knees. Then she surprised him by saying, 'My shift is pretty much over. Wanna grab some breakfast?'

Bruno Soutine came around, bound to the kitchen chair with thick black tape. He had the nasty taste of blood in his mouth and a monster headache. To his dismay, he'd also pissed himself. His only clean pair of jeans too. The last thing he wanted to do with his free time – assuming he had any left – was to visit the launderette.

A hand appeared on one shoulder, then on the other. Both were sheathed in latex, the kind of gloves worn by doctors. 'Relax.' His attacker stood behind him, out of Bruno's line of sight. 'Keep breathing. Nice and slowly.'

'What do you want?' Bruno tried to sound composed rather than scared.

'What do you think?' the man replied. 'I want the money back.'

'What money?' Bruno giggled nervously.

'You think it's funny?'

'I think you've made a mistake.'

'You're Bruno Soutine?'

Bruno considered lying, but what was the point? There was plenty of proof of his identity scattered around the flat. 'Yeah.'

'Then there's no mistake, my friend.' The man stepped in front of him: nothing unusual about him, nothing particularly athletic. Bruno was surprised the guy had been able to drag him back into the flat and sit him on the chair.

The man dropped a transparent plastic shopping bag onto the kitchen table. 'You tell me where the money is, right now, or the bag goes over your head.'

The flimsy bag was full of holes. Bruno imagined he'd die of old age before he suffocated. This was just a performance, an act designed to scare him. He felt a modicum of confidence return to his voice. 'Tell me about the money.'

'Don't fuck about.' The man was clearly English, but his accent gave no further clues about his identity. 'I'm not here for a chat. Give me the money you nicked and you get to live.' He pointed at the bag. 'Suffocation is very unpleasant. Not to mention slow.'

'You've made a mistake,' Bruno repeated. 'I haven't stolen any money.' If the guy wanted to stick the bag over his head, let him. Just get him out of the flat before Uloma turned up. Absolute worst case, the cleaning lady would get the bag off his head and call the police, see if they could work out what the fuck this was all about.

'Last chance.'

'Look, honestly, if I had any clue about what you were talking about, I would tell you. I don't owe anyone any money – I don't even have an overdraft at the bank.'

'If that's the way you want it.'

Bruno felt his confidence shatter into a billion pieces as the man placed a bottle of pills on the table. 'What're those?'

'Zopiclone.' The man turned the bottle around so he could read the label. 'Heavy-duty sleeping pills.'

'And what're they for?' Bruno almost choked on the question.

'To make sure you don't mess up your suicide.'

The breakfast rush at Romanov's Café was still some way off and they had a four-top to themselves. Pleasantly full, Declan Brady settled back in his chair. 'Quite a night, huh?' He had spared Laura Nixon the Philip Monkseaton story. It was a good tale, but not necessarily to everyone's taste and he didn't want to alienate the pretty cop. Over the years, Brady had learned the hard way that he had a niche sense of humour. Anyway, Monica Seppi, the woman who had appeared in the car park in nothing but a T-shirt and knickers, had given them more than enough to talk about.

The police sergeant had established the woman's back story with a minimum of fuss. Seppi was a twenty-eight-year-old Romanian who had worked in the UK for almost ten years. She told Nixon how she had been chatting to a couple of guys in a pub and then things went woozy. She suspected her drink had been spiked. They took her back to a flat and gave her more to drink. She blacked out. When she woke up, she was alone, on a dirty bed, covered with cuts and bruises. The smell of bodily fluids had made her gag. Crawling out of the place on her hands and knees, she had fled down the street.

'These assaults are far too common,' Nixon declared.

Brady gave a carefully calibrated response: not too empathetic, not too jaded. 'She didn't know the men who attacked her?'

'She says not.' Nixon looked doubtful.

'You don't believe her?'

Nixon wasn't totally convinced by the woman's story. 'But, then again, why would she lie? It wouldn't make any sense.'

How many people who end up in A and E can make any sense? By Brady's estimation, a pretty small minority.

'I need to go and write up my report.' The sergeant finished her coffee and signalled at a passing waiter for the bill. 'And I'll run a check on recent date-rape cases.'

Reaching for his wallet, Brady prayed his credit card would work. He had a vague sense of last month's bill not getting paid and his limit being breached. 'Isn't your shift over?'

'I can get overtime.'

'Handy.'

'I'm lucky. My boss'll approve it.' The bill arrived. Nixon scanned it while Brady dropped his card on the tip tray. 'We'll go halves,' she said briskly, not looking at him. 'I always pay my own way on the first date.'

'What about the second? Does the same rule apply?' The words were out of his mouth before his brain had time to engage.

'It depends.' Reaching into her pocket, she pulled out a card of her own.

He had to ask. 'Depends on what?'

Nixon kept her face expressionless. 'On whether it's any good or not.'

Out on the street, Brady basked in the euphoria of his card having not been rejected. 'Shall I give you a call?' he asked hopefully.

'I know where to find you. I'll pop by tomorrow to see how Monica's doing. Victim Support will be in touch, too. Hopefully, she'll remember a bit more about what happened, like where the flat was.'

'It couldn't have been too far from the hospital,' Brady mused. 'Her feet weren't so bad.'

'I think her feet are the least of her worries.' Nixon started off down the street. 'I'll see you tomorrow.'

Brady tried to remember his rota pattern. 'If I'm not there, get them to page me.' Exhaustion mixed with lust as he watched her disappear. Whistling a tuneless approximation of 'Step On', he strolled back to the hospital to pick up his car.

In the act of paying the extortionate parking fee, Brady was collared by Anna. The nurse was in a state of some agitation. 'It's terrible,' she cried. 'You have to stop it.'

Oh, fuck, Brady thought. Mr Fisher's gone and done it again. PALS'll rip me a new arsehole.

'They've handcuffed her to the bed,' Anna sobbed, 'like an animal. Why? What has she done?'

'Back up a minute. My brain's in shutdown mode.' Brady retrieved his amazingly still functioning credit card from the ticket machine. 'Who are we talking about here?'

Anna said something in Polish that Brady imagined might be questioning his intellectual capacity. 'Monica, the woman who came in last night, the police have just arrested her. They say she's an illegal. You need to come and sort this out.'

'But I've paid for my parking.' Brady looked hopelessly at the ticket sticking out from the machine.

'Come,' Anna repeated, taking him by the arm. 'You can get your car later.'

'All right, all right.' Grabbing the ticket, Brady let himself be led back inside. They took the lift in silence to the third floor where Anna pointed him in the direction of the Crespo Ward.

'She's in one of the rooms at the far end.'

'Aren't you coming too?' Brady's tone made it clear he didn't want to do this alone.

'I have to get home.' Anna pointed at a clock on the wall. 'The kids.'

Kids are the greatest excuse ever invented, Brady reflected. I must get some.

'I have to go.' Anna retreated into the lift, pressing the button for the ground floor in an attempt to prevent any further debate. 'Text me with how you get on.'

The main Crespo Ward was empty. It had been closed for more than six months as a result of the hospital administration's inability to keep a vomiting bug under control. The Crespo's private rooms, however, were still in occasional use. Brady found Monica Seppi in the first he came to, handcuffed to the bed by her ankle. Doped up since Brady had gone off shift, she showed no sign of recognising him. The doctor turned his attention to the sallow-faced woman perched on a chair in the corner, playing on her phone. 'Who are you?'

'Who are you?' was the hostile response.

Without his lab coat, Brady realised he didn't look the part. He fumbled with his ID. 'What are you doing with my patient?'

Putting away her phone, the woman came up with an ID of her own. 'Immigration Enforcement.'

'Home Office Na—' Brady choked off the insult before it fully escaped his mouth.

The woman gave him her best SS scowl.

'I'm not an illegal,' Seppi mumbled sleepily. 'You have no right to do this.'

Brady pointed at the handcuffs. 'There's no need for those. Take them off.'

'We need you to sanction the patient's release,' the woman said robotically, 'so she can be taken to a Home Office facility, ahead of a deportation hearing.'

Planting his feet apart and folding his arms, Brady adopted what he imagined – and hoped – was his most intimidating professional persona. 'My patient has been the victim of an extremely violent attack. She has serious physical and emotional injuries and needs to stay here, in my care, for the foreseeable future.'

Muttering to herself, the woman got to her feet. 'Play the martyr if you want, Irishman. I'll go and find your boss, get him to sign the release forms.'

'He's probably already on the golf course.' Brady watched the woman disappear through the door.

As the door slammed, he looked at his patient in mute helplessness. All he could do was contact Nixon and see if she could do anything to call off the dogs. He pulled out his phone, then realised he didn't have the sergeant's details. He didn't even know what police station she worked at. 'Fucking hell, Laura,' he groaned, 'why didn't you give me your bloody phone number?'

THREE

'Is that real?' Inspector Karen O'Sullivan looked at the V40 fragmentation grenade sitting on Commander John Carlyle's desk with some concern.

'Not any more,' the commander reassured her. 'The bomb squad made it safe.' He picked up the grenade and weighed it in his hand. 'They took out the explosive and let me keep it as a little memento.'

'I don't suppose it's every day someone sends you a bomb in the post.' The inspector took a seat.

'It's pretty unusual,' Carlyle joked, putting the grenade back on the desk, 'even for me.'

'Has there been any sign of Dawson?' Nick Dawson was a rogue undercover cop who'd disappeared after sending Carlyle his little present.

'Not a dickie bird.' Carlyle was relaxed about that. He was sure Dawson wouldn't be coming back. It suited everyone that the man was gone and forgotten.

'Anyway, we're all glad you're okay.'

'Me too.'

'Having a commander on the premises is seen as a vote of confidence in the station,' O'Sullivan continued. 'People hope it means Charing Cross isn't likely to get closed down any time soon. We're all pissed off with the cuts.'

'I wouldn't read much into my presence,' Carlyle advised. 'Although, hopefully, the most recent set of closures will be the last, for a while at least.'

'Let's hope so, or we'll end up with no bloody police stations left.'

'No police stations, no cops, just a dozen CCTV cameras for every person in London.'

'It's a complete joke,' O'Sullivan spat.

Carlyle could only agree. 'You can't police a city by remote control.'

'At least you took a stand.' O'Sullivan recalled how Carlyle had fought the commissioner, Virginia Thompson, in an unsuccessful attempt to stop a bunch of police stations being sold off on the cheap.

'Another great triumph,' Carlyle said sarcastically.

'The word was you were in deep shit.' Inspector O'Sullivan lowered her voice. 'People thought you were heading out the door.' She paused. 'Before you were nearly blown up.'

'Reports of my death are always greatly exaggerated.' Carlyle gestured at the grenade. 'That thing was never going to go off unless you pulled the pin out.'

'Yeah, but you didn't know that, did you?'

'No.' Carlyle thought back to the moment when he'd ripped open the envelope and the grenade had fallen out. He'd watched in horror as the thing had rolled across his desk and fallen onto the floor. At least, to his eternal relief, he hadn't soiled himself. In truth, he hadn't reacted at all.

'And you don't care that Dawson's still in the wind?'

'What's gone, and what's past help, should be past caring.'

'The wisdom of John Carlyle?'

'The wisdom of William Shakespeare. I'm more a *Don't let the bastards grind you down* type of guy.' Having had enough chit-chat, he asked, 'What can I do for you?'

'I just wanted to say we're looking forward to your talk.'

Carlyle looked askance. 'What talk?'

'You're scheduled to say a few words to the troops tomorrow night, followed by a Q and A. I sorted it out with your assistant last week.'

Bloody Joaquin. Carlyle cursed his PA. 'News to me,' he grumped.

'I'll be there,' O'Sullivan promised. 'The childcare's been sorted out.'

Carlyle recalled the inspector was a single mum with one kid, or maybe two. 'How's the family?'

'They're fine,' O'Sullivan confirmed cheerily. 'My daughter's about to start secondary school.' She mentioned an all-girls school in North London. 'And George, my boy, is doing his GCSEs. How's Alice getting on?'

'Good.' Carlyle had no recollection of mentioning his own daughter to the inspector but supposed he must have done at some point. He padded out his answer with 'She's enjoying Imperial. Wants to be a chemical biologist, whatever that is.'

'You must be very proud.'

Relieved, more like. Once the inspector had left, he called in Joaquin and cancelled his talk until further notice. The PA retaliated by dumping a large bundle of papers on his desk. 'This should keep you busy,' he said maliciously.

With great reluctance, Carlyle took possession of the printed material.

'There's the latest performance review of the station,' Joaquin explained, 'details of the major outstanding cases currently on our books. And a few other matters you should be aware of.'

I'll start with the 'other matters', Carlyle decided, after I've got myself a coffee.

As he beat a retreat, Joaquin issued the dread call, 'One more thing.'

Summoning his saint-like reserves of patience, Carlyle tarried in the doorway. 'Yes?'

'What colour do you want your office painted?'

'No more decorators,' the commander said. 'They keep following me around. It's impossible to get any work done.' He'd had the same problem at his old station. The fact that Paddington Green had been on the brink of being closed down at the time hadn't prevented some bureaucrat from organising its complete redecoration. Tiring of Carlyle's inability to decide on a colour scheme, the workmen had finally decorated his office with leftover stock from the repainting of the cells. A disgusting green called Memories of England, if he remembered correctly. Under no circumstances did he want a repeat. 'It's fine the way it is.'

Joaquin was unmoved. 'You don't have a choice. It's in the budget.'

After issuing a stream of curses, Carlyle opted for white. 'Nothing fancy.'

A café called Grind had recently opened near the police station. The place looked like a hipster hell, transplanted from Hoxton, with prices to match. Nevertheless, Carlyle gave it a go and was rewarded with good coffee and wonderful doughnuts. Better still, a relative dearth of patrons meant the place could feasibly act as an alternative office, away from Joaquin's disapproving gaze.

Settling in with a second Americano, Carlyle began looking through the papers the PA had given him. There was a letter from the Disciplinary Commission confirming his Written Warning. Having survived going head-to-head with the commissioner, he had come a cropper over his *derogatory and unprofessional behaviour* towards a Welsh inspector called Henry Jones. But it was a smack on the wrist, nothing more. You had to collect three Written Warnings before things got serious; since this was his first in several decades on the job, Carlyle felt he was doing okay. Plus, Jones had left the Met for a job with the Dyfed-Powys CID in Aberystwyth, so their paths were hardly likely to cross again. Carlyle happily tore up the letter and dumped it in the café's bin.

The latest missive from Human Resources touting the merits of early retirement was similarly filed in the rubbish. Elevation to the rank of commander had inflated his salary, and hence his pension, to the level where a reasonably comfortable retirement appeared well within his grasp. Rather than spreading a warm glow through his being, however, the idea worried him. What the hell would he do if he retired? The most likely answer was 'bugger-all', which was an extremely grim prospect.

Having dealt with the personal stuff, Carlyle turned his attention to a file marked *Private & Confidential*. Underneath was the instruction, *Not to be removed from CXPS under any circumstances.*

'Ho-hum.' Carlyle looked around. There were only two other customers on the premises, both staring intently at their phones. Deciding the Met's secrets were safe enough, he opened the file. Mostly, it contained stats about Charing Cross's performance, relative to the other remaining police stations in London. There were lots of graphs, pie charts and data on subjects ranging from absenteeism to clean-up rates for different types of crime. Charing Cross was a mid-table performer, not the best but by no means the worst. They'll never close it down, he concluded, thinking back to his conversation with Karen O'Sullivan. Wouldn't make any sense at all.

At the back of the file was a summary of current open investigations. Most of them were banal – phone thefts, domestics and shoplifting – but one caught his eye: 'Bruno Soutine. Suspicious suicide.'

O'Sullivan's name was against the case. Carlyle imagined the inspector's dilemma: call it a suicide and get it off your desk, or launch a murder investigation and come under immense pressure to get a quick result. Tough call.

Finishing his coffee, he tidied up the papers and left.

Standing in the doorway, arms folded, Declan Brady glowered at the empty bed.

'They took her away a couple of hours ago.' Anna was clearly upset. 'Not long after I came on shift.'

Bollocks. After his spat with the immigration woman, the doctor had gone home and crashed out. Now he was too late.

'Two men and a woman,' the nurse continued. 'They put Monica in the back of a car. When I asked where they were taking her, the woman told me to mind my own business.'

'It's like the bloody Gestapo,' Brady hissed, 'or . . .' he tried to come up with another example '. . . Pinochet's Chile. I mean, the poor woman's been disappeared. It's bloody unbelievable in this day and age.'

Anna expressed a similar sentiment. 'I called the police, but no one turned up.'

Brady cursed Laura Nixon. The pretty sergeant was looking very much like a busted flush, having failed to make good on her promise to return to the hospital to check on Monica Seppi's wellbeing. He struggled to summon up a scintilla of the excitement he'd felt when they'd first met.

Anna gestured in the direction of the lifts. 'Here's your girlfriend now. Maybe she can tell us what's going on.'

Brady turned to see Nixon walking down the corridor, a coffee cup in each hand. Out of uniform, in jeans with a leather jacket over a white T-shirt, she wore no make-up and had her hair pulled back into a ponytail. Her smile sent a jolt of energy through his chest, which almost lifted him off his feet. He imagined his dick beginning to get hard inside his grubby trunks. Delusions brought on by exhaustion, my arse.

'I'll leave you two to it,' Anna whispered, 'but don't mess the bed – we've got a new patient going in there in an hour. You can tell me everything later.' Grinning at Nixon, she scuttled off.

'Hey.' The policewoman held up the coffees for Brady's inspection. 'I've got a flat white or a double macchiato.'

A good rule of thumb on the ward was always to consume whatever gives you the most undiluted caffeine. Brady took the macchiato. 'Thanks.'

Nixon stared at the empty bed. 'You've moved Monica to a general ward?'

'Not exactly.' Brady explained what had happened, pausing to gulp down his coffee.

'A kidnapping.' Nixon was as outraged as the doctor himself.

'Not when the government does it, apparently.'

Nixon turned her anger inward. 'I should have come back sooner. Maybe I could have stopped them.'

'I don't know about that,' Brady countered, all thoughts about the sergeant being a busted flush having flown from his mind. 'It might have made things worse.'

'How?'

Brady had no idea. 'What are we going to do now?'

'I know who to call.'

'Ghostbusters?' His Pavlovian response brought him a smack on the arm.

'Be serious.'

'Sorry.' The urge to kiss her was almost overwhelming, but Nixon was already heading back down the hall.

'I know who to call,' she repeated. 'Don't worry, we'll get Monica back.'

Carlyle stalked the third floor of the police station, looking for O'Sullivan. Inevitably, the inspector was nowhere to be seen. Instead, he found himself face to face with an old ally.

'Inspector, nice to see you again.' Rita Vicedo's smile shone brightly as she shook his hand. Vicedo, a Catholic nun, ran an organisation called the International Network Against Human Trafficking. The Network regularly worked with the authorities to support trafficking victims caught up in police raids.

'They gave me a promotion. I'm a commander now.' Carlyle wondered how much longer he'd have to keep correcting people about his rank. He noticed the pass hanging from the woman's neck. 'I see you've joined the Community Safety Accreditation Scheme.' Recently introduced, it gave limited powers and access to non-police organisations whose work contributed to public order and security.

Vicedo fiddled with her ID. 'It helps when I'm working with you guys. I don't have to go around explaining who I am all the time.'

'Makes sense.'

A fresh-faced blonde woman appeared from behind Vicedo, and introduced herself as Sergeant Laura Nixon.

'Nice to meet you, Sergeant.'

Nixon gave Vicedo an indecipherable look. 'You two know each other?'

Carlyle confirmed it was so. 'What brings you back to Charing Cross?' he asked the nun.

'We're helping Laura track down a woman called Monica Seppi. It seems she was caught up in Operation Peregrino.'

'Operation Peregrino's the most recent round-up of foreigners by Immigration Enforcement,' Nixon chipped in.

Carlyle was already wishing he'd never asked.

'And Monica Seppi is a sexual-assault victim whose case I'm currently investigating. She was being treated in hospital when she was taken to an unknown location, pending deportation from the UK. The Home Office has declined to inform us as to where she is being held. I'm hoping Rita's contacts might be able

23

to help us where official lines of communication have failed.'

'So, we have one government agency refusing to talk to another and a, erm, private citizen having to try to step in and sort things out?'

'That sums it up,' Nixon replied. 'Not only is Monica Seppi the victim of horrible crime, she is a Romanian citizen. She came to the UK under her own steam and has been working here legally.'

'So why did the Immigration people pick her up?'

'That's something else the Home Office won't tell us,' Nixon grumbled.

'Maybe she lost her passport when she was attacked,' Vicedo speculated.

'She wouldn't necessarily take it with her on a night out,' Nixon said. 'But she certainly didn't have any papers when she arrived at hospital. When she was picked up, she couldn't immediately prove she wasn't illegal.'

You should keep an open mind. Carlyle wasn't too impressed by the sergeant's willingness to take the attacked woman's story at face value. On the other hand, Nixon's obvious brio encouraged him to cut her some slack. He turned back to Vicedo. 'It doesn't sound like the kind of case the Network deals with.'

'This is a favour for Laura,' Vicedo confirmed. 'She's supported us in the past, so when she came to me, I was happy to help.'

'Ridiculous as it sounds, Rita's our best bet for tracking down a woman lost in the system.' Nixon looked at Carlyle hopefully. 'Unless you could pull a few strings.'

'Let's see how Rita gets on before I jump in. It's never a good idea to escalate these things too quickly.' There was no way Carlyle was going to get involved with the Home Office. 'Keep me informed. My office is on the top floor. It's getting refurbished, apparently, so give it a week or so and we'll be ready for visitors.' He pretended not to notice the disappointed look on Nixon's face. 'I was looking for Inspector O'Sullivan. You wouldn't know where she is, would you?'

'She had to go out. I think there was some kind of problem with her kid at school.'

'Nothing serious, I hope.'

The sergeant displayed the sullenness of a non-parent. 'Dunno.'

'When she gets back, can you tell her I'd like a word about the Bruno Soutine case?'

'I've been working with the inspector on that.' Nixon's expression brightened slightly. 'What d'you need to know?'

Vicedo took this as her cue to leave. Carlyle perched on the edge of an unused desk. 'It's listed as a suicide. Is that right?'

'Looked like it,' was Nixon's verdict. 'Soutine took a fistful of sleeping pills and put a plastic bag over his head. Not exactly how I'd do it, but it got the job done.' She pushed out her lower lip. 'The cleaning lady found him. She was in a right state about it. We made all the standard enquiries, but they didn't throw up any major red flags. Didn't throw up much at all, to be honest. The guy seemed to be living quietly on his own. There was no note. No girlfriend, as far as we know. Or boyfriend. No family back in France – he came to London a couple of years ago from Marseille.'

'What did he do?'

'PT.'

Carlyle didn't understand.

'Personal trainer. He worked at a few gyms around Covent Garden and Soho, training fat bankers, ladies who lunch, and so on.'

Carlyle wondered if Soutine had ever worked at his own gym, Jubilee Hall, in the piazza. Maybe he'd seen him in there with a client. Then again, the commander's visits to the gym had become so infrequent it was highly unlikely.

'Seems he was good at it, too. Could charge more than a hundred quid an hour.'

Carlyle refused to be impressed: plumbers charged more than a hundred quid an hour.

'I went to a couple of the places Soutine worked at.' Nixon mentioned a couple of high-end clubs in the West End. 'Everyone says he was a nice guy, very professional. It seems he kept himself to himself, nothing out of the ordinary. They were all very shocked he'd topped himself but, hey, life goes on. It's a pretty transient business. People are coming and going all the time, so no one was crying their eyes out for a guy they barely knew.'

'It all sounds pretty straightforward,' Carlyle agreed. 'So why didn't O'Sullivan close the case?'

'You'll have to ask her.' Nixon looked vaguely surprised. 'I didn't realise she hadn't.'

'Ask me what?' A harassed-looking O'Sullivan strode across the room and dumped her bag on the desk, next to the commander.

'Why you've kept the Soutine case open,' they chorused.

'Bruno Soutine.' The inspector shooed Carlyle off her desk and sat down. 'There were various loose ends. One – where did the guy get the sleeping pills? He didn't have a prescription. As far as we know, he didn't even have a GP, and we didn't find any packaging or receipts in his flat. Two – someone smacked him about a bit, not long before he died. Why? This was a bloke who was supposedly a quiet, low-key guy. Three—'

Carlyle got the picture. 'Where does all this leave your investigation?'

'I'm keeping an open mind.' O'Sullivan shucked off her jacket. 'If it doesn't go anywhere in the next few days then we can close it. But there's no rush. I don't want to shut down prematurely, then have to reopen it.'

'No, I suppose not.'

'Don't worry, I won't leave it too long. We wouldn't want it dragging on the station's performance statistics, would we?'

Carlyle could not disagree. 'How's your family crisis?'

'False alarm.' O'Sullivan groaned. 'George got injured playing football. They feared he'd broken a bone in his foot, but it looks like it's only bruised. Just as well – he's got his mocks next week. What a nightmare if he'd had to hobble into the exam room with his foot in plaster.'

'I'm glad it's nothing serious.' Carlyle was interrupted by a text from his wife: *I'm round the corner. Fancy a coffee?* Making his excuses, he set off at a canter.

Helen was buzzing. 'I got a call from a woman called Imogen Edelman. She runs a consultancy advising NGOs. She's managing a major bequest coming to Avalon.' Avalon was the charity where Helen worked. 'We're getting an eight-figure sum.'

Carlyle took a moment to count up all the zeroes. 'Ten million?'

'At least.'

'Great.' Carlyle was genuinely happy for his wife. Running an international medical charity made police work seem extremely easy by comparison. The responsibility that came with the job was crushing and the constant fight for funding exhausting. No one was more deserving of a windfall.

'This'll be the charity's biggest single donation from a private individual *ever*. Plus, there are no restrictions on how we can spend it. Which means we can fund a whole bunch of projects either dormant or in danger of being shut down.'

'Who's the donor?'

'Imogen didn't say. At this stage, she's working with the executor of the estate to get the funds released. Hopefully it won't take too long. Then we'll meet up and talk about next steps.'

'Well done.'

'I didn't do anything,' she burbled. 'It landed in my lap.'

'You deserve a bit of luck,' Carlyle advised. 'Take it.'

'Oh, don't worry, I will.' Finishing her coffee, Helen rose to her feet. 'I need to get going. I'm going to do some shopping and then get started on dinner. Alice'll be round at seven.'

Carlyle looked at her blankly.

'You've forgotten, haven't you?' Helen's good humour ebbed slightly. 'Alice's bringing one of her friends for dinner. Don't be late or we'll start without you.'

After his wife had left, Carlyle took out his phone and googled Imogen Edelman. The woman's consultancy was called Edelman Helder & Simpson and its aim was 'helping non-profits achieve amazing results with outstanding people'. The client list included the Red Cross, various charities, a couple of banks and other businesses, and several unnamed high-net-worth individuals.

Great news . . . or was it? You get nothing for nothing in this world was how Carlyle saw it. The possibility of ten million quid appearing like magic started to make him feel a little uneasy. When he tried the EHS office number, the call was diverted to a mobile. After a few moments, Imogen Edelman's voicemail kicked in. Carlyle cut the connection without leaving a message. 'Don't be so paranoid,' he told himself. 'There's no reason to rain on Helen's parade.'

An unknown number popped up on the screen of her phone as it sat in its dashboard cradle. Imogen Edelman let it go to voice-mail. She was running late for picking the kids up from school. Whoever was calling could leave a message.

Edelman pulled away from the kerb, edging in front of a taxi whose driver gave an angry blast on his horn. 'Bugger off.' Edelman avoided making eye contact in the rear-view mirror. The phone's voicemail hadn't kicked in: whoever the caller was, it couldn't have been important.

Looking up from his phone, José Dias located the angry taxi driver in the line of traffic. London's roads were usually good for one punch-up a day or, at least, a violent argument. Invariably, they involved cabbies and cyclists or dallying pedestrians. Sometimes they could be quite entertaining.

On this occasion, however, José couldn't identify the object of the driver's ire. A couple of blasts of the horn failed to escalate into a full-blown dispute, so José went back to his refuse cart. He had pretty much reached the end of his route and it was about time to turn back and head for the waste depot. Finding an empty beer can by his feet, he kicked it into the gutter, next to a small box wrapped in plastic. Technically speaking, anything not lying on the pavement wasn't his problem – it could be left for one of the vehicle drivers to collect overnight – but José took his job seriously. Feeling a pang of guilt at kicking the can into the road, he stepped off the kerb, picked it up and tossed it into the cart, along with the box.

He was still standing in the gutter when the phone went. It was his sister. The woman only called when she wanted something, usually money. José considered ignoring her, then answered anyway.

'Hola, Beatriz.'

The girl didn't mess around with any small talk. 'There's this bill I need to pay . . .'

Sighing, José stepped back onto the pavement and wandered a little way down the street to a sheltered bus stop. If he was going to be tapped up, he might as well be sitting down while it happened.

'I'll get the money back to you in a week or so.'

He'd heard that before. Perched on a strip of uncomfortable red plastic, José looked up at the bus arrivals board. For some reason, the next 513 wasn't expected for another twenty minutes. No wonder no one was bothering to wait.

Beatriz finished her pitch. 'Cash works, but it would be better of you could put it straight into my bank account.'

I'm sure it would, José thought. Before he could reply, however, there was an almighty bang and the sky fell in on his head.

FOUR

Monica Seppi sat at a metal table in a windowless room under the watchful eye of a solitary security camera. Having been delivered to Crampton House Immigration Removal Centre at two in the morning, she had been processed and put in a cell with an Arab woman. Breakfast had been a tiny pot of yoghurt and a rice cake, washed down with some filthy coffee, lunch a sandwich from a packet with a sell-by date that was almost a month ago. Sometime in the afternoon, she had been brought to the interview room. After another wait, an immigration officer turned up, introduced himself as Edward Godson, and sat down.

After making a pantomime of looking for a pen, Godson started laboriously filling in a form on a sheet of grey paper. Seppi remained calm. Her anger had long since solidified into a basalt-type mass in her stomach. 'There's been a mistake,' she said firmly. 'I am not illegal.'

'That's what they all say, love.' Head bent, the officer ticked various boxes, filling in others in handwriting that was barely legible.

'I am allowed here to work. I pay my taxes.'

Why couldn't these people just shut up and do what they were told? Ted Godson rubbed his eyes. His lunch had settled in his stomach and he felt sleepy. The woman's English seemed good enough but still he spoke slowly, his voice slightly raised. 'If you're here legally, where are your papers?'

'I was attacked.' The woman fingered the cuts and bruises still clearly visible on her face. 'I was in the hospital and then they brought me here.'

Godson grunted. It wasn't his problem if the woman was legal or not. His only concern was to ensure she was properly processed before being shown the door.

'I was in the hospital,' Seppi repeated. 'Why would I have any papers?'

Bloody foreigners, Godson fumed. They come over here and exploit our health service. No wonder the NHS was on the brink of falling over. Any time his wife wanted to visit her GP, it took longer and longer to get an appointment because all the appointments had been taken by the Poles and Romanians. When you went to the clinic, the waiting room was full of people who didn't speak proper English. Tiffany, Godson's eighteen-year-old, needed a routine operation and they told her the waiting list would be more than a year. It was outrageous. The Godson family paid their taxes, always had, always would. They were *entitled*. And then somebody like this bitch waltzes in and gets what she wants, straight off the bat. It wasn't right, not right at all.

Godson wasn't a racist. He didn't have a prejudiced bone in his body. It was just common sense: the sooner all these people were sent packing, back to where they came from, the better. Brexit was supposed to have sorted all this stuff out. So far, however, it didn't seem to have made any difference at all.

'I want a lawyer,' the woman whined.

Ignoring her, Godson pushed the completed form across the table. 'This is your Removal Notice. It will be executed twenty-eight days from the date on the notice.' He didn't bother to point out the date on the top of the form was already four days old. 'You will be expected to pay for the cost of the removal process.

If you cannot pay now, the UK government will invoice you at your home address in your home country.' He paused, inviting her to read the form. 'You have to sign at the bottom, to signify you understand.' He offered her the biro. 'Do you understand?'

'I want a lawyer,' she repeated. 'And a smoke.'

'You want a cigarette?' He tapped the packet in his pocket with the pen, a crooked smile spreading across his face.

'You give me one?'

'What'll you give me in return?'

'I don't have anything. All my stuff got nicked.'

'That's not what I meant.' Rising from his chair, Godson tossed the pen on the table. With his back to the camera on the wall, he unzipped his fly. 'How bad do you want a Marlboro?'

Wrinkling her nose, Monica watched as Godson exposed himself. The guy smelt as if he hadn't washed in a month.

'How bad d'you want a smoke?' he grunted, coaxing a semi-erection from the nest of greying pubes.

How bad? Not that bad. Seppi shot out a hand and flicked the stirring member with her index finger.

'Ouch.' Godson took a half-step backwards, careful to keep his penis concealed from the CCTV. 'Fuck. That hurt.'

'Not as much as this.' Jumping to her feet, Monica stepped round the table and viciously kicked the man between his legs.

'Urghpfff.' Gasping for air, Godson folded himself away. 'You fucking bitch,' he hissed, 'I'll—'

'Now, now,' she chided, 'remember the camera.'

Still cursing, the immigration officer inched backwards to the door. 'Just sign the fucking form,' he demanded, 'and get ready to fuck off home.'

Bella Coleridge picked at her fingers. It was a bad habit, something her husband regularly complained about. Bella put it down to stress. Unfortunately, for her, stress came with the job. Three years as director of the Kidd Support Centre for abused and trafficked women had left her feeling drained and helpless.

'It's depressing, but not surprising.' Coleridge watched a ribbon of blood emerge from under the nail of her index finger. 'And you need to be careful.'

'I'm always careful.' Rita Vicedo sipped her tea without passing comment on her friend and colleague's minor act of self-harm.

'The police are part of this scam, too, Rita.' Coleridge sucked the blood from her finger. 'You can lose a lot of credibility by getting into bed with them.'

The nun raised an amused eyebrow. 'I don't get into bed with anyone.'

'Your licence to operate could be imperilled.'

Vicedo scowled. Bella was a good woman, but her use of jargon often teetered on the edge of gibberish. 'What does that mean?'

'Survivors'll be wary of working with you if they think you might pass on their details to the police. The Met is reporting more and more people to the Home Office. They talk to a police officer and the next thing they know they're getting a visit from Immigration Enforcement. They don't trust the police, and neither should you.'

'I trust the sergeant I'm working with on this. Laura Nixon is a good person. But she can't investigate a serious crime if she has no victim. Plus, if what she says is right, this Monica Seppi isn't even an illegal alien in the first place.'

Coleridge was unmoved. 'These days, it doesn't matter. If you don't have the right papers, no one is going to believe you. I mean, look at the *Windrush* generation.'

'Hm.' The only thing that surprised Vicedo about the illegal

33

attempts to deport Caribbean immigrants was that it had caused such a fuss. The English could be as sentimental as they were racist.

'The Centre helps undocumented victims to access services from the NHS and local government but it's getting harder and harder. The government declared it was going to create a hostile environment for illegal immigrants and it's the only promise they've ever kept. People aren't stupid. They know the dangers of coming onto the radar of any kind of government institution. The authorities are looking to deport as many people as they possibly can. They want to harry and chase undocumented migrants, including victims of crime, people who are already the most marginalised in society, the very people who have nothing. It's criminal.' Coleridge's outrage was genuine. 'We've made four separate formal complaints to the Metropolitan Police. We've not had a response to any of them. I even raised the issue with the commissioner, Virginia Thompson, when she came to visit the Centre a while back. She promised to look into it, but nothing happened. From where I'm sitting, the police are very much part of the problem.'

'I hear you.'

'Do you?'

'I always listen very carefully to your advice.'

Coleridge looked unconvinced. 'Just be careful.'

'I have the power of the Church to fall back on, if I need it. Like it or loathe it, the Holy Roman Church has both resources *and* staying power.'

'If only they used a bit more of both to help those most in need.'

Vicedo ignored the criticism. 'I promise you, I'm not siding with the police. I'm just helping a friend, who happens to be a police officer, in trying to trace this particular individual. Monica Seppi is a victim of crime, but also of bureaucratic failure and a lack of compassion. If I can possibly help her, why would I stand by and do nothing?'

Coleridge took a paper napkin from her pocket and wrapped it round her still bleeding finger. 'All we can do is fight for one person at a time, right?'

'One person at a time,' Vicedo agreed. 'If you can help me find Monica, I'm sure we'll be able to get her out.'

The director could not reject such a plea. 'Let me make a few phone calls,' she replied. 'There are only so many possibilities. I'm sure we can track her down sooner or later.'

Alice's friend was a perky American called Julie, who was in her second year at Imperial studying environmental geoscience. Dinner *chez* Carlyle was largely taken up with Julie trying to explain to the commander what environmental geoscience was. For Carlyle, pretending he understood was an effort in itself.

'At least Alice seems happy enough,' said Helen, once they had left.

'Yeah.' Although somewhat wearied by having to try to keep up with Julie, Carlyle was relieved not to have been presented with some geeky potential boyfriend. On an intellectual level, he knew boyfriends were none of his business; on a gut level, he had yet to come up with any idea of what an acceptable life partner for his only child might possibly look like.

After stacking the dishwasher, he retreated into the living room and flopped onto the sofa, next to his wife. 'I looked at the website for the charity consultancy sorting out your money.'

Helen stared into a mug of green tea. 'Avalon's money.'

'From what I can see, they look kosher.'

'Oh, they're definitely kosher. I can't see any reason why we won't get the cash. The board's very excited about it, like kids in a sweetshop, some of them. They've come up with a dozen different ways to spend the money already.'

'But you don't know who the actual donor is yet,' Carlyle pointed out. 'Depending on who it is, you might end up having reservations about taking it. I remember that rapper who wanted to make a big donation a while ago. When it turned out he'd beaten up his girlfriend, all hell broke loose.'

'Chase Race,' Helen winced. 'What a wanker.'

'You had to refuse his cash,' Carlyle reminded her.

'Yeah.' Helen sipped her tea, dismayed by the memory.

'Whatever happened to him?'

'The girlfriend ran off to America and ended up marrying some tech entrepreneur.'

'Good for her, I suppose.'

'Poor old Chase ended up on *I'm a Celebrity*.'

'Uh-huh.' Carlyle never ceased to be bemused by his wife's interest in trash TV.

'He came second a few years ago.'

Carlyle didn't know what to make of that. 'Best not to spend this cash till you know where it's come from,' he suggested. 'Just to be on the safe side.'

'Good advice,' Helen gave him a peck on the cheek, 'as always.'

He pulled her close. 'Any ideas on who your benefactor might be?'

'Could be almost anybody,' Helen mused. 'It's not really worth trying to guess.'

'No.' Carlyle didn't admit it, but he had a pretty good idea where the money was coming from. Fragments of an old conversation had been playing in his head since Helen had told him about the big bequest.

Why don't you make a donation to Avalon, the charity my wife runs?

He had made the suggestion to a contact called Victoria Dalby-Cummins. As well as being a rich widow, Dalby-Cummins was an ambitious gangster who wanted to lure Carlyle away from the Met to work for her. Carlyle had no interest in moving to the dark side, but had floated the idea of a charitable donation as a way of leveraging her interest for a good cause.

Make it a big one. I'm sure it'll be tax deductible.

Dalby-Cummins had died – in suspicious circumstances, naturally – not long afterwards. According to reports, her estate had been valued at £33 million and the money was being shared between various charities.

Carlyle imagined Dalby-Cummins had acted on his proposal, writing Avalon into the will before her death. At the time, he'd imagined he was being clever. In reality, swamping Helen with dirty money – if that was what he'd done – wasn't the greatest idea he'd ever had. Far from it. Keeping his mouth shut and his fingers crossed, he could only hope that his suspicions proved wide of the mark.

FIVE

Carlyle diverted to Grind on autopilot. Dallying over a black Americano and a pastry, he looked through a discarded copy of *Metro*. A small story on page two caught his eye: *IED Blows Up Binman's Cart*. A picture showed the destroyed rubbish cart smeared along the pavement. Amazingly, no one had been seriously injured. Even the binman, who'd had a bus shelter collapse on top of him, had walked away with just a few scratches and bruises.

His idling was interrupted by a call from Joaquin. 'Where are you?' The PA's tone indicated Carlyle was in trouble.

'I'm on my way in.'

'To Charing Cross?'

'Where else?'

An extended groan indicated he'd given the wrong answer. 'You're supposed to be in Liverpool Street for your course.'

Since being elevated to the rank of commander, Carlyle imagined he had been sent on more courses than any other person on the planet. The Met didn't seem to subscribe to the view that you couldn't teach an old dog new tricks. Or maybe it was just that someone had a budget to spend. 'What bloody course?' he snapped.

'Workplace Inclusion and Diversity Awareness Training,' Joaquin announced. 'The one you have to go on for calling some guy a pig-fucker.'

Carlyle cursed Henry Jones and wished a vicious crime wave on the Dyfed-Powys CID. 'It wasn't pigs,' he pointed out, 'it was sheep.'

'Same thing,' Joaquin said. 'You proclaimed him a man who had sex with animals.'

'As it happens, I didn't call the inspector anything at all, I simply—'

'Whatever. You have to go on the course.'

'I didn't know about this,' Carlyle persisted.

Joaquin muttered something in his native tongue. It clearly wasn't complimentary. 'I gave you the letter, right, the Written Warning?'

Carlyle confirmed that was the case.

'There was a bit at the bottom about having to do the course, as well, no?'

'Maybe.' Carlyle had no idea. He had read the words 'Written' and 'Warning' and torn the thing up.

'The course starts in thirty minutes. I'll text you the location.'

Carlyle admitted defeat. 'How's the office coming along?'

'Slowly. They might be able to start decorating soon. What colour do you want again?'

'White.'

'Boring,' was Joaquin's verdict.

'Boring is good,' Carlyle replied. 'Boring is what we're aiming for at all times from here on.'

Held in a new office development, north of the railway station, the Inclusion and Workplace Diversity Awareness course lived down to expectation. It was run by a nervous-looking American woman called Marge, who worked for a training company in the City, which was doubtless charging the Met a fortune so that the errant commander and others of his ilk could be re-educated.

The classroom had the air of after-school detention. The

eleven participants were all white; most were middle-aged or older; ten were men. As far as he could see, the various modules boiled down to 'be kind at all times', 'never say anything controversial' and 'don't try to be funny'. Thousands of pounds, plus VAT, for little more than one of his mother's oft-repeated pearls of wisdom: *You get more with honey than you do with vinegar.* Over the years his ma, God rest her soul, must have dispensed gallons of vinegar, without offering up so much as a teaspoon's-worth of honey. If she could see him now . . . He imagined her having a good laugh at his expense.

Sitting at the back of the classroom, he managed to keep his eyes open and his mouth shut until they reached the lunch break. Food had been provided on the basis that if the participants were allowed to leave the building they might not come back. Munching a desiccated cheese sandwich, Carlyle caught the eye of one of the other attendees, the only woman and, by his reckoning, the youngest on the course by at least a couple of decades.

'What d'you reckon, so far?' Before he could reply, the woman stuck out a hand. 'I'm Lottie Pearson, special adviser to the mayor.'

'Commander John Carlyle, Met Police.' He cleaned his fingers on a napkin before shaking her hand.

'Why are you here?'

'I got done for hurting the feelings of one of my inspectors. He misheard something I said.'

Pearson raised an eyebrow.

'A kind of intergenerational, transnational misunderstanding, if you will.'

'Bullying.'

Carlyle knew better than to quibble. 'Kind of depends on your definition of bullying, I suppose. What about you?'

'Transphobic behaviour.' Pearson bit into a carrot stick.

'I haven't graduated to that yet,' Carlyle quipped.

40

'I wasn't deemed guilty of negative attitudes towards transgender *people*,' the adviser explained, 'but of negative attitudes towards trans *activists*.'

'Uh-huh.' None the wiser, Carlyle wondered if this was a bit like a sanitised version of the Cultural Revolution. 'That seems to be a rather more specific kind of prejudice than I seem to specialise in.'

'Basically,' Pearson explained, 'I got dragged into a row with some transgender-rights campaigners and they outmanoeuvred me a bit. I was accused of undermining the fight for equality in gender identity.'

Carlyle had absolutely no idea what the woman was talking about. 'You wouldn't want to do that.'

'I would never want anybody to feel insecure or marginalised because of their perceived or actual gender identity.'

'No.' What the hell was this woman doing on a diversity awareness course? She already seemed a fully paid-up member of Generation Snowflake. He imagined Pearson must be one of the last people in the country who bought the *Guardian*. Maybe she even read it.

'The problem is, once people take offence, it's hard to get things back on track.'

'Tell me about it.' Carlyle felt a flicker of empathy. 'Being accused of something – anything – puts you on the back foot. Innocent or guilty, it's hard to recover.'

'I'm definitely innocent,' Pearson said brightly, 'but it looked bad. Things got a bit out of hand. The mayor was coming under pressure to sack me but he's a good guy – he sent me on this course instead.'

I would have let him sack me, Carlyle reflected, rather than put up with this crap. 'Lucky you.'

'It's not too bad.' Pearson seemed as determined to be cheery as Carlyle was to be grumpy. 'Some of it's interesting.'

41

'I must have missed that bit,' the commander declared, adding, 'At least there's only the afternoon session to go.'

Pearson gave him a funny look. 'You must have misunderstood. The course lasts for three days.'

'Three days?' Carlyle spluttered. 'We're stuck here for three whole days?'

'*You* are.' Pearson chuckled. '*I* get time off to go to the mayor's Victims' Summit.'

Carlyle spied an escape route. 'Sounds interesting.'

'It is,' Pearson confirmed. 'I organised it.'

'Must be good, then.'

'There's no need for the sarcasm.' Pearson stuck a straw into a small carton of orange juice. 'If you don't mind me saying so, you seem very jaded.'

'I'm a cop,' Carlyle countered. 'Cynicism is our first line of defence in the fight against crime.'

'Yeah, but you're management.' Sucking the juice through the straw made the special adviser look about twelve years old. 'When did you last fight any actual crime?'

Carlyle didn't go there. Instead, he asked, 'How did you know I was brass?'

'Well, you must be,' Pearson reasoned. 'All the people here are public-sector high-fliers. They've put their foot in it once too often but, for whatever reason, their bosses don't want to fire them.'

'I've never considered myself a high-flier.' Carlyle looked at his fellow classmates. Apart from himself and Pearson, all the others were sitting alone, staring at their phones.

'Some people are born great,' Pearson teased. 'Others have greatness thrust upon them.'

'That would be your boss, then, would it?' Carlyle knew next to nothing about the mayor, other than the oft-repeated fact he was the son of a bus driver.

'I'm not sure the mayor's reached the level of greatness yet,'

Pearson opined, 'but he's definitely on the way up. Come to the summit and I'll introduce you.'

'What about this?' Carlyle didn't want to sound too eager to do a runner.

'Speak to Marge. Tell her I've co-opted you for the summit. Her firm helped organise it, so she'll be happy to give you a credit against the rest of the course here.'

'Sounds good.' Carlyle began gathering up his rubbish. 'When do we leave?'

'The police are duty bound to report victims of crime to the Home Office if there are reasonable grounds to question their immigration status. But, equally, it is essential victims of crime can access the right support to help them recover and find justice. Without the confidence of victims to come forward and report crimes, we don't catch the perpetrators, justice isn't done and there's the risk there'll be more victims of crime down the line.'

The modest applause struggled to fill the City Hall auditorium. As the mayor stepped down from his platform, Lottie Pearson waved him over. 'Great speech.'

'You think?' The mayor dabbed the perspiration on his forehead with a handkerchief.

'I *know*,' Pearson deadpanned. 'After all, I wrote it.' She gave Carlyle a gentle nudge.

'You made some interesting points,' was the best the commander could immediately come up with.

Pearson made the introductions. 'Joe, I wanted you to meet John Carlyle. I met him at the I and D training.'

'Rescued you from detention, huh?' The mayor offered his hand. 'Joe Stanley.'

'Commander Carlyle's a bigwig in the Met,' said Pearson. 'I persuaded him to bunk off.'

Stanley's eyebrow arched up towards his fringe. For a man

who must be well into his fifties, he retained an impressive head of hair, with only a smattering of grey. 'An un-PC cop, who'd have thought it?'

'Just don't put me in front of the transgender-rights campaigners,' Carlyle joked.

'They're not here.' The mayor looked relieved. 'They've gone on a picket of Hampstead Ponds.'

'Some of the regulars at the women-only swimming pool are cutting up rough about allowing transgender women in,' Pearson explained. 'The whole thing's got a bit heated.'

'These things happen.' The mayor returned to matters closer to his heart. 'What did you *really* think of my speech?'

'I think it covered all the bases.' From the murky recesses of his brain, Carlyle dredged some management speak of his own. 'All government agencies have to work together to deliver effective services. At the same time, the government is committed to creating a hostile environment for illegal immigrants. Different people want different outcomes. There are no easy solutions. Then again, there never have been and there never will be.'

'Very good.' The mayor chuckled. 'I think you might even be able to give Lottie a run for her money in the wordsmithing department.' A callow-faced youth in an ill-fitting suit appeared and whispered something in his ear. Stanley nodded and turned on his heel. 'Sorry, I have to run.' He gave Carlyle an apologetic smile before heading for the nearest exit. 'Nice to meet you.'

'He likes you,' Pearson declared.

'Most people do.'

'I'm serious.' She gave him a playful smack on the arm. 'He found the bad-boy cop thing interesting.'

Carlyle felt his cheeks redden. 'I'm hardly Dirty Harry.'

Pearson looked at him blankly.

'I don't think being sent on a diversity course makes me a "bad-boy cop".'

'But this is just the tip of the iceberg, isn't it? I took a little peek at your service record. You've had quite the career, haven't you?'

Embarrassment turned to anger as the commander sensed he was being played. 'How the hell were you able to do that? We only met this morning.'

'A list of attendees on our diversity course was circulated in advance. I checked your career history . . . *interesting.*'

'You're stalking me?'

'I think there's something you might be able to do for us.'

The conversation was interrupted by a call from Helen. 'Can you come to my office?' It was a command, rather than a request.

'Erm,' Carlyle glanced at Pearson. 'I'm a bit tied up right now.'

'I wouldn't be calling if it wasn't important,' was his wife's strained response.

'Fine. I'll be there as quickly as I can.' Ending the call, he apologised to Pearson. 'Bit of an emergency. Why don't you come over to Charing Cross tomorrow and you can explain how you want to exploit me?' As an afterthought, he added, 'Perhaps you could sweeten the pill by using the mayor's expense account to take me to lunch.'

It took almost an hour to reach Helen's Fitzrovia office. City Hall's inconvenient location, coupled with problems on the Underground, meant getting across town was a struggle. To compensate for his wife's glare, he dialled up the famous Carlyle smile while he was introduced to the other person present.

'This is Imogen Edelman,' Helen explained, 'the adviser representing our major new donor.'

'Pleased to meet you.' Carlyle slipped into a chair. Edelman was a slight figure, largely hidden beneath the kind of seventies Scottish knitwear he imagined had long since been banned by the Taste Police. The dark rings under her eyes betrayed a lack of sleep. 'How can I be of help?'

'Somebody tried to blow Imogen up in her car,' Helen said flatly, 'and the police aren't dealing with it.'

Let the woman speak for herself. Carlyle invited Edelman to elaborate.

'Someone stuck a . . . device under my car.' The woman sounded calm, although her voice was strained. 'It fell off. A binman put it in his cart and it blew up.'

Carlyle recalled the *Metro* story about the guy in the bus shelter. 'How do you know?'

'Know what?'

'That it was stuck to *your* car?'

'CCTV footage,' Helen said, like it was obvious.

'Ah, right.' Carlyle clasped his hands in his lap, waiting for Edelman to go on.

'The police say they're taking the matter extremely seriously, but they haven't any idea why someone would do this.' Edelman's eyes filled with tears. 'It wasn't a big bomb.' Her voice cracked. 'They say it was a warning, but if the kids had been in the car . . .' She buried her head in her hands. 'I can't understand why anyone should do such a thing. It's terrible. And my husband's away. And—'

'Who's the police officer in charge?' Carlyle asked.

Edelman composed herself and pulled a business card from the pocket of her jeans. Chief Inspector David Holland. There was a phone number and email but no address. Carlyle didn't know the guy from Adam. Without missing a beat, he said, 'Dave's really good. He'll get to the bottom of this.' He handed the card back.

'He clocked off early to go to a dinner party.' Helen let out a snort of derision. 'Maybe you could put somebody better on the case.'

Maybe you could button it, my dear.

Edelman let out a small sob, nipping the impending domestic in the bud. 'It's horrible. I've been up all night, racking my brains, but I can't make any sense of it.' Pulling a paper tissue from the sleeve of her jumper, she blew her nose. 'I'm sorry to come to you but Helen said you'd be able to help.'

Carlyle bit down on his annoyance at being dragged into this mess. 'The first thing—'

He was interrupted by a knock on the door. A woman stuck her head into the room and addressed Helen. 'Sorry to disturb you, boss, but I've got Jonas on the line. I know you need to speak to him. Shall I put him through? His flight goes in forty minutes.'

I'll take it out there.' Apologising to Edelman – although not to her husband – Helen jumped to her feet and hustled out.

Edelman had another blow of her nose. 'I'm sorry,' she sniffed, 'I'm sure you must have more than enough to worry about already.'

'It's fine,' Carlyle reassured her. 'This is a very serious business. More than deserving of my attention. I can't really interfere in Chief Inspector Holland's investigation, but if I can help, I will.'

Leaning out of her chair, Edelman dropped her tissue into the bin underneath Helen's desk. 'Thank you.'

'There seem two plausible scenarios here. Either you were a victim of mistaken identity, or you've somehow made a serious enemy.' He paused, letting her take in what he was saying. 'The first, for obvious reasons, would be preferable.'

'Yes.'

'But, I have to say, mistaken identity seems pretty unlikely. A bloke who goes to the trouble of making a car bomb is pretty likely to stick it to the right car, even if it does fall off.'

Edelman blinked. 'How do you know it was a man?'

47

'Given the statistics,' Carlyle burbled, making it up as he went along, 'it's a more than reasonable assumption at this stage.' What were the actual statistics? He had no idea, but bomb-making was very much a male pastime. 'If you were the target, who could you possibly have annoyed so much?' He avoided adding 'that they wanted to blow you to bits'.

'I'm a normal person. We're a normal family. No one would want to hurt us.'

Carlyle scratched his chin. 'What about someone you've robbed of millions?'

The woman looked horrified. 'I haven't robbed anybody. I don't have millions.'

'Your business sometimes handles large sums for clients, big donations.'

'We don't handle the money. We simply make sure it goes to the right place, to the right charity.'

'All right, so let's follow the money for a moment. Who might not want it to go to charity?'

'What do you mean?'

'Say, for example, Helen left a million quid in her will, hypothetically speaking. Before her death, she decides she wants to give it to charity. I decide the cash would be better off in my pocket. I'd be fairly pissed off if you gave *my* money away.'

'But it's not your money,' Edelman pointed out. 'It's Helen's.'

'But I think I'm entitled to it,' Carlyle responded. 'It should be mine, therefore it is mine. It happens all the time. Families fall out. Disgruntled children go to court to try to claw the family farm back from the RSPCA, or the lifeboat people. Inheritances bring out the worst in people.'

'I'm sorry, but we don't disclose information about our clients.' Edelman stared at a black-and-white photograph on the wall behind Helen's desk. It showed a small child being treated in a medical clinic. 'Certainly not when it comes to individuals.'

Carlyle followed her gaze. 'They appreciate discretion.'

'They *demand* discretion. As it happens, though, we don't do many private bequests. It's mainly corporate clients.'

'What about this bequest to Avalon? Ten million's a lot of money.'

'I have to respect client confidentiality,' Edelman said stiffly.

'Client confidentiality comes a rather distant second to finding the lunatic who did this, wouldn't you say?' With Helen out of the room, he floated his theory about the identity of the donor. 'Who would be getting the money from Vicky Dalby-Cummins's bequest if it wasn't coming here?'

'Where did you get that name?' Edelman rocked backwards and forwards in her chair, as if she was in physical pain.

Bullseye. Carlyle was delighted and horrified at the same time. 'I knew Vicky professionally. She was a widow, with no kids. When Helen mentioned the size of the bequest, I put two and two together.'

'You guessed,' Edelman translated.

Carlyle was unapologetic. 'It's what policemen do.'

'I can't confirm the identity of my client.'

'I won't blow the whistle,' Carlyle promised, 'but you have more pressing concerns right now, especially when the client is dead.'

Edelman couldn't argue. 'Ms Dalby-Cummins came to us and outlined what she wanted to do.' Her voice sounded small and distant. 'It was supposed to be a long-term plan, given no one was expecting her to die so soon. However, all the necessary arrangements had been put in place. Executing the will should have been very straightforward.'

'There could be no doubt about the validity of the will?'

'Oh, no. Vicky had organised it all perfectly. She was very efficient – a great woman.'

She was also a criminal, someone who lived by the sword and died by it. Carlyle waited in silence for the rest of the story.

'The executor's been proving difficult, though.'

'Oh?'

'He's the brother, half-brother actually, Patrick Dalby. I think Patrick assumed he would be the sole beneficiary of the will. He didn't know it had been rewritten. When he found out, he became hostile. There was talk of a legal challenge, but it was just an empty threat. Going to court would be a waste of time and money. We haven't been served with any papers and I don't expect we will be.'

'Looks like the half-brother came up with a shortcut,' said Carlyle.

'He still wouldn't get the money,' Edelman replied.

'The guy put a bomb under your car. He's not exactly thinking straight.'

'We don't know it was him.'

The woman's infinite reasonableness grated. 'He's the only suspect we have,' Carlyle argued, 'so far. At the very least he should be brought in for questioning. Did you tell Chief Inspector Holland about this?'

Edelman looked at him as if it was a trick question. 'He didn't ask.'

'What about Helen?'

'I might have mentioned it. I can't remember.'

'Where can we find Mr Dalby?'

'I haven't got an address, but our lawyers will have it.'

'Get on to the chief inspector,' Carlyle instructed her, 'tell him about Patrick and put him on to the lawyer. With a bit of luck, he can find some bomb-making material in the guy's garage and it's case closed. Life can go back to normal and Helen – I mean Avalon – can get their cash.'

Edelman didn't seem overly impressed with this plan. 'Should I tell the chief inspector we've talked?' she asked.

'Leave me out of it,' Carlyle instructed. 'Let Dave think it's all his own work.'

'What about Helen? Should I tell her?'

'Better she hears it from me,' Carlyle replied, '*after* we've caught the guy.'

Helen was still on the phone when Carlyle left. Giving his wife a thumbs-up, he scooted for the exit. 'All done.' He chuckled. 'Problem solved. You can thank me when you get home.'

SIX

Monica Seppi was imbued with a perverse sense of wellbeing. To her surprise, being institutionalised was pretty liberating. Decision-making was taken out of your hands. Most of daily life's petty irritations simply fell away. On the negative side, her prison-issue tracksuit was beginning to smell, and the food was terrible. Overall, however, the accommodation compared favourably with the grotty room she rented in Wood Green at a cost of almost two hundred pounds a week.

Locked up for twenty-one hours each day, she had been overdosing on sleep and Martina Cole novels borrowed from the detention centre's apology for a library. The physical injuries were healing, and she was not the kind of person to dwell on the emotional damage her attackers had caused. Details of the assault that had left her hospitalised were slowly coming back. She studied each new piece of information, like a film student analysing a movie, frame by frame. With the distance of only a few days, the memories did not feel particularly real.

Her attackers were real enough. Justin and Peter – two guys she knew through a friend. They were drinking in a pub called the Lazy Donkey. They had bought the drinks; she had flirted a little. Everything had been under control, until it wasn't. She had been drugged – presumably – and blacked out.

The names had come to her while she was queuing for

breakfast on her second day of internment. She had spent the rest of the day thinking about what justice might look like. 'Don't get mad,' her dad used to say, 'get even.' She would get even.

Third on her shit list was Edward 'Ted' Godson. In the short-term, a kick in the nuts had done wonders for the man's professionalism; wary of another beating, the pervert had kept his distance and remembered his manners, relatively speaking. Still, Seppi had no doubts that he would revert to type soon enough.

Godson was well known among the inmates as a sexual predator. Most of the guards were willing to try their luck, cop a feel when the opportunity presented itself. Some would even try to trade a smoke or a few phone credits for the flash of a girl's tits or a quick hand job. But Godson was in a class of his own, assaulting prisoners on an industrial scale. That made him another arsehole to be dealt with.

First, though, she had to get out.

'The authorities want to move you to another centre.'

'Where?' Seppi placed her hands on the table and stared at the youth sitting opposite. It was hard to believe the specimen in the cheap suit was, in fact, a qualified lawyer. The boy's face was covered with spots and he looked like he had barely made it into his teens.

'Somewhere up north, probably. They usually have more capacity up there.'

Seppi glared at Godson, standing by the door of the interview room, out of range of another attack. 'I wanted a woman lawyer.'

The immigration officer glared back, his hands placed pro-tectively in front of his balls, like a footballer lining up in front of a free kick. 'You get what you're given.'

She responded by crooking her little finger and wiggling it at him.

Colouring, Godson placed a hand on the door. 'I'll leave you two to converse in private.' He added, not quite under his breath, 'For what it's worth.'

The lawyer looked on, confused. 'What was that all about?'

'Nothing.' Seppi stared at the card the boy had placed on the table. *Kevin Lofthouse, Junior Associate, Mellor & Ritchie.* Address in Camden Town. 'Well, Kevin,' she drawled, 'what are you going to do to get me released?'

'Well,' the boy nervously pushed his spectacles up his nose, 'it's not exactly what—'

'I don't want to hear excuses. Have you spoken to the embassy?'

Fumbling with his briefcase, the boy blushed from behind his spots. 'That's not my remit,' he stammered.

'What *is* your remit?'

'Well, it's a question of—'

'What they're doing here is wrong.' Monica stabbed the table with her index finger. 'I am not an illegal. I have papers.'

'You *say* you have papers,' Lofthouse said, 'but you cannot produce them.'

Seppi cursed, took a deep breath. After wrestling with her thoughts, she said, 'Speak to a man called Karol Lacko.' She spelt out the man's name. 'Write it down.'

The lawyer reluctantly did as he was told. It took him three attempts to spell the name correctly. Once he'd managed that, she gave him a phone number.

'Text him. Tell him it's urgent.'

'He works for the embassy?'

'He can get what I need.'

'They don't pay me to do this,' Lofthouse complained.

'It's just one lousy text.' She had a thought. 'And speak to the police.'

'Which police?'

'The ones who were investigating the attack on me,' Seppi

pointed to a selection of her bruises, 'before I ended up in this hole.'

'It's not what I'm here for,' the boy insisted. 'My job is purely to help you by facilitating the removal process.'

'What does that mean?'

'It means getting you out of the country as quickly as possible,' Lofthouse blurted.

'I'm your client.'

'Yes, but—'

'You do what I tell you.' Seppi leant across the table. 'Otherwise,' she whispered, 'I'll slice your balls off and make you eat them. Raw.'

Lofthouse squirmed in his seat. 'But you'll have been deported.'

Seppi smiled. 'I got in once, didn't I? I can come back.'

Lofthouse gulped at the prospect.

'Text Karol.' Seppi tapped his business card. 'And speak to the police. They won't be far from your office.'

'I'll see what I can do.'

'Good.' Seppi changed tack. 'Now, why are they moving me?'

'They're moving a bunch of people.' Tossed an easy question, Lofthouse brightened a little. 'The detention centre network's always running up against capacity constraints. It's normal. I wouldn't worry about it.'

Seppi sighed. 'Not when I've got so many other things to worry about, right?'

Grumpy at having to trek up to North London, his sugar levels falling dangerously, Carlyle held open the front door of Hampstead police station and ushered Emily Quartz onto the street.

'Thanks for bailing me out.'

'It's the least I could do for my favourite journalist.'

Ignoring his sarcasm, Quartz suggested lunch. 'My treat.'

Imagining being wined and dined in one of NW3's upmarket establishments, Carlyle's mood lightened. 'I think it's the least you can do,' he said cheerily.

In the event, she led him to a modest café, close to the tube station. Sitting at a dirty table, Carlyle sipped a lukewarm Americano before nibbling an over-engineered sandwich.

Oblivious to his dismay, Quartz swigged greedily from a can of Diet Coke.

'What happened?'

'It all kicked off.' Reflecting on her run-in with the Old Bill, Quartz stifled a burp. 'We were having our peaceful protest and then things kind of got out of hand.'

'"We" being . . .'

'The Ladies' Pond Association.' Quartz finished her drink and tore open a packet of chocolate raisins. 'The LPA represents pond users. It voted to oppose the decision of the Corporation of London, which runs Hampstead Heath, to let transgender women swim in the women-only pond and use the changing facilities. There's been a lot of debate about it – you might have seen some of the stories.'

Maybe.

'I don't have much of a view, one way or another. I mean, who would be against a friendly, welcoming and inclusive environment, right? For women *and* transgender women. But how do you decide who is a transgender woman? There was this guy – just a guy, even dressed like a guy – in the changing room. He was asked to leave but refused. It's causing a lot of anxiety. Some of our members are very upset.'

Carlyle muttered something vaguely sympathetic.

'Anyway, the LPA launched the *Our Pond Is Not Gender Fluid* campaign, which was what the demo was about. Some trans activists turned up and there was a bit of an argument. The police were called and three of us were carted off to the cells. The other two were released after an hour or so but I mouthed off a bit, so they left me to stew.' Quartz munched the last of her raisins. 'I have to say, your lot weren't very sympathetic.'

'In my experience,' Carlyle said, 'your average constable tends not to be *au fait* with the latest developments in sexual politics.'

'Snarky gits,' was Quartz's take.

'Gimme the name of the officer in charge and I'll see what I can do.'

She gave him a hopeful look. 'Can you get me off?'

'I can have a word. No promises.'

'Thanks.' Quartz began rooting around in her bag. 'I'm supposed to report back to the station in a fortnight. I wrote down the name of the guy I'm supposed to ask for.' She dumped a pile of papers on the desk. 'Hold on a sec.'

The papers spilt across the table, forcing Carlyle to catch them before they fell onto the floor. Catching sight of a name scrawled on the top sheet, he did a double take. 'What the fuck?'

Quartz continued rummaging. 'What?'

Carlyle tapped the papers with his index finger. 'Why're you interested in Bruno Soutine?'

'Here it is.' Quartz offered him a scrap of paper 'Ian Day. Know him?'

'Huh?'

'The guy I have to report back to. Sergeant Ian Day.'

'I'll have a word,' Carlyle repeated, shoving the scrap into his pocket. 'Tell me about Bruno Soutine.'

Quartz shrugged. 'He's the cryptocurrency guy.'

Carlyle groaned. First gender politics, now cryptocurrencies. It was another subject about which he knew the square root of fuck-all.

'I'm thinking of doing a story about him. Early days, though.

57

Whether I can get much that's new is questionable. He's a bit of a mystery man.'

'He's a bit dead.'

'Huh?'

'Topped himself in a flat in Covent Garden.'

Quartz shook her head. 'You must be thinking of someone else.'

'Bruno Soutine's dead as a dodo. I saw the report.'

Quartz was unmoved. 'Must be a different Bruno Soutine.'

'How many Bruno Soutines can there be?' Carlyle mused.

'More than one, obviously.' Quartz shoved the papers back into her bag. 'My Bruno Soutine is an international fugitive, last heard of in Montreal.'

'It could be the same guy,' Carlyle reasoned. 'He could have come to London to top himself.'

'No way,' Quartz said. 'Why would he do that?'

'Dunno,' Carlyle replied. 'Maybe he was depressed.'

'The guy isn't depressed,' Quartz insisted. 'Last heard of, he'd nicked thirty million dollars.'

'Millionaires can get depressed, too,' Carlyle supposed.

'Not this guy, he was living the dream,' Quartz asserted. 'How did your guy die?'

'He took a bunch of sleeping pills and stuck a plastic bag over his head. We found him in a tiny ex-council flat off Drury Lane. He worked as a personal trainer.'

'Definitely not the same Bruno Soutine. My guy founded a cryptocurrency for porn, then did a runner with the real money.' Quartz tapped the screen of her phone and handed it to Carlyle. 'Consensual Acts was set up by . . .' she wiggled her fingers in the air to signify quote marks '. . . "Bruno Soutine" as a porn site catering for all tastes.'

The home page looked like a million other porn sites. Careful not to seem too curious, Carlyle quickly handed back the phone.

'Clients bought ASTs, Adult Services Tokens, with cash. The idea was that the tokens would be used to pay for live sex acts on camera and other services.'

'A kind of dark web for self-abusers.' Carlyle had only the sketchiest idea of what the dark web was, but he imagined he was in the right ballpark.

'Very good.' Quartz chuckled. 'The thing never got off the ground, though.' She slipped the phone back into her pocket. 'You click on any of the links, nothing happens.'

'So, it was a con?' Carlyle needed it spelt out.

'Yeah. About a month ago, a guy who said his name was "Bruno Soutine" was tracked down by the *New York Times*. He claimed to have raised more than thirty million dollars from more than five thousand punters.'

'Thirty mill from five thousand wankers.' Carlyle tried to do the maths. 'That's . . . a lot, even on a per-head basis. Why would you hand over so much cash?'

'Money laundering.'

Carlyle waited for her to explain.

'An ICO – an initial coin offering – for a new cryptocurrency is a neat new way to clean up dirty money.'

'If you can get your real money back.'

'There's no such thing as "real" money,' Quartz corrected him.

'Eh?'

She looked at him like he was dim. 'How much is a twenty-pound note worth?'

Sensing a trick question, he hesitated. 'Twenty quid?'

Quartz gestured at the menu. 'Roughly the price of two full Englishes.'

This was like being back at school. Embarrassed by his lack of mental bandwidth, Carlyle scratched his head. 'Right.'

'Until the price of a full English goes up.'

Carlyle nodded slowly, hoping the motion might stop his brain seizing up. 'You get less for your cash.'

'Money is just a piece of paper printed by the government. It's only worth something because everyone believes it's worth something. *What* it's worth changes all the time.'

Carlyle had no idea what this had to do with Bruno Soutine and his dodgy website.

'The value of a pound changes every day, depending on what people think it's worth. It's the same with any currency, including digital currencies.'

'So . . . these tokens were not just for, erm, pleasure. They could be traded.'

'Right. Punters would buy ASTs. Performers would be paid in ASTs. But – unlike pounds, more of which are printed every day – the number of ASTs would be finite.'

'Which is important because?'

'The number of tokens is finite. But the demand for porn is infinite.'

'Pretty much,' he agreed.

'Therefore, over time, as more people want to use the Consensual Acts site, they should drive up the price of the tokens. The guys who bought in originally can sell at a profit. This was supposed to be one of the first schemes that allowed you to make money from the money-laundering process itself.'

'But "Bruno Soutine" sold the coins, pocketed the "real" money and did a runner.'

'Pretty much. According to media reports, a number of pretty nasty people are out of pocket. They're scouring the globe for him.'

'Maybe they found him . . . in Covent Garden.'

Quartz wasn't buying it. 'You wouldn't run a scam like this using your real name. The fake pornographer had a fake name – maybe your dead guy's where he got it from.'

Carlyle recalled Karen O'Sullivan's words – *Someone smacked him about a bit, not long before he died.* It looked like the inspector was right to keep an open mind. 'Maybe it wasn't suicide,' he speculated. 'Maybe some of the nasty people thought they'd found their man.'

'You think?' Quartz perked up, sensing a story.

Carlyle recoiled at the gleam in her eye. 'Do me a favour, keep this under your hat for now.'

After some further debate, Quartz finally agreed. 'As long as you give me the exclusive story in due course.'

'Deal.' Carlyle extended a hand and they shook. 'The nasty people – any idea who they are?'

Quartz shook her head. 'No one's rushed into print with the names of crooks dumb enough to be mugged by an online fraudster selling wank tokens.'

'Fair point.'

'Even if I had a list, I very much doubt Fran would publish it.' Francesca Culverhouse, founder of the Investigation Unit, was Quartz's employer. Carlyle had known her for years. It was Culverhouse who had introduced him to Quartz.

'How is the boss these days?' he asked.

'She's fine. As always, wanting more with less.'

'Give her my best.' Carlyle readied himself to leave. 'I'll speak to Sergeant Day for you. And I'll keep you posted on the Bruno Soutine investigation.'

Inspector O'Sullivan and Sergeant Nixon were on the third floor at Charing Cross, deep in conversation. As he approached, they fell silent.

'Bruno Soutine was murdered,' Carlyle said briskly. 'Case of mistaken identity.' He reprised the story of the cryptocurrency scammer. 'Looks like the real Bruno Soutine was mistaken for the fake one. That's why they killed him.'

The inspector was unconvinced. 'It's just a theory,' she pointed out. 'And we have no idea who "they" might be.'

'Correct.' Carlyle wasn't going to let such a detail derail the narrative to which he'd become attached.

'And the motive is questionable,' Nixon put in.

'Whaddya mean?' Carlyle was beginning to get a bit irked by their collective lack of enthusiasm for his stunning breakthrough.

'Why kill the guy?' the sergeant wondered. 'If they're trying to get their money back, surely they'd need him alive.'

'I don't know.' Carlyle made no effort to hide his exasperation. 'These are the blanks you guys need to fill in. As the only outstanding murder on our books, it's top of the to-do list.'

'What about Monica Seppi?' Nixon demanded.

Carlyle struggled to place the name.

'The Romanian assault victim who was illegally disappeared by Immigration Enforcement, the woman Rita Vicedo was trying to track down for us.'

'Have you found her?'

'Yes and no. They took her to Crampton House, a holding facility near Portsmouth, but by the time Rita tracked her down, they'd moved her again. I've got a line on the guys who assaulted her, though.' Ignoring the commander's obvious lack of interest, Nixon ploughed on. 'Peter Williamson and Justin Lansley were seen leaving a pub with Seppi the night she was attacked. I've got some pretty good CCTV images of the three of them heading down the street.'

'There's nothing to pursue if we don't have a victim.' Carlyle looked at O'Sullivan. 'How much time have you been giving this?'

'Not much,' the inspector reassured him. 'Sergeant Nixon is a highly efficient officer when it comes to time management.'

'I've been making some enquiries on my own time,' Nixon added, further burnishing her halo.

'Have you spoken to these guys—'

'Williamson and Lansley? Not yet. I need to speak to Seppi again first . . . if I can find her.'

'Monica Seppi's in Horsburgh.' A spotty youth invited himself onto the fringe of their conversation. Round his neck he wore a navy lanyard. The ID card in the plastic pocket said *VISITOR* in big red letters. He offered his hand to a nonplussed O'Sullivan. 'Sergeant Nixon?'

'I'm Nixon,' the real sergeant corrected him.

'Ah, right.' The boy dispensed with the handshakes and began handing out business cards. 'I'm Kevin Lofthouse from Mellor & Ritchie. I'm representing Monica Seppi in her deportation case.'

'How did you get up here?' Carlyle enquired.

'Mellor & Ritchie staff are pre-cleared for access. The guy on the desk downstairs let me come up.'

'New-ish protocol,' O'Sullivan explained. 'Waiting times for lawyers to get in to see their clients were getting ridiculous.'

'Hm.' Carlyle made a mental note to review the station's security arrangements.

Nixon flashed the lawyer a smile that made the poor sod swoon. 'You said Monica was where?'

Lofthouse composed himself. 'Horsburgh. It's on the outskirts of Dundee.'

'Has she remembered anything more about the night she was attacked?' Nixon asked.

'I don't know anything about that.' Lofthouse sounded defensive. 'I'm focused on dealing with the deportation process. Monica wants to know if you can get her replacement papers.'

'That's hardly our job,' Carlyle snapped.

'I haven't had a chance to speak to the embassy yet.' Nixon ignored her boss. 'I went down to Kensington High Street yesterday, but it was closed.' She led Lofthouse back towards the stairs. 'I'll give you a call as soon as I have anything.'

'I want you to focus on the Soutine thing,' Carlyle instructed O'Sullivan. 'You can't have people going off in all different directions, prioritising their own cases. That way lies chaos.'

A massive grin spread across O'Sullivan's face. 'Yes, sir.'

As the inspector failed to hide her amusement, Carlyle's irritation rose. 'What's so funny?'

'Well,' O'Sullivan coughed, 'if there's one man who's famous for going off and doing his own thing, regardless of what his bosses want, that would be *you*, sir.'

'Bollocks.'

'Your legend precedes you. Rightly or wrongly, there is no one – not one single person – in the entire Metropolitan Police Service who is considered less of a team player than you are.'

Carlyle couldn't really argue with that.

'Things might be a bit different now but, come on, people are going to raise their eyebrows if you start preaching about the chain of command after thirty years of being a sole trader.'

'I haven't been a solo operator for thirty years,' he replied, 'more like thirty-five.'

'So, cut Nixon some slack. She's a good cop and she could become a *great* cop. Give her some support. Get Monica brought back to London and I'll make sure we close both cases for you, Soutine *and* Seppi.'

SEVEN

For once, Carlyle couldn't hear any banging noises issuing from his office. 'How's the refurb coming along?' he asked.

'They say it's almost done. Should be finished tomorrow or the next day.' Joaquin's expression gave nothing away. 'You can look if you want.'

Against his better judgement, the commander stepped through the door onto a thick plastic sheet laid down to protect the carpet. Hands on hips, he breathed in the fumes as he contemplated the green paint plastered on every surface. 'For fuck's sake, Joaquin,' he called over his shoulder, 'I wanted *white*.'

Flouncing out of the building, he took refuge in Grind. Sitting in a corner with a black Americano, he called Rita Vicedo.

'We found Monica Seppi. They moved her to Dundee.'

'Can you get her back to London?' the nun asked.

'Probably.' Carlyle sighed. 'Although it'll probably only delay the inevitable. With the lawyer she's got, she doesn't stand a chance.'

'I can get her proper representation.'

'What she needs is proper documentation – assuming she is, in fact, legal.'

'You doubt her?'

'I've never even met the woman,' Carlyle pointed out. 'Why should I have a view, one way or the other?'

Vicedo didn't let his ill-humour rub off on her. 'I know, but you've seen many cases in your time.'

'I've seen enough to know every case is different.'

'And every case is worthy of our attention.'

'Resources are limited.'

'But human suffering is not.'

Spare me the homily. Carlyle had no time for pious words. 'Sergeant Nixon is trying to verify her identity at the Romanian embassy. It should be possible to get a factual answer to a factual question.'

A voice from above proclaimed, 'You'd have thought so, but it's not so simple.'

'Huh?' Carlyle looked up to see Nixon standing in front of him. 'What are you doing here?'

'Same as you.' Nixon held up a paper cup.

Carlyle ended his call with the nun. 'How long have you been eavesdropping?'

'You weren't exactly being discreet.' Taking a seat opposite him, Nixon placed her cup on the table.

'It isn't exactly official business. Anyway, I'm homeless till they get my bloody office sorted out.'

'Last time I looked, sexual assault was a crime,' the sergeant stated. 'That makes it official business.'

Carlyle circled back to her opening remark. 'What's not simple?'

Nixon looked around before leaning across the table. 'There are thirty-seven different women called Monica Seppi on the official database. Nineteen are dead. Seven are still at school. None of the others have a date of birth matching the one we were given.'

'Admin error?'

'There are only three in the same year. None of them has ever applied for a passport.'

This is why you should leave these things alone, Carlyle

decided. The more work you did, the more work you created for yourself. 'The woman *is* an illegal, then? Is that what you're telling me?'

'Her story certainly doesn't add up.'

'Then leave her to the immigration people. They can sort her out.'

Nixon looked surprised and miffed in equal measure. 'There's still the assault. I still want to go after the men who attacked her, Peter Williamson and Justin Lansley.'

In the face of the sergeant's determination, Carlyle's own resolve crumbled. 'I'll speak to the Home Office. I'll let you know if I get any joy.' After Nixon left, he put in the call. A double dose of patience finally got him put through to the head of Immigration Enforcement, a man called Jamie Worby.

Worby had the constipated telephone manner of burdened bureaucrats the world over. 'How did you get this number?' he spluttered.

Ignoring the question, Carlyle quickly explained what he wanted.

'That's a big ask. Do you have authorisation?'

'Barbara Reynolds pointed me in your direction,' Carlyle lied. Reynolds was Worby's ultimate boss, the CEO of Immigration Enforcement, a.k.a. the Home Secretary's 'Deportation Tsar'.

'Oh, yes?' Dropping Reynolds's name seemed to take the edge off the guy's tone.

'She said you would find this woman for me.'

There was a pause, followed by some muttering, before Worby said, 'What was the name again?'

Carlyle spelt out the surname, twice, and was rewarded with the sound of a keyboard being pummelled at the other end of the line.

More muttering was followed by a groan. 'Our IT system – it's a total bloody nightmare.'

'Tell me about it,' Carlyle empathised. 'Ours is the same.'

Worby bashed some more keys. 'The old system was bad enough, but the new one, bloody hell. Cost a fortune, too. Ended up almost two hundred per cent over budget.'

'They always do.'

More tapping. A few grunts. Then, finally: 'I've found your woman. She's in Horsburgh.'

Carlyle didn't let on he knew this already. 'Where's that?'

'Scotland.'

'Sod's law.' The commander sighed. 'I knew she'd be about as far away as possible.'

'We have to manage capacity in the system,' Worby explained.

Carlyle adopted a philosophical tone. 'These things happen. Anyway, I agreed with Barbara you would expedite the return of this woman to our custody.'

'That's not how it works.' The edge returned to Worby's voice. 'The woman is being readied for voluntary repatriation.'

Interesting use of 'voluntary', Carlyle reflected.

'Once the process starts, there can be no deviation.'

Carlyle had anticipated such an intransigent response. 'I understand, but your boss sees this as a special case. Monica Seppi is a criminal.'

'They're all criminals,' Worby proclaimed.

'Seppi is a *professional* criminal. We know for a fact she has committed a number of very serious offences against persons and property while on British soil. The British public wants to know you can't get away with this kind of thing. It is important for public confidence in the police – *and* the immigration service – that this violent *hooligan* is convicted, jailed and then deported in the full glare of publicity. It's absolutely the kind of story the *Daily Mail* likes to splash all over its front page. It'll be good publicity for both of us.'

Worby considered the commander's pitch, before declaring, 'It's still not in line with protocol.'

Carlyle ignored the man's concerns. 'You can send her down on one of your regular transports or I can ask some of my colleagues from Police Scotland to come and pick her up.'

'Let me get back to you.'

Carlyle knew he couldn't afford to let the man end the call without agreeing to send Seppi back to London. It was time to play his joker. 'We have a hearing scheduled at Southwark Crown Court tomorrow morning. The *Mail*'s sending somebody along and we expect other papers will be there, too. If the case gets thrown out because the police and the Immigration Service couldn't get their act together, the press'll go bananas.' He paused. 'Heads will roll.'

'All right, all right.' There was more tapping of computer keys and then: 'We've got a transport leaving Dundee at nine tonight. I can get Seppi to Southwark in plenty of time for the hearing.'

'Bring her to Charing Cross,' Carlyle said hastily, fearful of snatching defeat from the jaws of victory. 'We agreed with her lawyer that he could talk to her here first.'

'Suit yourself.' More tapping. 'Right. She's booked in.' Worby reeled off a reference number. 'I'll text you the tracking details.'

Just like using Amazon, Carlyle reflected.

'Don't forget to kick her out, when the time comes.'

'Wouldn't dream of it,' Carlyle promised. 'Rest assured, she'll get her just deserts. Congratulations, by the way, for taking one more violent threat to society off the board.'

EIGHT

If Ian Day was surprised to get a call out of the blue from a senior officer, he didn't let it show. The Hampstead sergeant knew nothing about Emily Quartz. 'I wasn't at the pond protest,' he pointed out equably, 'but I heard there were a few arrests. To be honest, the whole thing seems a bit weird. I can't say I'd be very happy if my missus was in a changing room and some bloke waltzed in and started getting his kit off.'

Carlyle could only agree.

'Doesn't mean we should get dragged into it, though.'

'I wanted to know if the investigation'll go anywhere.'

There was a pause, then Day asked, 'If you don't mind me asking, Commander, what's your interest in this?'

Carlyle cleared his throat. 'Quartz is the daughter of a friend.' It was a plausible fib, one the sergeant could hardly check.

There was another pause, followed by a weary sigh. 'Let me see what I can find out, sir.' After a couple of minutes, Day was back on the line with good news: no charges were being brought. 'You can tell your friend's daughter she's in the clear. The ponds manager wasn't very happy about it – he wanted the protesters prosecuted – but the Corporation didn't want the adverse publicity.'

'I'll let her know. I owe you one.'

An exchange of texts with Quartz revealed the reporter was

in the Royal Courts of Justice. Keen to be the bearer of good news in person, he strolled down to the Strand. Court fourteen was empty, save for a couple of gossiping clerks, plus Quartz, sitting in the public gallery, tapping on her laptop.

'Not a lot going on.' Carlyle took the seat but one beside her.

'There rarely is.' Quartz finished typing and closed down the document she was working on. 'The whole system is so inefficient. It never ceases to amaze me. It's a bloody miracle anything gets done at all.'

'The wheels of justice turn slowly,' Carlyle agreed.

'They hardly turn at all.'

'I spoke to Sergeant Day at Hampstead. The investigation relating to the pond protest has been dropped. There'll be no charges.'

'Good.' Abandoning the laptop for her phone, Quartz began checking her email.

You're welcome, Carlyle thought sourly. He watched the clerks disappear through a side door. 'Better not to have a repeat performance, though.'

'We haven't got any more protests planned.'

'Good.' Carlyle looked around the empty court. 'What's the hearing?'

'Been postponed.' Quartz didn't look up from the screen. 'The judge hadn't read the papers. They haven't even been able to agree a new time. Probably take months. Francesca won't be happy – she wants to publish this cryptocurrencies thing ASAP. This would have made a good news peg for it.'

Mention of cryptocurrencies got Carlyle's attention. 'Has this got anything to do with Bruno Soutine?'

Sensing his interest, Quartz put away her phone. 'Indirectly. A company called Sandringham Risk Consulting is suing its former compliance officer for fraud. It's alleged the compliance officer took backhanders to give a clean bill of health to a dodgy client called Kollision Financial Services. Kollision is believed to have links to Soutine, *my* Soutine, that is. Sandringham gave Kollision six million quid to invest in a basket of different cryptocurrencies. The cash disappeared.'

'Into the Bruno Soutine token scam?'

'Maybe. Kollision say they were hacked. SRC reckons it was an inside job.'

Carlyle considered the empty glass box of the dock. 'Who's on trial?'

'There are seven defendants in total. The most important are the SRC's compliance officer, a woman called Elena Doyle, and Tim Hitchcock, Kollision's CEO. The gossip is they were shagging but that's only a rumour. Hitchcock's wife is also a defendant so, as you can imagine, there's an interesting dynamic.'

'What's Hitchcock like?'

'He comes across as your typical spivvy City guy – pinstripe suit and too much gel in his hair. Been chasing one get-rich-quick scheme after another for decades. One theory is that he gave Soutine the six million to put into worthless tokens so they could split the proceeds further down the line.'

Feeling his leg start to cramp, Carlyle stood up. 'This guy Hitchcock,' he asked, 'where can I find him?'

'Back here,' Quartz deadpanned, 'in about nine months.'

The overnight drive down from Scotland had done nothing for Monica Seppi's mood. No one had explained why she was being delivered to a London police station, and a lukewarm shower had done little to ease her aches and pains. Breakfast was another cheap sandwich and a cup of stewed coffee. Finishing it, Seppi carefully put the packaging back into the paper bag in which it had arrived. Placing the bag in the middle of the table, she stared at Laura Nixon across the interview room table.

She recognised the policewoman from the hospital. 'Why am I here?'

'Peter Williamson and Justin Lansley.'

Seppi kept her face blank. 'Who?'

'The men who attacked you.'

The woman sounded more like a social worker than a cop. Seppi affected a tone of weary resignation. 'I have more important things to worry about now.'

'Hm.'

'Why am I being moved around all the time?'

'I'm sorry.' Nixon fiddled with her paper coffee cup. 'Sometimes you get caught in the system and it doesn't make a lot of sense.'

'Why did you bring me here? Am I under arrest?'

'Not at all. My job is to catch the men who attacked you. I need to speak to you about your assault.'

'If you want to help me, stop them deporting me.'

'That remains a matter for Immigration Enforcement.' To Nixon's eye, a short 'rest', courtesy of the Home Office, had done Monica Seppi some good. Her face still showed signs of the assault but she no longer looked like she'd been in a car crash. 'I spoke to the embassy – they have no record of you.'

'You can see I'm real.' Seppi grabbed the skin on her forearm. 'I exist.'

'I didn't say you weren't real,' Nixon said patiently, 'but they can't find your details.'

'An administrative error,' Seppi suggested.

Nixon opened a blue folder sitting on the desk. Removing two A4 photographs, she placed them on the table. 'These are surveillance camera images from the night you were attacked.' The sergeant tapped one of the images with a manicured nail. 'That's you leaving the Lazy Donkey public house, accompanied by two men, Williamson and Lansley.'

Leaning forward, Seppi peered at the pictures. 'Could be.'

'You don't recognise yourself?' Nixon scanned the woman's face but Seppi was giving nothing away.

'It could be me, it's impossible to say.'

'Do you remember going to the pub?'

'Maybe. I've been there before, for sure, but that night is still a blank.'

'And the men?'

Her reply was firm. 'No.'

'Peter Williamson and Justin Lansley. You don't know them?'

'No.' Rubbing her temples, Seppi asked for some pills and a bottle of water. 'I've got a terrible headache.'

'I'm sure I've got some paracetamol upstairs.' Nixon pushed back her chair and stood up. 'Wait here a minute.'

'Whaddya mean she walked out?' Carlyle looked at Nixon in disbelief.

'She said she had a headache.' The sergeant stared at a hole in the carpet. 'I went to get some paracetamol for her, and when I got back to the interview room, she'd done a runner.'

'Fuck's sake,' Carlyle complained. 'I went out on a limb for you to get this bloody woman and you lose her. The Home Office will kill me.'

'She wasn't under arrest.'

'That's not what I told the head of Immigration Enforcement.' He tried to remember the guy's name. Worby.

Jamie Worby.

If he found out they'd lost Monica Seppi, Jamie fucking Worby would be able to incinerate Carlyle's career with a single phone call.

'Don't worry, Commander, we'll find her.' Karen O'Sullivan didn't sound either convinced or convincing. 'She can't get far without any papers.'

74

'She seems to be doing pretty well so far.' Carlyle tried to focus on how best to cover this up. 'If we can find her, great. If not, we need to invent some kind of bureaucratic cock-up.' He looked at the crestfallen Nixon. 'When did she arrive at the station?'

'Just after five,' the sergeant confirmed. 'I signed for her myself.'

'Okay,' Carlyle decided. 'This is what we'll do . . .'

O'Sullivan watched Nixon scuttle off before turning to face the commander. 'That's your plan?'

Carlyle glared at her. 'Have you got a better one?'

The inspector had not.

'Then I propose you start trying to find the woman. If she doesn't turn up, we're all fucked.'

'Isn't that a bit melodramatic?' the inspector wondered.

'The only question Barbara Reynolds will have if she finds out about this is who to call first, the commissioner or the *Daily Mail*. One'll kill you, the other'll piss all over your corpse.'

'Urgh.'

'We also need to find out more about Monica Seppi – she's clearly not your average East European victim straight out of Central Casting.'

'The woman certainly seems to have a bit of gumption.' There was more than a hint of admiration in the inspector's voice.

'Nixon certainly met her match.'

'Poor kid.'

'It's a learning experience,' Carlyle declared.

'She won't be disciplined?'

'For what? Letting a member of the public leave the building? No way. Apart from anything else, if Nixon gets a kicking, you get a monster kicking, and I get a *monster-monster* kicking.' He looked at the inspector. 'And that can't happen, right?'

O'Sullivan agreed. 'By the way, I'm still digging on the Bruno Soutine thing. Have you ever heard of a company called Kollision Financial Services?'

It took Carlyle but a moment to place the name. 'Funnily enough, I have. They're involved in a court case where the chief executive is said to be mates with Bruno Soutine, although not necessarily *our* Bruno Soutine.'

'Very good.' The inspector mimed a round of applause. 'How do you know so much already?'

'I have my sources – mainly Google and Wikipedia.'

'It's amazing how much information's out there if you look for it,' O'Sullivan agreed. 'My boy, George, was at his friend Arjun's house. Arjun's dad is a forensic accountant. When George mentioned we were working on the Soutine case, the dad went into overdrive.' She held up her hand, thumb and forefinger a couple of inches apart. 'He sent George home with a folder this thick of articles.'

'You discuss your work at home?'

'Don't you?'

Carlyle had to admit that he did. 'My wife's input can be really helpful. She's got good judgement.'

'It can be good to get an external perspective,' O'Sullivan said, 'but I don't have that option, being a single parent.'

'No.' Carlyle couldn't begin to imagine how she did it, juggling both roles.

'There's plenty I *don't* tell the kids, but it's good they have some understanding of what I do at work. Especially when it stops me getting home sometimes. They need to know I'm only late when important work's keeping me back.'

'Maybe we should have a bring-your-kids-to-work day,' Carlyle suggested.

The inspector rolled her eyes. 'I think we've got more than enough on our plate for the moment, don't you?'

'Good point.'

'Anyway, after I read the stuff, I spoke to the forensic accountant – on the QT – and he did a bit more digging on Kollision's
boss for me.'

'Tim Hitchcock.'

'Yeah.'

This is what police work has come to, Carlyle thought
glumly, scouring the internet and begging favours from casual
acquaintances.

'I think he's got a soft spot for me,' O'Sullivan said.

'Huh?'

'The forensic accountant.'

'Ah.'

'Not that I'd get involved with a married man.'

Too much information. 'Glad to hear it.'

'At least, not when I'm friends with his wife.'

Moving swiftly on, Carlyle asked, 'Did he come up with anything interesting?'

'There's a list of business associates and Kollision investors.'
O'Sullivan pulled up an email on her phone and showed it to
Carlyle. 'Sixty-one names, including some senior Met officers,
a few MPs and even a junior minister. There's also some less
salubrious types.'

'Who can be less salubrious than a politician?' Carlyle ran
down the list. A few names were familiar, but nothing jumped
out at him. He handed the phone back to O'Sullivan before a
switch tripped in his brain and he grabbed it back. 'Hold on . . .
hold *on*.' He scrolled back up the list from the bottom, taking it
slowly. Somewhere around the middle, he found the name his
brain had belatedly processed: Patrick Dalby.

Carlyle admired the calming, off-white colour of David Holland's
walls. There was no hint of prison green anywhere in the chief

inspector's office. It was all the commander could do to refrain from taking a picture and sending it to Joaquin with a message saying, *This is what I want.*

The relaxing effect of the décor, however, could not offset Holland's annoyance at being forced to receive an unexpected visitor. 'I've got a budget meeting in five minutes,' was his opening gambit, 'and then I'll be tied up for the rest of the day.'

Carlyle had no sympathy for colleagues who liked to spend their working lives hiding in meetings. Getting straight to the point, he asked, 'How're things going on the car-bomb investigation?'

'Slowly,' Holland griped. The man was tanned and had a healthy air, indicating a familiarity with athletic pursuits of one sort or another. 'Imogen Edelman is a complete pain in the backside, hassling me for an update every five minutes.'

'She was almost blown to bits,' Carlyle pointed out. 'You can understand why she's nervous.'

'Mistaken identity,' Holland asserted flatly. 'We haven't found any reason why she would be the intended target.'

'What about Patrick Dalby?'

'Who?'

'Patrick Dalby is the half-brother of the recently deceased Victoria Dalby-Cummins.'

Holland checked his watch, inviting Carlyle to get on with it.

'Victoria left a sizeable estate – to charity. Patrick was contesting his sister's will.'

'What's the connection to Edelman?'

'Imogen Edelman runs a consultancy advising charities.'

'Yes, I know.'

'She helped redraft the will and has responsibility for delivering the bequest to the relevant charity.' Carlyle was careful not to mention *which* charity.

Holland considered this for a nanosecond. 'Your theory is

this guy tried to blow Edelman up in her car in order to stop her giving his sister's money away?'

'It's got to be a line worth looking at, in the absence of anything else.'

'Sure, sure.' Holland scooped up a bundle of papers from his desk and got to his feet. 'No need to worry, Commander. You can tell your wife we've got it all under control.'

Carlyle stiffened. 'Sorry?'

'Your missus runs the charity that's supposed to get the inheritance money.' Stepping round the desk, Holland invited Carlyle to take his leave. 'Edelman told me. She told me about Patrick Dalby, too. I just wanted to see how you were going to spin it.'

Busted. Embarrassed, Carlyle got to his feet. 'I didn't spin it,' he protested. 'I was just trying to help.'

'You're trying to get your wife her cash. Which is fair enough. Avalon does a good job. Nice people. Hearts in the right place and all that. But I don't like colleagues who won't give me the full picture. Your lack of full disclosure is troubling.'

Carlyle apologised.

Holland opened the door and ushered him out of the office. 'You're right, though. It's a lot of money – enough to kill for.'

'You're looking for Dalby, then?'

'Don't worry,' said Holland, 'we're tracking him down. I'll keep you posted.'

NINE

He found Helen watching a TV documentary about rich divorcees. She was less than impressed by his progress in hunting down Patrick Dalby. 'I can't believe you haven't sorted this out yet.'

'Looking for more donors?' Carlyle pointed at the TV in a doomed attempt to lighten the mood.

'This isn't a joke, John. Imogen's in bits. They've even hired bodyguards to protect the house and take the kids to school.'

'That's ridiculous.' The words escaped before he could clamp his stupid gob shut.

'Is it?' Helen paused the programme, the better to give him both barrels. 'What would you do if some lunatic came after us?'

I'd take care of it. Like I did before. Carlyle stopped short of mentioning Tuco Martinez, the crazy French gangster, who had threatened them a while back. Bad memories best left buried.

'In fact, what if Dalby does come after us or, more precisely, *me*?'

Carlyle dismissed the possibility with a scowl.

'But if he did?' Helen pressed him. 'What would you do? Would you treat it as a joke?'

'I'd sort it.'

'Very reassuring. I can see why people don't want to go into police protection.'

Don't rise to the bait, Carlyle told himself. 'Where's Imogen's husband?'

'Oh, so it's his problem, is it?'

'I didn't say that.'

Helen wasn't in the mood to listen. 'The kids could have been in the car when the bloody bomb went off, but the police aren't doing anything. They aren't keeping the family informed. And, worst of all, they aren't getting their finger out, trying to find the bloke who did it.'

In a situation like this, Carlyle had long since determined, all you could do was roll over and try to deflect the blame. 'This guy Holland, the chief inspector on the case, doesn't seem much cop,' he offered, trying to sound rueful, 'no pun intended.'

Helen wasn't having it. 'You're his boss,' she snapped. 'It's up to you to sort him out.'

'I'm not his boss,' Carlyle insisted. 'I hadn't even heard of the bloke until the other day.'

'Just sort it out. Find the bomber and put him in jail. Then, maybe, Imogen can start getting her life back and Avalon can have its money.' Pep talk over, she restarted her programme.

Carlyle watched glumly as some plastic blonde extolled the joys of embracing lesbianism after taking her banker husband to the cleaners in the divorce courts. Find the bomber and put him in jail. Yeah, sure, no problem, sweetheart. Consider it done.

'I can't believe this is happening.' Declan Brady tapped a teaspoon on the Formica tabletop. 'A decade of hard work – an *immense, monumental slog* – to get to this point and now it could all be down the drain.'

Laura Nixon finished her coffee and let her gaze wander towards the exit. After finally finding a time that worked for both of them, she had been hoping for something better than a visit to the hospital canteen. Declan was a nice bloke, but he never seemed to leave the place. Even worse, his only topic of conversation was the NHS, although, given all he seemed to do was work, that shouldn't have come as much of a surprise.

'I know mistakes are the portals of discovery and all that,' the doctor burbled, 'but only if you manage to survive them.'

'Huh?'

'PALS are going to kill me,' Brady continued, oblivious to Nixon's thought processes.

The sergeant tried to sound vaguely sympathetic while adding doctors to policemen on her *DO NOT DATE* list. At least she hadn't shagged the bloke – that would have made the whole situation exponentially more embarrassing.

'How can it be my fault? Samuel Fisher wasn't even on one of my wards.'

'He was the first time.' Nixon showed that she'd at least been listening to the blow-by-blow account of his downfall.

Brady began waving his teaspoon in the air, like an orchestra conductor. 'No one complained about *that*. Charlotte Monkseaton took the news that her poor old dad had been assaulted by the loony in the next bed in her stride.'

'It could have been worse.' Nixon had already heard the story multiple times. 'To be fair, not many people would be so relaxed.'

'Amy Spode certainly wasn't,' Brady grumbled. Spode's ninety-year-old father had been Fisher's next victim. 'The first bloody thing she did was demand the number of Patient Advice and Liaison Services. Didn't even ask how her dad was.'

Once an investigation had been opened it had taken PALS about two minutes to uncover the original attack on Philip Monkseaton. Brady was facing a disciplinary hearing, which could see him thrown out of the hospital. Even if he wasn't struck off, he would be unemployable.

'The woman's chasing compo,' Nixon suggested.

'I'm still fecked,' Brady concluded. 'The cover-up's what's gonna get me.'

'We all make mistakes.' Nixon explained how Monica Seppi had waltzed out of Charing Cross.

'Are you gonna be in trouble?' Brady asked, his own woes put aside for a moment.

'Depends on how the cover-up goes,' Nixon said. 'The boss is going to try and sort it out.'

'Lucky you. When things go wrong here, everyone runs for the hills – or the golf course, or the squash court.'

'Do people still play squash?' Nixon asked. 'Wasn't that, like, a 1970s thing?'

'Doctors do,' said Brady. 'A lot of things in the NHS are stuck in the seventies.'

There was a lull in the conversation as they watched an insanely fat bloke hobble past on crutches. Once he'd disappeared, Brady asked, 'Any hope of finding your woman again?'

'Not a chance,' Nixon replied. 'She could be anywhere.'

Sitting in a booth in the snug bar of the Lazy Donkey, Monica Seppi stared at the low piles of coins lined up on the table. Passing a tube station, she had robbed a busker, an old guy playing the accordion, grabbing the hat containing spare cash handed over by commuters. With the benefit of hindsight, it had not been her smartest ever move. The instrument made a hell of a racket and it wasn't much of a surprise when the haul was revealed to be less than five pounds. After paying for a tiny bottle of fizzy water, she had precisely £1.12 to her name.

Money, however, wasn't everything. Monica felt a sense of serenity as she contemplated the bubbles in her glass. In this moment, living her life was like watching a favourite movie – the outcome was predetermined, and it had a happy ending.

The pub was filling only slowly. No one hassled her to give up the table. Seppi watched a familiar figure arrive at the bar. After buying a pint and a packet of crisps, Justin Lansley scanned the room, looking for a seat. Catching his eye, she beckoned him over.

'Hey, long time no see.' Pulling out a seat, Lansley sat down opposite her.

Yeah, like a few days.

'You're looking good.'

Seppi accepted the fake compliment with a curt nod. The bruises on her face were fading, but the signs of her beating were still clearly visible.

'How's it going?'

'Good.' Seppi sipped her mineral water for the first time in almost an hour. 'Peter not around?'

'I might see him later.' Lansley drank a mouthful of lager.

'You guys know how to party, huh?' Another sip. A flutter of the eyelashes. 'Want to do it again?'

'Seriously?'

'Sure,' Seppi purred. 'I like a bit of – what do you English people call it? – slap and . . .'

'Slap and tickle.' Lansley started to grin.

'I *love* a bit of slap and tickle. Especially the slapping.' Seppi ran her tongue along her top lip. 'I don't mind being knocked about a bit. In fact, it turns me on.'

'Really?' Struggling to believe his luck, Lansley chugged more of his lager.

'This time it'll cost you, though. Last time was free. This time – two hundred.' She hoped it was a credible sum, but not too much.

Lansley considered the offer. 'Each?'

'A hundred each.'

'A hundred, total. Fifty quid each.'

After a bit of haggling, they settled on a hundred and thirty.

'Cash in advance.'

Lansley trotted off to a cash machine in a minimart across the road. When he came back, he handed over a selection of rubbery notes, topped up with a selection of coins.

'That's only half.' Seppi shoved the cash into her pocket.

'Peter'll give you his share when he gets to the house.' Still on his feet, Lansley downed the remains of his pint. 'Drink up, I'm going first this time and I want to get my money's worth.'

'Don't worry,' Seppi murmured. 'This will be an experience you'll never forget.'

'Look, this is a bit embarrassing, but I've got to be straight with you.' Wandering round the third floor of Charing Cross, phone clamped to his ear, Carlyle tried to sound contrite and hassled at the same time. 'Bottom line, there was a bit of a cock-up at our end.' He paused. 'We asked you for the wrong alien.'

'Useless bastards,' Jamie Worby growled down the line.

'We weren't looking for Monica Seppi at all. Rather, we were after a woman called, erm, Sandra Buzan. Date of birth, the first of August 2001.' Did that make the fictitious immigrant too young? No point in worrying about that now. He spelt the surname.

'The court must have loved that,' the head of Immigration Enforcement said drily.

Carlyle ran with the lie. 'We managed to spot the mistake before she arrived at Southwark but, yeah, the court wasn't very happy.'

'Doubtless an understatement. Who was the judge?'

Carlyle mentioned a beak he'd come across recently. 'Waterman.'

'Not a man to take any nonsense.'

'He was furious.'

'I can imagine.'

'Happily, I wasn't there.' At least that was true. Carlyle crossed his fingers that Worby wasn't the kind of guy to check the court listings for himself. 'But these things happen, right? It's not like the courts don't make mistakes themselves. I had this case once—'

'What went wrong?' Worby asked. Clearly he didn't want to listen to the commander trip down Memory Lane.

'Human error. You can't get the staff.'

'Tell me about it. Some of the people we use, my God.'

'My assistant handed me the wrong file. I gave him a right bollocking about it but it's like talking to a plank, you know. He's Spanish.' Wondering if he was laying it on a bit thick, Carlyle shut up.

'Have you told Barbara?'

'Not yet. I know your boss is busy, with the drink-driving charge and whatnot.' God had clearly been on Carlyle's side when Barbara Reynolds had been stopped in Birmingham at two in the morning after driving erratically in her BMW. The deportation tsar had been tested for drink and drugs and found to have twice the legal limit of alcohol in her blood. Ordered to appear before local magistrates, she was sent home but not before the media had been tipped off. According to *The Times*, Reynolds's resignation was in the post. 'The priority is to try to get this thing sorted out. That's why I was ringing. What I need right now is for you to send me this, erm, Buzan lady.'

'Where's she being held?'

'No idea.'

'Let me check.' Worby issued a sigh of such world-weary proportions you could imagine he'd been offered a final cigarette while standing in front of a firing squad.

Carlyle waited patiently while the official engaged in a bout of hand-to-hand combat with the state-of-the-art detainee tracking system. After a while, he came back on the line and confirmed what Carlyle already knew: 'We don't have a Sandra Buzan in custody.'

'Fuck.' Carlyle groaned theatrically. 'Are you sure? Maybe I've got the spelling wrong.' He waited patiently while Worby tried a couple of variants.

'It looks like no one of that name has ever been entered in the database.'

'Are you sure?' the commander repeated.

'Yes.'

'Where is she, then?'

'I'm afraid, Commander, that's your problem.' There was more than a hint of *Schadenfreude* in Worby's voice. 'I can't help you.'

'Fuck. What do I do now?'

'I'm sure you'll think of something.'

Carlyle uttered a few more curses.

'In the meantime,' Worby said, 'I'll need you to send Monica Seppi back to us.'

'Back to Dundee?'

'No.' More tapping. 'I need her to go to Colnbrook. It's the only removal centre with any capacity at the present moment in time.'

'Business is booming.'

'It's a never-ending fight to get rid of the buggers,' Worby said. 'The more we send back, the more turn up.'

'I'm sure you're on the case.'

'The whole thing's completely out of control.' It sounded like a well-rehearsed rant. 'The sooner we get proper control of our borders back the better.'

'Wasn't that supposed to have happened already?' the commander enquired innocently.

'It was *supposed* to,' Worby responded. 'Nothing much seems to have changed, though.'

Carlyle couldn't resist a little jibe: 'Maybe you could just start sinking their boats. Or shooting them as they approach Passport Control.'

'What?'

'Nothing. I'll get Seppi back to you right away.' There was something quite invigorating about such blatant lying. Ending the call, he almost expected a round of applause. Instead, he looked up to see the spotty lawyer, Kevin Lofthouse, standing in front of him. 'They let you in, again?'

'The people downstairs know me now.'

'All the more reason why they should keep you in Reception,' Carlyle fumed. There was no way civilians, especially lawyers, should be allowed to roam the police station unattended. He made another mental note – the first clearly having got lost somewhere in the pathways of his brain – to review the station's security arrangements. Channelling his inner bureaucrat, he wondered if a stern memo to all staff would do the trick. Unlikely, he decided, but a useful back-covering exercise all the same.

'Where's my client?' Lofthouse enquired.

The commander played dumb. 'Remind me, who do you represent?'

'Monica Seppi. The woman waiting to be deported.'

'The assault victim.'

'The assault victim waiting to be deported. Where is she?'

Carlyle signalled a sense of helplessness. 'How should I know?'

'I was looking for Sergeant Nixon but she's not here.'

And what am I supposed to do about it? Carlyle wondered. 'I'll get her to call you,' he promised, 'when I see her.'

The lawyer took his leave. Carlyle retreated upstairs to find Joaquin watching a movie on his computer.

'For God's sake,' Carlyle muttered, 'at least *pretend* to do some work.'

'Did you have anything in particular in mind?' Pausing the film, the PA looked at him expectantly.

'I want to send a memo to the staff.'

'A memo?' Joaquin's eyes narrowed. 'That's not your kind of thing, is it?'

'I think there's a need.'

'Hm. Are you feeling all right?'

Carlyle pointed at the PA's notepad sitting on the desk. 'Just take this down. It's to go to all Charing Cross staff, on the subject of station security.' Careful to go slowly and enunciate clearly, he dictated his missive. 'Get it typed up and let me see it before it goes.'

As Joaquin scribbled down his pearls of wisdom, Carlyle bounced into his office.

'What the fuck?'

'Maybe I should do a memo on swearing,' Joaquin suggested wearily.

'What?' Carlyle immediately reappeared in front of his desk.

'Nothing, boss.' Joaquin looked at him enquiringly. 'What's the problem?'

'It's still fucking green.' Carlyle jerked a thumb in the direction of his office. 'I thought they were going to redecorate.'

'They changed it,' Joaquin insisted.

'To a different green.'

'It's avocado.'

'Avocado's a colour they used for bathrooms in the 1970s. If I remember rightly, I asked for white. White – like a KKK convention.'

'What's a KKK convention?'

'Seriously?'

Joaquin looked at him blankly.

'You've never heard of the Ku Klux Klan?'

'Is it a rap group?'

Was the boy taking the piss? Carlyle decided base stupidity was the more likely explanation. 'It's a bunch of racists in America,' he explained, 'who used to march about burning crosses and wearing bedsheets over their heads. Come to think about it, they probably still do.'

Karen O'Sullivan appeared in the doorway. 'What've the Ku Klux Klan got to do with anything?'

'The commander's not happy with the decoration of his office,' Joaquin explained.

'Never mind about that,' Carlyle said hastily. 'What brings you up here to the home of bad taste?'

'We got a call about two men who've been seriously assaulted.' She mentioned an address in East London.

'Not our patch,' Carlyle pointed out. 'What's it got to do with us?'

'The call came straight into Charing Cross,' the inspector explained. 'A woman. She asked specifically for Sergeant Nixon.'

Carlyle put two and two together. 'Monica Seppi?'

'Could be,' O'Sullivan replied. 'Nixon's on her way to the scene now. I said we'd meet her there.'

By the time Carlyle and O'Sullivan reached the address, the victims had been taken to hospital. Nixon was in the living room, looking on as a pair of forensics technicians studied the copious blood stains on the carpet. The place smelt like a public toilet that hadn't been cleaned in months. Feeling faintly nauseous, the commander tried to breathe through his mouth.

'Jesus,' O'Sullivan groaned, 'whose blood is it?'

'Peter Williamson's,' Nixon replied. 'Or Justin Lansley's.'

'Or both,' grunted one of the technicians, 'most likely.'

'The guys who attacked Monica Seppi.' Nixon sounded quite pleased about it.

'She's toying with us.' Carlyle didn't like it.

'Both have suffered extensive groin and other injuries,' Nixon confirmed, 'which could yet prove fatal. Williamson, in particular, is in a bad way.'

'How old are they?'

'Late twenties?' Nixon guessed.

'And they were taken down by Monica Seppi?'

'Classic revenge attack,' was O'Sullivan's take.

'Even if they survive,' Nixon added, 'the paramedics say it's possible, maybe even likely, they'll never regain proper functionality.'

Carlyle winced. 'Where did they take them?'

'I'll have to check,' Nixon admitted. 'I doubt either of them is going to be in a position to talk to us for some time.'

'At least we have a prime suspect,' O'Sullivan chipped in.

'We have the *name* of a prime suspect,' Carlyle pointed out. 'Not the same thing.'

'You don't even have that.'

They turned to see Rita Vicedo standing in the doorway.

'What are you doing here?' Carlyle blurted.

'I called her,' Nixon admitted.

Carlyle glared at his underling but said nothing.

'All you have is a fake name.' The nun offered an apologetic smile. 'Sorry to be the bearer of bad news, Commander, but I think you've got a bigger problem on your hands than you might initially have realised.'

'Great.' Carlyle delegated O'Sullivan to liaise with the forensics team, while Nixon was dispatched to keep an eye on the victims. Leading Vicedo outside, he started down the road. 'Let's go and get a drink.' Up ahead was a crossroads, boasting a pub and a couple of coffee shops. 'I think I need some alcohol.'

The pub was called the Lazy Donkey. Rita Vicedo's chosen tipple was Guinness. Carlyle paid for a pint of the black stuff and a double Jameson's for himself and they retreated to a booth at the back.

'Cheers.'

'Cheers.' Vicedo took a taste. After wiping a line of froth from her top lip, she said, 'I checked you out.'

'Yeah?' Carlyle was surprised.

'I didn't realise a commander was so important.'

'You don't think I'm cut out for such a senior position?'

'I didn't think you were the kind of policeman who sits behind a desk all day.'

'As you can see, I still manage to get out and about.' Carlyle placed his drink on the table, as yet untouched. 'Whatever rank you are, you can't do the job properly without getting out of the office now and again.'

'But you're management. You could be the number-one big chief one day.'

'Commissioner?' Carlyle laughed out loud. 'That'll never happen.'

'No?'

'No,' Carlyle confidently asserted. 'I never expected to get this far.'

'But you're a good cop, no?'

'I try my best.' He took a nip of the whiskey.

Vicedo waved her pint pot in the direction of the street outside. 'This is a nasty one, huh?'

'It's certainly a confusing one,' Carlyle confessed. 'You have a woman who was attacked and incarcerated, then gives the authorities the slip and takes bloody revenge on her attackers. Who the hell is Monica Seppi? She certainly isn't playing the role of the stereotypical victim.'

'Well, for a start, she isn't the real Monica Seppi.'

First two Bruno Soutines, now two Monica Seppis? Everyone's at the identity-fraud game, Carlyle reflected. How many more John Carlyles might there be out there? he wondered.

'The real Monica Seppi was born in the Romanian city of Sibiu. She died when she was three years old.'

'And *our* Monica Seppi, if I can put it like that, stole this dead girl's identity?'

'It's one of a number of false identities she uses.'

'And what's her real name?'

'I don't know,' the nun confessed.

'So she's some kind of professional crook or fraudster?'

'Worse. The woman works – or maybe worked – for the Slovak Intelligence Service, SIS.'

'Slovakia, as in Czechoslovakia?'

'Separated from the Czech Republic in 1993, after the fall of Communism.'

Carlyle's confusion deepened. 'So she's not Romanian?'

'Who knows?' Vicedo shrugged. 'She might be. You can work for a country other than that of your birth.'

'I suppose so.' Carlyle was reminded of the Establishment types who'd spied for the Soviet Union back in the day. 'What's she doing in London?'

'What's any spy doing anywhere?'

Carlyle changed tack. 'How did you manage to find all this out?'

Vicedo recoiled slightly. 'Come on, Commander, you know better than to ask. I've gone out of my way to help you as it is. You can't ask me to betray my sources.'

'I really appreciate your help and I'm not asking you to betray anyone.' He tried to give her a stern look. 'But this is an active police investigation. You saw the mess back there – the woman is dangerous. It's a very serious business.'

'I am cooperating fully,' the nun said politely, '*and* I'm working hard on your behalf.'

'I need more.'

'I've given you as much as I can. The point is that you now

have a better idea of what you're dealing with. Like you say, this is a very dangerous woman. You have to proceed carefully.'

'I gathered that from back at the scene. I suppose her SIS background explains how she was able to cause such carnage.'

'She's a very highly trained operative,' Vicedo agreed.

'The question is, what's she gonna do next?'

'If you're lucky, she's already on her way back to Bratislava.'

'And if I'm not?'

The nun savoured another mouthful of Guinness. 'Who knows?'

'In the hands of God, eh?'

Vicedo's expression hardened. 'Don't make fun, Commander. This has nothing to do with God.'

'Sorry.' Carlyle stared at the table. 'I apologise.'

'Apology accepted. You will forgive me for being a little bit touchy on the subject but people in this country see the nun thing as a bit of a joke. It can be wearisome at times.'

'Blame Julie Andrews. She's the only nun most people have ever come across.'

'Ah yes, *The Sound of Music*. A British institution.'

'Have you seen it?'

'I've seen a clip on YouTube.' Vicedo's expression indicated she had been less than impressed. 'I'm more into Almodóvar and Buñuel.'

Carlyle said nothing.

'Anyway, I need to be going.'

Carlyle watched her finish her pint. 'Could I meet your source?' he asked.

Vicedo placed the empty glass on the table, a thoughtful look on her face. 'Let me see,' she said finally. 'It might be possible.' She offered up a smile that caused his calloused old heart to flutter as he reconsidered a lifetime of devout atheism. 'As long as you promise not to scare him.'

TEN

A gentle knock on the door had Declan Brady scrabbling to zip up his trousers. 'Shit. Just, erm, coming. I mean, hold on a minute.'

Making himself decent, the doctor swiped Pornhub from the screen of his phone and rolled off the bed. To his chagrin, he realised the door wasn't locked. Lifting his gaze to the heavens, he offered a silent prayer of thanks that whoever was after him hadn't just barged in. With his job hanging by a thread, the last thing he needed was somebody catching him knocking one out.

'One sec.' Taking a deep breath, he opened the door. Standing in front of him was Laura Nixon. Conscious of the bulge in his trousers, Brady buttoned his jacket.

'Sorry, did I wake you?'

'Killing time.' He coughed. 'They give you somewhere to crash when you're on call, but you never get much sleep. My all-time record is an hour and five minutes between interruptions.'

If he was looking for sympathy, the sergeant failed to oblige. 'I wanted to check on Justin Lansley and Peter Williamson.'

'The guys who were, um, attacked.' Brady tried not to think about the nature of their injuries. 'You can go and see them, but they're sedated up to the eyeballs. They're not going to be able to talk to you.'

'Just show me where they are and then you can buy me a

coffee.' Nixon looked down at the socks on his feet – one red, the other yellow – and smiled. 'I'll wait while you put your shoes on.'

'It was a pretty brutal attack.' Sitting in the hospital café, Declan Brady chomped happily on a Lion Bar. 'Those poor buggers are never going to be the same again.'

'They had it coming.' Nixon considered Justin Lansley and Peter Williamson, sleeping soundly in adjoining rooms upstairs, hooked up to an array of machines, enjoying the best the NHS could offer. Arguably, it was better than they deserved. 'They're the ones who attacked Monica.'

'Eh?' Brady shoved the remains of the bar into his mouth and crumpled the empty wrapper in his fist.

'We think Monica Seppi – the woman going by the name of Monica Seppi – attacked them in revenge.'

'Wow.' Brady's eyes grew wide. 'On her own?'

'As far as we know.'

Dropping the wrapper on the table, Brady let out a low whistle. 'She fucked them up pretty bad.'

'I know.' The sergeant tried not to sound too cheery about it. 'But this is all between you and me.' She began fiddling with the lid of her paper cup. 'The investigation is ongoing.'

'Sure.' Brady leant forward, forearms resting on the table. 'I understand.'

'We were looking at Lansley and Williamson for the original attack. Monica claimed not to know them, but it looks like she only said that because she wanted to take matters into her own hands.'

'If I were them, I'm not sure I'd want to wake up.' Brady defaulted to a standard noncommittal professional mode. 'There's a lot we can do with reconstructive surgery these days but, equally, there's plenty we can't. Both of them were savagely mutilated. The paramedics on the scene did a great job recovering what they could but . . .'

Now it was Nixon whose eyes grew bigger. 'They'll be eunuchs for the rest of their lives?'

'Too early to be definitive. Both have had emergency surgery, which went well, but rehabilitation could take months, more likely years. And there are limits to what we can do here. You might be looking at going to the US or France to get the best treatment.'

'I'd be surprised if these guys had health insurance.'

'Even if they did, it probably wouldn't do them much good. What you need, in a case like this, is some wealthy American hospital that wants to use you as a guinea pig for the latest pioneering techniques. There's bound to be some professor over there specialising in this kind of thing. The quid pro quo, however, is that you have to be paraded in front of the world as part of some twenty-first-century freak show.'

'Don't forget, these guys are sex offenders. Who would want to go out of their way to help them?'

'Good point.' Brady cracked open a can of cherry Coke and drank deeply. 'Bottom line, we'll just have to wait and see.'

'How are things going with your disciplinary hearing?' the sergeant asked.

'It rolls ominously on. My PALS hearing is tomorrow.' Brady glanced at his phone. 'In sixteen hours and thirty-five minutes, not that I'm counting or anything.'

'Good luck.'

'It'll be fine.' He sounded considerably less than confident.

Nixon got to her feet and started for the exit. 'Let me know when Lansley and Williamson wake up.'

'I will, if I'm still here.' He called her back. 'One final thing . . .'

'Yes?'

'Neither guy had a wallet on them – or any ID – when they were brought in. Did you find anything at the scene?'

'I don't think so.' Nixon tried to think back. 'I'll double-check.'

'Just a thought,' Brady offered. 'She might have robbed them, as well as, you know . . .'

'Good shout.'

'Maybe you can track their credit cards or something. Like they do on TV.'

'Like they do on TV.' Nixon rolled her eyes. 'I'll check it out.'

Third time lucky. After a couple of cancelled lunches, Carlyle caught up with Lottie Pearson at a restaurant near Tower Bridge, a stone's throw from City Hall. It had been quite the schlep, but the place was a step or two up from his usual establishments and he was happy to make the effort.

Filling his glass with carbonated water, Carlyle offered a toast to their delayed lunch date. 'We got there in the end.'

'Yes.' Pearson looked at him over the top of her menu. 'I was worried I was going to have to cancel *again* this morning. Something came up. Then it went away.'

'It's always pleasing when things sort themselves out.' Considering the menu, he plumped for the pasta. 'My father used to have a rule. Ignore a problem for a week. Then, if it's still there, try to sort it out.'

'Sounds like an interesting approach, although not necessarily one you should follow all the time.'

'Only now and again,' Carlyle agreed. 'And now I think about it, my da used to ignore his problems for a lot longer than a week.' As a waiter arrived to take their order, Carlyle let his gaze drift to the far side of the street. Despite the hour, a line of sleeping bags filled the length of the back of a succession of stores. While Pearson ordered her braised tuna, he counted fourteen figures, as oblivious to the passing pedestrians as the pedestrians were to them.

Pearson took a mouthful of wine as she considered the homeless. 'Shocking,' she admitted, once the waiter had left.

'Why don't you do anything about it, then?'

A spasm of embarrassment crossed her face. Or maybe it was annoyance. 'It's difficult.'

Carlyle couldn't resist yanking her chain a little. 'Isn't that why you got into public service, to make a difference?'

'It's *very* difficult.' After another sip of wine, Pearson launched into a pro-forma list of the mayor's key messages on rough sleeping. 'We've announced a fifteen-million-pound fund to buy homes for people on the street.'

Carlyle wondered how many homes you could buy in London for fifteen million quid, these days. Not many, he concluded. He watched as a head appeared from one of the sleeping bags and spat on the pavement. 'No one seems to have told those guys the good news.'

'We're doing what we can.'

'Yeah, I know,' Carlyle relented. 'I'm not giving you a hard time. It was ever thus.'

'Ah, yes, the confrontational but world-weary cop.' She looked at him over her wine glass. 'You've been doing your job a lot longer than I've been doing mine. Presumably you could already be retired with one of those nice fat pensions that are bankrupting the public sector.'

'Maybe. I haven't checked.'

'Why keep going if you don't think things can get better? What gets you out of bed in the morning?'

'Why do I do it?' It wasn't the kind of thing he thought about. Too much introspection was not one of his faults. 'To stop things getting worse, I suppose.'

She sat back, waiting for him to go on.

'Our veneer of civilisation is gossamer thin. We're more dependent on technology than ever before. If the Wi-Fi were to

99

go down, most of the population would have a mental break-down. If the power networks failed, and law and order broke down, we could go all the way back to the Dark Ages in a matter of days.' He snapped his fingers. 'Survival of the fittest – and no one around here's particularly fit.'

'What a cheery thought.' The waiter arrived with their food. Pearson drained her glass of wine and asked for another. Carlyle looked at three pieces of ravioli on his plate in dismay. Clearly, this was going to be one of those expensive meals that had you heading straight to the nearest Greggs afterwards to fill up. He carved off a dainty mouthful and chewed slowly while Pearson attacked her tuna with gusto.

Once the waiter had brought her replacement wine, she got down to business. 'The mayor's being harassed by some of his own activists, the trans people.'

'The ones you had a run-in with?'

'I'm not important enough for them to bother about any longer. They're moving up the food chain.'

'It's what these people do. It doesn't matter what the issue is, what cause they're fighting for, they all operate in broadly the same way: identify the non-believers and hound them out.'

'They've started turning up at Joe's house. His wife and kids are being targeted.'

Carlyle polished off the rest of his food while she filled in the details.

'The activists feel the mayor isn't doing enough to open up all-women shortlists to "all self-defining women", regardless of their legal gender.'

Carlyle scratched his neck. 'So, if I decided I was a woman, I could go on an all-women shortlist for a job at City Hall, even though I'm obviously a bloke?' This was a minefield inside a minefield inside a minefield.

'It's *extremely* complex,' Pearson confirmed.

Carlyle thought back to Emily Quartz and the row over swimming at the ladies' pond in Hampstead. He never ceased to be amazed by the ability of people to tie themselves in knots over the most random things. 'It's a hot issue. Although, I have to say, as a man of a certain age, I struggle to get my head around it.'

'I think the mayor struggles as well, given his own background. But he knows it's a legitimate issue. He's trying his best.'

'I'm sure.'

Pearson didn't seem to notice the lack of conviction in his voice. 'He certainly doesn't deserve the grief he's getting over it.'

'No.'

'But some people will always push these things too far.'

'There are always plenty of nutters about.'

Pearson gave him a look of disapproval. 'These people are committed to what they believe in,' she scolded. 'It doesn't make them nutters.'

They're total fucking nutters, no question about it, Carlyle thought, even as he apologised. 'It's a broad term. I was a bit loose in my language.'

'You can't say things like that any longer,' the woman huffed. 'I can see why they sent you on that course. You dinosaurs don't understand how far language has been weaponised by the patri- archy in order to—'

Isn't 'dinosaur' a term of abuse? Carlyle let it slide. 'What can I do to help the mayor?' he asked, cutting through the sermon. 'D'you want a uniform outside his front door?'

'That would go down like a lead balloon. If people thought Joe was hiding behind the police, his credibility would take a massive hit.'

'What did you have in mind, then?'

'I'm not sure.' Pearson bit her lower lip. 'Maybe you could have a quiet word, or something.'

'Smack them around a bit?'

The wine was beginning to make Pearson's face look flushed. 'I wasn't proposing violence!'

'Only joking,' Carlyle fibbed. 'That kind of thing went out of fashion in the 1970s. You couldn't get away with it, these days – there's always some bugger on hand to video it on their phone.'

'Do you miss being able to beat people up?' Pearson asked.

Carlyle wasn't sure if she was joking or not. 'That was before even my time. I started out on the picket lines during the miners' strike in the eighties. There was a bit of argy-bargy now and again, but mostly it was posturing.'

'Hm.' Her expression indicated that such ancient history lacked any relevance to the here and now.

Carlyle felt he might as well have been talking about the Napoleonic Wars or the Battle of Hastings. 'When I started pounding the streets of London, the days of suspects having "accidents" in police stations were pretty much over.'

'You make your job sound like social work,' she teased.

'It *is* social work,' he reflected, 'a lot of the time.'

'And that makes it boring?'

'Not necessarily. I mean, all jobs have their quota of boredom, right? Being a cop isn't any different. But you get to do some interesting stuff.'

'And make a difference.'

'Sometimes.'

Pearson warmed to her theme. 'That's what public service is all about, isn't it? Making a difference.'

'It's certainly what some people get off on, sure. Me? I do my job on the interesting days *and* the boring ones.'

'And which would you say this is?'

'This is interesting enough. I'll go and talk to your trans people and see if I can sort things out. Have a quiet word, try to agree a sensible way forward.'

Pearson seemed genuinely cheered by his offer. 'The ringleader's a guy called Jasper Wiggins.'

Carlyle couldn't resist. 'And is Jasper a bloke or a self-defining woman?'

Pearson ignored his mickey-taking. 'Jasper's been arrested a few times, at demos and things. Last year he pleaded guilty to assaulting a police horse on an anti-globalisation demo. He was given a fine and a community-service order.'

'Sadly, there's no deportation to Australia, these days.' Before she could tell him off again, Carlyle added, 'Leave it with me. I'll have a quiet word, without breaking any bones. Or using any insensitive-slash-inappropriate-slash-threatening language.'

'I really appreciate it. And Joe'll be very grateful.'

'Let the mayor know he owes me one.' Carlyle tapped his temple with a finger. 'He's gone into my favours book, on the debit side.'

'Do you have anything in mind when it comes to paying his dues?'

'No, but I will one day. All debts have to be settled in the end. Just make sure that when I do come calling he doesn't suffer a bout of amnesia.'

'You'd better name your price quick,' Pearson advised. 'Special advisers tend not to last very long.'

'I'm sure you'll be the exception that proves the rule. He likes you.'

'And how would you know that?'

'Well, he didn't sack you when you had your run-in with the trans activists. And he sent you here to talk to me.'

Pearson waved a hand in the air, gesturing at the wider restaurant. 'I did this off my own bat.'

'In that case, you'd better remind your boss that he owes you, as well as me.'

'I will.' Pearson laughed.

The waiter appeared and took their plates. 'Would you like to see the dessert menu?'

Absolutely, Carlyle thought. I'm still bloody starving.

'The bill, please.' Pearson looked at Carlyle. 'If that's okay?'

'Sure.' Carlyle reached for his phone to google the nearest Greggs. 'I never have pudding.'

ELEVEN

'Helen Carlyle?'

'Helen Kennedy, yes.' The Avalon CEO hadn't taken her husband's name. It annoyed her when people assumed otherwise but it was usually an honest mistake. She looked up from her papers, proofs of the charity's latest annual report. The man standing in front of her looked about thirty. Expensively dressed, his face was partially hidden behind thick-framed spectacles. The shaven head was probably a response to the onset of male pattern baldness. A black canvas messenger bag hung from one shoulder. 'Can I help you?'

Placing the bag on the table, the man sat down. 'You've got my money.'

'Sorry?' Helen mimicked confusion even as she realised that Patrick Dalby, the disinherited bomber, was right in front of her.

Fucking hell, John! Why didn't you nick this lunatic like I told you to?

Avoiding eye contact, she scanned the restaurant. Mercifully, the lunchtime rush was still an hour away and none of the other tables was occupied. As a smiling waitress approached, Helen gave a sharp shake of her head to send the woman retreating behind the bar.

'You know who I am?' Dalby seemed calm, in a mad-bomber type of way.

'Yes.' Helen saw no point in pretending otherwise.

'Who the fuck d'you think you are?' Dalby growled. 'Working with that bitch Imogen Edelman, plotting to steal my inheritance.'

Helen took a deep breath. 'I can understand why this is rather difficult for you but—'

'Shut the fuck up.' Dalby took a translucent plastic box from the bag. It was around half the size of a shoebox. Inside was what looked like a fist-sized lump of modelling clay with a mess of wires sticking out of it.

A bomb? Are you kidding me?

Clenching her jaw, Helen forced herself to think of Alice. If she was going to die, she wanted her daughter to be the last thing on her mind before everything went blank.

'I know all about you – you're married to the bent cop, your daughter goes to Imperial, you have coffee here every day.'

Dalby opened the box, removed the device and tossed it across the table. 'Here.'

'Shit.' She caught it by reflex.

'Tell Edelman you don't want my money, or the next one will be real.'

Blinking away a tear, Helen said nothing. Staring at the assemblage in her hands, she didn't see him leave the restaurant.

Paying for her coffee, Helen left a large tip and returned to work. After a series of mind-numbing meetings, she went home and had a long, hot bath. By the time her husband came in, she was ready for him.

It took about fifteen minutes to get over the preliminaries – her wanting to kill him for being hopeless and him trying to sound calm, almost professional, without appearing blasé – and set about analysing what had happened.

'I don't understand.' Helen gulped a mouthful of wine. 'Why

did he try to blow up Imogen with a real bomb and then toss me a fake one?'

'The guy's a nutter,' was Carlyle's professional opinion. When he'd explained to Lottie Pearson that 'nutter' was a broad term, he wasn't kidding. In the Carlyle lexicon, it covered a range of personality disorders from snowflake to serial killer. 'Trying to make sense of his thought processes is a waste of time.' Rather than let his wife drink alone, he cracked the seal on a bottle of Jameson's purchased from Tesco on the way home. Filling a glass with a generous measure, he sat on the sofa next to her. 'Maybe he didn't have any more explosives.'

'That's reassuring.'

'There's no point in fretting about it.' Carlyle tasted the whiskey, letting it lie on his tongue for a moment before enjoying the gentle burn in his throat. 'Did you speak to Imogen about what happened?'

'Not yet. She's spooked enough already.'

'Good. Leave her to me. I'll sort this out.'

'You said that before,' Helen snarled. 'On this very sofa. *And* when you were in my office. "All done," you said. "Problem solved."'

'It *will* be sorted. Patrick Dalby's made his last bomb, real or fake, I promise you.'

'The whole thing should have been sorted already.'

Carlyle couldn't argue. 'Chief Inspector Holland's looking for him.'

'The guy you said was totally useless?'

'I didn't say he was *totally* useless,' Carlyle backtracked.

'"Doesn't seem much cop" was your exact phrase, if I remember correctly.'

You always do, Carlyle reflected. 'That's not the same as "totally useless",' he said lamely.

'Either way, he hasn't caught the guy.' Helen finished her wine and refilled her glass.

Carlyle had to acknowledge the accuracy of his wife's observation. 'I'll kill the little fucker,' he vowed.

'Which one?'

He had to think about it for a moment. Both. 'Dalby.'

His wife gave him a cool look. 'Putting him in jail will suffice, thank you, as long as it's for a nice long time.'

Murder would be rather more satisfying, Carlyle thought.

'How long will he get, once you catch him?'

'Not long enough.'

'Justice will take its course,' Helen said primly. 'Meantime, have you spoken to Alice?'

'Yes. She took it in her stride.'

'A right chip off the old block.' Helen didn't mean it as a compliment.

'And campus security has been informed.'

'Will that be enough?' Helen fretted. 'The guy knows she's at Imperial. What if he goes back to making real bombs? He blew up Imogen in her car.'

'He blew up a rubbish cart,' Carlyle corrected her. 'The bomb squad say it wasn't big enough to do much damage to the car.'

'What about if it had set the petrol tank alight?'

Good question. He moved swiftly on. 'I suggested to Alice she come home for a few days, but she wasn't interested. She has her life to get on with – which is a very healthy approach. You can't live in fear. You can't let the terrorists win – and so on and so forth.'

'Easy for you to say. You didn't have Dalby sitting right in front of you.'

'Hey, look, you know I'm not going to let this little scrote do any harm to you or Alice.' He slipped an arm round her shoulders and was relieved she didn't shrug it off. 'I made a mistake in leaving it to Dave Holland to handle but, rest assured, I'll deal with Dalby personally. By this time tomorrow, he'll be in jail, or in hospital. Or both.' Pleased with his little speech, he tossed back the rest of his whiskey.

'One other thing.'

'What?'

'Dalby said you were "bent". What's that all about?'

Christ on a fucking bike. Where to begin? 'Long story.' Carlyle poured another inch of whiskey into his glass. 'Remember my old sergeant, Umar Sligo?'

'I remember Umar,' Helen said coolly. 'He's the guy who married the stripper from Everton's and got sacked for exposing himself to his female colleagues. How could I forget such a colourful character?'

'He married an exotic dancer who worked in Holborn's leading, ahem, nightspot and ended up resigning instead of having to go in front of a disciplinary hearing.'

'Same difference,' Helen decreed.

'Yes, well, when he left the police, Umar went to work for a posh pimp called Harry Cummins.'

'Good for him,' Helen said sarcastically.

'It all ended very badly. Harry was killed in a turf war by an old-time gangster called Vernon Holder, along with Umar and his girlfriend.'

Helen slurped her wine. 'Whose girlfriend?'

'Huh?'

'Umar's girlfriend? Or Harry's?'

'Harry's. But Umar was shagging her at the time.'

'Christ, this *is* complicated.' Helen placed her wine glass on the coffee table. 'I can see I'm going to have to pay close attention.'

'Harry's dead,' Carlyle recapped, 'leaving behind a small business empire based on girls and drugs. Harry's wife, your benefactor Vicky Dalby-Cummins, took over the running of the business.'

'Harry the posh pimp had a wife *and* a girlfriend, then?' Helen's disapproval was clear, but Carlyle wasn't sure if it was the pimping or the playing away that was the main cause of her ire.

'Harry and Vicky led separate lives. He more or less lived in his club. She had a farm and never came to town.'

'Some marriage.'

'Each to their own,' Carlyle declared. 'Anyway, it was a bit of a surprise when Vicky arrived in London and took over the reins of the business. Even more surprisingly, she then went into partnership with Vernon Holder.'

'The old-time gangster who killed her husband.' Helen's expression said, *See, I am paying attention.*

'The old-time gangster who *allegedly* killed her husband . . . who then disappeared.'

'Jeez, a real *roman noir.*'

'Eh?'

'Pulp fiction, sweetie.' She gave him a patronising pat on the arm. 'The kind of stuff you'd like to read if you ever had the time.'

'Yeah, well, it gets worse. The strong suspicion is that Vicky had Vernon Holder done in. According to urban legend, Vernon's body was fed to the pigs on her farm.'

'Not exactly a typical Avalon donor, then.' Helen eyed her husband suspiciously. 'How well did you know her?'

'I met Vicky a few times.' Carlyle kept it simple. 'She attracted the interest of the Met on a fairly regular basis.'

'Imogen thought she was an impressive woman.'

'She certainly kept us all on our toes,' Carlyle agreed.

'When she got run over, it was an accident, right?'

'That was the verdict.' Carlyle thought back to the day Dalby-Cummins was taken out by an octogenarian driver outside her club, the Chapel. 'But I have my doubts.'

Helen's eyes grew wide. 'You think the half-brother was behind it?'

Carlyle was sceptical. 'He didn't know then he'd been cut out of the will.'

'All the more reason for him to do her in,' Helen reasoned.

'I'm pretty sure it was business-related, rather than a family thing,' was Carlyle's take.

'Either way,' Helen declared, 'you couldn't make it up.'

'Like you said, a pulp novel.'

'Or one of those BBC4 crime dramas with subtitles.'

'Life is stranger than fiction.'

'Yeah, but the cops in real life aren't nearly as good-looking.' She gave him a peck on the cheek. 'Only joking.'

'I know you were, sweetheart.'

'Seriously, though, this is why I don't ask you about your work.'

'And why I don't bring it home.'

'But,' Helen yawned, 'to come back to the original question, why did the tosser with the Plasticine say you were bent?'

'Vicky was involved in one of my investigations,' Carlyle explained. 'Some people had an interest in claiming I was on the take, but I wasn't. She offered, but I refused.'

'She offered you a bribe?'

'She offered me a job.'

'Blimey,' Helen teased, 'and here was me thinking you were unemployable outside the Met.'

'I probably am.' Carlyle chuckled.

'How much did she offer?' Helen asked.

'Huh?'

'What was the salary?'

'We didn't get into that.'

'Would've been interesting to know what she thought you were worth.'

'Not really. It was a non-starter. I'm a cop.'

'Still, would've been interesting.'

Carlyle wasn't having it. 'Change sides and you're lost. If I'd wanted to take that path, I'd have done it a long time ago.'

'And you'd probably be in jail right now.' Helen burrowed deeper into his embrace. 'Which would not be good.'

'It wouldn't be good at all,' Carlyle agreed.

Helen was silent for a while, then asked, 'The donation, was it your idea?'

Carlyle stiffened.

She sat up. 'It was, wasn't it?'

'A possible donation to Avalon was mentioned,' he admitted, 'but I didn't know about the will.'

Helen jabbed him in the chest with an index finger. 'So this is all your fault, then?'

'What?'

'Dragging Alice into some gangster-family dispute.'

'That's hardly fair. I mean—'

'So much for not bringing your work home,' Helen complained. 'Get out there and nail the bastard.'

'Sounds like a plan.' Carlyle could feel the whiskey taking a gentle hold of him. 'What did you do with the bomb, by the way?'

'It's in a desk drawer in my office,' Helen said, calming down a bit.

'We'll need that.' Carlyle kissed her forehead. 'It's evidence.'

TWELVE

Around two hundred punters had filled the Montgomery Suite of the Swarbuck Kensington Hotel. The audience for the London Cryptocurrency Seminar was almost exclusively male; men of all ages, sizes and demeanours. If the entire crowd had paid the stated £275 entrance fee, plus VAT, someone was having a very profitable day.

Carlyle's warrant card got him into the room without opening his wallet. The first scheduled speaker – due on stage in ten minutes – was Tim Hitchcock, CEO of Kollision Financial Services, and alleged partner in crime of Bruno Soutine. Kollision was sponsoring the event and Hitchcock would explain how you could make a killing trading digital currencies.

Inspector O'Sullivan had sent him a photo of his quarry. Carlyle scanned the room until he realised Hitchcock was standing barely five feet in front of him, deep in conversation with a red-faced fellow in a loud pinstripe suit.

'Mr Hitchcock.' The commander interposed himself between the two men. 'I was wondering if I could have a word.'

Hitchcock's smile said *Fuck off.* He pointed towards a podium at the far end of the room. 'I was about to give my speech.'

'Your talk can wait.' Taking a firm hold of the man's arm, Carlyle started marching him towards the nearest exit.

'Let go of me.' Hitchcock tried to wriggle free, but Carlyle refused to release his grip. 'This is assault. You have no right—'

'We can do this the easy way,' Carlyle hissed, 'or the hard way.' Ignoring the bemusement of various onlookers, he dragged Hitchcock in his wake. 'Either we have a quiet word outside, or I embarrass you in front of your, erm, followers.'

'Let go of me,' Hitchcock squealed, 'or I'll call the police.'

'I *am* the police.'

Hitchcock stopped struggling.

Carlyle released the man's arm and flashed his ID. 'Kindly stop obstructing me in my duties or I'll put you under arrest.'

'You can have two minutes.' The CEO rubbed his arm vigorously. 'Then I have to make my speech.'

Leaving the conference room, they headed down a corridor to a vestibule containing two high-backed chairs. Plonking Hitchcock in one, Carlyle took the other. 'Patrick Dalby.'

'What about him?'

'You know him?'

'He's one of our early-stage investors.'

'Where can I find him?'

'How should I know? I'm not his keeper.'

Carlyle took a deep breath, vowed to remain calm. 'In two minutes, you can be on stage, spouting your spiel . . . or you can be standing in the foyer, in handcuffs, waiting for your ride to take you to a cell at Charing Cross police station. Up to you.'

'This is harassment.' Hitchcock looked down the corridor, hoping to be rescued.

'It is,' Carlyle agreed. 'And it will be followed by violence if you don't tell me where Patrick Dalby is, right now.'

'You wouldn't dare.'

A swift smack in the face ended that particular debate.

'Ow, you bastard.' Hitchcock's eyes filled with tears as he held his nose.

So much for remaining calm. Carlyle felt the slightest frisson

114

of shame; it passed in an instant. He geared up to give Hitchcock another slap. 'Where's Dalby?'

Hitchcock reared backwards, almost toppling his chair. 'You can try his club,' he blurted. 'When he's in London, Patrick likes to hang out at the Cromwell Club.'

Carlyle knew the place. The Cromwell Club was a top-end members' club in Knightsbridge. He had been there only once – as a guest of Vicky Dalby-Cummins – but it was a memorable occasion. It looked like Patrick had managed to get his hands on his sister's membership, if nothing else.

'Is he there now?'

'I've no idea.'

Carlyle lifted Hitchcock from his seat by the lapels of his jacket. 'You'd better not be lying to me.'

'I'm not.'

There was only one way to find out. Carlyle hadn't finished with Mr Hitchcock but the rest of their conversation would have to wait. 'Do your speech,' he commanded. 'Then go back to your office and wait for me. Once I've dealt with Mr Dalby, I want to have a word about Bruno Soutine.'

Hitchcock backed away, muttering something about consulting his lawyer.

'Hurry up,' Carlyle called after him. 'You don't want to keep the punters waiting.'

Sleek, appraising, unruffled, the receptionist at the Cromwell Club looked like she'd stepped straight off the catwalk. The badge on her tunic gave her name as Klara. She considered the commander with an appraising eye. 'I'm sorry, but the membership waiting list is not currently open.' The accent was more East European than West London, but the arrogance was universal.

Carlyle took the rebuff with a degree of good grace. 'I'm not looking to join, Klara, thank you.' Placing his ID on the reception desk, he let the woman study it at length. 'I'm here to see one of your members, a gentleman by the name of Patrick Dalby.'

'I'm afraid we don't disclose—'

Carlyle ignored the protestations about member confidentiality. 'Just tell me if he's here.'

Klara reached for the house phone. 'Let me call my manager.'

Carlyle clamped his hand over the receiver. 'Do as I ask, right now, or I'll call in a vanload of police officers and we'll have everyone out on the street for inspection. You can spend a couple of hours shivering in the rain.'

Klara took a moment to swallow her annoyance at the rude cop. 'Mr Dalby's in the Hambleton bar,' she said softly. 'First floor and on the right.'

Upstairs, a couple of dozen people were in the bar, maybe half on their own, all but two of them men. Realising he had absolutely no idea what Dalby looked like, Carlyle retreated to the landing. Ignoring a sign proclaiming *All phones must be switched off*, he called Helen.

'Have you sorted it out yet?'

'I'm dealing with it right now.'

Helen didn't sound reassured. 'Get on with it, then. I had Imogen on the phone for almost an hour this morning. She's losing it.'

Carlyle kept his voice low. 'You didn't tell her Dalby paid you a visit?'

'No. She was in enough of a state as it was.'

'Good. Now, what does this guy look like?'

Helen could always be relied upon to provide a sufficiency of information with a minimum of fuss. 'Bald, with NHS specs.'

Carlyle stepped back to the entrance and spied his target sitting at the far end of the bar, reading a newspaper. 'Bingo. I've got him. Problem solved.'

'You said that before,' she reminded him.

'A hundred per cent guaranteed this time,' he promised, 'or your money back.'

'I gave up trying to get my money back on you a long time ago,' his wife drawled.

Carlyle laughed out loud. '*Caveat emptor*, baby.' As he hung up, he felt a tap on his shoulder. 'Excuse me, sir.' A bearded member of staff pointed at the sign. 'Phones are not allowed on the first floor.'

'My mistake.' Putting the phone away, Carlyle pulled out a pair of handcuffs. The man's eyes widened, but he said nothing. 'I won't do it again.' Stepping inside the bar, Carlyle marched up to Dalby. 'Patrick, I've been looking for you.'

Dalby tossed his paper onto the bar. 'Who are you?'

Without breaking his stride, Carlyle placed the palm of his hand on the man's chest and gave a hard shove.

'Whoaaa.'

As Dalby fell from the stool, the commander gave him a sly kick in the ribs to encourage him to stay down. 'I'm the guy who's come to arrest you.' He slapped on the cuffs.

'Fuck off,' Dalby squealed. 'What are you doing?'

Carlyle gave him another kick for good measure. 'Stay there,' he growled, 'and shut up.' Climbing onto the still warm stool, he beckoned over the bartender. 'I'll have a double macchiato,' he said, taking a moment to catch his breath, 'and a phone I'm allowed to use.'

Hiding behind their MacBooks and their flat whites, club members pretended not to gawp as the handcuffed, dishevelled Patrick Dalby was escorted from the premises by a couple of uniforms. A few minutes later, Karen O'Sullivan appeared to confirm that Dalby was on his way to Charing Cross.

'Lucky for you no one filmed the arrest,' the inspector observed drily.

117

Carlyle pointed to the *All phones must be switched off* sign. 'Always one step ahead.'

'Just as well they didn't have CCTV in the bar, then.'

Hm. Carlyle hadn't considered the possibility. 'Better to be lucky than smart,' he reasoned.

'Did you need to smack him about so much?' the inspector wondered. 'His lawyer'll have a fit when he sees the bruising.'

'Dalby resisted arrest,' Carlyle proclaimed. 'He fell off his stool. If his lawyer wants to cause a fuss, he can sue the club.'

'Good luck with that argument.'

Carlyle adopted a sombre demeanour. 'In all seriousness, Patrick Dalby's a dangerous guy. I didn't want to take any chances.'

'In that case, why didn't you have any back-up?'

'There wasn't any time. I was acting on a tip-off, but I couldn't be sure he'd be here. Then, when I found him, I didn't know how long he'd stay. I had to nab him before he did a runner. Far better to arrest him here than in the street . . . You know what it's like.'

'I know when I'm being spun a line,' she said, without malice.

'This is a proper result,' Carlyle insisted. 'We've stopped a serious danger to the public. Pats on the back all round. No need for the long face.'

The inspector stared off into the middle distance. 'Are we gonna hand him over to Chief Inspector Holland?'

'Not a chance. Holland'll only stuff things up.'

'I know it's important, but this is still below your pay grade. Plus, you appear to be conflicted.'

Carlyle frowned. 'How did you know about that?'

'Dalby was ranting about your wife as they shoved him in the wagon,' O'Sullivan explained. 'I can't see how you can be anywhere near this.'

'That's why it's going to be your investigation.'

'Thanks a lot.' O'Sullivan groaned.

'I need you to grip this. Dalby can't be allowed to walk.'

'Do we have enough to charge him?'

'We've got a confession of sorts.' He brought the inspector up to speed on Helen's earlier confrontation with Dalby. 'You need to get a statement from my missus – as well as the fake bomb.'

O'Sullivan's eyes widened. 'She's still got it?'

'In a desk drawer,' the commander said nonchalantly, 'in her office.'

O'Sullivan rolled her eyes. 'Your wife's involvement represents a serious conflict of interest,' she repeated. 'You should've let someone else make the arrest.'

'There wasn't any time.'

'At the very least, you shouldn't have smacked the guy around.'

'I didn't,' Carlyle repeated patiently. 'His injuries are both minor and self-inflicted.'

'He'll need to be examined by a doctor.'

'That can wait a day or two. Process him slowly.'

'You're the boss,' said O'Sullivan, clearly not happy with what he was proposing. Once she'd left, he called Helen and told her to pass on the news of the arrest to Imogen Edelman.

'You won't let him slip through your fingers?' The anxious tone to Helen's voice was unusual and unsettling in equal measure.

'Don't worry, we won't mess this up. I'm having the case reassigned to an inspector at Charing Cross, Karen O'Sullivan, who's very good. You'll have to give her a statement.'

Helen was less than enthused at the prospect. 'Can't you leave me out of it?'

'Do you want this guy put away or not?' Carlyle countered brusquely. 'He basically confessed to you about planting the bomb on Imogen's car.'

'I've still got the fake bomb he made. Won't that be enough?'

'No, it will not.' Things had come to a pretty pass when his own wife didn't want to cooperate with the police. Carlyle took a couple of deep breaths and lowered his voice. 'Inspector O'Sullivan will come over to your office to pick up the box with the phoney device in it and to take your statement. Just keep it simple and factual.'

'Will I have to go to court?'

Carlyle took another breath. 'We'll cross that bridge,' he said calmly, 'if and when we get to it.'

Edward Godson stood outside his back door and lit up a post-evening-meal cigarette. The rain had only recently stopped for the first time that day and the neighbours had remained inside. The sound of a distant motorbike rose and fell but otherwise there was quiet. The detention-centre guard luxuriated in the calm of his surroundings. There was never much peace at work and home was pretty much the same. Tonight, however, he had lucked out: his wife had gone to the bingo with her sister while his daughter was in the pub with her boyfriend. Godson might have fancied a pint himself, but the idea of having to make small talk with the boyfriend – a useless lump called Jason – had put paid to that idea. Other than Godson's daughter, the boy's only interests were smoking dope and internet porn. Godson had no interest in drugs and preferred to keep his online habits to himself.

Anyway, he had no need of the pub. A couple of cans of lager in the fridge and a wildlife documentary on BBC2 meant he was well set. An interest in natural history programmes was a sure signal that middle age had taken over, but he found them calming after a difficult shift at Crampton House. Taking a long drag on his Marlboro, he hawked up a wad of phlegm and spat it into the long grass. His wife had been on at him to get it cut, but tending the garden was the last thing he fancied after work. Today's shift had been relatively uneventful – three assaults and a solitary suicide attempt. Tomorrow promised nothing but more of the same.

The job took its toll, mentally as well as physically. Godson was a firm believer in a hostile environment for illegals, but even he could see the net swept up some pretty pathetic specimens. On the other hand, there were some right bitches, too. Godson winced as he thought back to the woman who'd had the temerity to kick him in the balls. He tried to recall her name, but it had long since slipped his memory. He hadn't bothered reporting the cow. If there was any justice, she'd already be back wherever she'd come from. That was a far worse punishment than anything Her Majesty's government could come up with. Meantime, it was back to business as usual. There were always plenty of victims to be exploited. The last woman Godson had propositioned had been perfectly accommodating. Closing his eyes, he brought up a mental image of the look on the woman's face – a unique mix of disgust, dismay and disbelief, overlaid by a veneer of resignation – which sent a pleasing spasm through his groin.

A faint noise off to his left caused him to blink. Godson looked around the garden. Nothing. Probably next door's cat on the prowl again.

'Fucking Ossie.' The neighbour was a Tottenham fan and he'd named the family pet after one of Spurs's old players. Appropriate, Godson thought, given that the animal had no balls. Spurs had never been a team of fighters. He took a long drag on his cigarette and exhaled into the darkening night sky. Through the smoke he caught a flash of movement at the edge of his vision. Whatever it was, it was bigger than a cat.

He turned his head.

'What the—'

The cigarette was knocked from his mouth as something cold and metallic smashed into his jaw.

'Fuggg.'

Godson sank to his knees. The cigarette was in front of him, its tip glowing in the weeds, next to what looked like one of his teeth. He spat out a gobbet of blood before a blow to the crown of his skull sent him fully into the ground. This place really could do with a tidy, he thought. Before he could try to get up, a boot contacted with the side of his head and blackness swallowed him whole.

Godson woke up on the kitchen floor. Bound hand and foot, his mouth covered with duct tape, he was sitting with his back against the fridge. His skull felt as if it had been cleaved with an axe. Every time he drew a breath, it felt like a corkscrew was being driven into his chest.

'Are you ready for me now, pig?' The woman stood over him, drinking from one of his cans. He recognised her from the detention centre – the psycho who'd kicked him in the balls. His gonads shrivelled at the memory.

What are you doing here?

Why are you drinking my fucking lager?

He struggled to remember the woman's name. It wouldn't come. Then again, why would it? Why would he keep a useless piece of information like that in his brain?

So many women, so easily forgotten.

Throwing back her head, the woman finished the lager. Crushing the can in her hand, she tossed it into the sink. Godson had never felt so violated in his life.

'Cheap shit.' Wiping her mouth with the back of her hand, the woman declared herself dissatisfied with his choice of booze. 'Not that I'm surprised.'

Fuck this. Godson summoned up whatever reserves of defiance he could scrape together. 'I'm gonna fucking kill you,' he screamed.

Muffled by the tape, his words came out sounding like 'MMMMMMMMWWWWWWWWWAAAAA.'

'We'll deport your corpse.'

'WWWWWWWFFFFFFSSSS.'

'And make your fucking family pay the fucking bill.'

'UUUUUUFFFFFFFLLLLLL.'

Christ, the pain was killing him. His chin fell to his chest and he was bemused to note a monster erection had bloomed in his trousers. How the hell could he possibly have a hard-on at a time like this? For the first time in his life, Edward Godson wondered if there might be something wrong with the wiring in his brain.

A whirring noise put an end to any fleeting bout of self-psychoanalysis. Out of the darkness a yellow plastic tube appeared in front of his face. The thing looked like an electric toothbrush on steroids. At the end of a 50-centimetre shaft a small circular grinding tool turned at 35,000 r.p.m. Godson knew the speed because he had the exact same piece of kit in his garage. Maybe it was one and the same. He tried to think of the last time he'd used it, but his mind began to disintegrate as the grinder came closer.

'Holy Jesus,' Godson wailed, 'save me from this fucking monster.'

'HHHHHHHHHMMMMMMMRRR.'

'Brace yourself.' The woman's voice betrayed no trace of either glee or malice. 'This is going to hurt.'

'NNNNNGRHHHAAAAAGG.'

'It's going to hurt a lot.'

Monica Seppi. The name finally came to him. There was no way he would ever forget it now, not as long as he lived . . . *if* he lived. His life expectancy had suddenly collapsed to the point where it could be measured in mere minutes. Godson wondered who would find him first: would his wife come back from the bingo before his daughter got in from the pub? Either way, both of them were in for a hell of a shock.

THIRTEEN

The offices of Kollision Financial Services occupied the top floor of a mixed-use development in Fitzrovia, which had been built on the site of a decommissioned hospital. His arrival was expected and the commander was quickly shown into a large office with a view towards Soho. From behind a desk almost as big as Carlyle's kitchen, Tim Hitchcock fiddled with his phone. Other than the sticking plaster that straddled his nose, the CEO showed no real signs of the smack he'd taken from the long arm of the law.

'How did the conference go?' Carlyle approached the desk, only to be intercepted by a large, hulking man who looked like an ex-heavyweight boxer gone to seed.

'Colin Spooner, Tim's legal adviser, TRX Associates.' The man did not offer a handshake. 'My office is filing a complaint against you for aggravated assault as we speak.'

'Knock yourself out ... no pun intended.' Carlyle affected an air of insouciance as he flopped into a chair. 'Taking that line means your client goes from being a cooperating witness to a co-conspirator but, hey, it's your choice.'

Hitchcock looked at his lawyer. 'What's that mean?'

'The guy's talking shit,' the lawyer said. 'He's just trying to scare you.'

'Yes and no,' Carlyle said amiably. 'I *am* trying to scare you, but I'm *not* talking shit. Mr Hitchcock has turned up in not one, but *two* current police investigations. Very serious investigations. I'm sure you can appreciate how unusual that is.'

'I haven't done anything,' Hitchcock whined. 'I'm the victim here.'

'There are no victims,' Carlyle continued. 'Only people who have made bad choices. Your mistake was to get into bed with some very nasty people, like Patrick Dalby and Bruno Soutine.' The CEO started to protest but he talked over him: 'Whether it was poor judgement on your part, or maybe a lack of basic due diligence, I don't know. The fact that you're *directly* connected to a bomb-maker and a dead man whose identity was stolen by a cryptocurrency fraudster might be a coincidence.' He paused. 'Or it might be indicative of a deeper conspiracy. At this stage, you could make a pretty good argument either way.'

'What dead man?' Spooner asked. 'And what bomber?'

'We'll get to that,' Carlyle promised. 'First we need to agree where we all stand.' He addressed the lawyer: 'I am minded to consider your client as an innocent onlooker in this mess, not least because he did, eventually, provide me with some useful information, which led to the arrest of Patrick Dalby, thereby taking a homicidal maniac off the streets.'

Hitchcock looked surprised and confused. 'Patrick's not a—'

'Your mate,' Carlyle growled, 'tried to blow up a woman in her car.'

'None of this has anything to do with my client,' Spooner proclaimed, his composure waning.

'I am prepared to take that assertion on face value,' Carlyle said. 'However, if you try to destabilise my investigations by lobbing a spurious complaint into the mix, I would have to reconsider Mr Hitchcock's role in all this.'

'I can assure you,' Spooner spluttered, 'there is nothing spurious about—'

Carlyle fixed his gaze on Hitchcock. 'These are very grave

matters – murder, attempted murder, extortion – so, if I had reasonable grounds to suspect you are other than a cooperating witness, I would have no choice but to take you into custody immediately.'

The lawyer wasn't having it. 'He's bluffing, Tim. Worst-case scenario, I'd have you out in a matter of hours.'

'During which time, your arrest will be all over the internet and your investors will be running for the door.'

'My investors are all incredibly loyal.' Hitchcock's claim lacked much conviction.

'This would certainly offer an opportunity to test that theory.'

The chief executive stared out of the window for a few seconds. 'Bollocks,' he said finally. 'I'll drop the complaint.' His lawyer started to protest, but Hitchcock indicated the decision had been made.

Spooner tried to make the best of his client's U-turn. 'What about showing a bit of goodwill,' he haggled, 'and getting the SRC case dropped?'

Carlyle frowned. 'SRC?'

'Sandringham Risk Consulting.'

'Ah, yes, one of your loyal clients.' Carlyle recalled the legal action at the Royal Courts of Justice, which Emily Quartz was keeping an eye on. 'They gave you millions to invest, only to see their money vanish in a puff of digital smoke.'

'They knew the risks,' Hitchcock grumbled. 'They're like a lot of folk, fine with risk when they're making money, not so much when they're losing it.'

'The SRC claim is a complete joke,' Spooner chimed in. 'It should never have made it to court.'

'Nothing to do with me,' Carlyle pointed out, 'but I'll see what I can do.' Given it was a civil case, he would be able to do the square root of nothing, so it was an easy promise to make. 'Meantime, tell me about your connection to my dead man.'

Hitchcock frowned. 'What dead man?'

'Bruno Soutine.'

'I don't know where you got that from.' Hitchcock raised an eyebrow. 'You must be mistaken.'

'I don't think so.' Carlyle explained about the dead personal trainer.

'Some guy with the same name,' Hitchcock shrugged. 'A coincidence. *My* Bruno is alive and well. In fact, I had a text from him just last night.' He offered his phone to Carlyle. 'See for yourself.'

Reluctant to don his glasses, the commander squinted at the message: *Funds on the way, ETA 2 weeks max.*

He handed the phone back to Hitchcock. 'What does that mean?'

The CEO took a deep breath. 'We have a fund—'

'Before you continue,' Spooner interjected, 'can we agree nothing said in this room will go any further?'

Carlyle gave a solemn nod. 'Agreed.'

'And nothing uncovered in the course of this investigation will be used, in any way, against my client.'

That depends, Carlyle thought, on where the investigation goes. 'Mr Hitchcock is an innocent onlooker in my investigations.'

Choosing to take that as sufficient assurance, the lawyer invited his client to continue.

'We have a fund,' Hitchcock repeated, 'SDS Four.'

'SDS stands for Special Digital Situations,' Spooner explained. 'There are four different funds that were set up to invest clients' money. The first one was very successful. The next two less so.'

'And SDS Four has completely fucking sunk without a trace,' Hitchcock added.

The lawyer took up the tale, 'Rather unwisely, as it turns

out, the fund manager decided to hand all the cash over to Mr Soutine and his Consensual Acts project.'

Hitchcock offered a pithy market commentary: 'With the benefit of hindsight, it was a fucking insanely stupid thing to do, but Esther, the fund manager, genuinely bought into the whole AST concept.'

Carlyle recalled Quartz's explanation of Adult Services Tokens as a cryptocurrency for porn. Money for . . . He quickly shut down that line of thought.

'Esther got gold fever,' Hitchcock sighed, 'believing digital wanking would be a licence to print money. The forecasts were fantastic . . . literally. After it became clear we'd been taken to the cleaners, we tried to put a brave face on it, saying we were hacked, but no one fell for that. We consciously and willingly handed the fucking money over, like the mugs we were.'

'And that was Sandringham's six million?' Carlyle asked.

'Yeah. Along with money from a few others. Eight and a half in total.'

'Where's Esther now?'

'I don't know, and I don't bloody care,' said Hitchcock. 'I hope she's face down in a gutter somewhere. The stupid bitch should be in court instead of me.'

'What about Bruno Soutine?' Carlyle pointed at the CEO's phone. 'The one who's still alive. Where is he now?'

'No idea.' Hitchcock had slid down his chair to the point at which he was barely visible behind the desk. 'He could be literally anywhere in the world. And, before you ask, it's impossible to trace his location when he sent the text. He uses all kinds of encryption and fancy anti-tracking shit. Plus, he's always on the move.' Carlyle started to ask another question but was cut off. 'And I don't know *who* he is, either. Bruno Soutine was never going to be his real name, was it?'

'Which makes Ms Blake's investment decisions all the more puzzling,' Spooner said. 'You might even say troubling.'

Carlyle looked at him blankly.

'Esther Blake. The fund manager.'

Emily Quartz had raised the issue of money laundering. 'Could Ms Blake be in on the scam?' Carlyle asked.

'She got gold fever,' Hitchcock repeated. 'Any alternative explanation is just too horrible to contemplate.'

'What happened to the real Bruno Soutine,' Spooner asked, 'the personal trainer?'

'Somebody fed him a bunch of sedatives and stuck a plastic bag over his head.'

'Not a nice way to go,' said Spooner. 'You don't think it was suicide?'

Carlyle shook his head. 'We think he was mistaken for the guy who stole his name.'

'But how could you mistake a personal trainer for a crypto-currency expert?' Hitchcock seemed genuinely bemused.

'No one seems to know what the fake Soutine looks like so . . .' A thought crossed his mind, interrupting his train of thought. 'Your Ms Blake—'

'Not our Ms Blake any longer,' Spooner said hastily.

'She hasn't met the cryptocurrency Bruno Soutine, has she?' Spooner looked at Hitchcock.

'Not as far as I know,' said the CEO.

'Even so,' Spooner reasoned, 'she wouldn't have mixed them up.'

Hitchcock was not convinced. 'For all we know, Esther could have sent the money to a fucking personal trainer.' He wiggled an index finger in the air. 'Fat finger.'

Carlyle didn't follow.

'Fat finger – press the wrong button. You know, you mean to sell a million shares in Shell and you buy a million instead.

Happens all the time.' Hitchcock looked at Spooner. 'Maybe that's what happened. Maybe Esther made a mistake and tried to get the money back.'

The lawyer looked profoundly unconvinced. 'Why kill the guy? You'd never get your money back.'

'Would a fat-finger error get us off the hook with SRC?' Hitchcock asked hopefully.

'We don't have sufficient insurance cover,' his lawyer advised.

'Fuck.'

Carlyle reflected on the text on Hitchcock's phone. *Funds on the way* . . . 'Will you get the money back?' he wondered. 'Is there any chance Soutine will actually return the cash?'

The two men look at him as if he was mad.

'He's yanking our chain.' Hitchcock let out another sob. 'The money's gone. It's never coming back.'

'What about Patrick Dalby?' Carlyle speculated. 'Could he have killed the trainer?'

'Why?' Spooner wondered.

'Why not? The guy clearly has a screw loose.'

The lawyer dismissed the idea, but Hitchcock was more open-minded. 'What date are we talking about?' he asked the commander. 'When was this guy murdered?'

Carlyle consulted the calendar on his phone. 'A week ago yesterday.'

Hitchcock checked his own diary. 'Nah. Patrick's in the clear for that, at least. We were shooting at his farm in Sussex.' He offered up the address, unbidden. 'And, no, before you ask, I didn't know about his explosives fetish. Patrick was always moaning – about the performance of his investments, about missing out on this thing or that thing, about his sister's inheritance going to some bitch at a charity.'

Hitchcock clearly didn't know about his guest's connection to the bitch at the charity. Clenching his jaw, Carlyle said nothing.

'I can't say I noticed much of a change,' Hitchcock mused, 'but he must've flipped. I've known Patrick since university and I've never seen him hurt a fly. With the benefit of hindsight, I can see how Vicky's estate slipping through his fingers might've pushed him over the edge. Of course, if I'd had any inkling he was planning such a horrendous act, I'd have reported him to the police immediately.'

Sure you would. Carlyle ignored the self-exculpation. 'If it wasn't Esther Blake and it wasn't Patrick, who might have killed this poor sod in Covent Garden?'

The two men looked at each other. 'Dunno,' they chorused.

'Let's leave it there.' Carlyle rose from his chair. 'If I have any other questions, I'll be in touch. In the meantime, if you can think of anything else that might be germane, let me know.'

Germane. Not a word he had used in a while.

Eager for the meeting to be over, Spooner followed him to the door. 'Let me show you out.'

At Charing Cross, Patrick Dalby was lawyered up and saying nothing. Handing Karen O'Sullivan the address of Dalby's farm, Carlyle instructed the inspector to arrange a search warrant in double-quick time.

'How did you get that?' the inspector asked, impressed by the speed of her boss's sleuthing.

'I have my sources,' Carlyle replied, giving nothing away. 'If Dalby made the bomb down there, we've got him whether he talks or not.'

'I got your wife's statement,' O'Sullivan confirmed, 'and also the fake bomb Dalby handed her.'

'If we can get some physical evidence of the *real* bomb, we can prove he's not some fantasist and we're home and dry.'

'I'll go down there myself to oversee the search. We don't want the locals stuffing it up.'

'Get Sergeant Nixon to do it.' The inspector had a family to look after: she didn't have time to be running about the countryside. 'She's more than capable.'

'Will do.' O'Sullivan gave a nod of gratitude from one parent to another and hustled off to get the warrant.

Carlyle was about to look in on Dalby when he was interrupted by a call from Jamie Worby, the head of Immigration Enforcement.

'Monica Seppi,' Worby boomed, 'where the hell is she?'

Having learnt his lines, Carlyle didn't miss a beat. 'I thought we handed her back to you guys, as agreed.'

'Colnbrook never received her.'

'No?'

'As far as I can tell, Seppi was never returned to the system.'

'Are you sure?' In Carlyle's mind, the gentle surprise suffusing his tone was worthy of an Oscar. 'It's probably a mix-up in the paperwork. Let me see what I can find out.'

'Do that, Commander. This has become a matter of some considerable urgency.'

'I'm going into an interview with a suspect but I'll deal with it straight after that.'

'Not good enough.' Worby let out a strangled groan. 'Do it now. Immediately.'

'Excuse me?' Who the fuck d'you think you are? Carlyle bridled. If it came to a pissing contest, he wasn't sure he would outrank the Home Office man, but it wasn't certain he would lose, either.

'If this woman's slipped the net, there'll be hell to pay.'

'What makes you think that could have happened?'

'An immigration officer called Edward Godson was tortured and murdered in his own home last night.'

'So?'

'Godson worked at Crampton House Immigration Removal

132

Centre. Seppi allegedly had a run-in with him when he was there.' Worby paused, inviting him to join the dots.

Oh-oh. Carlyle thought of Peter Williamson and Justin Lansley, the two guys Seppi had hospitalised. His brain went into intelligence-gathering mode. This conversation might be his one opportunity to pump Worby for information that could help cover his back. 'What kind of a run-in?'

'She assaulted him,' Worby continued, 'in a most violent and unprovoked manner.'

'Isn't it normally the other way round?'

Worby ignored the question. 'These people are little better than animals. Attacks on staff are regrettably common. Godson didn't even bother to report it. It only came to light when we checked back through the footage from the security cameras.'

These people are *treated* like animals, which is not the same thing. Carlyle kept fishing: 'And you think Seppi was responsible for this killing?'

'Seppi is the prime suspect. A neighbour saw a woman leaving Godson's house around the time of the attack.'

'Witnesses are notoriously unreliable.'

'There's CCTV coverage of a woman in the street outside.'

Fuck.

'Although the quality's not good.'

'That's unfortunate.'

'If the media get hold of this, they'll go crazy.'

'You'd better find Seppi, then,' Carlyle declared shamelessly, 'and quick.'

'How can we have her,' Worby complained, 'if she's running around the country killing public servants?'

Carlyle dismissed the possibility. 'Bet you a pint she's lost in the system somewhere.'

Worby wasn't in the mood for a wager. 'She's missing and it's your fault.' He sounded like he wanted to reach down the phone and throttle the obtuse copper. 'You'll pay for this, mark my words.'

'That remains to be seen,' Carlyle said equably. 'Let me see what I can find out.' Worby started to speak, but Carlyle cut him off with a curt 'I'll call you back.'

Abandoning thoughts of quizzing Patrick Dalby, he went off in search of Laura Nixon. The sergeant, however, was already on her way to search Dalby's farm. A call to her phone went straight to voicemail. Carlyle hung up without leaving a message. 'Bollocks.'

After a few more curses, he tried Rita Vicedo.

The nun picked up on the second ring. Carlyle was straight to the point. 'Things are getting badly out of control here. I need to speak to your source, immediately.'

FOURTEEN

Vicedo's contact was a pudgy young man who introduced himself as Karol Lacko. They met in a safe house belonging to the International Network Against Human Trafficking in east London. Before they got down to business, Lacko opened his laptop and insisted Carlyle watch a YouTube video.

'It's only a minute.'

Irritated, Carlyle peered at the time code on the screen. 'One minute and twenty-two seconds.'

'Bear with me.'

Carlyle glanced at Vicedo.

'It's just a minute,' the nun parroted.

'All right.' Carlyle sighed. 'Let's see it.'

Lacko hit play. 'I'll explain at the end.'

The clip showed six people walking around a room passing basketballs to each other. Three wore black shirts; three wore white. Carlyle was asked to count the number of passes made by the whites. About two-thirds of the way through the clip, a seventh person, wearing a gorilla suit, wandered into the middle of the action, beat their chest and walked out of shot. The ball-throwers continued passing the basketballs.

While Carlyle tried to keep count, Lacko took off his spectacles and began cleaning the lenses with a paper tissue. As the video finished, he put his glasses back on and blinked, as if seeing the world afresh.

'Did you see the gorilla?'

'Sure I saw the gorilla. It was rather hard to miss.'

'About half of people who take the test don't see the gorilla,' said Lacko.

'Very interesting,' Carlyle said sarcastically.

'Stay with it, Commander,' Vicedo advised. 'You might learn something.'

'The invisible gorilla experiment is very famous,' Lacko explained. 'It shows how people miss a lot of what goes on around them.'

'Plus,' Vicedo added, 'they have no idea how much they're missing.'

'That doesn't surprise me,' Carlyle grunted. 'Try getting any decent information out of eyewitnesses at a crime scene. People are hopeless at the best of times.' Slightly miffed no one was interested in whether he had counted the number of passes correctly, he invited his hosts to get to the point.

'The gorilla we're talking about here is corruption,' Lacko explained. 'Project Gorilla was the name given to a wiretapping operation conducted by the Slovakian security services, an investigation into an alleged bribes-for-contracts scandal. Millions of euros in development funds were being diverted into the pockets of officials and criminals.'

Carlyle began to see where this was going. 'The Slovak Intelligence Service, as in the people Monica Seppi works for?'

'The people she used to work for.'

'What happened?'

'I'll get to that.'

'As soon as you like.'

'You're the one who asked for this meeting, remember?' Vicedo upbraided Carlyle for his bad attitude. 'Let Karol tell his story.'

Told off by a nun. Carlyle tried to look suitably chastened. 'Sorry.' He signalled for Lacko to continue.

'The SIS was tracking this gorilla.'

'The gorilla of corruption?' Carlyle ignored Vicedo's glare. He hated it when people couldn't get to the point.

'Right.'

'And the powers that be didn't like that.'

'Inevitably, there were plenty of important people who wanted to ignore the gorilla. In fact, they wanted it dead and buried. When the investigation got too close to the truth, it was closed down.'

'The usual kind of thing.'

'Do you realise how jaded that makes you sound?' Vicedo chided.

'By the time you get to my age, you're supposed to be jaded.'

The nun muttered something Carlyle didn't catch in a language he didn't understand. He turned to Lacko. 'Why was the investigation stopped?'

'A new prime minister took office and the government wanted to draw a line under the past.'

'Again, not exactly unheard of,' Carlyle commented. 'Politicians are genetically programmed to sweep things under the carpet.'

'Not everyone was happy with this decision,' Lacko continued. 'Transcripts of the wiretaps were leaked online. The leak caused a big storm back home.'

Vicedo took up the tale. 'Monica Seppi was a senior security agent working on Project Gorilla. Her real name is Zuzana Klek.'

Carlyle felt the questions piling up in his brain faster than he could ask them. 'She's not Romanian, then?'

'That was just a cover,' Lacko confirmed.

'Zuzana resigned her job and disappeared before the transcripts were leaked,' said Vicedo. 'She's the one the SIS thinks dumped the files online.'

'In protest at the investigation being dropped,' said Lacko. 'Project Gorilla became an obsession for her. She always was very headstrong and determined.' He added, somewhat wistfully, 'A real tigress.'

You fancy her, Carlyle deduced, but you're supposed to kill her. It was quite the dilemma. 'You're here to find her?'

'I want to help her.'

'Which means what?'

Vicedo closed down the line of questioning: 'Karol didn't come here to be put on the spot.'

'I don't mind, Rita.' Lacko scrutinised Carlyle. 'I can talk to you in confidence, right?'

'I know how to keep my mouth shut,' Carlyle confirmed.

'Yeah, so, I worked with Zuzana in SIS. We were quite . . . close.'

In your dreams, Carlyle thought. He couldn't blame the boy for trying to punch above his weight in the boxing ring of love. He could see how the woman could turn the heads of much finer specimens than poor Lacko.

'When the shit hit the fan, I told them I was the best person to get her to come out of the shadows.'

This was no time to beat around the bush. 'Your bosses, they want her dead?'

Lacko looked pained. 'They want her silent. If she dies – quietly – fine. If she ends up rotting in an English prison under a fake name, fine. If she retires to the sunshine, fine. They don't really care what happens to her, just as long as she stops causing trouble back home.'

Carlyle wondered what might have become of the woman if Immigration Enforcement had managed to deport her. There was every chance she would already be dead. The thought made him feel better about leading Jamie Worby a merry dance.

'Like they say in my country,' Lacko continued, '*If the eyes don't see, the heart doesn't hurt.* People want the whole thing to go away – they see it as an unwelcome reminder of previous scandals from before Slovakia joined the EU. The government insists the documents leaked online are fake. Powerful people want it, like you say, to stay under the carpet.'

'See the size of the mess you've dragged me into?' Vicedo asked archly.

Blame Sergeant Nixon. Carlyle wondered how the sergeant was getting on with searching Patrick Dalby's farm.

'Zuzana can be a very dangerous woman,' said Lacko.

'I realised that,' Carlyle quipped, 'when she sanded off Edward Godson's genitals.'

Lacko grimaced. 'I heard about that.'

'We know all about Edward Godson,' Vicedo said grimly. 'He was a sexual predator allowed to roam free in the prison system.'

'Doesn't mean you can do that to him,' Carlyle argued.

Vicedo refused to condemn the attack. 'You should deal with men like him – there are plenty of them about.'

'I'll add it to my to-do list,' the commander said wearily.

'It was his bad luck to come across Zuzana,' Lacko ruminated. 'She is not the kind of woman to forgive and forget.'

'She brought him to account,' Vicedo asserted. 'Good for her.'

Carlyle was slightly taken aback by the nun's hard-nosed attitude. Then again, she did run with the crew who'd given the world the Spanish Inquisition. 'How am I going to find the multi-talented and incredibly troublesome Zuzana Klek?' he asked. 'And what should I do with her?'

'Zuzana can drop out of sight for long stretches at a time,' Lacko advised.

'I don't mind her dropping out of sight. It's when she reappears we have a problem. Edward Godson's the second time she's taken things into her own hands. There simply cannot be a third.' The commander stared at each of them in turn. 'Where might she be?'

'You don't find her,' Lacko said. 'She finds you.'

Lacko left first. Vicedo agreed they would wait five minutes before following him out. Carlyle thought the whole George Smiley arrangement was a tad OTT, but he played along.

'What are you going to do?' Vicedo asked, while they waited for the last couple of minutes to count down.

Carlyle didn't have a clue. 'All ideas gratefully received.'

'Karol is genuinely sorry for what's happened. He wants to avoid a diplomatic incident.'

'He's besotted with a killer.'

'Karol tries his best. He's done many good things over the last few years. Supported the Network, both here and in Slovakia. Helped a lot of victims.'

Carlyle took her word for it. 'If he comes with your seal of approval, that's good enough for me.'

'Thank you, Commander.' Vicedo started towards the door. 'Rest assured, if Karol comes up with any more useful information, he'll pass it on, through me.'

'I would expect nothing less.' Carlyle followed Vicedo outside. As she was locking up, a taxi trundled down the road. Sticking out an arm, he brought it to the kerb and ushered her inside.

Traffic was light, by London standards, and they made good progress, heading into the centre in companionable silence. Trundling along Old Street, Vicedo pushed the intercom button. 'I need to get out here, please.'

As she pulled out her purse, Carlyle held up a hand. 'Don't worry, I'll get this.'

As the driver pulled over, Vicedo took a scrap of paper from her pocket. 'This is the address of Monica Seppi's – or Zuzana

Klek's – flat.' She handed it to Carlyle. 'In case you want to take a look.'

The walls of his office were still avocado. 'What happened to the decorators?' Carlyle asked wearily.

'They say it'll be done next week.' Joaquin pointed at a pile of papers on his desk. 'You need to read those.'

'All of them?' Carlyle was horrified.

'The ones on the top are the most important.'

Trying to ignore his surroundings, Carlyle sent his PA packing and sat down to do some reading. Top of the pile was a draft of his proposed all-staff security memo about the need to restrict access to Charing Cross's inner sanctums.

Dear colleagues . . .

Almost immediately, his eyes glazed over. Dropping the note onto his desk, the commander allowed himself to be distracted by the siren call of his phone. Twenty minutes evaporated as he considered the latest football transfer rumours. Eventually, Sergeant Nixon called from Patrick Dalby's farm.

'Result.' Nixon sounded slightly high, like she'd just finished a ten-K run, or overdone things in a kickboxing class. 'There's enough fertiliser and shit down here to blow up half of London.'

'Fertiliser and shit,' Carlyle parroted, pleased that her grasp of technical detail pretty much matched his own.

Nixon brought her high spirits under control. 'All the relevant details will be in my formal report, sir. Suffice to say, we have found plenty of evidence supporting the thesis that explosive devices were manufactured at the farm. And I have a preliminary confirmation from Forensics that the bomb which blew up the dust cart was made from the materials we've found here.'

'Preliminary confirmation?'

'They're sure Patrick Dalby's our guy.' Nixon cleared her throat. 'One hundred per cent.'

Carlyle waved a triumphant fist in front of his face. 'Excellent, well done, Sergeant. I'll give Mr Dalby the good news right away, see if it encourages him to talk.'

Whistling 'We Are The Champions', Carlyle strode into the interview room. The atmosphere, poisoned by the prisoner's terrible body odour, was foetid. Without introducing herself, Dalby's lawyer raised her chin in the direction of the clock on the wall. 'Time's running out. You'll have to charge my client or let him go.'

'Fair enough.' Carlyle tried to speak and breathe through his mouth at the same time.

'Well?'

'Seeing as we've uncovered a veritable bomb-making factory at your client's farm, with a cornucopia of evidence linking him to the attempted murder of Imogen Edelman, I think we'll be charging him.'

A wave of resignation swept across Dalby's face. He started to speak, but his lawyer shut him up.

Desperate for some fresher air, Carlyle retreated to the door. 'I'll get the paperwork ready. Shouldn't be too long.'

The lawyer started berating her client before he had even left the room. Enjoying her volley of abuse, Carlyle resumed whistling as he headed down the corridor. Returning to his office, he discovered an urgent message waiting for him from Lottie Pearson, the mayor's special adviser. With some reluctance, he returned her call.

'Jasper Wiggins and a bunch of his comrades staged a vigil outside the mayor's house. A brick was lobbed through the living-room window. Fortunately, no one was home at the time. But what I don't understand is this – why isn't anyone doing anything about it?' By 'anyone', Pearson meant the police in general and Carlyle in particular. 'I mean, you were going to have a word with him.'

'Things have been a bit hectic.'

'Jasper and his pals weren't even arrested. They were given a warning and sent on their way.'

That's one way of saving on the paperwork, Carlyle reflected. In reality, it was a bit of a miracle they were even caught in the first place. The local cops must have been keeping an eye on the house despite the mayor's reluctance to have a police presence there.

'It's outrageous,' Pearson complained. 'What do you have to do these days to get arrested? Next time, someone'll end up hurt.'

'Let me speak to the officer in charge,' Carlyle offered. 'What's his name?'

'Dunno, but it's all online.' Ending the call, she texted him a link to a YouTube video featuring a 'powerhouse transgender activist' called Miss P. A bunch of people were standing in the street, surrounding a uniformed police sergeant, arguing the toss. If it hadn't been for Pearson's primer, Carlyle wouldn't have had a clue what was going on. Helpfully, however, the hapless copper's epaulette badge was clearly visible. It was a simple task to identify him as Sergeant Harry Black, based out of Kennington. A call to the station revealed Black had gone off duty. Pulling rank, Carlyle demanded Black's personal phone number.

'Sophie?' The background noise indicated the sergeant was enjoying a post-shift pint.

'Sadly not.' The commander apologised for calling him when he'd gone off duty.

'No problem. What can I do for you, sir?'

'I've been watching you on YouTube. The mini-protest outside the mayor's house.'

'Dirty bastards,' the sergeant grumbled. 'You can't do anything, these days, without some little wanker filming it.'

'Tell me about it.'

The noise receded as Black found a quieter spot to talk. 'I imagine things were a lot easier in your day.'

I'm not so old, Carlyle thought, irritated. Then, to his considerable dismay, he realised he was. A lot of the things that had gone on when he'd started on the force you couldn't hope to get away with now. But it was ever thus: a smart copper simply had to adapt. 'A brick got thrown through the mayor's window – correct?'

'Yeah,' said Black, warily.

'But there were no arrests?'

'It was impossible to work out who threw the brick. We've got video of the incident but it's impossible to clearly identify the perpetrator.'

'I understand.' Carlyle wanted to sound as reasonable as possible, to avoid the sergeant clamming up on him.

'If you don't mind me asking, sir, what's your interest in this?'

'One of the mayor's people asked me to look into it. But, don't worry, I'm not looking to cause you any trouble.'

Black sounded less than reassured. 'What *are* you looking to do, sir?'

'One of the protesters was a guy called Jasper Wiggins.'

'A right idiot.' Black snorted. 'Rich-kid revolutionary. Went to Eton, same as that dickhead politician.'

Which particular dickhead politician? Carlyle wondered. There were so many of them.

'Did you know Wiggins's dad's some bigwig at the BBC?'

'Better than his dad being a judge,' Carlyle supposed. 'These snowflakes all have important parents. Otherwise they'd have to stop fucking about and get a job in Starbucks.'

'We've had him in the cells before. He was caught vandalising a Range Rover, but his dad pulled some strings and he got off.'

'Way of the world.' Carlyle wasn't interested in the details.

'I'd love to be able to give him the shoeing he so richly deserves.'

'Like you said, you can't get away with that kind of thing, these days.'

'More's the pity.'

'But we still have options.'

There was a moment's silence and then Black asked, 'How d'ya mean?'

'When you get in tomorrow, I want you to review the CCTV footage and decide there's enough to arrest young Master Jasper for criminal damage. Bring him in. Let him stew in the cells while you lean on his mates to finger him for it.'

The sergeant was less than enthused. 'Seems a lot of effort for not much reward.'

'One way or another, the little bugger has to be made to back off. If this doesn't work, we'll try another approach.'

'My boss won't like it. He got a right bollocking over the Range Rover thing.'

'Any complaints, tell him to speak to me.'

'The chances of getting Wiggins into court,' Black complained, 'never mind convicted, have got to be slim to none.'

'We can cause him a lot of aggravation in the meantime, though.'

'I hope the mayor appreciates all the effort we're going to on his behalf.'

'Me too.' Somehow, Carlyle doubted it. Next up, he spoke to Emily Quartz. 'I need you to help with my Plan B.'

'Nice to speak to you, too, Commander.'

Carlyle was unmoved. 'Ours is a transactional relationship,' he said, 'based on enlightened self-interest. I want something, I call you. You want something, you call me. What's wrong with that?'

'Nothing.' The reporter laughed. 'In fact it's refreshing.'

'My thoughts exactly.'

'A bit like Tinder sex.'

'Er, I wouldn't know about that.' Carlyle felt his cheeks begin to burn. Moving swiftly on, he asked, 'What do you know about a guy called Jasper Wiggins?'

'With a name like Jasper, and a cop asking about him, I'm thinking he must be a posh boy gone off the rails.'

'Not a bad guess.' Carlyle explained his interest in the transgender-rights activist.

'I'm surprised he hasn't waded into the argument over the ladies' pond.' Quartz chuckled at her own joke.

'I'm sure it's on his radar, but Jasper's got other things to worry about right now. He's going to be arrested on suspicion of lobbing a brick through the mayor's front window.'

Quartz immediately understood where this was going. 'You want me to write a story about him being nicked.'

'This'll be Jasper's fifteen minutes of fame. I was thinking you might shine a light on his antisocial behaviour, in the context of this whole trans thing.'

Quartz was reticent. 'If we look at "the whole trans thing", as you put it, I would be conflicted because of the row at the pond.'

Not as conflicted as if I'd let my colleagues in Hampstead charge you with various public-order offences, Carlyle thought. 'No one will make the connection,' he said. 'The problem with the pond is old news. It's gone away.'

'Not for the Ladies' Pond Association. They've got another meeting about it next week.'

Carlyle sensed leverage. 'Maybe I could make representations to the Corporation.' The Corporation of London, which ran Hampstead Heath, decided who could and couldn't use the 'women-only' pond. 'But I need you to do the Wiggins thing first.'

'I could pitch the idea,' Quartz said, 'but it's not really the Unit's thing. Francesca's more interested in taking on the rich and powerful, not smearing some kid who's got a bit carried away on a demo.'

Carlyle was irritated by her continued lack of enthusiasm. 'The kid's a hooligan,' he pointed out. 'And his arrest has got to be a story. He went to Eton. His dad is head of something or other at the BBC.'

'But "posh public schoolboy gone bad" is such a cliché.' Quartz sighed. 'And everyone at the BBC's head of something or other.'

'It's a story,' Carlyle insisted. 'If the Investigation Unit won't run it, maybe you could sell it to one of the tabloids.'

'Maybe.' Quartz still didn't sound overly keen. 'I'd need a good picture.'

'I'll get you one.' Carlyle saw a headline swim before his eyes in a large font: *Shame of BBC Boss's Son.* 'It'll be a nice little exclusive for some lucky organ.'

'Leave it with me.'

'I'll let you know when the guy's been formally charged.'

'Fine.' It sounded like *Whatever.*

'As a quid pro quo, I'll speak to the Corporation,' Carlyle promised. 'Plus I'll let you have the latest on Tim Hitchcock.'

At mention of the Kollision CEO, Quartz perked up noticeably. 'You know why he killed himself?'

Why he killed himself?

WTF?

Why hadn't he heard about that? Carlyle took a moment, trying to hide his surprise.

'Now *that* is a story,' Quartz continued. 'I'd be very interested in the inside line on why he ended it all.'

'First things first,' Carlyle said calmly, 'find a home for the Wiggins story and then I'll let you have chapter and verse on Hitchcock.'

'Exclusively?'

'Exclusively.' Killing the call, Carlyle shouted, 'Joaquin, get in here.'

After a carefully calibrated delay, the PA appeared in the doorway. 'A guy called Tim Hitchcock has committed suicide.' Carlyle spelt out the surname. 'Like the film director.'

Joaquin scribbled on a notepad. 'Like the, erm, film director.'

'Alfred Hitchcock.'

Joaquin looked none the wiser.

'Never mind.' Carlyle groaned. 'I need all the paperwork relating to *Tim* Hitchcock and I need the name of the senior officer who attended the scene.'

'On it.' Joaquin wandered back to his desk.

'Quickly,' Carlyle called after him. 'This is important.'

FIFTEEN

Tim Hitchcock had taken a dive off the balcony of his Notting Hill flat. The report was uninformative and the officer in charge of the investigation had signed off on the provisional verdict of suicide, pending an autopsy. Heading down to the third floor, Carlyle filled Karen O'Sullivan in on the latest developments. 'The guy hit the pavement at precisely one minute past three. He almost hit a woman walking down the street looking at her phone. She took a photo and put it on Twitter and it was trending five minutes later . . . hashtag pavement pizza.'

The inspector wasn't amused. 'Maybe he was pushed.'

Carlyle's heart sank. 'What makes you say that?'

'Patrick Dalby was released before one o'clock,' she announced. 'That's more than enough time to get over to Notting Hill and deal with the bloke who shopped him.'

'What?' Carlyle felt like he'd been punched in the face. 'We charged Dalby. He should be sitting in prison by now.'

'It didn't happen. The paperwork wasn't completed in time.'

'And we didn't ask for an extension?' Carlyle stamped his foot in frustration. 'Fuck. *Fuck*. FU-UCK.' A few officers looked up from their desks, wondering what the fuss was about.

The inspector signalled for him to lower the volume. 'Dalby's lawyer hustled him out of here the minute the detention period expired,' she said quietly. 'These things happen.'

'I should have used the fucking Terrorism Act,' Carlyle hissed.

'We'll have to re-arrest him.'

'We'll have to find the bastard first.' Carlyle groaned. 'Start with the lawyer.' He realised he had never even asked the woman her name.

'Miranda Curtis is a real piece of work,' O'Sullivan groused. 'She won't lift a finger to help us.'

'You know her?'

'I've had a couple of run-ins with her.' A pained expression crossed the inspector's face. 'She knows how to press your buttons.'

Carlyle had no time for Machiavellian lawyers. 'Track her down. Tell her if she doesn't hand over her client immediately, we'll arrest her, too.'

'For what?'

'I'll leave that to your discretion.' Carlyle retreated towards the stairs. 'Just make sure the woman cooperates.'

'And where are you going?' O'Sullivan asked plaintively.

'Parallel enquiries,' was all Carlyle offered. 'This has to take top priority. I'll see you back here, later on.'

From behind her desk, Helen gave him a murderous look. 'Whaddya mean you let him go?'

'*I* didn't let him go. *We* ran out of time to question him. It was an administrative thing.' Carlyle shifted his weight from foot to foot. After some umming and ahhing, he had decided it would be better to deliver the bad news in person. 'There was a mix-up with the paperwork and—'

'But you're the boss, right? You have to take responsibility for letting a maniac like Patrick Dalby waltz out of the door.'

'That's one way of looking at it.'

'Oh, and what would be the other way to look at it?' Helen

cranked the sarcasm up to eleven. 'You were only obeying orders? Never heard that one before.'

'It's my responsibility,' Carlyle said quietly. 'We are making every effort to return Dalby to custody as quickly as possible.'

'Don't give me your PR bullshit. Save it for the outside world.'

'It's true,' Carlyle insisted. 'He won't get far.'

'And, in the meantime, what am I supposed to tell Imogen Edelman? The poor woman's a nervous wreck as it is. She hasn't been able to get back in her car since the ... since the thing. She'll have a complete bloody breakdown when she finds out.'

'There's no need to alarm her unnecessarily. We should sit tight and wait till Dalby's back under lock and key. With a bit of luck, she doesn't even need to know.'

'And what if you don't get him? What happens if he flees the country?'

Either way, Carlyle thought, Imogen Edelman's safe. 'He's not going to target her again.'

'You don't know that.'

Carlyle hated it when Helen had him on the run. He gritted his teeth, 'I know we'll have him back behind bars as quickly as possible.'

'What about when the press gets hold of it?' Helen fretted. 'It would be terrible if Imogen were to read about this online. We have to tell her.'

'One step at a time. We'll cross that bridge when – if – we get to it.'

'You and your bloody bridges.' Helen picked up a pencil and threw it at his head, missing by a good distance. 'How could you be so totally, utterly useless?'

Let her vent, Carlyle told himself. Answering back will only get you into more trouble.

Helen looked around for something else to throw at him.

Finding nothing immediately to hand, she asked, 'What are you going to do now?'

'We're chasing Dalby's lawyer and . . . a few other things.'

'Such as?'

'I'm going to speak to a Colin Spooner. He works for a guy called Tim Hitchcock, a business associate of Dalby's. Spooner should have some ideas about where Dalby might be.'

'Speak to Hitchcock too,' Helen commanded.

That might be difficult. 'I'll let you know how I get on.' Carlyle rose from his chair. 'Meantime, leave Imogen be. We can take a view at the end of the day whether we need to tell her or not.' Leaning over the desk, he kissed the top of her head. 'I'll see you back at home.'

'I'll be late.'

Probably no bad thing, Carlyle decided. 'Okay.'

'I've got the Sandland hearing starting at five.'

Carlyle was reminded that Patrick Dalby wasn't the only scumbag on Helen's radar. 'The sex pest.'

'*Alleged* predator.'

Carlyle frowned. 'I thought he was bang to rights.' Christopher Sandland was a doctor who'd been caught bartering medicine for sex in one of the charity's Asian projects. He wasn't the first predator who'd worked for Avalon and, doubtless, he wouldn't be the last.

'Innocent till proven guilty and all that.' Helen sighed.

Carlyle instinctively felt it was a matter for the local police – accusations of a cover-up could be more difficult to deal with than the original offence – but Helen's trustees wanted the matter dealt with internally. 'At least it should be quick.'

'It's scheduled for four hours.' Helen rolled her eyes. 'Chris is fighting it all the way.'

'Sometimes that's the only plan people can come up with,' Carlyle reasoned. Play for time. Delay, frustrate, embarrass, and hope something comes up and saves your arse before you finally go down.'

Conveniently, the offices of TRX Associates were only a block from those of Avalon. Carlyle made his way through two different receptions, acquiring three visitor badges in the process, only to be told by Colin Spooner's secretary that the lawyer wasn't in.

'I can wait.'

The woman couldn't have looked less happy if he'd dropped his trousers and taken a dump on the carpet. 'Mr Spooner may be some time, I'm afraid.'

'I need to speak to him,' Carlyle said blandly. 'It's a matter of some considerable importance.'

'He might not be back today.'

'Call him,' Carlyle's tone dropped several degrees, 'or send him a text. Let him know a police officer needs to speak to him.' He contemplated the workspace. 'Meantime, I'll go and have a chat with a few of Colin's colleagues, see what they can tell me.'

The secretary scowled. 'About what?'

'About what I need to know,' Carlyle said cryptically. 'Just call him.'

'He won't pick up. He doesn't like to be disturbed when he's in the Masons Arms.'

Carlyle recalled the pub he'd passed on the way in. 'He's in the boozer? Why didn't you say so?' Leaving the woman muttering to herself, he divested himself of his various visitor badges and exited the building.

Walking back down the street, he got a text from O'Sullivan informing him Dalby's lawyer had, like her client, gone to ground. Cursing, he entered a large, gloomy establishment, largely devoid of punters. Spooner was sitting in a booth at the back, mechanically eating a packet of crisps. On the table in front of him, a half-finished pint of beer sat next to a pile of three slim A4 plastic files.

As Carlyle approached, the lawyer looked up, his face devoid of expression.

'Bloody Harriet. She's supposed to say I'm in a meeting.'

'I beat it out of her.' Carlyle pulled up a stool and sat down.

'Really?' Spooner wiped a crumb from the corner of his mouth. 'I would have quite enjoyed watching that.'

'Just kidding. I only use violence as a last resort . . . or if I'm in a bad mood.'

Spooner raised an eyebrow. 'What kind of mood are you in at the moment?'

Carlyle gave the question some thought. 'Could go either way,' he decided.

'Well, I don't want to push you over the edge but I'm a bit busy.' Spooner gestured at the files. 'Stuff to do.'

'I just want a quick word.'

'I'm afraid I don't like being disturbed when I'm working.'

'Probably not a good idea to have your office in a pub, then.'

Tossing the crisps packet onto the table, the lawyer looked hopefully towards the bar. 'Are you at least gonna buy me a drink?'

Carlyle declined the invitation. 'This is purely business. I need to know what happened to Tim Hitchcock – and where I can find Patrick Dalby.'

'Tim fell off his balcony.' Spooner reached for his pint pot and drank about half its remaining contents. 'As for Patrick Dalby, I'm not the man to ask. I only met the guy a couple of times. Don't know him at all. If he's done a runner, I wouldn't know where to start looking for him.' Finishing his drink, he stood up. 'If you're not buying, I'd better get my own. Forgive me if I don't offer you one.'

Watching Spooner make his way to the bar, Carlyle reached

for the files. The first two were of no interest, but the third related to TRX's work for Kollision Financial Services. Waiting for the man to return, Carlyle began reading it.

'Hey, you're not supposed to be looking at that.' Reappearing at Carlyle's shoulder, Spooner made a grab for the file, spilling some of his beer over the policeman in the process.

Carlyle jerked the folder out of reach. 'You shouldn't have left it on the bloody table.' Sticking it under his arm, he made a performance of brushing his jacket. 'And if you get any more sodding beer on my coat, I'll nick you for assault.'

'Fuck off.' Spooner stumbled back onto the banquette.

'Not very articulate for a lawyer, are you?' Carlyle waved the file in the air. 'If I understand this right—'

'You probably don't,' Spooner scoffed.

'If I understand this right,' Carlyle repeated, 'Kollision was involved in various different court cases, not only the one against Sandringham Risk Consulting.'

With no stomach for an extended argument, Spooner stared dolefully into his beer. 'You'll leave me out of it, right?'

'This is just to get me up to speed,' Carlyle promised. 'I won't do anything with it.'

'Fine.' Spooner took a sip of his pint. 'There are six different cases under way, with another couple pending. Every time we get sued we sue right back.'

'Mr Hitchcock must have had deep pockets.'

Spooner let out a pained yelp. 'His bills alone are well into seven figures. If we don't get any money from Kollision, I'm fucked. My partners might not care about me working down the pub, but if we get stiffed on our fees, I'll be out on my ear.'

Carlyle offered to speak to whoever was now in charge at Kollision about paying their bills. 'You think it was suicide?'

Spooner didn't miss a beat. 'Yeah. It was all getting a bit much for Tim. You saw him on one of his better days, but he was getting worse and worse. Basically, he'd got himself into a hole and didn't have the first clue about how to get out of it.'

Carlyle waited for him to continue.

'Tim was basically Bruno Soutine's point man in London,' Spooner blurted.

'The cryptocurrency guy?'

'Yeah, the one who stole the personal trainer's identity. And, before you ask, no, I don't think Tim knew his real name. I certainly don't.'

'Did Hitchcock know it was all a scam?'

Spooner smiled. 'Who knows how much thinking was actually going on? But, come on, you have to believe in fairies to think that something like that'll make you rich.'

'If it seems too good to be true, it probably is.'

'Right. People were given plenty of warnings, too, but greed is such a powerful emotion, know what I mean?'

Carlyle understood perfectly. 'What about Patrick Dalby?' he asked. 'Where does he fit into all of this?'

'They were old university pals. Dalby was an early investor in Kollision but I got the impression he wasn't as big a deal as he liked to make out. He latched onto the Soutine thing as a get-rich-quick scheme. Dalby was the kind of guy always on the lookout for an easy score. I think he was broke.'

'What about his farm?'

'Tim said it was heavily mortgaged.'

'It would explain his desperation to get his hands on his sister's money.'

'I didn't know anything about that,' Spooner said hastily. 'What kind of crazy bastard would try to blow up a woman in her car?'

'The kind of guy,' Carlyle speculated, 'who might have killed the real Bruno Soutine?'

'Maybe. Sounds like he's completely lost the plot.' Spooner

took another drink. 'Surely his lawyer knows where he is.'

Carlyle had a sudden urge for a whiskey. He pushed it away. 'She's AWOL, too.'

'Now *that* I might be able to help you with.' Spooner's expression brightened a little. 'Miranda Curtis and I go back a long way. We went out together for a while. Long time ago.' His face darkened again. 'She dumped me. Said I was a crap shag.'

'These things happen.' Carlyle wasn't interested in the guy's lack of sexual prowess. 'Where can I find her?'

'You have no right to be here.' Leaning against the frame of the front door, Miranda Curtis played with an unlit cigarette. Patrick Dalby's lawyer was trying to create a *Don't fuck with me* vibe. To Carlyle's mind, however, it was no more than posh-girl posturing. When he didn't respond, she asked, 'How did you find me, anyway?'

'It wasn't hard.' Carlyle had tracked the woman down to her mother's house in Kew. He didn't mention he'd been tipped off by a guy she'd dumped because he was crap in bed.

'You can't come in.'

Carlyle was unmoved. 'Want me to arrest you, and we can debate that down at the station?'

Grumbling to herself, Curtis led him through the hallway to the back of the house. Through an open door, Carlyle spied the mother watching *Countdown* on TV.

Arriving in the kitchen, Curtis folded her arms. 'What do you want?'

Leaning his backside against the sink, Carlyle tapped the breast pocket of his jacket. 'We have an arrest warrant for your client.'

'Which one?'

'Don't fuck about.'

'Patrick.'

'Where is he?'

'I wouldn't know.' Curtis lifted the cigarette to her lips, eyeing the lighter on the kitchen table. 'We left the police station and went our separate ways.' She attempted to pre-empt further questioning by adding, 'I tried to call him earlier but got his voicemail.'

'Maybe he went back to the farm.' Carlyle lifted his eyes to the ceiling. 'I mean, he's not here, is he?'

'Of course not.' Grabbing the lighter, she fired up the cigarette and took a succession of rapid puffs, ignoring her visitor's obvious displeasure.

Carlyle refused to be smoked out. 'You have to bring Dalby in, or we'll be coming after you, too.'

Curtis tapped the ash from the cigarette onto a saucer sitting on the kitchen table. 'Is that a threat?'

'I want Patrick Dalby back in custody by the end of the day.' He started back down the hall. 'Otherwise I'll arrest you and leak it to the papers.'

'Promises, promises.' The lawyer's mocking laughter followed him all the way out.

The journey back to the Underground station took him down a narrow alley cut through a row of terraced houses. Catching up with emails on his phone, Carlyle was only dimly aware of a figure coming towards him. Trying to step out of the way, he realised too late the man was deliberately blocking his path.

'Excuse me.' By the time Carlyle looked up, the man's fist was almost in his face. He tried to duck, only to be rewarded by a sharp blow to the cheek. Stumbling backwards, his main concern was not to drop his phone. A succession of punches changed his priorities. Beaten to the ground, he adopted a foetal position, waiting for his attacker to relent.

SIXTEEN

Carlyle wondered if he was going to puke. The lump on his temple felt as big as a chestnut. The paramedics had given him the all-clear, but a fistful of painkillers had yet to make a meaningful dent in a headache that felt like someone was trying to scoop out his brains with a corkscrew.

'Did you see his face?'

'I smelt him . . . It was Dalby.'

Karen O'Sullivan gave him a funny look.

'I'd recognise his BO anywhere.'

'Not sure that would stand up in a court of law.'

'When I catch up with the little shit,' Carlyle said grimly, 'a court of law's going to be the least of his worries.' After taking his beating, he had retreated to Curtis's mother's house. The old woman had opened the door and let him in without comment. Informing him her daughter had left, she returned to her TV programme, leaving Carlyle to his own devices. Deciding that the woman must be suffering from some form of dementia, he retreated to the kitchen, called an ambulance, then O'Sullivan, and brewed himself a cup of tea. Forty-five minutes later, a pair of paramedics turned up on bicycles and declared his injuries to be 'essentially superficial'. After handing him a packet of painkillers they cycled off in search of more worthy victims. Inspector O'Sullivan, who turned up ten minutes later, was no more sympathetic than the paramedics.

'You basically let the guy walk right up to you without noticing.' At least she didn't laugh in his face.

'That's not exactly how it happened,' Carlyle muttered.

'And now he's done a runner with Curtis.' O'Sullivan shook her head. 'You've made a right mess of this, Commander, if you don't mind me saying so.'

Everyone's a critic. Carlyle downed another couple of pills to try to ease his pain. 'I was the one who tracked down the lawyer,' he pointed out, 'on my own.'

'Come on,' O'Sullivan grinned, 'it wasn't hard – she was at her mum's.'

'Still, I did it.'

'Yes, well done.' She belatedly adopted a more sympathetic tone. 'Don't worry, we'll get them, soon enough. Why don't you go home? Get some rest and we can see where we are in the morning.'

'Good idea,' Carlyle agreed. 'I've had enough for one day.'

By the time Helen returned to the flat, Carlyle's aches and pains had been eased by a couple of beers, chased down with a generous amount of Jameson's. Requisitioning a bottle of Sauvignon Blanc from the kitchen, Helen poured herself a large glass before joining him on the sofa.

'Bloody Sandland.'

Christopher Sandland was the alleged medicine-for-sex doctor. Carlyle was cheered his memory did not appear impaired by his beating on the mean streets of Kew. 'How did it go?'

Helen took a mouthful of wine. 'Not only did the shameless charlatan not resign, he informed the trustees he'll launch a claim for wrongful dismissal if he's sacked.'

'He's bluffing.' Carlyle hoped he was telling his wife what she wanted to hear. 'Go for the jugular.'

160

'The trustees won't back me. They're too scared of the potential for bad publicity if they take him on.'

'You could leak it to the press.' Finishing his whiskey, Carlyle placed his glass on the coffee table. 'Get it out in the open. Bounce the trustees into action.'

Helen rejected the idea. 'It's too risky. If I was caught leaking material from an internal investigation, I could get the sack.'

'You could get the sack anyway.'

'Whaddya mean?' Helen's face darkened. 'I'm the one trying to deal with this mess. Why would *I* get the sack?'

'All I'm saying is . . . when things like this blow up, somebody usually gets thrown under a bus.'

'That's what I'm trying to do, throw Chris fucking Sandland under the bus.'

'Which is the right thing to do. Unless this bloke gets sacked and publicly hauled over the coals, there's the danger the charity will be accused of trying to cover things up.'

'That's what the trustees want, a cover-up.'

'It won't work,' Carlyle predicted. 'These things always come out in the end.'

'A very helpful observation,' Helen snapped. 'Thanks a lot.'

'I'm just saying—'

'Well, don't, all right? I've had enough of this shit for one day.' Turning the tables, she asked, 'And I don't suppose you've caught Patrick Dalby yet, have you?'

'We're closing in on him.'

'That's a no, then,' Helen scoffed. 'You've failed to sort it out – again.'

'I *am* sorting it out.' Carlyle was miffed his wife hadn't shown any concern over the bruises on his face.

'Not fast enough.' Helen finished her wine. 'I'm going for a long hot bath.' She struggled to her feet. 'You'd better give Imogen a call.'

161

Carlyle fiddled with his phone, waiting for her to leave the room. With no intention of calling Imogen Edelman, he was happy to be diverted by a message from Emily Quartz. The text contained a link to an online story Quartz had published minutes earlier. It covered Jasper Wiggins's arrest, along with a potted history of the boy's political activism and a nod to his father's job at the BBC. Carlyle forwarded the story to Lottie Pearson, then called Harry Black, the officer he'd prevailed upon to nick Wiggins.

'He's still claiming he didn't throw the brick,' said the sergeant, 'but there's enough to send a file to the CPS. Just about.'

Carlyle had no intention of leaving Wiggins's's fate to the Crown Prosecution Service. 'What's his home address?' he asked. 'I'll take it from here.'

The Wiggins family home was a large detached house in Highgate, far removed from the hoi polloi. Walking up the short drive, Carlyle pressed the doorbell for three seconds and waited. It was late-morning. Hopefully, the adults would be out at work.

No one stirred.

A second blast on the bell brought, equally, no response.

Third time around, Carlyle kept his finger on the bell until an upstairs window opened. A girl's head appeared, her nose ring glinting in the weak sunlight. 'Bugger off,' she shouted, 'or I'll call the police.'

Smiling up at her, Carlyle adopted his most pompous voice. 'I am the police, madam.'

There was some shouting, followed by the sound of footsteps. Finally, the front door opened, and Carlyle found himself face to face with a skinny youth devoid of clothing, save for a pair of sagging underpants.

'You must be Jasper.' Carlyle presented his ID and stepped inside. 'Go and get dressed and I'll put the kettle on.'

'We've got a Nespresso machine,' was the only response the dazed youth could muster.

'Even better,' Carlyle replied. 'I'll get busy.'

It took the best part of fifteen minutes for Wiggins to throw on a pair of jeans and a sweatshirt. Padding into the kitchen, he began rummaging through a drawer full of teabags. 'Molly wants a white tea.'

Sitting at the breakfast bar, Carlyle gazed out across the expansive garden at the back of the house. 'Good thing I'm not in a hurry.' Fuelled by two espressos, he had a nice buzz going on and was feeling pretty good about things.

'She's pissed off you woke us up.'

Carlyle eyed the clock on the wall. 'It's almost afternoon.'

'We had a late night.' The boy yawned in slow motion. 'It took ages to get out of the police station.'

'You shouldn't throw bricks through people's windows,' Carlyle suggested.

Wiggins selected a teabag and dropped it into a mug. 'I didn't do anything.'

Carlyle waved away his protestations of innocence. 'Get your girlfriend her tea. Then we'll talk.'

When Wiggins reappeared for a second time, the sweatshirt had been replaced by a shirt with a flower pattern. Carlyle signalled for him to take a seat.

'You got yourself into a bit of a mess, huh?'

'It's the Feds, man.' The boy's accent was completely bogus, more Hackney than Highgate. 'They've got it in for me. It's sick.'

We're not 'the Feds', you moron. Carlyle bit down on his contempt. 'All the more reason,' he said gently, 'why you should steer clear of trouble.'

'You sound like my dad,' Wiggins griped. 'A total sell-out.'

A total sell-out with a nice house close to Hampstead Heath, Carlyle reflected. He took a deep breath. 'I'm sure you've been stitched up, right enough. Which is why I'm going to do you a favour.'

Wiggins looked at him suspiciously. 'Whaddya mean?'

'I'll make this go away.'

'You can do that?'

'Sure,' Carlyle said airily. 'Consider the case dropped. We'll make sure the papers know it's been a mistake, too.'

Wiggins plucked a plum from a fruit bowl on the counter and weighed it in his hand. 'And why would you do that?'

'Why d'ya think?' Carlyle adopted a conspiratorial tone. 'Because Joe Stanley doesn't want to see one of the good guys get done by the, erm, Feds.'

Mention of the mayor caused Wiggins's face to crumple in disgust. 'The mayor hates me, man.'

'The mayor respects people with beliefs, people who try harder, people at the cutting edge of political discourse.'

'What?' Wiggins put the plum back into the bowl.

Carlyle tried again. 'The mayor doesn't want to be surrounded by yes men all the time. He likes you because you're true to your beliefs.'

The kid was still struggling to understand the line he was being spun. 'You know the mayor?'

'I've known him a long time.' Carlyle thought back to his fleeting conversation with Stanley. 'He's a smart guy.'

Wiggins let out a hoot of derision. 'He should back our demands.'

'He does. For him it's only a question of timing.'

'Huh?'

Was the kid really so thick? Carlyle wasn't sure *he* wasn't being strung along, rather than the other way round. 'Joe needs people like you to lead, so the rest can follow.'

Wiggins considered this for a moment, then said, 'There's gotta be a leader in any struggle, right?'

'And the mayor knows you are that man.'

'Person.'

'Right.' Carlyle was growing increasingly confident of the boy's gullibility. Perhaps his little deception would work after all. 'He knows good people like you are hard to find and he doesn't want your, ahem, progress stalled by a run-in with the police.'

'But you are the police. Why're you here?'

'I'm here to, well, apologise for what happened.'

'Officially?'

Carlyle thought of the six-figure sum doubtless wasted on the boy's education, not knowing whether to laugh or cry. He gave a solemn nod. 'We're sorry for what happened. The demo got out of hand. It could've been handled better.'

'That's not much of an apology,' Wiggins whined. 'It was a peaceful protest until your lot turned up.'

Carlyle wasn't going to genuflect any further. He slid off the stool. 'Try to keep off our radar for a while,' he suggested. 'Otherwise, even the mayor may not be able to keep you out of jail.'

'I wasn't going to jail,' the boy said defiantly. 'My dad said it was all bullshit.'

'I wouldn't test that theory if I were you.'

'Is that a threat?' The boy scowled.

'Just a bit of friendly advice,' Carlyle backtracked. 'And the next time you see the mayor you should say thanks.'

The news that Patrick Dalby was at large did not go down well with Imogen Edelman. After much wailing (her), apologising (him) and promising to do better (him again), Carlyle finally managed to end the call and bring the self-flagellation to a close. Resisting the temptation to hurl his phone into the gutter, he looked up and was rewarded, like Saul on the road to Damascus, by the emergence of a vision trading under the name of Gail's Café. Gail's was an upmarket chain, with prices to match, but if ever there was a time for an overdose of caffeine and sugar this was it. Scuttling inside, he ordered the largest pastry he could find.

Demolishing the bun in double-quick time, he was enjoying a second Americano when a woman in black jeans and a battered leather jacket took a seat, uninvited, at his table. Somewhere in her thirties, she had a hard, pinched look, her blonde hair was pulled back in a ponytail and her face was freshly scrubbed, devoid of make-up. Carlyle imagined he could make out a faded bruise on her cheek, but he couldn't be sure.

A pair of glacial blue eyes looked him up and down, giving no indication of being in any way impressed by the specimen in front of her.

'Can I help you?' Carlyle tried to sound insouciant, as if approaches from fierce-looking women in cafés were a common occurrence for a man of the world such as himself.

'You've been looking for me.'

'I have?'

The woman's expression made him feel like a praying mantis about to be decapitated.

'I was at your police station. Your colleague let me walk out.'

Oh, shit. He cleared his throat. 'Zuzana Klek.'

'One name among many,' she said blithely. 'Monica Seppi will do for now.'

'As you wish.' Wondering if the woman was armed, Carlyle squirmed in his seat. 'I will always defer to a trained assassin.'

Enjoying his discomfort, Seppi ran her tongue along her lower lip. 'Don't worry, Commander, I'm not here to do you any harm. I just want to talk.'

'Glad to hear it.'

166

'I understand you are a sensible man, pragmatic.'

Who told you that? Carlyle wondered. He kept silent, preferring to let the woman do as much of the talking as possible.

'I think we have a shared interest in resolving this situation, don't you?'

'I'm open to suggestions.' Carlyle signalled to the waitress behind the counter for another coffee. 'Would you like a drink?'

Seppi accepted his offer, asking politely for a pot of green tea. 'I thought it might be better for us to talk here, on neutral ground if you like, rather than me going back to the police station and turning up in your office.'

'Very considerate of you.'

'Although, I have to say, I think you might want to think about improving your security arrangements.'

'It's in hand,' Carlyle said defensively. He made a mental note to get his damn memo out as soon as possible. 'We're upgrading our procedures.'

'No one challenged me.' The drinks arrived and Seppi filled her cup almost to the brim. 'It was all very lax.' She took a sip of her tea. 'The guy on the door even wished me good day as I left. More like a hotel than a police station.'

'We're a service provider,' Carlyle said lamely. 'We have to be polite at all times.'

Seppi moved on. 'What did Karol tell you about me?'

'You know about our meeting?'

She gave him a pitying look. 'I *told* him to take the meeting.' Reaching forward, she placed a hand on Carlyle's forearm, causing him to recoil, more in frustration than anything else. There was nothing he liked less than being taken for a fool, other than, maybe, proving himself one. 'There was no way you would be able to work out what was going on by yourself. I needed Karol to give you a push in the right direction.'

'You and Karol are working together?' It was hard to see how he was going to come out of this looking like anything other than a prize idiot.

'He still works for our government and he needs to be careful. But I've known him a long time and he won't turn me in.'

'He's a friend?'

'I would describe him as a reliable acquaintance.'

'He explained about the situation back home.'

'I can't go back to Slovakia. They'd kill me. Or throw me in prison for the rest of my life. Hard to say which would be worse.'

'Hm.'

'Which is why it was so unfortunate to be arrested by your immigration people.'

Carlyle held up a hand. 'Nothing to do with me.'

'Maybe. I didn't know such things happened in England.'

'You were unlucky.'

'Not as unlucky as some.'

Carlyle did not challenge the assertion.

'My luck changed, though, when you brought me back to London, didn't it?'

'I wish I hadn't bothered,' he blurted.

'I couldn't believe it when I just left,' Seppi crowed. 'Even in Slovakia, the cops are more switched on than that.'

'Did you come here to wind me up,' Carlyle enquired grumpily, 'or was there a point to this little meeting? I'm not going to blame my people for what happened. Our usual customers at the station are drunks, pickpockets and mugged tourists – far less problematic.'

'Drunks, pickpockets and tourists.' Seppi took another sip of tea. 'It must be very boring.'

'You've certainly livened things up.'

'It wasn't deliberate. I was trying to keep a low profile, mind my own business. If those guys in the bar hadn't attacked me, none of this would have happened.'

'Those guys are still in hospital,' Carlyle pointed out. 'They'll never be the same again.'

'My only regret,' Seppi said flatly, 'is I didn't kill them.'

'You didn't make that mistake with the other guy,' he struggled to remember the dead man's name, 'the detention-centre guard.'

'Edward Godson was a coward. He was a tough man when you were locked up and he could sell you a cigarette for a blow-job. Outside, not so much.'

'Nothing gave you the right to kill him, though.'

'If I were you, I would be more worried about putting my own house in order,' Seppi growled. 'You should discipline your sergeant for letting me go. In fact, you should probably get rid of her altogether. The woman clearly doesn't have what it takes.'

'Sergeant Nixon is a good police officer.' Carlyle gulped his coffee. 'She was trying to help you. She thought you were a victim of crime.'

'Ha.' Seppi finished her tea and refilled the cup. 'If there is one rule in life you should live by, it is this: *Never be a victim.*'

'You certainly had your revenge.'

'Those men all got what they deserved.'

'Nixon was only trying to help. You dropped her in it.'

'Dropped her in it?'

'You caused her a big problem. And me, for that matter. I tried to help you – against my better judgement, as it happens – and look at the mess I'm in. I should have left you in the hands of Immigration Enforcement.'

'Those idiots.' Seppi snorted. 'And that moron of a lawyer they gave me. A boy who wanted me deported as quickly as possible. The whole thing was a sham.'

'He tried to help you, too.'

'And where would all that help have got me?' she hissed. 'A one-way ticket to an unmarked grave.'

Carlyle didn't know what to say.

'And what about all those people who don't escape? What happened to me, it happens to thousands of women every month. They get kicked out to fend for themselves. We hear about the famous English fair play, what a joke. You think your country is so great? Why would anyone come here if they didn't have to? You think people come here for fun? Because they like the weather?'

We're getting a bit off the point, Carlyle thought wearily. 'We were trying to help you,' he repeated.

'I didn't need help.'

'We didn't know that.'

'I would have got out of that detention centre myself, one way or another.'

Carlyle didn't doubt it. He looked nervously at the teapot, imagining how Seppi could use it as a weapon. On the plus side, the café was filling with lunchtime customers so there would be plenty of witnesses. Keen for her to get to the point of their meeting, he signalled for the bill.

'I wasn't going to go home to be killed.'

'You could apply for asylum.'

'Not now.'

'No, I suppose not.'

The waitress brought the bill and a card reader. Carlyle waved his Visa card over the machine and pocketed the receipt. 'Presumably now you want my help. Otherwise you wouldn't be here.'

'Asking for help is one thing,' Seppi said. 'When it's unsolicited, that is when the problems arise.'

Carlyle wasn't going to debate the point any further. 'What d'you need?'

'I want my passports back.'

Plural.

'We don't have them. We didn't know who you were, remember?'

'They'll be among the things your people took from my flat.'

Eh? Carlyle recalled the scrap of paper Rita Vicedo had given him as she was getting out of the taxi. Casually putting his hand in his pocket, he was relieved to find it was still there.

'Karol gave you the address, so you could get there before my former colleagues in the security services cleaned it out.'

'Um, yes.' Lacko must have given it to the nun, who, in turn, had given it to Carlyle, who had stuck it into his pocket and forgotten all about it.

Excellent work, Commander.

Misreading the mixture of emotions on his face, Seppi offered, 'Perhaps I can do you a favour in return.'

SEVENTEEN

'It's a result.' Leaning against the reception desk, Declan Brady ran a hand across his three-day-old stubble. 'Samuel Fisher had a heart attack while stalking his latest victim – bang,' the doctor slammed a fist into his palm, 'fatal. No more bed hopping for him . . . and no disciplinary hearing for me.'

One of the nurses skipped by. 'You're a lucky boy, Declan,' she grinned, 'and no mistake.'

'You're off the hook?' Having written off the doctor as a near miss in the relationship stakes, Laura Nixon was vaguely irritated at being back in the hospital so soon. A female patient was claiming money had been stolen from her bedside table; the police had been called and a report had to be filed. The sergeant would have delegated the chore but no one else was available. All the constables had been sent to cover a Chelsea game and the community support officers were on strike, objecting to being treated like dirt and openly disparaged as 'plastic policemen'.

'Looks like it.' The doctor couldn't have looked any happier if he'd found a tenner on the pavement.

'The families of Fisher's victims have dropped their complaints?'

'It's more the hospital's trying to sweep it under the carpet.'

Nixon didn't understand.

Brady tried again. 'What we had was a situation in which Mr

Fisher was about to start riding his latest victim when he fell off the bed. He cracked his skull and that was it. Game over. The family kicked up a hell of a fuss. One of Fisher's sons started complaining about the quality of his father's care and threatened to sue the hospital. The bloke went absolutely mental when Patient Liaison told him what his old da had been up to.'

'I'm not surprised. No one wants to be told their old da is a serial sex offender.'

'No, I suppose not,' Brady agreed. 'But they calmed him down in the end. A deal was struck – PALS dropped all investigations into the assaults and the family won't take legal action against the hospital over the circumstances of his death.'

'Neat.'

'It is, kinda.'

Nixon thought about it for a moment. 'Won't the other families kick up a fuss, though? The ones whose relatives Fisher attacked before?'

'As for the original complaints against Mr Fisher, PALS will put them on the back-burner for six months, then declare they couldn't dig up enough evidence to adjudicate.'

'Christ, and I thought the police were bad when it came to burying bad news.'

'Common sense ruled in the end,' Brady insisted. 'And, most importantly, my career is saved.'

'Lucky for you.'

'Better to be lucky than smart,' the doctor observed. 'But enough of that. What brings you back to my door?' When Nixon explained about the missing money, he feigned disappointment. 'And here was me thinking it was my rugged medical charm.' When she didn't respond, he adopted a more professional persona. 'I don't suppose you've got a line on the woman who was grabbed by the immigration Nazis?'

Nixon shook her head. 'She's disappeared into the system

somewhere.' Her phone started to buzz. The screen said, *Commander.* 'Sorry.' Retreating down the corridor, she waved the phone at Brady. 'Gotta take this.'

'I'm going to text you an address,' Carlyle announced. 'Meet me there in twenty minutes.'

The address Rita Vicedo had provided was located in a featureless building containing a selection of newly built flats that were struggling to sell in London's post-boom property market. Carlyle had neither the keys nor the lock-picking skills required to gain entrance unaided. Luckily, the block had a concierge, a moonlighting student called Arjun.

Arjun inspected the commander's ID with great care before returning it. 'You should speak to the managing agents,' he suggested politely.

'I don't have time, I'm afraid.' Carlyle clocked Nixon approaching the front entrance. 'So, unless you want my sergeant to arrest you for impeding a police investigation, let's do this my way.'

Unmoved by the threat, Arjun buzzed Nixon into the building and reached for the phone sitting on the desk. 'It won't take a minute to give them a call.'

Carlyle beat him to it. He placed the phone on top of a textbook entitled *Understanding Hydraulics* as Nixon stepped up to the desk. 'We need a quick look round. Five minutes. We'll be gone before you know it.'

'I have to follow the standard protocols,' the young man insisted. 'It's my job, after all.'

'Time is of the essence.' Nixon tapped a steel-toed boot on the tiled floor. 'You wouldn't want us to have to kick the door in, would you?'

'Is there a body in there?' Arjun's eyes grew wide, his imagination going into overdrive. 'We don't want any trouble.'

'There's no body,' Carlyle replied, 'and there won't be any trouble. Just give us a key, go back to your studies, and we'll be in and out in a flash.'

The flat had the vaguely desolate air of somewhere occasionally occupied but never properly lived in. Nixon stood in the middle of the living room, hands on hips. 'What are we looking for?'

Before Carlyle could reply, the front door opened and a peeved-looking middle-aged man walked in. 'What are you doing?' he demanded.

'Police.' Carlyle held up his ID. 'Who're you?'

'Rory Gooding, the managing agent.' He fished out a business card and handed it to Carlyle as Nixon disappeared into a bedroom.

'How did you get here so quickly?' Carlyle glared at the concierge, who had appeared behind his boss. Peering into the room, the young doorman seemed disappointed not to be staring at a corpse lying in a pool of blood.

'He was in the neighbourhood,' Arjun offered meekly.

'Good thing I was,' Gooding grunted. 'You shouldn't be in here without a warrant.'

'Someone was here before us.' Nixon reappeared, waving an empty shoebox. 'Any idea who?'

'Presumably the tenants,' Gooding replied.

'There's more than one?' asked Carlyle.

Gooding hesitated, then said, 'The flat is let to a couple.'

'The man,' Carlyle pressed. 'What does he look like?'

'You shouldn't be here,' the agent repeated.

Carlyle resisted the urge to throttle him. 'Tell me what the guy looked like and we'll go.'

'I've never met him.'

'Overweight. Late twenties. Thick-rimmed glasses,' Arjun offered. 'I've spoken to him a few times. Seems a nice enough bloke. Foreign. His English was good, though.'

Karol Lacko. 'When did you last see him?'

'Dunno.' Arjun screwed up his face as he thought about it. 'A week ago? Maybe a bit more.'

'And the woman?' Nixon asked.

'She was here yesterday,' Arjun confirmed. 'In and out in ten minutes.'

Looking for her passports, Carlyle thought, which she thinks we've got.

'She never said much. Stern-looking babe.' Arjun corrected himself under Nixon's harsh stare. 'I mean, she seems like a very serious person.'

Tell me about it. Carlyle let the concierge run through a basic description of Monica Seppi, then hustled Nixon out of the building.

'How did you get the address?' the sergeant asked, as they approached the tube to take them back to Charing Cross.

'Rita Vicedo came up with it.'

'I need to give her a call.'

'Leave her to me for the moment,' Carlyle instructed. 'The immigration people are still on our case. If this all blows up, I'll have to take the blame. No point in getting you dragged into it.'

'But it was my fault we lost Seppi in the first place,' Nixon admitted.

'Never apologise, never explain.' The sergeant looked puzzled by Carlyle's advice, so he continued, 'We all make mistakes. I appreciate you holding up your hand, but if all the good people take responsibility and get canned, what does that leave us with? Muppets who pass the buck.'

'Um, okay.'

'This Seppi thing's gone completely pear-shaped.'

The sergeant could not dispute his analysis. 'It's all very weird, going off in all different directions.'

'Which is why I'll deal with the Home Office, and Rita.'

'Thanks, Commander.'

'I have a rule – I try to judge colleagues solely on my experience of working with them.' He worried that he was sounding like an old fart but kept going. 'I've been working in the Met since before you were born, more or less, and I've found good people are few and far between, certainly far rarer than you would hope. In my opinion, you're a good cop.' Nixon blushed. 'And so is Inspector O'Sullivan.'

'Karen's great,' Nixon agreed.

'Hopefully, you've both got long and successful careers ahead of you. No point in stuffing things up because of some minor spat with the immigration Nazis.'

'That's what Declan called them.'

'Who?'

'The doctor at the hospital who saw Monica when she first came in,' Nixon explained.

'Smart bloke.'

'It's a bit harsh, don't you think? I mean, Immigration Enforcement's got a job to do, right? We've got to keep illegals out, for sure. That's what taking back control is all about.'

Fuck's sake, Carlyle groaned. There I was, singing your praises, and you suddenly go all racist on me. 'I'm with Dr Declan,' he declared. 'It's easy to pick on the weakest and most vulnerable in society, especially when you've got the weight of the state behind you. Seems to me that's *exactly* like the Nazis.'

'You sound like a right old leftie,' Nixon scoffed.

'I have no political allegiances,' Carlyle pronounced solemnly. 'I hate all politicians equally.'

'But you believe in law and order?'

'Absolutely I believe in law and order, especially for those who need it most, those at the bottom of the pile.'

'Monica Seppi hardly seems like one of the weakest and most vulnerable.'

Carlyle couldn't dispute that. 'What's the situation with the guys in hospital?' he asked.

'Williamson was released a couple of days ago. Lansley's still in. He'll be there for a while.'

'Nasty.' Carlyle didn't want to think about it.

'Given how things have moved on, there's not much likelihood of us pursuing the original case against them.'

'Best to let it drop,' Carlyle agreed. 'I mean, it's not like Monica Seppi's going to make a complaint, is it?'

'You'd arrest her if you got the chance, wouldn't you?'

'Chance would be a fine thing.' Carlyle raised his gaze to the grubby heavens. 'You never know, but I'd be amazed if we ever saw her again.'

In his office he found a crumpled man in a cheap suit. 'Jamie Worby.' The head of Immigration Enforcement shook Carlyle's hand without getting out of his seat.

The commander slid behind his desk. 'You should've told me you were coming.'

'Monica Seppi.' Worby dialled down the temperature to somewhere below freezing. 'You've got some explaining to do.'

Having rehearsed this conversation in his head, Carlyle didn't miss a beat. 'As far as I can ascertain, we handed the woman back to you and you've lost her.' All he could do was stick to his story and hope for the best.

Worby tried to look menacing but he didn't have the face for it. 'There is absolutely no record whatsoever,' he blustered, 'of any documentation that serves to back up your version of events.'

'All proper paperwork was completed at our end,' Carlyle insisted. 'I know you've been having problems with your new IT system, but I didn't realise things were this bad.' To bolster his narrative, he deployed a few facts he'd gleaned from the internet about the Home Office's latest IT debacle. 'What was it you did

178

the other day? Tried to deport a dozen Asian doctors because you said they were from Pakistan when, in fact, they were born and bred in Blackburn?'

Worby's face went red as he bemoaned 'quotas' and 'software issues'.

Having pushed the bureaucrat onto the back foot, Carlyle sought to press home his advantage. 'You need to get your own house in order before you come round here having a pop at me. I read you've spent four hundred million on this new computer system of yours. More than double the original estimate. More than a year late.'

'All right, all right.'

'Sounds like a total nightmare. Then again, all IT projects go off the rails, don't they?'

'That's your line, is it?' Worby's face was almost beetroot now. The man looked like he wanted to commit an act of serious violence on the commander's person.

'Monica Seppi was handed back,' Carlyle responded. 'How the hell should I know what you've done with her?'

'Bullshit. What's your game?'

'I don't play games. If I make a mistake, I hold up my hand. I don't pass the buck – unlike the Home Office.'

'You never returned the prisoner,' Worby hissed.

'Maybe she's been deported already,' Carlyle said blithely. 'Like the woman who was supposed to be in Cardiff but was eventually found in Caracas.'

Worby's face began to twitch. Carlyle idly wondered if the man might be having a stroke. Deciding that would be too much to hope for, he waited patiently for him to rise from his chair. The Home Office man headed to the door, like a Napoleonic soldier on the retreat from Moscow. That'll teach you to fuck with me, pal, Carlyle thought. 'Let me know if you manage to find the woman.'

Worby skulked out, only to be replaced by Joaquin.

'What was all that about?' the PA asked.

'It was about *you* letting a guy into my office who shouldn't be in there.'

'What else was I supposed to do with him?' Joaquin pouted.

Having no answer, Carlyle shooed him out.

Peace having finally descended in the office, he called Rita Vicedo.

'Where's Karol Lacko? I need to see him right now.'

'No idea.' The nun seemed taken aback by his brusque tone. 'I haven't spoken to him since our meeting at the safe house.'

Carlyle throttled back his irritation. 'How well do you know him?' he asked.

'Well enough. I told you, Karol's one of the good guys.'

'He might be one of the good guys but he's playing some kind of game here. I'm being used and I don't like it.'

'You asked for the meeting, remember?'

'All that means,' Carlyle groused, 'is I'm being *well* played. And I like that even less.' He filled her in on his conversation with Monica Seppi and his subsequent visit to the apartment she had shared with Lacko.

'Sounds like you should have checked it out sooner,' was Vicedo's verdict.

'The point is I don't know what the hell is going on and I need your pal to shed some light on things.'

'Let me see if I can find him for you. Again.' The line went dead. I suppose, Carlyle thought glumly, that's what happens when you try to get one of God's little helpers to do your job for you.

Pondering the chances of being bailed out by divine intervention, he realised the walls had finally been repainted. The avocado was gone, replaced by the off-white he'd been asking for.

Hallelujah!

Leonard Cohen started singing in his ear. A sense of peace cloaked his soul. His reserves of optimism and goodwill started to rise.

Monica Seppi hadn't come to London just to fool an ageing London cop in the twilight of his career. He'd done his best, even if it wasn't much. And even though it had all gone wrong, the world hadn't stopped turning.

'Get over yourself,' he muttered. 'Just get over yourself.'

Leaving the station, Carlyle had almost reached Covent Garden piazza when he got a call from Emily Quartz. He answered the call with a cheery 'hello', only to be greeted by what sounded like a full-scale riot from the other end of the line.

'It's all kicked off again,' she blurted. 'The Ladies in Charge were having a meeting and a bunch of activists turned up.'

'Ladies in Charge?'

'That's what they call the Executive Committee at the pond.'

'And you just happened to be there as well, I suppose.'

'I was having a swim,' Quartz explained. 'I had to get out when a shoe nearly hit me on the head.'

Having mentally clocked off, Carlyle couldn't muster much in the way of sympathy.

'Can you come up here?' Quartz asked. 'We don't want any arrests, but the situation needs calming down.'

I don't think so. 'I'm on my way to a meeting,' he lied effortlessly. 'I'll be tied up for at least a couple of hours, I'm afraid.'

Quartz was in no mood for excuses. 'You need to come, now,' she urged him. Right on cue, the noise levels in the background ratcheted up a decibel or two. 'Jasper's here.'

'Jasper Wiggins?' So much for the boy heeding Carlyle's instruction to stay out of trouble. Ditching his fictitious meeting, the commander set his autopilot for the nearest tube station.

'Along with his mates and some of the people who were here last time,' Quartz confirmed. 'It's gonna get ugly.'

'It's gonna get *very* ugly,' Carlyle promised, 'when I get my hands on the little shit.

By the time he made it to the pond the excitement was over. The activists had headed off in search of other battles to fight while the Ladies in Charge had retreated to a tearoom in Highgate. Quartz, suitably apologetic for dragging Carlyle up for nothing, invited him to join them. After a quick look at the epicurean delights on offer, he readily agreed.

'I'm sorry about this, Commander.' Mary, the Ladies' Pond Association's chair, nibbled a biscuit. 'It was very kind of you to come up at such short notice.'

No notice, Carlyle thought. He added a significant debit to Emily Quartz's account in his favours book. Before leaving, he vowed to remind the journalist of the need to start making some sizeable deposits.

'I hope we didn't make you miss an important meeting.'

'What?' Biting into a raisin Danish almost as big as an old seven-inch single gave Carlyle time to get his story straight. He chewed the mouthful of pastry at length, before swallowing and washing it down with a very agreeable Ethiopian blend of coffee. 'It'll be fine. My team will make sure I'm brought up to speed in the morning.'

'I expect you must have a very big team of people working for you,' said another woman, whose name he hadn't caught.

Carlyle looked around the table. Eight expectant faces gazed back at him, seven of them well north of sixty, plus Emily Quartz, who seemed amused by the way he was holding court. This was the biggest audience he'd had in years. Carlyle wiped a crumb from the corner of his mouth. 'I'm very lucky I've got a lot of good people I can call on. Still, I'm not the kind of man who thinks you can delegate everything. I like to roll my sleeves up and do my share of the heavy lifting.'

'A very commendable attitude,' Mary said. 'I was wondering if you could tell us how you got on with our friends at the Corporation of London?'

'Huh?' Carlyle looked at Quartz.

'You were going to speak to the Corporation about our little problem,' the reporter reminded him.

'The Corporation simply won't listen to what we have to say,' complained one woman. 'The other side simply has to say, "Jump," and they say, "How high?" It's not very balanced at all.'

'It's not fair,' said someone else.

'I understand your concerns.' Carlyle slipped into his 'professionally sympathetic' mode. 'And I wish I had better news. Clearly this is a thorny problem. The Corporation understands your position but it, ahem, feels caught in the middle of this. Inevitably, some people will end up being unhappy, even if it can manage to reach a sensible compromise.'

'I don't want to share a changing room with a man,' somebody on the other side of the table piped up, 'even if he is wearing a bikini.'

'There's a men's pool and a mixed pool,' another pointed out, 'so there's plenty of choice.'

'Why on earth,' said a third woman, 'if there are three pools, can't biological women have sole access to one of them?'

Carlyle held up his hands in mock surrender. 'I hear what you're saying, but I'm not the man you have to convince.'

'The commander's trying his best,' said Quartz.

The others seemed less than convinced. 'I understand,' said Mary, gently placing a hand on his arm, 'that the police are not responsible for the running of the ponds but, surely, they should be doing more to stop the kind of loutish behaviour we see from the so-called "activists" who seem to have jumped on this particular bandwagon.'

'If you want to file a complaint, we can go to the police station.'

Carlyle's offer provoked an outbreak of grumbling around the table.

'I'm sorry, Commander, if we don't like your idea,' Mary's pained expression mirrored those of her comrades, 'but the last time this happened, we were the ones thrown into the cells.'

By now it was clear he was only going to disappoint his audience. The faces around the table were displaying various degrees of frustration, bordering on hostility. How do I get myself into situations like this? Carlyle wondered. Taking a deep breath, he gave it one last go. 'I know the local officers will be fair and even-handed,' he prattled, provoking further murmurs of dissent. 'I'll . . .' he was about to say 'pop in and have a word' but he'd made too many such promises recently and had yet to keep any of them, so he downgraded the commitment to '. . . I'll keep in touch with Emily and make sure I help where I can.'

The feeble offer did nothing to improve the mood of the group. Finishing his pastry, he took his leave as quickly as politeness allowed.

Quartz followed him to the door. 'I'm sorry about that. The Ladies in Charge can be a bit daunting. They don't take any prisoners.'

'They ambushed me, right enough.'

'They're trying to work their way through a very difficult situation.'

'Change can be difficult.'

'There's change and there's change. I mean, come on, this is a big deal for the Ladies in Charge. Activists like Jasper will get bored and turn their attention to something else. They'll have destroyed something these women value, and for what?'

It sounded like a perfectly valid point, but Carlyle – as he thought he'd made clear – had no easy solution hidden up his sleeve. He did, however, have an idea. 'Wiggins lives near here.'

He pointed up the road. 'Why don't we go and pay him a visit?'

'I saw the guy in action,' Quartz grumbled, 'useless little so-and-so. I don't feel the need to see him again anytime soon.'

'C'mon.' Carlyle led her along the road. 'You'll get the chance to discover the boy in his natural habitat. It'll be fun.'

Jasper answered the bell far more speedily than he had on Carlyle's first visit. And he was dressed, which was another bonus. The welcome, however, remained on the frosty side of cool.

'You're the copper who was here before.'

'At least we know there's nothing wrong with your memory.'

Ignoring the sarcasm, Wiggins looked the commander's companion up and down. 'Who's she?'

'Emily Quartz,' the woman herself piped up. 'I'm a journalist.'

'She's interested in the dispute at the pond,' Carlyle improvised.

Wiggins raised a fist in the air. 'The fight goes on.'

Carlyle was suddenly reminded of Wolfie Smith, the comedy Che Guevara. He kept the thought to himself; neither Wiggins nor Quartz was even born in the heyday of the Tooting Popular Front. 'Are your parents in?'

The boy idly scratched a nipple through the thin fabric of his ripped T-shirt. 'Whaddya want them for?'

'It was a yes-or-no question.'

The boy thought about it for longer than seemed strictly necessary. 'No.'

'Good.' Inviting himself inside, Carlyle brushed past the boy and headed into the open-plan kitchen-living area.

'Hey.'

'Back already?' Sitting on a sofa, Molly, Jasper's girlfriend, eyed him suspiciously from behind a mug of – presumably – white tea.

Carlyle identified himself to the other couple in the room – at first glance a man and a woman – who were sitting on the floor.

'I hear there was more trouble at the pond.'

'Nothing to do with us.' Wiggins flopped onto the sofa and draped an arm over Molly's shoulders. Quartz hovered uncertainly behind them.

'Looks like we're in trouble again,' Molly drawled, flicking V-signs at Carlyle with her eyes.

'We're supporting equality and fairness,' Wiggins trumpeted, to no one in particular.

'You think the pond should allow self-identifying trans women in women-only spaces?' Quartz asked.

'Definitely,' Wiggins squealed. 'It's only right, innit?'

'Someone's got to stand up to those rich white women,' the woman sitting on the floor proclaimed. 'They're always trying to hold things back. It was the same with the lesbians. Back in the day, they tried to keep them out, too. It's the same thing now – prejudice, pure and simple.'

'Society moves on,' her companion opined. 'They've been left behind.'

Wait till it happens to you, sunshine, Carlyle thought. He pointed an admonishing finger in the direction of their host. 'You're a right shit magnet, Jasper, aren't you?'

The young activist seemed taken aback by the policeman's suddenly hostile tone. 'You can't come in here, to *my* house, and—'

'It's not your house,' Molly pointed out, 'it's your parents'.'

The boy did not appreciate being corrected. 'It's the same thing.'

Carlyle shook his head. 'I got you out of trouble and now you jump right back into it.'

'That was different.' The boy pouted. 'No windows got broken this time.'

'I nearly got hit by a shoe.' Quartz's revelation was met with general disinterest.

'This antisocial behaviour cannot be allowed to continue,' Carlyle pronounced.

'What antisocial behaviour?'

Carlyle turned to see a well-dressed, middle-aged woman standing in the doorway, looking professionally pissed off.

'Who're you?' Carlyle asked, causing Jasper to giggle.

'This is *my* house,' the woman snarled. 'I'm Jasper's mother, Sonia Wiggins. Who are *you*? And what are you doing here?'

'It's the Feds,' the man sitting on the floor chortled, 'and this is a bust.'

Molly had seen enough. Without saying anything, she slipped off the sofa and left the room. The other two followed her, leaving Jasper to face his mother alone.

Carlyle made the introductions.

'What's wrong with you, Jasper?' Sonia Wiggins was steadily working herself into a rage. 'Why do you bring this . . . nonsense into our home?'

The boy sat, stock still, head bowed. 'Gender dysphoria,' he said quietly, 'is a serious issue.'

'And so is bringing the police to our door,' his mother replied. 'You know how traumatic it was being in the cells. Do you want to go back there?'

'This is the policeman who got me off the brick thing,' Jasper explained. 'He's keeping me *out* of jail.'

For the moment, Carlyle thought.

Jasper's mother gave no indication of wanting to shake Carlyle's hand. 'What are you doing in my home?' she asked again.

'There was a fracas down at the pond,' Carlyle explained.

'*Another* fracas,' Quartz put in.

Carlyle tried to sound generous in his assessment of the boy's behaviour. 'I know Jasper is campaigning for things he believes in—'

'Lots of people believe in this stuff,' the boy whinged.

'They do,' Carlyle agreed, 'but things are getting a wee bit out of hand. There was the incident at the mayor's house and now this. Jasper's developing an unfortunate habit of being in the wrong place at the wrong time. Next time, it could be considerably more serious.'

Sonia Wiggins was not impressed. 'This is classic police intimidation,' she spouted.

The mother appeared to be one of those aggressive middle-class types – *I pay your salary* – who wanted public servants to know their place and do as they were told without demur. Carlyle could see where the boy had acquired his sense of arrogance and entitlement. He remained calm. 'I'm trying to help your son stay out of trouble.'

'Jasper's being victimised, pure and simple.' Sonia ran a hand over her boy's hair as she moved into the kitchen area. Opening a massive fridge, she pulled out a small bottle of water and took a drink. 'First he's arrested for no reason and now you invade our home.'

'He's been here before,' Jasper pointed out, keen to wind his mother up even further.

'No one's invading anything,' Carlyle said. 'All we're trying to do is ensure you don't get into any more trouble.' He tried to make eye contact, but the boy wasn't having it. 'Did you speak to the mayor?'

'Joe Stanley's useless.' Sonia guzzled more water.

'The mayor understands and supports the goals of Jasper and his, erm, people in promoting equality and fairness. He believes in constructive and respectful dialogue, rather than confrontation.'

'Change,' Jasper chuntered, 'is only coming from the barrel of ma Uzi.'

'Eh?' Carlyle considered the possibility the kid – rather than just being a dick – might seriously have a screw loose.

'Zig Domino.' The boy smiled. 'He's a rapper.'

'Oh.' Carlyle looked at Quartz, whose expression said, *Who knew?*

'Jasper,' his mother said wearily, 'why don't you go and play with your friends? Leave this to me.'

The boy seemed happy to oblige. Once he'd gone, Sonia Wiggins returned her attention to her unwelcome guests. 'You have no right to be here.'

'We were invited in,' Carlyle said.

'Well, I'm inviting you to leave.'

'Why do you think Jasper is so interested in trans rights?' Quartz asked.

Sonia Wiggins was flummoxed. 'What kind of a question is that?'

'I'm curious.'

'He's a sensitive boy. He believes in safe spaces for everyone.'

Carlyle tried to be conciliatory. 'There's nothing wrong with that, but he needs to avoid getting into trouble. He's not being victimised, and no one's out to get him, but if he's arrested again, I may not be able to get him out.'

'He's *my* son, who made *you* his guardian angel?'

Carlyle could feel his reserves of patience and goodwill dwindling, fast. 'I'm making a big effort here, Mrs Wiggins.'

The woman refused to yield any ground. 'No one asked you to.'

It was pointless arguing any further. Carlyle let her show them the door.

'Mummy's boy,' Quartz proclaimed, once they were down the drive and out of earshot. 'I'm glad I'm not Jasper's girlfriend.'

'Poor Molly's got her work cut out, right enough.'

'Where do things go from here?' Quartz asked.

'It's a classic dialogue of the deaf.' Carlyle couldn't see any way of reaching a compromise. 'I don't think it'll end well,' he concluded. 'If I were you, I think I'd start looking for somewhere else to go swimming.'

EIGHTEEN

Carlyle was woken from a black, dreamless sleep by a knee in the small of his back.

'That's yours,' Helen grumbled, from somewhere under the duvet. 'Switch it off.'

The phone was buzzing on the floor. Scooping it up, he stumbled out of bed and into the hallway.

'Yes?' he whispered.

Rita Vicedo sounded annoyingly bright. 'Sorry, Commander, did I wake you?'

Carlyle carefully closed the bedroom door before retreating into the kitchen. 'Why would I be asleep, given it's the middle of the night?'

'It's only just after one.'

Wait till you get to my age, he thought. You're doing well if you can make it past ten. 'What's so important it couldn't wait till the morning?'

'I've found Karol Lacko.'

He tried to sound grateful for the tip-off. 'That's good.'

There was a pause, voices in the background. Then Vicedo announced, 'He's dead.'

'Ah. That's not so good.'

'I'm here with the police and the ambulance people.' She gave him the address.

Carlyle stifled a yawn. 'I'm on my way.'

The nun pointed to a length of rope hanging from a metal beam. 'They cut him down about ten minutes ago.'

'Uh-huh.' Carlyle wished he'd taken time for a coffee before leaving home. He looked around the empty warehouse. 'How did you find him?'

'He sent me a text.' Vicedo handed Carlyle her phone. The message was simply the address, plus the words, *My decision.*

'Suicide?'

'Looks like it.' Vicedo watched the remaining emergency-services personnel moving out. 'Forensics took a good look, but it seems they're not treating it as a crime scene. And I couldn't see anything suspicious.'

Carlyle was prepared to take her word for it. Having worked with the authorities for so long, Rita Vicedo knew how to analyse a crime scene better than most cops. 'Who's the officer in charge?'

'An inspector called Claire Buscombe.'

'Don't know her.'

'I've worked with her before. She's good.' Again, the nun's judgement was good enough for Carlyle. 'She left to write up her report.' Vicedo handed him one of the inspector's business cards. 'You can call her.'

Carlyle shoved it into the back pocket of his jeans. 'Maybe later.'

The last thing he wanted to do was to get caught up trying to explain his interest in Karol Lacko and, by extension, Monica Seppi. That would only serve to complicate matters terribly. 'Does she know you called me?'

'No. I told her I was a friend of Karol's and he'd supported some of my organisation's projects. I called 999 when I got the text and came over here myself.' She lowered her voice. 'I didn't go into any of the secret-service stuff . . .'

191

Project Gorilla. Carlyle lamented the waste of one minute and twenty-two seconds on the stupid video Lacko had made him watch. 'Good call. All that stuff would only be a distraction if this is written off as a straightforward suicide.'

'That's what I thought.'

Carlyle pointed at the rope. 'Why d'you think he did it?'

'Karol suffered from depression. And he tended to be a bit of a drama queen – he lived too much in his head.'

'He was a geek?'

'He was a nice, genuine guy. He liked opera and *Game of Thrones*.'

'Lots of people like *Game of Thrones*. Doesn't mean they top themselves.' It had already crossed Carlyle's mind that Monica Seppi could have killed her colleague and made it look like suicide. He had no doubt the woman was capable of it, but what possible motive could she have? Lacko was the only person trying to help the rogue agent make good her escape.

'The whole Project Gorilla thing was getting him down,' Vicedo offered. 'And he couldn't get a girlfriend. I think he was a bit in love with Zuzana Klek.'

'Monica Seppi.'

'Yeah, right. The way he talked about her, you could tell he was smitten.'

'I guessed that. Presumably she didn't reciprocate?'

'I don't think so.'

'Did you ever meet her?'

'Once, at a drinks event. She came as a favour to Karol, to be his guest, but she was clearly uncomfortable being there. I think she left after maybe twenty minutes. I remember Karol being upset about it. He tried to put a brave face on it but I could see he was disappointed.' Vicedo contemplated the rope sadly. 'I didn't realise he was struggling so badly.'

Carlyle regretted getting out of bed simply to see the spot

where a bloke he barely knew had topped himself. What he needed was a line on Seppi's passports. 'Sometimes people chase things – or people – precisely because they know they're unattainable. I mean, if you end up getting what you want and it's a disappointment, where does that leave you?'

'That's pretty deep, for—'

'For a cop?'

'For this time in the morning.' Vicedo offered him a feeble smile. 'Certainly for a cop at this time in the morning.' She started for the exit. 'I'm going to light a candle for Karol. And say a prayer for his immortal soul. You should join me.'

'Rush hour.' It was barely 5 a.m., yet Carlyle counted fourteen worshippers scattered among the pews of St Etheldreda's. All but two were women.

'People visit the church at all hours of the day or night,' Vicedo explained, her voice barely more than a whisper. 'It's the only one kept open round the clock.'

Carlyle contemplated the large, gloomy building, amazed by its size. 'I must have walked past this place literally thousands of times over the years, but this is the first time I've ever been inside.'

'These are people you don't usually see. Cleaners, kitchen workers, porters, taxi drivers, shop assistants. They come here on their way home after the night shift or on their way to work.'

'Invisible.'

'They're still people. They have a right to be here.'

'I wasn't suggesting otherwise.' Carlyle felt a stab of embarrassment. Was he imagining it, or was the nun becoming steadily more hostile towards him? They had worked together before and she had always been professional, friendly even. Now he detected a coolness, a dislike even, that dismayed him. He imagined she had developed a sense they were no longer on the same side – she was trying to help people while he was trying to persecute them. It was, the commander felt, unfair. Official policies aimed at harrying illegal immigrants might be making it harder for her to help trafficking and other victims, but that was hardly his fault.

'Some of these people may be illegal,' Vicedo continued. 'Now is a good time for them to visit.'

'God is listening?'

'God is always listening, but the Home Office isn't. Immigration Enforcement only come during office hours.'

'They raid churches?' Carlyle thought about Jamie Worby. How long would it be before the Home Office man was back on his case about the missing Monica Seppi?

Vicedo looked at him like he was an idiot. 'They've paid St Etheldreda's a visit three times in the last year. There isn't a church in central London that hasn't been targeted.' Tiring of his ignorance, she wandered towards a table filled with lines of beeswax votive candles, flickering in the gloom, illuminating a quote from Christ on the wall behind: *I am the light of the world; the one who follows me will not walk in darkness, but will have light and life.*

Vicedo reached for a candle. 'Will you join me?'

Carlyle politely declined. 'Not my thing.'

Lighting the candle, she placed it at the back of the table. 'You are a funny man, Commander.'

'It has been said.' Unable to decide what to do next – whether to go home or to work – he took a pew while Vicedo bowed her head and offered a prayer for the late Karol Lacko.

After she finished, he extended an olive branch of sorts. 'Shall we get some breakfast?'

Vicedo didn't take up the offer. 'I have work to do. And I need to clear out Karol's things.'

'His things?'

'This was Karol's church,' Vicedo explained. 'He visited three or four times a week and came to confession here.'

'And he left some stuff here?' O Father, forgive me for the various sins I'm about to commit.

'He used a locker in the storeroom.'

'Well, let's check it out.'

He invited the nun to lead the way, but she stood her ground.

'I can't let you do that.' She folded her arms. 'For a start, you don't have a search warrant.'

'I really need to see what's in the locker.' He tried to sound firm, but not hectoring. 'You know I'm in the middle of an important ongoing investigation and—'

'And you want me to let you steal Karol's things?'

The church door opened, and a man of late middle age walked in, head bowed. Carlyle tried to decide whether he was a worker coming off the night shift or a homeless guy looking for shelter. Normally, he could size a person up in an instant, but this guy was borderline. Walking between Carlyle and Vicedo, the man crossed himself and took a pew near the front. Carlyle turned his attention back to the nun. 'I'm not going to steal anything,' he promised. 'I don't even have to *touch* anything. I just want to see what's in there.'

Wrestling with her conscience, Vicedo eyed him suspiciously. 'What are you searching for?'

'I don't know, that's the point.' He hoped Lacko hadn't told her about Monica Seppi's passports. 'I only need a quick look.'

An old woman slipped past them and headed out onto the street. The nun considered the dilemma for several more seconds. 'You don't have the authority,' she decided finally. 'Snooping on Karol's things would be a violation of his rights.'

Why was the woman being so stubborn? 'I wouldn't be snooping,' Carlyle lied, failing to hide the irritation in his voice. 'And, anyway, Karol won't mind, seeing as he's dead.'

It was a stupid thing to say. Her face darkened. 'I'm disappointed in you, Commander. I didn't know you could be such an ignorant man.'

You sound like my wife. Carlyle imagined Helen laughing her head off. Maybe he should introduce the two women to each other. Doubtless they'd get on famously.

'Ignorant and prejudiced.'

'Me?' He struggled to keep his voice down. 'I'm not the one whose Church says poor old Karol should be burning in Hell because he topped himself.'

'Ignorant, ignorant, ignorant.'

Some of the supplicants had finished their chats with the Lord and their spat was beginning to attract an audience. Holding up a hand, Carlyle sued for peace. 'Sorry, you're right. I apologise. Let's start this conversation again.'

The nun said nothing.

Taking her silence as consent, he refined his pitch. 'Why don't we do this? You can clear out Karol's locker and I can watch. I won't touch anything, or take anything away, but I might ask you a question or two about what you find. How about that?'

Vicedo did not reply. Instead, she stepped between two rows of pews and disappeared through a side door. It was as much of an invitation as he was going to get. Carlyle followed her into a dusty storeroom, filled with broken furniture and boxes of prayer books. There were various items of lost property, including a moth-eaten fur coat, a walking frame and a bike. In the far corner stood a row of half a dozen battered grey metal lockers. They were about four feet tall and a foot wide. Vicedo already had one open. He watched in silence as she emptied the contents onto a wobbly table, including a couple of T-shirts, a pair of trainers and two red Lever Arch files stuffed with papers. 'Nothing worth stealing,' the nun declared.

'What about the documents?'

Vicedo inspected each file in turn. 'They're not in English. Slovak, presumably. It's not a language I speak.' Her phone started to ring. She looked at the screen and said, 'I have to take this, in private. Excuse me a minute. Don't touch anything.'

As soon as she had left the room, Carlyle sidled over to the open locker and stuck his nose inside. Beneath a couple more files, he found an executive-style briefcase. Reaching inside, he grabbed the case and placed it on the table. Happily, it wasn't locked. A quick rummage inside yielded a wad of euros, a phone and two passports. Carlyle quickly stuffed the passports and the phone into his jacket pocket and shoved the case back inside the locker. By the time Vicedo reappeared, he was engrossed in the latest football news on his own phone.

'Sorry.' Vicedo stared at the open locker. 'You didn't take anything, did you?'

Carlyle continued to stare at his screen. 'No,' he lied. 'I waited for you.' Out of the corner of his eye, he watched the nun retrieve the briefcase. 'Anything interesting?'

The nun pulled out the roll of banknotes. 'There's money.'

'How much?'

Vicedo began counting. 'A lot.'

'Is it real?'

She tossed the commander a bundle of fifty-euro notes. 'Why would it be fake?'

'You never know. Hundreds of thousands of fake notes are seized every year, so God knows how many are floating about undetected.'

'Do you have to take the Lord's name in vain so often?' Vicedo lifted her gaze to the heavens. 'And why do you have to assume the worst in people all the time?'

Because I'm a cop? Sensing a trick question, he kept his trap shut.

'Karol wasn't a criminal.'

'No, but he was a spy, of sorts. God kn— I mean, who knows what he was really up to? I'm not a betting man but I would hazard a guess this whole mess goes far beyond Project Gorilla and some little local difficulty in Slovakia.'

'Maybe,' Vicedo conceded. '"What a tangled web we weave, when first we practise to deceive."'

'Yes, yes. Very good.' Carlyle rubbed a note between his thumb and forefinger before holding it up to the pale glare of the bare light bulb. 'Looks real to me, although I'm no expert.' He handed the cash back to the nun, who shoved it into the bag.

'Where would Karol have got this money?' she wondered.

'Maybe he was on the take.'

'On the take?'

'Bent. Corrupt.'

'He wasn't that kind of person.'

'Where the money came from,' said Carlyle, 'is less important now than where it's going. Does Karol have any next of kin?'

'I don't think so. He certainly never mentioned any family.'

'Well, maybe it should be used as a donation to the Church – or the Network Against Human Trafficking for your good works.'

Vicedo looked at the case doubtfully. 'I'm not sure it would be right to take Karol's money without checking first.'

'I wouldn't fret about it. I'm told the Lord works in mysterious ways.'

The nun glared at him.

'I'll find out if Karol has any family, and a will for that matter,' Carlyle said hastily, 'so we can make sure the money goes to the right place.'

Leaving the church, he tried to make some sense out of what had happened. Two suicides in short order – Tim Hitchcock and Karol Lacko – was unusual but not necessarily suspicious; both men had been under severe pressure and people often cracked under pressure. The alternative theory, that they had been killed by persons unknown, was too troubling to consider seriously. Karen O'Sullivan had already transferred Bruno Soutine from the suicide pile to the murder pile, and Carlyle didn't want to create more work for Charing Cross's finest than was absolutely necessary.

He had breakfast at a greasy spoon near the British Museum while reviewing the loot pinched from under the nose of Rita Vicedo. Any pangs of guilt at deceiving a woman of God were more than offset by the need to draw a line under this trouble-some Slovakian business. In this case, he decided, the ends more than justified the means. Gorillas and cover-ups were of no par-ticular interest. All he wanted was Monica Seppi, a.k.a. Zuzana Klek, off his patch for good.

One of the passports was German, in the name of Ingrid Schubert, the other Canadian, for an Angela Luther. Each had a photograph of Seppi. In the Luther version, she sported a short, spiky haircut and a deep frown. As Schubert, the hair was longer and her expression softer.

'Okay, genius,' he mumbled to himself, 'you've got the pass-ports. What're you going to do now?' With no way of contacting the woman herself, he had to sit tight. He looked around the deserted café, still awaiting the breakfast rush, half expecting Seppi to swan in and take a seat at his table. When that didn't happen, he shoved the passports into his pocket and turned his attention to the phone he'd swiped at the same time. The sleek black Samsung was locked. Not having a clue what the code might be, Carlyle didn't even try to guess. Instead, he pulled up a number on his own phone and made a call.

'A bit early, isn't it?' Dudley Carew harrumphed. Carew Forensic Services – i.e. Dudley and his daughter, Gloria – was Carlyle's go-to consultancy for all technological matters. 'I thought you civil servants never started before ten.'

'The older you get, the earlier you rise.'

Dudley agreed. 'It's rare, these days, I'm not up and about before six. Normally, I'd have read the paper and be well on the way to finishing the crossword by now. But the Super Fiendish is proving more than a little tricky this morning so I'm all ears. What d'you want?'

Carlyle explained about the locked phone.

'By your standards,' Carew said drily, 'that's a rather modest request. Bring it round – during office hours – and I'll take a look at it for you. We've got software for that sort of thing.'

It was exactly what Carlyle wanted to hear. 'Jolly good.' On a roll, he decided to push his luck. 'There's one other thing.'

'There always is with you, Commander.' Carew gave a weary sigh. 'You get your foot in the door and then you keep on taking. You're a man without scruple or shame.'

He didn't argue the point. 'D'you know anything about fake passports?'

'What kind?'

'German and Canadian.'

'Thinking of emigrating?' Dudley teased. 'Are you tiring of this green and pleasant land of ours?'

'They're not mine,' Carlyle explained. 'I'm sitting here with a couple of fake passports and they look pretty authentic to me.'

'They're probably real.' Carew sniffed.

'They're definitely fake.'

'Depends what you mean by fake. There're fake *passports*, which are very hard to do these days, what with all the security features, and fake *identities*, which are much easier to come up with. With fake ID, birth certificate et cetera, you can apply for a *real* passport.'

'Sounds appealing.'

'Running off into the sunset's a common middle-aged fantasy. I thought someone like yourself would have a bit more

200

imagination, although if you really wanted one, I might know a man who knows a man type of thing.'

Carlyle fleetingly considered the possibilities. 'Best to stick to the matter in hand,' he decided.

'Probably for the best,' Carew agreed. 'Details?'

Carlyle read out the name and number from each booklet.

'That should be enough to get me started. I'll see what I can find out when I head into the office – bring them round later.' There was a pause. 'I suppose we're talking your usual rates?'

At mention of money, Carlyle felt himself blush. 'Perfect.'

'Given the Metropolitan Police Service has a budget of almost three billion pounds,' Carew drawled, 'I appreciate you can do with all the pro bono help you can get from us little people.'

It was a familiar complaint, to which Carlyle had no answer. 'Thanks for your help,' he said. 'I'll be round later on.'

A visitor was waiting for him when he arrived at the police station. Carlyle made no effort to hide his dismay. 'What are you doing here?'

'Nice to see you, too.' Abigail Slater, ambulance chaser deluxe, was an old adversary. The defence lawyer had abandoned her usual power dressing for some expensive running gear. She looked flushed.

'Get mugged in the park?' Carlyle quipped.

'God help the mugger who tries it on with me,' Slater drawled, chugging on an iced coffee while the commander organised a visitor pass. 'I run into work, these days.'

'I see.' Carlyle led her to the lifts, trying to recall the last time they'd crossed swords.

A more generous and less confrontational person might have described Slater as a respected opponent. Carlyle simply saw her as a pain in the arse. At the same time, they were, in lots of ways, pretty similar. If Carlyle ever needed a lawyer, Slater would be the first person he'd call.

'Better to get one's exercise done first thing, I find, otherwise the day gets away from you.'

'Yes.' Getting into the lift, Carlyle asked, 'To what do I owe the pleasure?'

'I thought I'd drop by and have a word.'

'You could've called.'

'I could,' she gave him a reptilian smile, 'but I didn't.'

Reaching the top floor, Carlyle showed her into his office.

'This is best discussed face to face.' Slater flopped into a chair. 'I heard on the grapevine you're looking for Miranda Curtis.'

'News travels fast.'

'Miranda has always been a bit . . . controversial.'

That's rich, Carlyle thought, coming from you.

'And when you take on a client like Patrick Dalby, you're asking for trouble in my opinion.'

'You know Dalby?'

'Only by reputation.' Slater's face had lost its beet colour and she looked tired. 'But Miranda and I go back a long way.'

Carlyle sensed there was no love lost between the two lawyers. This was confirmed when Slater explained why she'd jogged his way.

'I wanted to let you know where to find her.'

NINETEEN

As always, there was a price to pay for Abigail Slater's help. In this case, the lawyer wanted a deal for one of her clients. Carlyle listened patiently while she told him the tale of a hapless businessman accused of fiddling expenses to pay for an expensive Brazilian girlfriend half his age. 'It's a story as old as life itself.'

'He's guilty?'

'One hundred per cent he's guilty. But surely the Crown Prosecution Service has better things to do than go after people like Harry?'

'White-collar crime is still crime,' Carlyle pointed out.

'My client is full of remorse, especially now he's broke and his girlfriend's done a runner.'

Carlyle raised an eyebrow. 'If he's broke, how come he's a client of yours?'

'I always get cash in advance,' Slater purred. 'You never want to be waiting in line with all the other creditors.'

'Good to know.'

'In this case, the client does not have enough remaining credit to cover the cost of going to court so we want to settle. We'll offer a guilty plea if Harry gets a suspended sentence and a reasonable schedule for repaying his debts – like a couple of hundred years.' She laughed at her own joke. 'You know what I mean, long but vaguely credible.'

'And you can't take this to the CPS yourself?'

'Jodie Morris is handling it.'

Carlyle realised he was being dealt a useful card. 'I know Jodie reasonably well.' He smiled. 'I've done her a couple of favours in the past.'

'The Kenyon case.'

Carlyle's smile disappeared. Sammy Kenyon had been one of his collars, a nasty thug, who had been looking at an extended spell behind bars until Jodie Morris had messed up the prosecution. Kenyon had walked. Carlyle, swallowing his annoyance, had graciously shouldered some of the blame, rather than dump the whole mess on his colleague at the CPS. 'We don't talk about that,' he muttered.

'I'm not looking to reopen old wounds, Commander, I just want you to call in a favour with your pal at the CPS. Jodie hates me – I've embarrassed her in court too many times in the past – and now she sees a chance to get back at me. I need you to persuade her to see reason.'

Carlyle thought about it for a moment, before deciding, 'I can do that.'

'Excellent.' Pulling a scrap of paper from her jacket pocket, Slater tossed it onto the desk. 'You'll find Miranda there, shacked up in her little love nest.'

'With her client?'

'No.' Slater looked vaguely offended by the question. 'Contrary to the prurient imaginings of police officers, lawyers rarely, if ever, shag their clients. As it happens, Miranda's got a girlfriend, an Australian water polo player.'

'You don't have any inkling where Dalby might be?'

'You'll have to work that out for yourself,' said Slater. 'That's what they pay you for, after all.'

Carlyle said nothing.

'I heard Dalby smacked you one.' Slater grinned.

Is there anything you *don't* know? Carlyle involuntarily touched his cheek. 'I was blindsided.'

'It happens.'

'What Patrick Dalby did to me is nothing compared to his various other crimes. He's a dangerous man. We need to get him back behind bars.'

'All right, all right.' Slater held up a hand. 'Spare me the sermon. What I *can* give you – because I'm in a good mood with all these endorphins running round my brain after jogging over here – is a bit of extra leverage with Miranda.'

'Oh?' Slater must *really* hate Curtis to go out of her way to stitch her up like this. Carlyle knew better than to enquire about the details.

'The water polo player's here illegally. Her visa ran out more than a year ago. If Miranda doesn't cooperate you can threaten to have her girlfriend deported.'

Carlyle didn't fancy taking that to Jamie Worby. 'I'm not sure Immigration Enforcement targets Australians.'

'Maybe they should. When people think of illegal aliens, they imagine refugees from Syria or Libya, but most of them are Commonwealth citizens who haven't sorted out their paperwork.'

'I didn't know human rights was one of your things.'

'It isn't. But knowledge is power. Miranda's not the type to resist pressure. She'll give up Dalby in an instant if she thinks you can get her lover sent to some crappy detention centre.'

'Worth a try.' Carlyle picked up the scrap of paper and studied the address. 'Woodstock?'

'Not the one with the hippies,' said Slater. 'The one in Oxfordshire.'

Once Slater had jogged off, the commander dispatched the ever-willing Sergeant Nixon to pick up Miranda Curtis.

'It'll be routine,' he promised. 'Either she tells us where

Patrick Dalby is, or you can arrest her and bring her back here. Her girlfriend, too, if she's around.'

'What's the charge?'

Carlyle scratched his head. 'Whatever gives you the maximum leverage for the minimum amount of paperwork.'

'Righty-ho.' Nixon departed for the shires, leaving the commander free to consult with Dudley Carew.

Arriving at the offices of Carew Forensic Services, he was greeted by Gloria, Dudley's daughter. Fresh-faced and friendly, Gloria looked impossibly young in a pair of torn jeans and a U2 T-shirt. Dudley must have had you when he was north of fifty, Carlyle imagined. Father and daughter didn't talk about Gloria's mother. Sensing the story didn't have a happy ending, he had never asked.

'Dad's gone to lunch.'

'Already?' Carlyle checked the time on his phone. 'It's barely time for a mid-morning snack.'

'He's been up since before six. Plus, he likes to beat the rush.'

'Fair enough.'

Gloria proffered a sheet of CFS-headed A4 paper. 'He did check out those passports you asked about, though.'

Carlyle scanned the notes. 'Ingrid Schubert and Angela Luther are terrorists?'

'They were, back in the day. They were members of the Red Army Faction, or the Baader-Meinhof gang, in Germany in the 1970s and 1980s. Presumably using the names was someone's idea of a joke.'

'That's a bit obscure.'

'Yeah. Schubert died in prison in 1977. We don't know what happened to Luther. If she's still alive she would be over eighty by now.'

Carlyle read through the notes a second time. 'Presumably the chances of her living in London are pretty slim.'

'Dudley ran a few databases and found the Angela Luther passport, the Canadian one, had been used as ID for a rental agreement on a flat in Belsize Park that was taken out two months ago.' Gloria waved at the piece of paper in Carlyle's hand. 'I don't suppose Haverstock Property Services would get the reference.'

It looked like Monica Seppi had another bolthole. In the absence of any other leads, Carlyle was keen to investigate the address right away. First, he handed Gloria the Samsung phone he'd taken from St Etheldreda's. 'Dudley said you'd be able to unlock this for me.'

'Sure.' Gloria plugged the phone into her desktop. Humming to herself, she tapped at the keyboard a few times before handing it back to Carlyle.

'As easy as that?' The commander, a complete technophobe, was suitably impressed.

'If you have the right software, it's very straightforward.' Gloria invited him to reset the password.

'One-two-three-four,' Carlyle recited. 'Bear it in mind, should I forget.'

Gloria highlighted the foolishness of such basic security.

'I know, but . . .' Carlyle checked the contents of the phone. In total, he found one photograph – Monica Seppi, unsmiling, in a restaurant – and two numbers, simply listed as A and B. There were no texts, and no log of any calls being made.

'Is that all for today, sir, or is there any further assistance we can provide?'

'That's it,' Carlyle confirmed cheerily. 'You've been very helpful.'

Walking down the street, he tried each number in turn. No one picked up and neither call went to voicemail. 'Belsize Park it is, then.'

The address was a top-floor conversion in the middle of a row of terraced houses. No one answered the bell. He tried the ground-floor flat and got no reply either.

'What next?' He found the front door was locked. It looked solid and his B and E skills had never been up to much, so, as a last resort, he called Haverstock Property Services.

'I suppose you've got a warrant.' The letting agent sighed, when Carlyle identified himself and requested access to the property.

Carlyle didn't miss a beat. 'Yes.' He reckoned it was fifty–fifty that when the agent arrived she wouldn't ask to see it. If she did, it was fifty–fifty he could sweet-talk her into letting him in anyway. 'I'm trying to be as discreet as possible, though. I don't want to cause you any embarrassment.'

The woman wasn't reassured. 'You *are* a cop, right?'

'It would be pretty strange to make all this up, don't you think?'

'You'd be surprised. Some of the weirdos you get are . . . well, *weird.*'

'I don't want to cause you any trouble, but I'm at the property now and—'

'All right, all right. I need to look in on another letting nearby, anyway. Give me fifteen minutes.'

Carlyle got a coffee from a café down the road and returned to see a woman approaching the flat from the opposite direction. She wasn't as well attired as he'd expected but at least she was prompt. Extending a hand, he gave her a big smile. 'Haverstock Property Services?'

The woman stopped in her tracks, keeping her distance. 'Immigration Enforcement. Who are you?'

'How was I to know there was a bunch of Albanians living underneath Monica Seppi's flat?' Retreating to his office, Carlyle had stashed the passports in his desk, while trying to decide on his next move. Unable to decide on a plan of action, he had wandered down to the third floor to catch up with his colleagues. 'I had to make my excuses and get the hell out of there.'

Laura Nixon, holding an ice pack to her busted lip, wasn't particularly sympathetic. 'At least no one gave you a smack for your trouble.'

'I'm very sorry.' Carlyle tried to look apologetic. 'I didn't think Miranda Curtis would turn violent.'

'It wasn't Curtis,' the sergeant pointed out. 'It was her bloody girlfriend.'

'I heard she was athletic.'

'Thanks for the heads-up,' said the sergeant, sarcastically.

'There was no reason to think she'd turn violent,' the commander reflected. 'She's a water polo player.'

Karen O'Sullivan looked nonplussed. 'What's that got to do with anything?'

'She won't be playing any water polo where she's going,' Nixon asserted.

'You arrested her?' Carlyle asked.

'They're both in the cells – in Oxford.'

Shit. Just as well he hadn't explained about the Aussie's tenuous immigration status or she could have been on a plane home already, taking with her his leverage over Curtis.

Sensing his dismay, the sergeant added, 'I couldn't very well bring them back down here, could I?'

'No.' Carlyle realised he would have to take a trip out of town, after all.

'There wasn't much choice,' said O'Sullivan. 'Laura had to bring in the local constabulary.'

'Hm.'

'Thames Valley insisted on making the arrests,' the sergeant added. 'You can't assault a police officer and get away with it.'

'I'd better get up there.' Carlyle wondered whether he should

209

go by car or take the train. 'You did the right thing,' he grudgingly told the sergeant. 'I appreciate it, taking one for the team.'

A signal failure had shut down Paddington, forcing him to go to Oxford by road. The two-hour drive did nothing for his mood and he arrived at the St Aldates police station starving hungry, with a blinding headache. Gobbling down a Mars Bar and four painkillers, he chugged a bottle of fizzy water as he marched into a dingy interview room.

Handcuffed to the desk, Miranda Curtis greeted his appearance with a disgusted tut. 'I should've known you'd be behind this.'

Carlyle wasn't in the mood for an argument. He took a seat. 'All I want is Patrick Dalby.'

'Fuck off.'

Carlyle took a deep breath. 'My sergeant got smacked around. *I* got smacked around . . . but it comes with the job, sometimes.' He gestured at the cuffs. 'I'll make this all go away if you tell me where to find your crazy client.'

The lawyer was unmoved. 'This is harassment, pure and simple. I'll have you for this.'

The commander thought about all the similar threats he'd heard during the course of his career. This one wouldn't make the top fifty. Probably not even the top hundred and fifty. 'You know your girlfriend's in the country illegally, don't you?'

'Whaddya mean?' Curtis tried to look shocked, but Carlyle could see she understood where he was taking the conversation.

'Give me Dalby, or I'll make sure she's on a plane back to Australia in the next twenty-four hours.'

'You couldn't.'

'I have extremely good contacts with Immigration Enforcement. As you can imagine, we work very closely together, these days. And they have quotas to meet. They would be more than happy to do me a favour.'

'It's simply an admin error. I can get it sorted.'

'Not from inside here.'

'They wouldn't send her back,' Curtis insisted.

'Why not? Deporting some nice white girl would have novelty value, if nothing else. The Home Office would love a chance to claim it's not institutionally racist. If it turns out there's been a mistake, your girlfriend can always argue her case in Sydney.'

'She's from Melbourne.'

'Whatever.' Carlyle's knowledge of Australian geography was pretty much non-existent. 'The point is, I can get both of you out of here and back home in the next hour or so, or it's a night in the cells, followed by a court appearance for you and deportation for . . .' He didn't know the water polo player's name.

'Hannah.'

'Give me Dalby or it's deportation for Hannah.' He drummed his fingers gently on the table. 'What's it to be?'

In the event it took almost four hours to spring the pair. The matter was kicked all the way up to an assistant deputy chief constable who had to be roused from her bed to approve their release. Happily, the woman took matters with good grace and approved Carlyle's request on the nod. He dozed on the way back into London and arrived home armed with breakfast from a new café, recently opened on Drury Lane. His wife, not yet out of bed, greeted him suspiciously.

'Long night?' Helen took his offering of a croissant and a latte, placing them carefully on the bedside table. 'Where've you been?'

Carlyle recounted his trip to Oxford.

Helen was less than impressed. 'You basically blackmailed the poor woman by threatening her girlfriend.'

Carlyle felt a flash of anger boom in his breast. Sometimes his wife's thought processes seemed deliberately obtuse. 'That "poor woman", as you put it, a lawyer no less, was obstructing a police officer in his duties, aiding a fugitive – a fugitive *you* want behind bars more than anyone else.'

'He's her client.'

Why was she being so contrary? 'Ms Curtis has gone way, way beyond the boundaries of any acceptable client-lawyer relationship.' Carlyle shook his head. 'God knows why. I gave her a great deal, under the circumstances.'

Helen kept niggling away. 'Dalby's still in the wind. You haven't found him.'

'I know where he is,' Carlyle protested. Curtis had finally revealed her client had fled to Mexico. Airline records confirmed Dalby had arrived in Cozumel the day after attacking Carlyle.

'You know what country he's in. That doesn't exactly narrow it down much.'

'The local police'll find him.'

'You hope.' Helen yawned. 'He could be anywhere.'

'The main thing is he's not *here*.' Carlyle suddenly felt immensely weary as the night's events caught up with him. Kicking off his shoes, he pulled back the duvet and crawled into bed.

Helen took that as her cue to get up. 'I want him behind bars. So does Imogen.'

'One step at a time.'

Helen pulled on a pair of jeans.

Despite his tiredness, Carlyle felt a little twitch in his groin as he contemplated his wife.

'Do we even have an extradition treaty with Mexico?' she asked, reaching for a T-shirt.

'We do. I checked.'

'Well, get on with it, then.'

'I just need a little rest.' He patted the duvet hopefully. 'You could join me, if you want.'

Helen had no interest. 'I've got work to do,' she said flatly. 'There's another meeting on the Sandland thing.'

Carlyle didn't want to get into yet another discussion about the sex-pest doctor. 'You should sack him,' he advised, 'like yesterday.'

'You worry about Patrick Dalby,' Helen responded, 'and I'll worry about Chris Sandland.' She disappeared into the bathroom.

Carlyle glanced at her breakfast, untouched on the bedside table. 'Don't you want your croissant?'

'You have it,' Helen replied. 'Just don't lie there for too long – it'll bugger up your body clock.'

TWENTY

The phone was vibrating on the bedside table.

'Hello?'

'You sound like you were asleep,' Emily Quartz said cheerily. 'Did I wake you?'

'No, no.' Carlyle blinked at the ceiling. 'I'm, erm, in a meeting. Give me five minutes and I'll call you back.' He reluctantly rolled out of bed. After a quick wash and a cup of steaming black coffee, he was fit to talk.

'You got it wrong,' was her opening gambit. 'You told me to look at the father, but it's the mother we should be interested in.'

Carlyle wondered about a second cup of coffee. 'Whose mother are we talking about?'

'Jasper's.'

He recalled the fierce woman who'd kicked them out of the family home.

'Sonia Wiggins is a board member at Sandringham Risk Consulting, the people who're suing Kollision to get their six million quid back.'

'The six million that ended up in the pocket of cryptocurrency scammer Bruno Soutine.'

'Right.'

'So Sonia knew Tim Hitchcock, Kollision's CEO?'

'More than that,' Quartz said breathlessly. 'I think she killed him.'

'You have no actual evidence for any of this.'

'That's the next step.' They were sitting in the café on the top floor of Foyles bookshop on the Charing Cross Road. 'I have to find the evidence, write the story and get the lawyers to approve its publication.' Sipping peppermint tea, Quartz showed no sign of being cowed by his lack of enthusiasm for her theory. 'Then you can arrest her.'

'As simple as that, huh?' Carlyle fiddled with his empty demitasse. The double espresso had been a mistake – he'd gone from being unconscious to being sufficiently wired to run a marathon. Well, a half-marathon . . . or a five K, at the very least. 'Let's go through it, piece by piece. Tell me what you think happened.'

'All right.' Quartz slurped her tea. 'Sonia Wiggins is well known in financial circles in the City. She's one of those establishment types who flits effortlessly from job to job. Went to an expensive private school, studied German at Oxford and worked for the giant vampire squid.'

'Huh?'

'Goldman Sachs.'

'Ah, right.' What Carlyle knew about business and finance you could have written on the back of a postage stamp, but even he had heard of Goldman's.

'She was there for a decade before leaving to work at a hedge fund run by some internet entrepreneur.'

'Seems a bit high-powered to be living in Highgate with some BBC pen-pusher.'

'Jasper's dad is husband number two. Husband number one fell off a boat at a party and drowned in the Thames.'

Carlyle raised an eyebrow.

'No sign of foul play,' said Quartz. 'I read the coroner's report. It was definitely an accident.'

The journalist had certainly done her homework. Carlyle was

impressed. You could give Dudley and Gloria Carew a run for their money, he thought. Almost.

'Some time later, Sonia hooked up with Jasper's dad. Jasper was born a couple of years before they married. There was also a daughter, but she drove a motorbike off a cliff in Ibiza a couple of years ago.'

'Another accident?'

'Drink and drugs.'

'Sonia Wiggins has had more than her fair share of bad luck over the years.'

'In her personal life, yes. Professionally, she seems to have done pretty well. She's been at SRC for almost a decade. In addition, she has a couple of non-executive directorships, plus a separate consultancy gig at a company called Thorpe Kirwan. Thorpe Kirwan's interesting – its areas of expertise include cyber-security and cryptocurrencies, and Kollision Financial Services is one of its clients.'

'So,' Carlyle reasoned, 'with SRC and Kollision at logger-heads, Sonia had a conflict of interest.'

'Yes, because she was involved with both companies.'

'Interesting.'

'There's more than that.' Quartz's grin was so large, it seemed like it might swallow her face. 'Sonia was shagging Tim Hitchcock.'

Carlyle thought back to their conversation in the Royal Courts of Justice. 'I thought you said Hitchcock was supposed to be shagging somebody else.'

'Elena Doyle, SRC's compliance officer, one of his co-defendants in the fraud trial.'

'Right.'

'You can shag more than one person at a time, you know.'

'Hm.' Carlyle was reluctant to go there. 'Sonia's not one of the defendants?' he asked.

'No. In fact, she's one of the main prosecution witnesses.'

'That can't be right.' Carlyle frowned. 'The conflict of interest destroys her credibility.'

'I'm guessing she hasn't mentioned that to her lawyers. Now that Mr Hitchcock is no more, she can try to keep it under wraps.'

'Is that sufficient motive for murder?' Carlyle wasn't sure.

'There were lots of reasons for killing Hitchcock,' Quartz argued. 'For a start, he was a right sleazebag. The guy had girlfriends all over the place.'

'The dirty bugger.' Carlyle was torn between being appalled on the one hand and jealous on the other.

'I think Doyle was just a fling, one of many. Sonia, on the other hand, was a long-term thing.'

'Strange carry-on,' Carlyle mused. 'She didn't strike me as the kind of person who'd put up with that kind of behaviour.'

'There's no accounting for taste.'

'You can say that again.'

'Plus, she was cheating too.'

Carlyle was conscious people at nearby tables were starting to tune in to their conversation. 'Keep your voice down.'

'Sorry.'

'How do you know all this?' he asked.

'I have my sources,' she whispered theatrically. 'They're confidential.'

'You want my help on this,' Carlyle insisted, 'there has to be total transparency.'

Quartz looked doubtful.

'Who would I tell?'

'I can't—'

But she didn't have to. It came to him in a flash. 'Molly,' Carlyle blurted. 'Jasper's girlfriend.'

Quartz didn't deny it. 'Molly Arnold's well known in activist circles. I tracked her down on Facebook through Jasper. She hates Sonia, thinks Jasper's tied to his mother's apron strings and she won't let him grow up.'

'Young Molly might have a point.' Carlyle ran a hand across his chin. He needed a shave. And a shower. He hoped Quartz couldn't catch a whiff of his BO. It wasn't in the Patrick Dalby league, but it was still unpleasant. 'And she confirmed Sonia's affair with Hitchcock?'

'Yeah. Jasper told her about it. It's not exactly a family secret. The parents have a fairly open marriage. His father's boffed various women at the BBC over the years.'

Boffed? It wasn't a word he'd have expected Quartz to use.

'He's come a cropper, though, up on some harassment charge for inviting a colleague to have a threesome with him and Sonia. It hasn't made the papers – yet.'

'The *Mail* would love that. Presumably Sonia'll kill *him* when she finds out.'

'Molly says Sonia knows all about it.'

'She'd have let her husband have a threesome?'

'I don't know about that, but Molly said she thought it was funny.'

'Blimey.'

'Interesting family.'

'Yeah, but how do we get from Sonia, erm, *boffing* Tim Hitchcock to killing him?'

'Now Hitchcock's dead, Kollision'll probably collapse or settle out of court. Either way, Sonia won't have to take the stand and explain what she was doing working for Thorpe Kirwan, or her relationship with Hitchcock.'

'Conflicts of interest are pretty common,' Carlyle reasoned, 'not necessarily a cause for embarrassment, even. Same when it comes to the extramarital stuff. Add it all up and it still doesn't lead you to murder Tim Hitchcock. Not if you're as direct and composed as Sonia Wiggins.'

Quartz dangled another titbit in front of him. 'What if Thorpe Kirwan was on the trail of the missing six million?'

'Wouldn't that be a good thing?'

'Not if Sonia was involved in scamming SRC with her errant lover and wanted to keep it hidden.'

Carlyle didn't follow.

'Maybe she got a cut of the cash,' Quartz speculated, 'in return for being Hitchcock's spy at SRC.'

'Very hard to prove. Impossible, probably.'

'But it would make sense,' Quartz insisted. 'If Tim Hitchcock was in bed with Bruno Soutine, and Sonia Wiggins was in bed with Hitchcock – both literally and metaphorically – the last thing she'd want is anybody to find the cash and expose her in the process. She's a crook.'

'Even if she was crooked,' Carlyle mused, 'that's a long way short of being a killer.'

'Getting rid of Hitchcock pulls the plug on Kollision and any hope of SRC getting its money back. From Sonia's point of view, it all goes away. That's a pretty good motive, if you ask me.'

It sounded more convoluted than the plot of a Bernie Gunther novel. Carlyle pointed in the direction of the stairs. 'We're in the wrong place. Crime Fiction's on the first floor.'

'So's True Crime.' Quartz wasn't going to let him infect her with his doubts. 'Trust me, I'm definitely on to something here. Sonia Wiggins is the key to all this.'

'You don't have any *evidence*,' Carlyle reminded her.

The reporter would not be swayed. 'I'm going to keep digging.'

'Do that.' Carlyle got up from his stool. 'But keep it low-key. And be careful.'

Quartz laughed off his advice. 'Yes, *Dad*.'

I'm probably old enough to be your granddad, Carlyle thought unhappily, rather than your father. He liked the girl well enough, but doubted she was sufficiently streetwise to be poking around in a can of worms like this. 'I'll make some discreet enquiries of my own,' he promised. A woman carrying a tray appeared at his side, keen to take over his freshly abandoned seat. 'Let's stay in regular contact.'

Rather than return to the police station, he took a detour to the Masons Arms. Colin Spooner was ensconced in the same spot as before. Surprisingly, the lawyer seemed happy to see him. He saluted the commander with his pint pot. 'Thanks for sorting the Kollision people.'

'Erm, my pleasure.' Carlyle had completely forgotten about the promise he'd made on his previous visit. He took a seat.

'We finally got our bills paid last week.' Spooner took a mouthful of lager. 'Thank God. I was crapping myself – it was a big number.'

'Glad to be of assistance.'

Spooner sensed it was time for a bit of quid pro quo. 'I suppose you're here about Esther Blake?'

The name rang only the quietest of bells in Carlyle's brain.

'The fund manager at Kollision who handed over SRC's money to Bruno Soutine's Ponzi scheme,' Spooner reminded him. 'She's back in town, looking for a new job, I hear.'

Carlyle was confused. 'Why would anyone hire her? She lost so much money.'

Spooner gave him a *Don't be stupid* look. 'Losing money's part of the game . . . as long as it's not your own.'

'Good to know.' The commander turned to his intended line of enquiry. 'I'm interested in a firm called Thorpe Kirwan. I understand they did some consultancy work for Kollision and might have had a line on the missing money.'

Spooner made a face. 'The name doesn't ring a bell. That doesn't mean much, though. People were in and out of there all the time. Tim used consultants like toilet paper.'

'What about a woman called Sonia Wiggins?'

'Yeah, I knew Sonia. Met her a few times; one of Tim's

girlfriends, probably one of the most serious ones. She was at a dinner I was at once. Smart woman.'

'You must know she works for Sandringham Risk Consulting,' said Carlyle.

'That wasn't something that was ever discussed.' Spooner looked sheepish.

'She works for Thorpe Kirwan, too.'

'One of these people who collects a portfolio of jobs.' Spooner finished the last of his pint. 'I know Tim thought very highly of her. He told me once he wanted her to leave her husband but she wouldn't, because of the money.'

'What money?'

'Sonia's husband's. Apparently he's loaded.'

Carlyle slowly digested that morsel. 'I thought he worked at the BBC.'

'His brother made millions with some biotechnology business before dying in a helicopter accident on holiday in New Zealand with his wife and kids.' Spooner stared into his empty glass. 'They were doing a tour of *Lord of the Rings* locations, or maybe it was *Game of Thrones*. Either way, very sad. But Sonia's husband was the only living relative, so it all went to him. Tim reckoned the money was the only reason she didn't get a divorce. He was distraught when she dumped him and hooked up with Patrick Dalby. Now that was a real cluster—'

'Wait, wait, wait.' Carlyle held up a hand, struggling to process what he was hearing. 'Hold on one second. Sonia Wiggins dumped Tim Hitchcock for *Patrick Dalby*?'

'That's right.'

'Are you kidding me?'

'Well—'

'And you didn't think of mentioning this earlier?'

'I didn't know it was important,' Spooner protested.

'What the fuck?' Even by the standards of the legal profession, this guy was proving himself to be an extreme arse. Carlyle took a moment to calm himself down.

'Tim didn't talk about it much. I think it was the final nail in the coffin of his friendship with Patrick. Things had been heading south ever since Patrick remortgaged his farm to invest in cryptocurrencies through Kollision.'

Carlyle deployed his powers of hindsight. 'Bad move.'

'Blinded by greed,' was Spooner's verdict. 'He thought it would be his chance to make a lot of easy money.'

'I'm sure he wasn't the only one.'

'By no means,' Spooner agreed. 'I'm just glad I didn't jump in myself. I've always taken the view that if you don't understand something, you shouldn't put your money in it.'

Carlyle could only agree. He would no more put his modest funds into anything digital than place it all on a nag in the three-thirty at Kempton Park. 'How much did he lose?'

'I dunno,' Spooner admitted, 'but it would've been a lot. Inevitably, he blamed Tim.'

A not unreasonable view, Carlyle thought. 'So Dalby got the woman but lost the cash needed to keep her in the style to which she'd become accustomed?'

'I would say that pretty much sums it up.' Spooner waved his glass at Carlyle. 'Wanna drink?'

Carlyle declined.

'How did you get on with Miranda Curtis?' the lawyer asked when he returned from the bar.

'She's no longer helping us with our enquiries.'

'She's in the clear?'

'Yes, I think so.'

Spooner's eyes narrowed. 'And what about me?'

'Don't worry, you're off the hook, too.' Carlyle got to his feet. 'Enjoy your pint.'

TWENTY-ONE

Could he use Sonia Wiggins to lure Patrick Dalby back from Mexico? Carlyle struggled to come up with a cunning plan as he walked down the street. Head bowed, deep in thought, he narrowly dodged a succession of oncoming pedestrians before coming to a halt at a road crossing. The lights were against him, but a convenient gap had opened up in the traffic. As he stepped off the kerb, he felt a hand on his shoulder. Turning, he found himself facing a young woman with spiky bleached blonde hair and rimless spectacles. He did a double-take. 'Angela Luther, I presume.'

Monica Seppi let out a throaty laugh. 'Very good, Commander. I assume that means you've found the passports.'

'Yes.' The lights changed and he led her across the street. 'They're at the station.'

'You can keep the Schubert one as a memento. I only need Luther's.' Seppi pointed towards a gloomy-looking Italian restaurant further down the street. 'I'll see you in there at seven. You can buy me dinner.'

'Sure, why not?' A bowl of spaghetti and some house red would be a small price to pay to get the woman off his hands.

'Bring the passport.'

As a further gesture of goodwill, Carlyle offered to return the phone he'd swiped from the church.

223

Seppi wasn't interested. 'Get rid of it,' she commanded. 'It's no use to anyone.'

'Okay,' he agreed meekly.

'Drop it into a sewer.' She started off down a side street. 'But bring the money.'

'The money?' She was gone before Carlyle could explain that it was now being used for a higher purpose. 'Shit.' He felt a spasm in his guts as he realised he'd dug himself a massive hole.

Heading back for the station, he cursed himself for telling Vicedo to keep the cash. He'd acted in haste, spurred on by the fact that it was always easy to be generous with other people's money. With the benefit of hindsight, he should have realised that the money was Seppi's – not Lacko's – and that she would want it back.

'You fucking idiot,' he growled, to the alarm of passers-by in the street. 'You total fucking idiot.' He continued chuntering to himself, like a lunatic. 'Well done. You've really gone and dropped yourself in it now.'

When Carlyle got back to the office, Joaquin brought him a hard copy of the Tim Hitchcock file and a mug of green tea. 'I need a bit of peace and quiet,' Carlyle instructed, 'so absolutely no interruptions.'

'You won't be disturbed,' Joaquin promised, closing the door as he retreated from the room.

Sipping his tea, the commander sifted through Hitchcock's autopsy report. The man had had high levels of alcohol in his system. There were no signs of any assault, although hitting the pavement at terminal velocity would most likely have covered a multitude of pre-existing injuries.

'No one's claiming he was pushed,' said a voice above him. 'The coroner's inquest will be a formality.'

Carlyle looked up to find Karen O'Sullivan standing in front of his desk. 'I thought I told Joaquin I wasn't to be disturbed,' he grumbled.

'Joaquin's gone to his rollerblading class.'

'Now?' Carlyle cursed the Met's flexible working policies, which his PA managed to stretch to the extreme.

'He's part of a troupe,' the inspector explained. 'They're very good. Semi-professional, almost.'

'If only he could manage such heights at work.'

'It's good to have a pastime. Good exercise, too.'

'Hm.' The commander was unconvinced. 'What d'you want?'

O'Sullivan overlooked his gruffness. 'Just checking in on the Monica Seppi thing,' she said casually. 'I don't suppose there've been any developments? Poor old Laura Nixon's still stressing about it.'

'Er, no.' Carlyle didn't want to bring his colleague into the loop. 'But tell Nixon not to worry. It'll sort itself out sooner or later, if it hasn't already.'

'Will do.'

'What're you up to?' Carlyle asked, keen to move off the subject of the Slovakian killing machine.

'A few odds and sods. Nothing particularly exciting.' O'Sullivan mentioned the case of a missing teenager who'd run away from home. 'It's more like being a social worker.'

'I know the feeling.' Closing the Hitchcock file, Carlyle reached for his phone.

O'Sullivan took the hint. 'Right, well, I'll be off. I'm having dinner with the kids for once.'

'Good idea. See you tomorrow.'

After she left his office, he called the CPS, speaking to a couple of people before getting through to Jodie Morris. Keeping the small talk to a minimum, he brought the conversation round to Abigail Slater's client, the pilfering businessman with the Brazilian squeeze.

'What an idiot,' the prosecutor proclaimed. 'Men are so predictable.'

225

Carlyle didn't challenge the sweeping generalisation.

'It's ridiculous we're not pursuing it.'

Had he heard her right? 'Whaddya mean?'

'The guy's guilty, but we don't have the bandwidth to deal with trifling cases like this right now,' Morris explained. 'The latest round of budget cuts is killing us and we're having to bin a whole bunch of investigations.'

No need to call in the favour, then. My lucky day, Carlyle mused. 'Does his lawyer know?' he asked.

'It's Abigail Slater,' Morris wailed. 'Which is the icing on the fucking cake.'

Carlyle said nothing.

'She'll be informed in the next few days.' Morris grew wary. 'What I definitely don't need is you giving her a heads-up.'

'No need to worry,' Carlyle chuntered. 'Slater and I have never been on good terms.'

'What is your interest, then?'

'Erm, the guy's wife is a friend of a friend. They asked if I could find out what was going on.' Pleased with his powers of invention, Carlyle embellished his tale. 'She was worried his legal costs might blow a hole in her divorce settlement.'

'The guy's supposed to be skint. There's a report from a forensic accountant that says he hasn't got a bean to his name.'

On a roll, Carlyle couldn't stop. 'His missus thinks he's got stuff hidden away.'

'In that case, the divorce court can sort it out,' Morris replied. 'But don't go tipping off the wife, either. It'll all come out in the next few days, through the proper channels.'

'I won't mention anything until it's been officially confirmed.' Ending the conversation as quickly as possible, he immediately called Slater with the good news.

'I knew the CPS would fold,' the lawyer crowed.

You've changed your tune, Carlyle reflected.

'I expect Ms Morris has been fretting for some time about how to get out of this particular hole.'

'I think she's got a lot on her plate,' Carlyle commented.

'I needn't have bothered getting you to make the call at all.'

'It was still worth doing.' Carlyle was irked by her attitude. He hadn't been expecting the lawyer to shower him with praise, but, still, she could have been more gracious towards the bearer of such good news.

'When are they going to let me know officially?'

'It could be a while yet. Just remember to act surprised when you get the call. I'm not supposed to be giving anyone a heads-up.'

'You didn't tell Morris you were calling on my behalf, did you?'

'No, of course not.'

'Good.' Slater finally showed a little gratitude. 'Thanks for the call. I'm sure Jodie would've made me wait as long as possible for confirmation.'

'Your client will be happy.'

'Happy, no. He's still distraught at being dumped by the girlfriend. Once he gets over that, though, he might begin to realise he's a very lucky boy.'

'Now he only has the divorce to worry about.'

'It'll be a breeze by comparison,' Slater declared. 'His wife's lawyers will never find the money.'

Carlyle was surprised by the aside. 'Jodie said he was broke.'

'There's broke and there's broke,' the lawyer offered cryptically.

Carlyle didn't probe any further. 'I kept my end of the deal,' he pointed out, 'so I assume we're quits.'

'I wouldn't say that,' Slater huffed. 'You still owe me. I delivered you Miranda Curtis, did I not?'

'You did,' Carlyle confirmed.

'And you got what you wanted?'

'Yes. Although Curtis's girlfriend did assault my sergeant.'

'Those water polo players can be quite something.' Slater chuckled. 'Are you going to deport her?'

'I don't believe so,' Carlyle replied.

'Aha, I see you're finally getting better at this game. Why play that card now when you can keep it in your back pocket for future use?'

'That's one way of looking at it.'

'In effect,' Slater reasoned, 'I've managed to do you multiple favours in exchange for the quarter-favour you did for me.' When Carlyle queried her accounting, she added, 'All you did was preempt Morris's phone call. You didn't get her to agree a deal.'

'Yes, but—'

'Getting the deal was the ask, not just making the call.'

Carlyle gave up trying to argue his case.

'At some point in the future, I'll come looking for you to repay the favour. When the time comes, I don't want any mewling and puking.'

'You never get any of that from me,' Carlyle promised wearily.

'Glad to hear it. Always nice doing business with you, Commander.' Slater hung up.

Feeling slightly battered, Carlyle retrieved the Angela Luther passport from his desk and headed off to face his next challenge.

The restaurant was called Umberto's. Inside, the place looked like it hadn't been decorated since the middle of the last century. Still, it was pretty full as Carlyle scanned the main dining room. Monica Seppi was sitting at a table at the back, facing the door, drinking a glass of red wine. The clock above the entrance to the kitchen showed two minutes to seven.

'You're early.'

'I can think of worse crimes.' Tossing the passport onto the table, Carlyle sat down.

'True enough.' Seppi reached for the bottle sitting on the table. 'Would you like a drink?'

'Why not?' Carlyle let her half fill his glass, before topping up her own. He took a sip. 'Very nice.'

'I went for one of the better wines on the menu,' Seppi drawled, 'seeing as you're paying.' Picking up the passport, she lifted herself half off the chair and shoved it into the back pocket of her jeans.

'Don't you want to check it?'

'Why would you try to trick me, Commander? You want me out of here even more than I want to leave.'

'True enough.'

She stuck out a hand. 'Which leaves only the issue of the money.'

'I don't have it.' Carlyle took a gulp of his wine.

A flash of anger crossed Seppi's face, but she quickly brought it under control as she withdrew the hand. 'Explain.'

'You know about Karol hanging himself?'

'I heard.' Irritation trumped sorrow in her voice. 'He was such a weak man. Sentimental. Ultimately unreliable.'

'Ultimately, well, yes, I suppose so.'

'He had the passports?'

'Yes.'

'And the cash?'

'He stashed the euros in a locker in a church. I was able to retrieve the passports but not the cash.'

'Who has the money now?'

'God.'

'God,' Seppi said coolly, 'or that fucking nun Karol was working with?'

Carlyle didn't want to place Rita Vicedo in the sights of the

Slovak ninja. Trying to come up with a suitable response, he became conscious of people approaching their table. He looked up to see a hard-faced woman flanked by two men. The woman seemed vaguely familiar. Reaching into her pocket, she pulled out an ID.

'Immigration Enforcement.'

Shit. Carlyle belatedly recognised the agent from Belsize Park. It looked like the woman hadn't been hunting a gaggle of Albanians after all. Her boss, Jamie Worby, clearly wanted to catch Monica Seppi more than he'd let on.

The chatter around the room began to die down as the diners sensed some free entertainment coming their way.

'Hold on a second.' Pushing back his chair, Carlyle was preparing to bluff his way out when Seppi took matters into her own hands. Giving the table a firm shove, she jumped up, smashing a fist into the face of the nearest agent. As the guy pitched forward, she downed the second guy with a sharp stomp on his kneecap. The commander was still wincing at the sound of breaking bones when Seppi grabbed the female agent by her collar and delivered a vicious headbutt, which sent the woman's nose to all corners of her face and blood across the checked tablecloth.

A stunned silence descended on the restaurant for a fraction of a second before the screams of the injured agents had those not already fleeing for the door reaching to cover their ears. A woman vomited into a bowl of soup while her dining companion videoed the scene on his phone.

'Wow!' an American voice cried. 'It's like a Tarantino movie.'

The agent who'd had his kneecap relocated to his ankle was in a particularly bad way: white as a sheet, his eyes had rolled back in his head. Foaming at the mouth, he had pissed on the floor. His female colleague had retreated under a table. Not realising his lucky escape, the agent who'd been punched in the face came back for seconds, only to be dispatched, face first, into a plate of pasta.

'That's one way to do it.' Carlyle's admiration for Seppi's

fighting skills was tempered by the realisation he would be the one left to clean up the mess.

'What the fuck?' Seppi stepped over the body of the knee-capped agent, fists raised.

'This was nothing to do with me.' Carlyle took a careful step backwards. 'I had no idea they were on your tail.'

'They followed you here.'

'You don't know that. They could've been following *you*.'

Seppi scoffed at the idea.

'Anyway, it's all a bit academic.' Glancing at the man still filming on his phone, Carlyle lowered his voice to a whisper. 'You'd better get going.'

'I need the money,' she hissed, heading for the door. 'You've got twelve hours to get it back.'

'We've got at least twenty different versions of events.' Jamie Worby looked at Carlyle with a mixture of disgust and dismay. The Home Office man made no attempt to take control of the crime scene, but it was clear he wanted answers.

Taking a deep breath, Carlyle defaulted into SBM, Standard Bullshit Mode. 'Witnesses are notoriously unreliable. People freeze. They can't deal with what's happening in real time.'

'I can't believe none of them had the gumption to film it on their phone.'

'That is a bit of a surprise,' Carlyle agreed. While the immigration agents were being helped into ambulances, he had forced the one guy who had managed to film the incident, an IT consultant called Derek, to delete the footage. The commander had explained to Derek and his girlfriend that they were 'compromising a top-secret undercover police investigation'. He gave them a stern warning that if they breathed a word about events in the restaurant they would be charged with a raft of offences that would land them both in jail. The pair, who had tickets for

Hamilton, didn't want to hang around to debate the matter.

'You didn't come to the assistance of my people,' Worby noted.

'It all happened so fast.' Carlyle shrugged.

'And you let her get away,' Worby snarled.

'My first instinct,' Carlyle said primly, 'in line with standard protocols, was to call for back-up, along with medical assistance for your colleagues, as well as the other diners.'

'Half of whom seem to have fled before they could be questioned.'

'People simply have no sense of civic duty any longer,' Carlyle said sadly. 'Helping the police is no longer the second nature it once was.'

'That's what happens when you have a city full of foreigners,' Worby complained, 'people who don't understand our standards and values.'

'This'll be good for Immigration Enforcement, though.'

'Three agents seriously injured, and no arrest.' Worby considered the chaos of the restaurant. 'Not to mention all the claims we'll get for damages. How is this in any way good for us?'

'Your brave officers unthinkingly put their lives on the line to take a dangerous alien off the streets. People will love it. Mark my words, you'll get an OBE for this, maybe even a knighthood.'

Worby eyed him suspiciously. 'Are you kidding?'

'You'll be heroes in the *Mail* tomorrow,' Carlyle insisted.

'We'll see,' Worby grunted.

Carlyle gave him a reassuring pat on the shoulder. 'Bet you a pint.' When Worby didn't take it up, he asked, 'Why are you putting so much effort into chasing down one illegal anyway?'

'Monica Seppi's a special case. I've seen more than my fair share of bureaucratic cock-ups in my time, but this one takes the biscuit. I don't like losing people, especially when they go on to kill.' Worby sighed. 'Then there's the little matter of having MI5 on my case, which I don't like at all.'

'Oh?' Carlyle tried not to look too interested.

'Yes, the Security Service wants this woman, too, for some reason.'

'Blimey.'

'Blimey's right. Monica Seppi – if that's her name – isn't your average illegal.'

Carlyle played dumb. 'What is she, then?'

'Nobody's telling me anything.' Worby poked a broken plate with the toe of his shoe. 'There are forces at play going way beyond our pay grade, Commander.'

'We're in the middle of a right mess,' Carlyle agreed.

'Which brings us to the key question,' Worby said slowly. 'What were you doing here when my people arrived?'

'We got a tip-off that the lady would be here.' Sergeant Nixon appeared at Carlyle's side with a big, friendly smile for the Home Office man. 'Anonymous.'

'Obviously.'

Nixon ignored Worby's sarcasm. 'The commander didn't want me going in alone. He volunteered to do it instead. It was very brave of him.'

Embarrassed, Carlyle looked down at the splattered floor. To his surprise, he felt Nixon take his arm.

'If you'll excuse us,' said the sergeant, 'I need to take him to the hospital for some tests.'

'But there's nothing wrong with him,' Worby complained.

'He might be physically okay, but that doesn't mean there isn't any psychological damage.' Picking her way through the mess, she led her boss towards the door.

'Bollocks,' Worby called after them. 'You're taking the piss.'

Outside, Carlyle walked past the row of waiting ambulances and continued down the street.

'Where're you going?' Nixon demanded. 'I wasn't joking

233

about going to the hospital. You need to get a check-up.'

'I'm fine.' Turning right at the corner, Carlyle lengthened his stride. 'Seppi never laid a finger on me.'

'But the stress.'

'Nothing that can't be sorted out with a drink.' Leading the sergeant down a side street, he ducked inside a nondescript pub. At the bar, he pointed to one of the bottles lined up on the back shelf.

'Jameson's, please.'

The barmaid gave him a friendly nod. 'Ice?'

Carlyle saw no merit in diluting hard liquor. 'No ice,' he said briskly, 'no water. Straight.'

'Shall I make it a double?' the woman asked.

'Good idea.' As she got to it, Carlyle turned to Nixon. 'What're you having?'

The sergeant looked around, embarrassed. 'I'm still on duty,' she pointed out. 'You are, too.'

Carlyle watched as the golden liquid was poured into a shot glass. 'I won't tell if you won't.'

Nixon reluctantly took a Diet Coke and they retreated to a table near the door.

'Your chosen tipple, is it?' Nixon raised her glass in a mock toast.

'Yeah.' Carlyle took a mouthful of whiskey, letting it linger on his tongue before swallowing. 'I'm not a big drinker but I like the occasional taste.'

The sergeant looked at him doubtfully.

'Seriously. I don't drink much. I'll have a couple of drinks a week, maybe. Certainly not every day.'

'You don't have to explain yourself to me, Commander.'

'Just a simple statement of fact.'

'Sorry. That came across as a bit censorious, didn't it?'

Yes. 'No.' Carlyle was coming to the view that the sergeant

was a bit wet. 'How did you get into the job?' he asked, expecting a familiar tale of a family connection – fathers or uncles who'd been on the force, or maybe an older brother.

'I was headhunted.' Nixon sucked her Coke through a straw, with an artlessness that made him squirm. 'After I graduated, I was working in compliance in the City. It was boring, but then I got approached about the Met's graduate training programme.'

'Ah.' Carlyle was vaguely aware of the scheme, which aimed to broaden the range of people coming into the service. 'I suppose that means you'll be in charge of me soon enough.'

'I don't know about that,' Nixon blushed slightly, 'although the aim is to make superintendent in five years.'

'Good for you.' Carlyle wondered what O'Sullivan thought of that. The inspector had fought her way up the hierarchy without the help of any training programme.

'Karen's been a big help,' Nixon said, almost as if she was reading his thoughts. 'She's a great mentor.'

'Yes,' Carlyle agreed. Finishing his drink, he ignored the sergeant's disapproving look and headed to the bar for a refill. On his return, he held it up for her inspection. 'Only a single this time, the last one for tonight.'

Nixon's expression softened a little. 'I suppose after what happened in the restaurant you could use it.'

'Yeah.'

'What *did* happen in there?'

Carlyle wasn't for going into the details. On the other hand, Nixon was part of what might loosely be called the Seppi investigation and she deserved an explanation of sorts. 'I managed to track down Monica Seppi. I was going to nick her when a bunch of Immigration Enforcement goons waded in and all hell broke loose.'

'You were going to bring her in?' Nixon sounded unconvinced.

Carlyle tried to look surprised by the question. 'The woman's

235

wanted in connection with the murder of a prison officer, Ted Godson, not to mention the very serious assault on those two blokes.'

'Peter Williamson and Justin Lansley.'

'Exactly.'

'They're the guys who started all this off by attacking Seppi in the first place.'

'Stupid bastards.'

'She got her revenge, though.' Was there a hint of admiration in Nixon's voice or did he imagine it?

'How are those two gentlemen getting on with their, erm, recovery?'

'Slowly, I should imagine.'

'Quite.'

'I'll check, sir.'

'No particular need. And don't call me "sir" when we're sitting in the pub. It makes me sound like a schoolteacher.' Nixon blushed again and Carlyle quickly returned to Monica Seppi. 'She's got a lot of explaining to do.'

'There's plenty we don't know.' Nixon sucked the last of her drink from the bottom of the glass. 'What started out as a fairly routine investigation seems to be getting increasingly complicated with every passing day.'

'You can say that again. I doubt we'll ever get to the bottom of it.' Carlyle crossed his fingers. Whatever the truth was, he didn't want it coming out.

Nixon refused to be put off by such a defeatist attitude. 'We can try,' she insisted.

'We certainly can.' He affected enthusiasm for the challenge. 'Absolutely.'

'What I don't understand,' Nixon continued, 'is why so many different agencies are piling in. As well as Immigration Enforcement, a whole bunch of other folk turned up. Someone said they were from the Security Service.'

236

'Yeah?' Trying to come across as uninformed and disinterested at the same time, Carlyle took another mouthful of whiskey. 'What's all that about?'

Nixon had no idea. 'There remains a lot more to Monica Seppi than meets the eye. I have to say, I wish I'd never come across the woman.'

'Whatever game's afoot, it'll sort itself out.' Finishing his drink, he stood up. 'Now, I have to get going.'

'Before you go, I need a witness statement from you – if you don't mind.'

Carlyle looked round the bar. 'Here?'

'Back at the station.'

'I'll meet you at Charing Cross.' Carlyle ignored her protests as he bolted for the door. 'Type something up and I'll sign it when I get back.'

TWENTY-TWO

'Whaddya mean, the money's gone?' Sitting in the back pew at St Etheldreda's, Carlyle watched a pale young man emerge from the confessional and scuttle from the church. For a fleeting moment, the commander wondered about going into the box and unburdening himself. *Forgive me Father, for I have sinned. And there's plenty more to come.* Somehow, he didn't imagine it would do much good. God wasn't going to get him out of this mess. Only cold, hard cash could achieve that.

'I've spent it.' Rita Vicedo gave him a defiant look. 'All nineteen thousand and twenty-five euros.'

'Is that how much it was?' Nineteen thousand euros translated to about seventeen thousand quid, Carlyle guessed.

Vicedo nodded.

'And you've given it all away?'

The nun was unrepentant. 'What did you think I'd do?'

'Well . . .' Carlyle had no idea. You should have pocketed the cash along with the fake German and Canadian passports, he told himself. Yet again he'd been too clever by half. 'Story of my life,' he groaned.

'What?'

'Nothing. I'm just surprised you found a use for it so quickly.'

'Our funding is pretty much hand-to-mouth.' Vicedo tucked a strand of hair behind her ear. 'When you get a windfall, you spend it. There's no point in sitting on cash when it can be put to good use.'

Carlyle uttered an expletive.

The nun tutted. 'There was a programme in South London which had run out of money,' she continued. 'The council had stopped supporting it. They're looking after a dozen women and children. Without this windfall it would have had to close at the end of the month. Karol's gift will help them keep going for a little while longer. He'd like that.'

'It wasn't Karol's cash.'

'Maybe not,' the nun shot back, 'but it wasn't yours either.'

'No,' Carlyle conceded, 'but spending it has put me in a bit of a hole.'

Vicedo demanded an explanation.

'It's Monica Seppi's. She wants it back.'

The nun offered no sympathy. 'You might've seen that coming.'

'I could say the same to you,' Carlyle sniped. 'But it's *me* she's coming after.' He gave her a quick update on the Slovakian's latest adventures.

Vicedo's eyes grew wide. 'There was a fight in a restaurant?'

'It wasn't much of a fight.'

'Were you hurt?'

'I'm fine,' Carlyle assured her. 'I just need the money.' He pointed to a poster advertising the good works of the Church. 'D'you think we could get a loan from Father Burns's Fighting Fund?' Father Burns was in charge of St Etheldreda's and three other churches in central London. The Fund supported everything from roof repairs to educational projects in West Africa.

'You mean steal from the Church?' Vicedo was scandalised.

'I was thinking of it more as correcting an administrative error.'

'I don't even know if the Fund has nineteen thousand euros,

or anything like it. They lost a fortune when Father Burns's predecessor, Father Sunderland, thought he'd invest in crypto-currencies. The poor man thought he could earn money to support our charitable work. In the event, he managed to lose more than seventy thousand pounds in something called Ripple.'

Carlyle had never heard of it.

'Neither had I,' the nun confessed. 'When he realised what he'd done, Father Sunderland tried to cover it up. The losses only came to light after he had a heart attack and Father Burns was brought in to replace him. When he recovered his health, Father Sunderland was sent to a parish in Bolivia.'

'One with no internet access, I hope.'

The nun gave him a funny look. 'How did you know that?'

'Just a guess.'

'Father Burns reckons it will take decades to restore St Etheldreda's finances.'

'A sorry tale.'

'But not an uncommon one.' Vicedo sighed. 'Men and their vices dog progress at every turn.'

'I wouldn't be so hard on poor old Father Sunderland. Lots of people have had their fingers burnt trying to make money out of cryptocurrencies. At least it's not as bad as abusing little boys.'

She smacked his arm.

'Well, it's not.' Another smack had him muttering about the penalties for assaulting a cop.

'I should hit you harder,' Vicedo grumbled. 'Your lack of empathy makes you unfit to be a police officer.'

'What lack of empathy?'

'Sometimes it seems like you treat everything as a bit of a joke. You don't know how to deal with victims properly.'

'I'm the victim here,' Carlyle wailed. By now he was feeling genuinely sorry for himself.

Vicedo would not be moved. 'I can't help you. Whatever

hole you've dug yourself into, you'll have to get out of it on your own.'

The commander racked his brains, wondering how he might come up with the cash that would save him from Monica Seppi's wrath. There was only one person he knew who might be able – and willing – to hand over that kind of cash without asking any questions. With a CV that included stints as a cop, a drug dealer and an art dealer, Dominic Silver was Carlyle's oldest mate. Unfortunately, Dom was out of the country and not returning his calls.

His other potential source of funds was the Charing Cross CI fund. However, turning Seppi into a confidential informant would be insanely risky. Handing a snitch so much cash wouldn't pass unnoticed; if it led to an investigation, even Carlyle would struggle to bullshit his way out of a disciplinary hearing. It would be impossible to come up with a story that was even remotely credible. Reluctantly, he binned the idea.

What he needed was access to funds no one could connect to him, which no one would miss and which wouldn't have to be paid back.

Easier said than done.

Returning to the police station, he was intercepted by Sonia Wiggins. 'Jasper's been arrested again,' she announced, 'and they won't let me in to see him.'

Carlyle groaned. 'Let me see what's going on and I'll come back and let you know.'

A familiar voice behind him declared, 'Mr Wiggins has a right to see his lawyer.'

Carlyle turned to face Abigail Slater.

The lawyer didn't offer a handshake. 'The poor boy's being victimised by your colleagues.'

The commander bit down on his scepticism. 'What's he done now?'

'He hasn't done anything,' Sonia Wiggins screeched. 'That's the point.'

'Calm down, Sonia.' Slater took Carlyle by the arm and walked him out of earshot. 'You owe me a favour,' she hissed, 'and now's a chance to repay it in double-quick time.'

Carlyle wasn't going to quibble in front of the mother.

'Jasper and two of his friends were arrested three hours ago on public-order offences. I don't know the details yet because I haven't been able to speak to my client. We've been kept waiting for over an hour. It's a disgrace.'

'You should have called me.'

'I tried. Several times.'

'Sorry, I've been out dealing with another matter.' He pointed to the entrance. 'Come with me and we'll see what's going on.'

Having installed Sonia Wiggins in his office, Carlyle led Slater down to one of the interview rooms. 'I'll let you talk to Jasper and then he can see his mum. You were lucky I turned up when I did. Another twenty minutes and he'd have been on his way to Wormwood Scrubs for the night.'

'I can feel a claim for false imprisonment and wrongful arrest coming on,' Slater half joked.

'You don't even know the details yet,' Carlyle pointed out. 'I'm going above and beyond here.'

When they reached the interview room, Slater took a seat at the table. 'I suppose a cup of coffee's out of the question?'

On cue, there was a knock and Nixon's head appeared round the door. 'There you are.' Stepping into the room, the sergeant handed Carlyle a sheet of paper. 'Your statement regarding the fight in Umberto's. I need you to read it and sign it.'

'I'll sort it out straight away.' Carlyle felt himself redden slightly under Slater's amused gaze.

'I heard about that,' said the lawyer. 'Quite a mess.'

'Something and nothing.' Carlyle looked pleadingly at Nixon. 'Could you get Ms Slater a coffee, please?'

'Americano,' said the lawyer. 'Black.'

'I'll see what I can do.' Looking somewhat miffed, the sergeant disappeared.

'Umberto's used to be quite fashionable,' Slater recalled. 'Now it's just for tourists and the pre-theatre crowd.'

'Hm.' Carlyle carefully folded his statement and stuck it in the inside pocket of his jacket. 'By the way, did you know Sonia Wiggins was having an affair with Miranda Curtis's client, Patrick Dalby?'

Slater did not answer the question. After an extended pause, she said, 'The private lives of clients' parents are not my concern.'

'I assumed you know Sonia, which is why you're representing Jasper.'

'Never assume, Commander.'

'How did you end up with Jasper as a client, then?'

'Sonia's a friend of a friend. They contacted me last time he was arrested but I was unavailable. I don't think they thought much of his last lawyer, so when it happened again I got the call. This time, luckily for Jasper, I was free.'

'I've bent over backwards to help this kid.' Carlyle explained about Lottie Pearson and their attempts to stop Jasper and his activist pals hounding the mayor. 'But he keeps getting into trouble.'

'Sonia blames his girlfriend.'

'I've met Molly,' said Carlyle. 'She seems okay.'

'According to Sonia, Molly's the driving force of Jasper's little group. Fifty years ago, it would've been feminism. Thirty years ago, animal rights. Then, anti-globalisation. Now it's this non-binary stuff about your gender identity not being exclusively male or female. My daughter's always trying to explain it to me but, frankly, I find it all rather boring.'

'You have a daughter?' Carlyle couldn't recall if the lawyer had ever mentioned kids before.

'According to her, I'm a TERF, a Trans Exclusionary Radical Feminist.'

'Hm.'

'It's a term of abuse aimed at feminists who aren't "woke" – like Germaine Greer, for example.'

The Ladies in Charge would love to meet you, Carlyle thought. Before he could explain about the pond dispute, the door opened and a clearly chastened Jasper Wiggins appeared, chaperoned by a support officer.

Wiggins took a seat opposite Slater. 'I hope you're better than the last lawyer.'

'Ms Slater's very good,' Carlyle advised. 'And when you've finished speaking to her, you can talk to your mum.'

As he was leaving, Nixon appeared with Slater's coffee, plus a spare, which she offered to the commander.

'Don't I get one?' Wiggins whined.

'Here you go.' Carlyle took the paper cup from Nixon and passed it to the boy.

Wiggins removed the lid and stared at the inky liquid with dismay. 'No milk?'

'Don't worry,' Slater reassured him. 'We'll get you out of here as quickly as possible and then you can have whatever you want.'

Carlyle ushered Nixon out of the door before the boy could complain further. They walked to the end of the corridor before he asked, 'What happened this time?'

'The mayor was making a speech at the Covent Garden Residents Association,' Nixon explained. 'Jasper and his pals attacked him as he was getting out of his car. Luckily, we had people there to deal with it. No one was hurt but there was some damage to the vehicle and Jasper threw a punch at a policewoman.'

'The boy's a total idiot,' Carlyle declared. 'Who else got arrested?'

'Three arrests in total: Jasper, his girlfriend and a third woman.'

Carlyle thought back to the people he'd met at the Wiggins house in Highgate. Maybe the third woman was part of the other couple with Jasper and Molly. 'Are the other two still here?'

'We haven't transferred any of them yet,' Nixon confirmed.

'Why don't you bring Molly up? Put her in one of the other interview rooms.'

'You going to have a little chat with her?'

'Why not?' Carlyle reasoned. 'She can't be any harder to deal with than her boyfriend.'

'I'm going to be straight with you.' Carlyle jerked a thumb towards the door. 'Jasper's down the corridor talking to his mum . . . and his lawyer.'

Molly Arnold rolled her eyes. 'Why haven't I got a lawyer?' she whined. 'I'm entitled.'

'Yes, you are.' Carlyle wondered why he was bothering with this nonsense. 'Do you have a lawyer?'

'Don't you have to provide me with one?'

'You want one?'

'Why not?'

'I'll sort it out.' He got to his feet. 'They'll probably be in touch tomorrow. In the meantime, you can go back to the cells and we'll arrange transport.'

'Transport?'

'We don't keep prisoners here overnight. You'll be held in a prison, probably in London, no further away than Birmingham at any rate, I'd expect.' He let that sink in. 'We'll let the lawyer know where you end up and they'll come and see you.'

'Birmingham?' The girl's eyes began to glisten. 'You're fucking with me.'

'It's just the way it works.' Carlyle shrugged.

'But you want to offer me a deal,' she speculated hopefully. 'That's what all this is about, isn't it?'

Carlyle was happy to let her dangle a little longer. 'I don't know we're in deal territory yet,' he said.

'What *do* you want, then?'

'I want to understand about your little group and why you seem to get into so much trouble all the time.'

'And then we can get to a deal?'

'You sound like you've got something in mind.'

She wiped away a tear. 'Might have.'

'I can't believe you've sent him back to the cells.' Sonia Wiggins paced Carlyle's office like a caged animal while Abigail Slater looked on. 'It's outrageous.'

'This is a serious matter,' Carlyle intoned solemnly from behind the relative safety of his desk. 'The mayor isn't going to thank me if we don't deal with it properly.'

'You're doing his dirty work,' Wiggins snarled. 'Wait till the papers hear about this.'

'I'd think carefully before talking to any journalists.' Carlyle looked at Slater. 'Jasper's had several run-ins with the mayor now. He's already been in the press and is going to come out badly in any newspaper story, however it's written.'

'And you aren't?' Wiggins shot back.

'I'm only doing my job.'

'You're just—'

'The commander's right.' Slater invited the woman to take a seat. 'It wouldn't be good for Jasper to get stereotyped as a rich-kid troublemaker. I'm sure we can sort this out quietly.'

'How?' Wiggins reluctantly sat down.

'While you were talking to Jasper,' said Carlyle, 'I had a word with Molly Arnold.'

'The little bitch,' Wiggins hissed. 'This is all her fault.'

'Sonia, please.' Slater didn't conceal her irritation. 'You're not helping.'

'But it's true,' Wiggins persisted. 'Jasper had never been in any trouble before she came along.'

'Molly's keen for everyone to move forward,' said Carlyle. 'To that end, she gave me a list of things Joe Stanley can do to help resolve the situation.'

'She made some demands,' Wiggins translated. 'That certainly sounds like Molly.'

'I promised I would take them to the mayor,' Carlyle said, 'and, in exchange, your son will take a sabbatical from throwing bricks through windows and vandalising cars.'

Jasper's mother couldn't have given two hoots about his deal. All she wanted to know was that her boy would be coming home.

'I'm going to go downstairs and have everyone released,' Carlyle confirmed. 'No charges will be brought.'

Slater was suitably grateful. 'We appreciate you going the extra mile.'

'Better late than never,' Wiggins muttered.

Ignoring the woman's spectacular gracelessness, Carlyle continued, 'I need you to make sure Jasper stays out of trouble now. This is absolutely the last time I can help him. If there is another incident – however minor – we'll throw the book at him.'

Under the commanding gaze of her son's lawyer, Sonia Wiggins finally issued a grudging 'Thank you.'

'Jasper's entitled to express his views, but he has to respect the law, and also the mayor. I'll see if we can arrange a truce in this ongoing squabble. In the meantime, though, you must keep Jasper on a short leash.'

'Yes, yes.' Wiggins pushed herself out of her chair. 'I'll wait for him downstairs.'

Carlyle shuffled some papers on his desk. 'One more thing, before you go.'

'Yes?' The woman sank back into the seat.

He looked up slowly. 'I understand you knew Tim Hitchcock.'

Wiggins eyeballed him for several moments.

'The CEO of Kollision,' Carlyle added gratuitously. 'Jumped out a window after the company lost a load of money.'

Wiggins didn't nibble at the bait. 'Such a shame,' she said blandly, 'I knew Tim was under a bit of pressure, but I had no idea things were so bad. Tragic.'

'Very sad,' Carlyle agreed. 'And what about Patrick Dalby?'

'What about him?'

'He seems to have disappeared.'

'I heard,' Wiggins said casually, 'that he ran off to Mexico.'

'You haven't heard from him since he's been there?'

'No.' Wiggins's eyes narrowed. 'Why would I?'

'Just a question.'

'A question that has nothing to do with the matter in hand,' Slater observed drily. She offered Carlyle one of her less hostile scowls. 'That's enough fishing, I think.'

'Just making conversation.'

'Yes, well, thank you again for all your help, Commander.' The lawyer ushered Wiggins towards the door. 'I'm sure we'll be in touch again soon.'

After they left, Carlyle enjoyed a moment of calm. Then he called Nixon and asked her to process the release papers for Jasper, Molly and the third activist, whose name he still didn't know. Next, he rang Lottie Pearson.

'I hope you're ringing to tell me those little sods are finally going to jail.'

'I've done a deal.'

The mayor's aide groaned theatrically. '*Pffff.* You can't do deals with Jasper. It won't work.'

'I've done a deal with Molly Arnold. We can do business with her.'

'Maybe. What's the plan?'

'I'll talk you through it in the morning.' Carlyle suddenly felt too weary for any further politicking that day. 'You can buy me breakfast.'

TWENTY-THREE

Laughter was coming from the squad room on the third floor. A group of officers Carlyle didn't recognise were in good spirits, exchanging high fives as they chugged beer. The commander sidled over to Laura Nixon, who was at a nearby desk, completing the paperwork required for the release of Jasper Wiggins and his comrades.

'What's with the party?'

'Operation Squirrel,' the sergeant explained. 'They've had a monster result.' Operation Squirrel was a long-running anti-drugs operation, focused on McVeigh Heights, a social-housing development near Seven Dials. 'They hit the right flat at the right time.'

'Any arrests?'

'Four. One guy who is registered as living there and three blokes who say they were just visiting for a chat.'

'Yeah, right.'

'They all claimed to know absolutely nothing about the drugs and cash we found in the flat.'

Cash? Carlyle wandered over and congratulated the celebrating officers. Declining a half-hearted offer of a beer, he inspected a trio of plastic shopping bags piled up on a nearby desk. 'How much d'you get?'

'We haven't done a full inventory yet,' said the lead officer, a lean, shaven-headed inspector, who introduced himself as Charlie Kearns. 'A decent amount, though.'

'I'd reckon eighty grand,' one of the other officers ventured, 'at least.'

'That's just a guess,' said Kearns. 'We haven't counted it properly yet. Could be anywhere between fifty and a hundred plus, I reckon.'

'Minus what we spent in the off-licence,' someone else quipped, to a round of guffaws and clinking beer bottles.

Kearns glared at the comedian. 'That's a joke, sir,' he clarified, for Carlyle's benefit. 'We paid for the booze ourselves.' He tipped his beer bottle at the plastic bags. 'The money we found in the flat – I bagged it up personally. It hasn't left my sight since.'

'This stuff should be logged and in storage by now. You can't leave it lying around.' Carlyle lifted the bags from the table. 'I'll put it downstairs.' There were a few murmurs of discontent, but he cut them off. 'You've done a good job, but if we're going to get the result your hard work deserves we have to maintain the chain of custody.' Kearns put down his beer and reached for the evidence, but Carlyle kept a firm hold of the bags. 'Leave them to me. I'll check them in for you. Finish your party, then get some rest. It's been a long day.' Turning on his heel, he walked towards the door, bags in hand. 'And, again, well done. Great result for Charing Cross. Just what we needed.'

Evidence Storage was in the basement, along the corridor from the station's abandoned canteen. Carlyle took the lift down, wrestling with his conscience as he descended. He had been handed an obvious solution to the Monica Seppi problem, but recycling the impounded cash in such a manner was theft, pure and simple. Was it worth the risk? With the money yet to be properly counted, the chances of getting away with it were high, though less than a hundred per cent. Pushing himself to put a number on it, Carlyle estimated the chance of any shortfall being noticed at less than five per cent. On that basis, he calculated the chance of being identified as the culprit at less than one per cent.

A less than one per cent chance of blowing up his career, in exchange for getting rid of Seppi, who might otherwise bring him down anyway.

Should he take the punt?

His head said, 'Yes.' His heart said, 'No.'

Or was it the other way round?

Either way, it was now or never. Coming out of the lift, Carlyle stepped into the empty corridor. Fortunately, the CCTV in this part of the building had been switched off when they closed the canteen, ending the regular disputes over people nicking bananas and such. He ducked into the darkened cafeteria, remembering the dinner ladies who'd worked in the kitchen for decades before being unceremoniously let go to save a few quid. Sticking the bags on the abandoned service line, he pulled out a wad from each until he had amassed a pile approximating seventeen grand. Shoving the cash into his pockets, he hurried back into the corridor.

The evidence locker was manned by civilian staff only during office hours. With the place to himself, Carlyle tagged each bag and logged them into the station's computer system. In the morning, the cash would be counted and deposited in a nearby bank, in line with standard protocol. Placing each bag in its own secure locker, he headed back upstairs.

Nixon caught him as he approached the exit. 'Jasper's gone home with his mum.'

'I think I'd have preferred a night in the cells,' the commander joked, hoping he didn't look too guilty and his pockets didn't look too full.

The sergeant didn't notice anything amiss. 'I feel a bit sorry for Jasper. Between his mother and his girlfriend, I don't see how he'll ever escape being under the thumb.'

Carlyle edged towards the door. 'So long as he stays out of trouble, I couldn't care less.'

'Are you off?'

'I think we can all call it a night.'

'What about your statement?'

Shit. It was still in his jacket pocket. Carlyle pointed skywards. 'I left it in my office. I'll sign it in the morning.'

Nixon was annoyed by his failure to complete such a basic task. 'We need to get it sorted out before Immigration Enforcement turn up.'

'Eh?'

'The main guy just called to set up a meeting for tomorrow morning.'

'Jamie Worby?'

'He'll be here at ten.'

'And I thought I was in charge,' Carlyle grumped.

'Sorry, Commander, but you'd disappeared.'

'Couldn't Joaquin have just taken a message?'

'He's gone.'

'The little shit,' Carlyle hissed. 'If he's fucking rollerblading again, I'll kill him.'

'He's in a troupe.'

'I know he's in a bloody troupe but he's still got a day job.'

'He wasn't here,' Nixon repeated, 'so the call got put through to me. The guy was very blunt.'

'He's a wanker.'

Colouring slightly, the sergeant made it clear that his use of language made her uncomfortable.

'It's a technical term,' Carlyle insisted. 'Plus, in Worby's case, it's true. He could wank for an international select eleven.'

Nixon stood her ground. 'You can't say things like that, sir.'

'Yes, yes.' Carlyle's powers of resistance had dissipated to the point where he could argue no longer. 'Sorry.'

'Whatever you think of him, he'll still be here in the morning.'

'Fine.' Carlyle bolted for the door. 'I'll see you then.'

'Not much of a statement,' was Helen's verdict. Handing him back the sheet of paper, she went back to her crossword. 'Doesn't exactly paint much of a picture of what happened in the restaurant.'

'That's the idea.' Carlyle took the last mouthful of the generous measure of Jameson's he'd awarded himself after returning home. That it was his third of the evening was not something he felt the need to share with his wife. 'It's a witness statement, not a crime novel.'

'Pardon me, but I thought most of the stuff the police came up with was a work of fiction.'

Too tired to take the bait, he held out a hand. 'Gimme your pen.' Helen handed it over. Carlyle signed and dated the statement, and dropped it on the coffee table.

'Dishonest,' Helen took back the pen. 'Twisted.'

'What?' Conscious of the stolen money – currently sitting in his sock drawer – he felt his cheeks burn. He hoped Helen took his flushed look as a side effect of his drinking, rather than a sign of a guilty conscience.

She tapped the newspaper with the pen. 'Four down. Dishonest or twisted.'

As a rule, Carlyle was hopeless with crossword puzzles. This time, however, it came to him in a flash. 'Bent.' He blushed even harder.

'Very good.' She filled it in and threw him another clue.

'No idea.'

They repeated the exchange a couple of times before Helen gave up. 'I suppose I should have known you getting one right was a complete fluke.'

'Yes,' he agreed, happy to keep the conversation on the crossword.

Helen tossed the paper onto the table and dropped the pen on top of it. 'I saw Imogen Edelman today.'

Carlyle braced himself for another bollocking for his failure to bring Patrick Dalby to justice. By immense force of will, he tried to summon up some empathy for the woman who'd been targeted by the crazy car bomber. 'How's she doing?'

'They've dispensed with the bodyguards but she's still struggling.'

'It's good they've ditched the security.' Carlyle wondered about another drink. He decided against it. 'That's an important step in getting back to normal.'

'There's no getting back to normal,' said Helen, 'while that lunatic's still at large.'

'What do you want me to do?' Carlyle asked, exasperated. 'Go to Mexico to find him?'

'Why not?'

'Well . . .' Carlyle was the kind of guy who had a deep natural aversion to travelling beyond zone one of the tube map. The prospect of a trip to the Americas held no appeal whatsoever. 'Apart from the fact we don't have the budget, I have other things to do.'

'Like what?'

Like what? Carlyle didn't want to get into all the Monica Seppi stuff. Instead, he mentioned the Bruno Soutine case. 'We're under a bit of pressure to close the book on that one. You know what it's like – an unsolved murder is the last thing you want against your name.'

Helen was somewhat mollified. 'One of the girls was a client of his. She was very upset about it.'

'What?'

'Corinne.'

The name meant nothing to Carlyle.

'Dylan's mum.'

He looked at her blankly.

She looked at him like he had Alzheimer's. 'Dylan was one of Alice's playmates at nursery.'

'But that's got to be, like, more than fifteen years ago.' Carlyle wondered if he'd ever met the woman.

'We still keep in touch. Dylan's studying in the States now.'

'Good for him.'

'Corinne's firm moved offices a couple of years ago. They're round the corner from Avalon. We have a coffee every few weeks.'

Get to the point. Carlyle resisted the incredibly strong urge to chivvy his wife along.

'I saw her last week and we were talking about it.'

'And you didn't think to mention it?'

'How was I supposed to know it was one of yours?' Helen protested. 'Anyway, we've had more pressing things to worry about of late, don't you think?'

Carlyle bit down on his frustration. 'What did Corinne say?'

'She was hacked off. A good personal trainer's hard to find.'

'She didn't have any idea who might have killed the poor bugger?' Carlyle asked.

'Of course not. She did say, though, that the guy was a bit of a player. He liked to get it on with his clients, the female ones.'

'She was shagging him?'

'I dunno. Corinne's going through a divorce and—'

Carlyle had heard enough. 'You'd better give me her number.' He'd go and have a chat with her. Better still, he'd get O'Sullivan to do it.

Helen reached for her phone to text him. 'You won't tell her I thought she might be sleeping with him?'

'I won't say a word,' Carlyle promised.

TWENTY-FOUR

'Joe's very pissed off.' Lottie Pearson poked at her granola. They were sitting in a very expensive chain café on Charing Cross Road, just north of Leicester Square. 'He thought you were going to sort this out.'

'This is me sorting it out.' Carlyle gazed out of the window. A group of workmen were standing around a large hole on the far side of the road and the traffic was backed up in both directions. Tempers were getting frayed to the accompaniment of a symphony of horns. Carlyle, who'd never owned a car in his life, always felt smug at the sight of a jam. Why anyone drives anywhere in this city, he thought, is beyond me.

'Six thousand pounds' worth of damage to the mayor's official Daimler doesn't look like it's being sorted out.'

'I wouldn't have thought the son of a bus driver would want to be seen swanning about in a car like that,' Carlyle teased.

'He inherited it from his predecessor.'

'That doesn't mean he has to use it. Surely it's bad for his image.'

'What's bad for his image,' said Pearson, 'is a bunch of agitators dogging his every move, making him seem like the enemy.'

Whose enemy? 'They're your people,' Carlyle pointed out. 'But, look, Molly'll keep Jasper under control – no more harassment of the mayor – in exchange for a place on your new Trans Equality Commission.'

'How does she know about that?' Pearson scowled. 'It hasn't even been announced yet.'

'No idea, but she wants a job.'

'That's not going to happen,' Pearson declared. 'You were supposed to get these people off our back, not hand out rewards for their bad behaviour. Get a grip.'

Feeling his patience begin to unravel, Carlyle went on the offensive. 'There are more than eight million people in this city,' he snapped. 'We have crumbling infrastructure, a housing crisis, terrible air pollution and God knows what else, and what are you doing about it? Setting up a bloody commission to investigate a problem no one knew existed until five minutes ago and which no one cares about apart from a bunch of self-absorbed snow-flakes.' His voice had risen steadily, and they were beginning to get a few stares from nearby tables. Pausing, he dialled it down a couple of notches. '*You* get a grip. I'm doing my job, how about you do yours?'

Taken aback by his outburst, Pearson stared at the remains of her breakfast for several moments before muttering, 'I'll see what I can do.'

'Thank you.' On a roll, Carlyle slurped his coffee. 'While you're at it, there's something else you can help me with.'

Under the circumstances, Carlyle was happy enough to pick up the tab. As he was in the process of tapping his card against the waitress's device reader, he looked up to see a familiar figure approaching on the far side of the road from the direction of Trafalgar Square.

My next appointment. Pocketing the receipt, he settled back into his seat, waiting for Monica Seppi to take the seat recently vacated by Lottie Pearson. Organising back-to-back meetings had been a good idea. It was shaping up to be a productive morning.

The money he'd swiped from the police station was in a plastic supermarket bag at his feet. A quick handover under the table, avoiding the gaze of the café's CCTV, would rid him of Seppi for good.

The traffic had started moving. He watched Seppi join a gaggle of pedestrians hovering on the far kerb, next to the roadworks, waiting for the chance to cross. The drivers of the slow-moving vehicles showed no inclination to let anyone pass. Seppi tried to force the issue, stepping into the gutter, only to be forced back onto the pavement by an unyielding delivery vehicle.

You might be able to kill people with your bare hands, Carlyle thought, but you're no match for white-van man.

A lorry trundled past, obscuring his view. By the time it had passed, Seppi had disappeared. Trying to locate her, Carlyle became conscious of a crowd gathering around the hole. A couple were pointing at something inside, while one of the workmen tried to keep them back. Another workman stood in the middle of the road, stopping the traffic again, while making a phone call. Almost immediately, the sound of sirens rose out of the background hum. Sliding out of his seat, Carlyle went outside to investigate.

'Monica Seppi's dead?' Laura Nixon looked at him in disbelief.

'Someone slit her throat on Charing Cross Road.' Carlyle tried not to sound too happy about it. In truth, the murder was pretty convenient.

'And you saw it?'

'Not exactly.'

'Who did it?' the sergeant asked.

'No idea.'

'Did you give a statement?'

259

Not another bloody statement. 'I didn't see anything.' He closed the conversation before she could quiz him further. 'Look on the bright side. With Seppi gone, you can drop the original assault case.'

'That's one way of looking at it,' Nixon huffed, stalking off.

'It's the only way of looking at it,' Carlyle called after her. Retreating to the nearest gents toilet, he locked himself into a stall and transferred the stolen cash from the carrier bag back to his pockets. Down in the evidence room, he found a middle-aged civilian worker called Dave Richards reading the *Sun* and eating a bacon roll. Richards had a paper napkin tucked into the collar of his shirt and there was a large blob of brown sauce on his chin. Trying to hide his disapproval, Carlyle asked to see the seizures from the McVeigh Heights raid.

'The cash was taken to the bank this morning,' Richards reported dully, 'in line with our operating protocols.'

'Of course, yeah, sure.' Carlyle beat a hasty retreat. How was he going to return the stolen wad now?

Returning to the third floor, he found it deserted. Empty beer bottles from the impromptu party the night before had been left strewn about, along with the remains of a monster takeaway from the Indian restaurant on the Strand.

What a pigsty. Carlyle pitied the poor cleaners. It was shocking how people behaved when they felt someone else would clean up the mess. Opening a window, he tried to freshen the atmosphere a little.

Fretting about the mess gave him an idea. Stepping over to the desk at the centre of the chaos, he sat down and looked around, carefully considering his surroundings. To his right was a steel filing cabinet. On top of the cabinet stood a large banana plant. Together, they kept him hidden from the security camera hanging from the ceiling in the far corner of the room.

Calculating his actions were obscured, Carlyle surreptitiously slipped the cash from his pockets and dropped it onto the floor, nudging it with his toe under a pile of empty containers, a copy of last night's *Standard* and some half-eaten naan bread. Hopefully one of the cleaners would pocket the windfall and no one would be any the wiser.

'There you are. I was coming to find you.'

Carlyle swivelled in his chair to see Karen O'Sullivan walking towards him. Jumping to his feet, he moved smartly away from the desk.

'The boys had a bit of a result last night, I hear,' the inspector said, wrinkling her nose at the lingering smell of curry.

'Doesn't mean they couldn't tidy up after themselves,' Carlyle grumbled. 'Surely they wouldn't tolerate a mess like this in their own homes.'

O'Sullivan refrained from speculating about her colleagues' standards of domestic cleanliness. Instead, she announced, 'I had a chat with Corinne Fleming.' When the name didn't register, she added, 'Your wife's friend, the client of Bruno Soutine.'

'Ah, yes.' Helen's belated tip. 'Did she have anything interesting to say?'

'She didn't have anything on who might have killed him, but she went red as a beetroot when I asked her if they'd had sex.'

'Busted.'

'She said it was only a couple of times. According to her, Soutine advertised it as part of the service.'

'Advertised it?'

'Well, he made it clear it was an option, as a no-strings kind of thing. According to Ms Fleming, he claimed about ten per cent of his female clients took him up on it.'

Carlyle raised an eyebrow. 'How many clients did he have?'

'Eighty-two.'

'That's very precise.'

'Fleming goes to a small gym off Jermyn Street. I paid them

a visit. They knew all about Bruno Soutine. He even had a desk there, which is where I found his client list.' O'Sullivan pulled a pile of papers from her bag and handed them to the commander.

'Mostly women.'

'By my calculations, he was having it off with about half a dozen.'

Having it off. Not a phrase you heard much, these days. Carlyle's eyes darted up and down the list until something jumped out at him. 'Well, well.'

'A name you know?'

'A name I've heard of.' Carlyle gave the list back to O'Sullivan. 'Let me take it from here.'

Sitting outside Bar Italia was a good place to watch the world go by. Carlyle lingered over a double espresso before calling Colin Spooner.

The lawyer sounded hassled. 'I've been under the cosh – a Russian client who's having problems getting his British visa renewed. The Home Office is playing silly buggers with the paperwork.'

'They're pretty good at that, in my experience.' Carlyle wondered if he was off the hook with Jamie Worby. It would probably take a while for news of Monica Seppi's death to reach Immigration Enforcement.

'You'd have thought they had better things to do,' the lawyer griped. 'The client's stuck in Zurich. I've got to go and see him, try to sort it out.'

'There are worse places to be stuck,' Carlyle reflected.

'The Immigration Enforcement people seem to take a perverse pleasure in messing people about. It's like a perk of the job.'

Carlyle moved on to Esther Blake, the fund manager who'd lost millions of her clients' money. 'I need to speak to her urgently.'

Spooner's visa woes were instantly forgotten. 'Has there been a development in the Hitchcock case?' he asked.

Realising he'd disclosed too much, Carlyle backtracked. 'It's a question of tidying up loose ends.'

Taking the hint, the lawyer backed off. 'Fair enough. Hold on a sec and I'll dig it out.'

'Sure, no problem.' Carlyle waited patiently while the man sifted through his contacts.

'Here we go.' Spooner slowly recited a phone number and an email address.

'You wouldn't know where she lives?' Carlyle asked hopefully.

'No.' There was a pause. 'But I know where she works out. A place called TERR.'

'What?'

'T-E-R-R. Esther goes there pretty much every day. At least, she did when she was working at Kollision. A right gym bunny.' Spooner didn't make it sound like a compliment.

'Tim was always going on about how toned she was.'

'Was he fucking her?' The question slipped out without any thought behind it.

'Only in his dreams.' Spooner chuckled. 'He'd have been in there like a rat up a drainpipe, but Esther didn't stand for any nonsense in that regard. She was a crap fund manager, but she could look after herself.'

'Was she a crap fund manager?' Carlyle wondered. 'I can't work out whether she was a mug, a crook, or simply unlucky.'

'It comes down to the same thing in the end,' the lawyer theorised.

'Maybe.' Carlyle wasn't sure.

'Anyway, sorry, but I've got to run. Check out TERR. It's worth a punt, I'd have thought. Esther's bound to turn up there, sooner or later. I mean, if she's still looking for a job, what else has she got to do at the moment?'

TWENTY-FIVE

TERR was a ten-minute walk from the café. The reception area looked more like a high-end hotel than a gym. Standing at the front desk, Carlyle was conscious of lowering the tone as he watched a steady stream of well-heeled and well-maintained individuals wandering in and out.

Refusing to confirm or deny whether Esther Blake might be on the premises, the receptionist went off to speak to her manager. Watching her disappear through a door marked *STAFF ONLY*, Carlyle began casually thumbing through a brochure, as if he could afford membership. Predictably, the booklet didn't contain any prices. He did, however, learn that TERR stood for Train, Eat, Recover, Repeat.

A fairly boring existence. Carlyle felt the carefully constructed smugness of a man who hadn't done any training himself for far too long.

'Are you the policeman?'

'Huh?' He looked up to see a fresh-faced, tanned young woman standing in front of him, ready for her workout, with a small towel draped round her neck.

'Esther Blake.'

'If you could give me five minutes, I'd appreciate it.'

'I can give you as long as you want.' Blake led him towards a cluster of comfortable-looking armchairs. 'Given I'm not gainfully employed at the present time.'

Carlyle handed her a card. 'I heard you left Kollision.'

'Nothing to do with Tim falling out of the window.' She giggled. 'That was just karma.' Once they had settled in a quiet corner, she said, 'I'm guessing what you *really* want to talk about is Bruno Soutine. The question is which one?'

Carlyle hadn't expected the woman to be so up front. 'Both.'

'Aha. I see the police are making some progress with their enquiries.'

'We might have made more if you'd come forward off your own bat.'

Blake took no offence. 'I've been away. I needed a break, you know?'

Carlyle was vaguely sympathetic.

'How did you find me, anyway?'

'I was told this was your gym. I took a punt you might be here.'

'Very good.' Blake mimed giving him some applause. 'This place is my home from home. It costs a fortune, so I might as well get my money's worth. If I didn't come at least once every day, I think my head would probably explode with all the stress.'

At least once a day? Bloody hell. 'Why did Hitchcock fire you?'

'He didn't fire me. I quit.'

Whatever. 'You fell out over the tokens investment.'

'Hardly. Tim *loved* it. He thought the timing was perfect and he was tickled by the idea of cryptocurrency for porn. Cyberwanking he called it.'

'It was risky, though?'

'Not specially,' she replied briskly. 'We got in at the ground floor and there was a clear window to make an excellent return. The thing gets hyped, millions of ordinary punters pile in behind us, pushing up the price of the stock and giving us a very profitable exit.'

'Regardless of the ultimate success or failure of the scheme.'

'Exactly. By the time ASTs have taken off – or crashed and burnt – we'd be long out of it.'

'*Caveat emptor.*'

'You got it. Not exactly an investment for widows and orphans but, like your visit here, worth a punt.'

'Except your scam was derailed when the money was stolen.'

'It wasn't a scam.' Blake sounded irked. 'And the money wasn't stolen.'

'Where is it, then?'

'The company we invested in, CA Holding Corporation, is in an investment phase. When you're in an investment phase, money gets spent.'

'CA as in Consensual Acts, the name of the website?'

'Right.'

'And what did the money get spent on?'

'The usual stuff – salaries, IT, marketing, advisers.'

That doesn't tell me much. Carlyle changed tack. 'Tim Hitchcock said he thought the money had been stolen. Sandringham Risk Consulting thought so too, which was why they sued Kollision.'

'They got cold feet,' Blake claimed. 'It happens. People make an investment and then they change their minds. Well, too bad. You make a decision, you've got to own it. Consensual Acts was – still is, as far as I know – registered as a corporation in the Cayman Islands. It has an office and the required infrastructure.'

'If it's all above board,' Carlyle wondered, 'why does the owner hide behind a fake name stolen from your personal trainer?'

'It added to the mystery of the project. People love the cloak-and-dagger stuff. SRC were gagging for it, believe me. They couldn't hand their cash over quick enough.'

Carlyle was less than convinced. He moved on. 'Why use the name Bruno Soutine?'

'That was my fault,' Blake admitted. 'I mentioned I was using this great trainer and Brad liked the name.'

'Brad?'

'The Consensual Acts guy. And before you ask, that's not his real name, either. I knew him as Brad Smith . . . like that's not fake, right?'

'But how could you deal with people when you didn't know who they were?' Carlyle didn't understand it.

'That's just part of the game.'

'Sounds crazy to me.'

'It's like any game. It only makes sense in a certain context.'

Esther Blake was clearly a major-league bullshitter. Trying to reorder his thoughts, Carlyle shifted in his seat. 'You were playing the game.'

'Yep.'

'And Bruno Soutine was collateral damage . . . Then Tim Hitchcock kills himself.'

'Tim didn't jump,' Blake said. 'He was pushed.'

'You know that for a fact?'

She shook her head. 'Just an educated guess.'

'Who pushed him?'

'The same guy who killed Bruno Soutine.'

'And who's that?'

'Haven't you worked it out yet?'

I haven't got a fucking clue. Carlyle tried to keep his cool. 'If I knew who it was, I wouldn't be asking the question.'

'Fair point.' Blake jumped to her feet. 'I need to go hit some things and get my heart rate up. See if you can work it out before I get back.'

Esther Blake reappeared, sipping from a small bottle of water, towel still round her neck, having hardly broken sweat. She dropped into the chair next to him. 'Worked it out yet?'

267

'No.' After idling away an hour on his phone, Carlyle still had no idea.

'I'm disappointed,' she teased. 'I'd have thought it was pretty obvious.'

Carlyle refused to be riled. 'Sadly not.'

'You need to think it through.'

'Not when you can tell me.'

But Blake was determined to spin it out. She put the cap on her water bottle. 'How did you find me?'

'I told you, I took a punt.'

'I know, but *who* told you where to look?'

'Colin Spooner. He told me you worked out here every day when you were at Kollision.'

'And Colin is?'

'Tim Hitchcock's lawyer.'

'What else?'

'I don't know,' Carlyle said, exasperated. 'A man who . . . likes a pint?'

Blake smiled, squeezing out a few more seconds before her big reveal. 'Colin,' she said finally, 'was – is, I dunno – the boy-friend of a guy called Patrick Dalby.'

Carlyle's head started to swim. 'What?'

Blake's amusement seemed to grow in proportion to the policeman's discomfort. 'You've heard of Patrick Dalby, right?'

Carlyle took a couple of deep breaths. 'Oh, yes, I've heard of him.'

'He's a very dangerous man.'

'I know that.'

'He attacked me once.' Blake's tone was matter of fact. 'Needless to say, he didn't get very far.' She nodded towards the gym. 'The kickboxing came in very handy.'

'I didn't realise he was bisexual.'

'Patrick would fuck anything,' was Blake's verdict. 'The guy's a complete user. When it came to Colin, the relationship was really just a way to keep an eye on what was going on at Kollision.'

Carlyle was confused. 'Why would he need Spooner for that?' he wondered. 'I thought Dalby and Hitchcock were mates from way back, at university?'

'They were at university together,' Blake acknowledged, 'but I don't know how close they were. I'm not sure Patrick's ever had a genuine relationship with anyone in his life.'

Carlyle conceded the point.

'Colin definitely was a lot closer to Tim, professionally speaking, than Patrick was,' Blake continued. 'Remember, Tim was supposed to be the guy who could make Patrick rich – richer than his sister, no less. Patrick wanted to keep tabs on him 24/7.'

'So Colin was Patrick's spy in the office?'

'You can imagine the pillow talk.'

Carlyle preferred not to. 'Did Patrick get on with his sister?' It was a question he should have asked before now.

'He was incredibly focused on competing with Victoria. Ironically, I'm not sure she even noticed. She was too busy dealing with her own shit.'

'There was certainly enough of that.'

'I met Victoria a couple of times when we were trying to get her to invest with Kollision. I liked her – she seemed comfortable in her own skin. But, then, what do I know? Patrick said she was married to a gangster.'

'He was a pimp,' Carlyle nitpicked.

'He died, too, right?'

'Unlucky family.'

'Yeah, well, Patrick didn't like the brother-in-law. Mind you, Patrick didn't like anyone much. He was obsessed with getting rich quick. That was why he piled into ASTs.'

'I thought the money you put into Adult Service Tokens was SRC's?'

'Mostly. A bunch of other' – Blake wiggled her fingers in the air to signify quotation marks – '"favoured investors" were allowed to pile in as well. In the end, Kollision invested – *I* invested – more than ten million of clients' money, including SRC's six.'

'Jeez.' Carlyle tried to imagine how he'd feel blowing ten million quid on fictitious wank tokens.

'Tim liked to make out I was throwing other people's cash around like a drunken fool, but I was instructed to do it. Cryptocurrencies were super-hot – Bitcoin was heading for the stars and everyone got gold fever. At one point, Patrick was ringing me like a dozen times a day – *Have you put me in yet? Am I fully invested?* All the bloody time.'

'Isn't investing in Adult Service Tokens different from putting your money in Bitcoin? I mean, even I'd heard of Bitcoin. Surely it's a bit more established than something dreamed up by a guy called Brad Smith.'

'The punters were desperate to get into *anything.* They didn't care what it was supposed to be bankrolling – porn, drugs, arms . . . dog biscuits – it didn't matter. They thought it was a one-way bet. Tim didn't put in his own money, though, which tells its own story.'

'Did you put money in?'

'Absolutely not.' Blake looked affronted by the suggestion. 'Far too risky. I have to earn my money. I look after it.'

'You told investors it would come off.'

'It *might* come off – and even if it didn't you could make money in the meantime – but the risk was high. You had to have nerves of steel. Either that, or you could afford to lose your cash without a second thought. Like I told you, SRC went in willingly, then got cold feet. Everyone was a grown-up.'

'Including Dalby?'

Blake smiled. 'Patrick seemed to think he'd pony up some

cash and be a billionaire within a week. He got very angry when it didn't happen.'

'How much did he lose?'

'A couple of mill.'

'Ouch.'

'At the same time, I heard some charity was trying to screw him out of his sister's estate. That was what *really* pushed him over the edge, I think.'

Carlyle said nothing.

'To be honest, I can understand it. Imagine some bloody do-gooder comes along and nicks your family's money.'

Time to recap. 'What you're telling me is Patrick got his lover – Colin Spooner – to kill Hitchcock?'

'Well done. You got there in the end.' Blake wiped an imaginary bead of sweat from her brow with her towel. 'Happily, Patrick blamed Tim for the ASTs fiasco, not me. Otherwise it might've been my death you were investigating.'

'And Bruno Soutine?'

'Ah, yes, poor old Bruno.' Blake's face clouded, but only for a moment. 'Not much in bed but a good trainer.' She patted her leg. 'Great for my thighs.'

Carlyle didn't pass comment. Instead he asked, 'Patrick got Colin to kill him too?' He was mortified that the lawyer had taken him for a fool.

Blake nodded. 'Patrick was pissed off I was sleeping with Bruno and not with him.'

Carlyle thought about the poor sap with the plastic bag over his head. 'It wasn't about the money at all, then?'

'Sexual jealousy, pure and simple. Colin *thought* it was about the money, though. Patrick spun him a line about the real Soutine and the fake Soutine being one and the same, a kind of double bluff, if you like.'

'The whole thing sounds totally crazy.'

271

'Patrick *is* crazy.'

'Colin Spooner isn't.' Carlyle's thoughts turned towards getting a conviction.

'His defence would be temporary insanity, I'd imagine. Colin took a punt on ASTs, too. Not as much as Patrick but, again, money he couldn't afford to lose. He started drinking heavily and I think he was going to lose his job.'

Carlyle thought back to one of his earlier conversations with the lawyer. 'He said they'd promoted him.'

'I'd check that, if I were you.'

'It's on my to-do list.' Carlyle felt embarrassed at his basic oversight. 'This theory of yours—'

'It's not a theory, Commander. Patrick, sicko that he is, rang me up to boast about it. Thought it made him some gangster type, like his brother-in-law.'

'The brother-in-law was a pimp,' Carlyle repeated.

'Detail was never Patrick's strong point.'

'But Colin's a lawyer. How could he be so stupid as to get involved in this?'

Blake burst out laughing.

'Sorry, dumb question.'

'People do silly things for love.'

'Not many commit a double murder.'

'I always thought Colin lacked emotional intelligence. In my experience, it's often true of professionals. Give them a narrow set of tasks to do and they're fine, but it doesn't make them properly functioning human beings.'

Once Spooner was behind bars, there would be plenty of shrinks to try to work out what was going on in the guy's head. Carlyle tried a different tack. 'Why would Spooner put me on to you, if you could tell me all this?'

'Because he doesn't think he's going to get caught.'

A pained expression settled on Carlyle's face as he thought

272

back to Spooner's Russian client and his supposed visa problems. 'He said he was going to Zurich.'

'And you believed him?'

'Well . . .'

'I'll bet you anything he's chasing after Patrick.'

'Who was last heard of in Mexico.' Carlyle stifled a curse. 'I'm going to need a formal statement.'

'No way.' Blake's mood darkened. 'It's one thing getting all this off my chest but I'm not going to be involved publicly. I can't have any of this nonsense hanging over me.' When Carlyle started to protest, she talked over him. 'It would kill my chances of getting another job stone dead. My reputation would be completely trashed. I'd always be the woman who lost clients' money and got her boss killed into the bargain.'

Carlyle could see her point.

'And for what?' she continued, getting more angry as the words spilled out. 'What good would it do? It won't bring Tim back from the dead. Or Bruno, for that matter.'

'What about the money?'

'What about it?' She waved the water bottle at him. 'It's only money.'

'Other people's money.'

Blake looked him straight in the eye. 'That's the only kind you should ever gamble with.'

TWENTY-SIX

'Have you signed your statement about the riot in Umberto's restaurant yet?' Laura Nixon asked, more in hope than expectation.

'It was hardly a riot.' Carlyle made a half-hearted sweep of his desk before admitting, 'I'm not *entirely* sure where I put it.'

The sergeant let out a deep sigh. 'I'll print you off another copy.'

'Thanks.'

'It looks like things have been overtaken by events, anyway. They reckon they caught the guy who cut Monica Seppi's throat on CCTV. Haven't been able to identify him, though.'

'Big surprise,' Carlyle grunted. 'He's probably back in Slovakia by now. Or wherever.'

'Rita Vicedo told me her real name was Zuzana Klek.'

'Maybe.' Carlyle no longer had much interest in the tale. 'She had lots of aliases.'

'She's still pissed off with you, you know.'

'Seppi?' Carlyle chuckled. 'From beyond the grave?'

Nixon shook her head. 'Rita ... You'll have to make it up to her.'

Carlyle was unmoved. It would take a while longer for him to get over his own irritation with the crusading nun.

The sergeant moved on: 'Zuzana Klek hasn't been formally identified yet. D'you want me to sort it out?'

Carlyle thought about it for a moment. 'Nah,' he decided. 'Let the Home Office or the Security Service deal with it. Not our problem.'

Nixon looked at him doubtfully. 'Are you sure?'

'This started out as a routine assault case and blew up into ... well, God knows what. Let's cut our losses and put it down to experience.' Jamie Worby and his Immigration Enforcement goons could run around chasing a dead woman, if they so wished. Hopefully, they would have less time to hassle people who were still alive as a result.

'You're the boss.' Nixon didn't sound very happy about it. She took her leave.

'Correct,' Carlyle muttered, as he sifted through a pile of papers, 'I'm the boss. The big fucking boss. He who must be obeyed. Or not.'

'What?'

Blushing slightly, Carlyle looked up to see Charlie Kearns, leader of the McVeigh Heights raid, standing in the doorway. 'Nothing.' He invited the inspector to take a seat.

Kearns slumped into a chair and ran a hand over his stubbled head. He had dark rings under his bloodshot eyes and looked rather the worse for wear.

'More partying?' Carlyle was beginning to wonder if there was a drinking culture at Charing Cross. He thought about writing another memo: *The Dangers of the Demon Drink*. Surely, these days, people didn't need to be told how to behave.

'It was one of the guys' birthday,' Kearns explained. 'We made a night of it. Ended up in Kane's Garden.'

Carlyle was aware of the grubby strip club on Parker Street. 'That used to be Everton's.'

'Did it?' Kearns couldn't look any less interested. 'Before my time.'

'I guess it would be.'

'It's a good place to go.'

I'm not sure our female colleagues would agree. Carlyle was relieved Karen O'Sullivan wasn't listening to this conversation.

'Helps with bonding, which is more important than ever, what with the cuts an' everything.'

Thecutznivryfink.

'Yeah.' Carlyle was unconvinced.

Small talk over, Kearns pulled a familiar mass of banknotes from his jacket pockets. Leaning out of his chair, he tossed the cash onto the commander's desk.

Carlyle considered the money, said nothing.

'One of the cleaning crew handed it in downstairs,' the inspector explained. 'They found it in the squad room.'

'Bloody hell.' Why did people have to be so honest? Carlyle cursed the cleaner for not keeping the cash he'd dropped under the desk. 'Good they didn't pocket it.'

'They're a decent bunch.' Kearns rubbed the stubble on his chin. 'There's fifteen grand there.'

More like seventeen. Carlyle said nothing.

'It's from the McVeigh Heights raid.'

'Is it?'

'Where else would it be from?'

'But I took the bags down to the lockers.' Carlyle thrust out his lower lip in contemplation. 'You saw me.'

'You must have dropped it.' Kearns eyed his superior with more than a little suspicion.

'Are you sure? You'd have thought somebody would've noticed at the time.'

'We were all half-cut,' Kearns admitted, 'or, at least, well on the way to being half-cut.'

You weren't that pissed, Carlyle thought. The inspector's fishing irritated him.

'How could it end up on the floor?' Kearns wondered.

'You tell me.'

For a few moments, the two men glowered at each other, until Kearns turned to the question that was really troubling him. He nodded at the cash. 'What are we going to do with it?'

Carlyle frowned, playing dumb. 'Whaddya mean?'

'The money we impounded has already been logged and banked.'

This was exactly the situation Carlyle had been trying to avoid. He cursed the all-too-honest cleaner for a second time. 'How much went to the bank?'

'It doesn't matter what the number is,' Kearns sniffed, 'as long as it's the official number and it doesn't change. If we turn up with more cash now – cash left lying around on the floor, for Chrissake – then we're gonna look pretty stupid, if not a little bit bent. There'll have to be an external review. All the evidence from McVeigh Heights will need to be re-examined. The CPS will have to be informed. The chain of custody will become an issue and—'

Carlyle held up a hand to stop the man before he worked himself into a complete frenzy. 'McVeigh Heights was proper police work. You and your team did a good job.'

Kearns seemed unsure whether it was a statement or a question.

Carlyle grabbed a handful of notes and waved them in the air. 'And this cash is essentially untraceable, right?'

They were getting down to the sharp end of things. Beads of sweat appeared on Kearns's brow. He wiped them away with the sleeve of his coat. 'How d'ya mean?'

'Could someone query the official figure?' Carlyle asked. 'Claim we lost some?'

'Lost' meaning 'nicked'.

Kearns looked unsure. 'Who are we talking about? The people we nicked in the flat at McVeigh Heights? Or just anyone?'

'Primarily the people who were nicked.'

'Well, they claim they know nothing about anything, so how would they know how much cash we found?'

'Right. So that's them sorted. What about anyone else?'

'What about them?' Kearns looked pained, like he was in the witness box facing hostile questioning from an aggressive defence lawyer.

Carlyle tossed the cash onto his desk and tried again. 'Could anyone – anyone at all – actually *prove* money's gone missing?'

'No, I don't think so.' Kearns slowly climbed off the fence. 'I can't see how.'

'So we have deniability.' Sitting back in his chair, Carlyle steepled his fingers together. 'Even if the finger was pointed at us.'

'We have deniability,' Kearns agreed.

'And we're gonna get a conviction on McVeigh Heights.'

'Definitely.' Kearns turned bullish. 'We're gonna get a result, no doubt at all.'

'And when we do, the cash in the bank will be confiscated under the Proceeds of Crime Act and it won't matter to its former owners.'

Kearns's gaze returned to the notes on the desk. 'What about *that* cash?'

Carlyle stroked his chin. 'Let's give it to charity.'

'The Combined Benevolent Fund?' The inspector's expression was hard to read. Perhaps it was relief, relief that his superior wasn't suggesting they keep the cash. Equally, it might have been disappointment at seeing such a sum slip through his fingers.

'I had something else in mind.'

'Yes?'

'An anonymous donation to a bona fide charity that the Met works with on a regular basis.' Carlyle scooped up the cash and dropped it into a desk drawer. 'I'll make sure it finds a good home and we'll say no more about it.'

Kearns remained less than ecstatic. 'If you're sure it's the best way forward.'

Carlyle counted off the pluses on his fingers. 'We avoid the paperwork. The McVeigh Heights case doesn't become a car crash. The cash goes to a good cause. And *you* avoid getting clobbered for losing it in the first place.'

'But I didn't lose it,' Kearns protested.

Carlyle stared him down.

'All right,' the inspector agreed. 'We'll go with your plan.'

Another day, another speech: 'We have to accept that there is a widespread groundswell of opinion that supports a hostile environment for illegal immigrants. That might create problems, certainly in terms of the way that individual cases are handled. But, at the same time, the Home Office has a job to do. We have to recognise that – it is the reality of the Britain we live in today. Politics is the art of the possible. We have to work within the framework we find ourselves in, while retaining our humanity.'

As Joe Stanley stepped down from the platform, Lottie Pearson ushered him in the direction of the commander.

'Interesting speech,' Carlyle lied.

'Nice of you to say so.' The mayor offered him a perfunctory handshake.

'I wrote it.' Pearson beamed.

Another aide appeared and whispered something in the mayor's ear.

'I'll be right there,' Stanley replied. 'Give me one minute.'

'I'll let them know.' The aide made for the nearest exit.

'It never stops.' The mayor gave Carlyle a weak smile.

'Like Groundhog Day,' Carlyle suggested.

'Yeah. But, look, I wanted to thank you personally for sorting out the little problem we discussed.'

'Erm, my pleasure.' Carlyle looked at Pearson.

'I appreciate your help.' The mayor was already walking away.

'What about the thing you were going to do for me?' Carlyle called after him.

The man didn't stop walking.

'That's been sorted, too,' Pearson assured him. 'The mayor spoke to the chief executive of the Corporation of London about the Hampstead ladies' pond and he agreed to put changes to the admissions policy on the back-burner. Plans to open up the women-only pond to men who self-identify as women will not be progressed for the next couple of years.' When Carlyle started to protest that the can had just been kicked down the road a bit, she quickly added, 'That really was the best we could get. The Corporation doesn't like being told what to do by the mayor or anyone else and we have no power to force them to take any particular course of action. I listened in to the conversation and, trust me, it was robust.'

'Hm.'

'I also got Molly Arnold to endorse the move. If there's any pushback in the media, she's given us a supportive quote to use.'

Carlyle tried to be positive. 'I'm pleased Jasper's girlfriend is turning into a useful ally.'

'We announced the Trans Equality Commission last week. Molly's on it.'

'Everyone has their price.'

'Given it carries a stipend of five thousand a month, plus expenses, I'd say she drove a hard bargain.'

'So long as she keeps her hopeless boyfriend under control.'

'Yes, well, there's good news and bad news on that front.'

Carlyle was always a man to have the bad news first.

'The bad news is Molly dumped Jasper. I think it happened about five minutes after the commission was announced.'

'Bollocks.' Carlyle wondered how they would resolve the Jasper problem now. 'Surely that invalidates the deal.'

Pearson disagreed. 'I like Molly. So does the mayor. We think she'll do a good job. She'll play the game.'

'You mean she wants to climb the greasy pole.'

'She's ambitious. What's wrong with that?'

'She reneged on your deal,' Carlyle countered. 'You can't ignore that, or she'll always have you over a barrel.'

'I think I can handle Molly,' Pearson said. 'Plus, you haven't heard the good news yet.'

'Go on, then, what's the good news?'

'Young Jasper took the break-up very badly.'

'Well, you would. No one likes being dumped.'

'His way of dealing with it was to jump on a plane and head for Thailand. His mother told Molly he's gone travelling for at least a year.'

'Result.'

'With a bit of luck, he won't be back this side of the next election.'

'Shame he didn't take his mum with him.'

'Molly says that might happen yet. Jasper's parents have split up. The family seems to be falling apart.'

'Couldn't happen to a nicer bunch.'

Leaving City Hall, Carlyle called Emily Quartz and updated her on the swimming pond. Like Carlyle, the journalist took a moment to get over her initial disappointment and focus on the positives. 'I suppose it's better than nothing.'

'At least it gives the Ladies in Charge time to plan their next move,' Carlyle suggested.

'I'm sure they'll be grateful for your help.'

'They need to take control of the situation and come up with a useful compromise,' Carlyle replied. 'And avoid getting arrested in the meantime.'

TWENTY-SEVEN

The black plastic urn looked like an outsized reusable coffee cup. Carlyle watched Laura Nixon ceremonially place it on his desk. 'What's that?'

'The ashes of Monica Seppi.' The sergeant took a seat. 'Or, rather, Zuzana Klek. Or, rather, Angela Luther. Luther's the name on the death certificate.'

Hardly matters now, Carlyle thought. 'When did they cremate her?'

'Last week,' Nixon confirmed. 'I picked her up this morning.'

'Why?'

'Common sense,' the sergeant reasoned. 'We don't want the woman's remains left lying around, in case somebody starts digging into who she really was.'

'There can't be much chance of that.' Carlyle crossed his fingers. 'What are you going to do with them?'

'I thought you might want them,' Nixon gave him a sickly smile. 'A memento of one of your more bizarre cases.'

'I'm not likely to forget.' He waved away the idea, but the sergeant had jumped from her chair and was already halfway through the door. 'You can't leave them here,' Carlyle called after her, but it was too late. Nixon had made good her escape.

For fuck's sake. Carlyle glowered at the urn. 'You're still a fucking pain in the arse,' he hissed at the dead woman's remains.

After issuing a few more curses, he lifted his head and redirected his ire.

'Joaquin . . . JOAQUIN.'

The PA appeared in the doorway.

Carlyle pointed at the urn. 'Get rid of that for me, will you?'

'No way.' Crossing himself, Joaquin took a step backwards, muttering, in Spanish, something that might have been a prayer.

'For God's sake,' Carlyle wailed, 'you're no more religious than I am. Take it away.'

Joaquin was unmoved by his pleas. 'Dealing with dead people isn't in my job description.' He edged out of the room. 'And, anyway, I need to get going. If I'm not careful, I'll be late for my rollerblading.'

Wandering through the Wenger Ward, Nixon was approached by a nurse sporting the name badge Anna Meronk.

'You looking for Dr Brady?'

'That's right.'

Grinning, the nurse lowered her voice. 'Here to arrest him?'

'No,' the sergeant frowned. 'Why?'

'The stupid sod's gone and done it this time.'

Done what? Nixon had planned to bring Brady up to speed on the Monica Seppi saga. Instead, it seemed she was being dragged into an entirely different soap opera.

'You missed the excitement.' The nurse pointed towards an exit. 'Declan was marched off the premises by Security about an hour ago. He got into a big argument with the relatives of a patient and ended up thumping some bloke. Patient Liaison'll have him out on his ear for that.'

'I see.' Nixon stared at an empty bed, unsure what to do next.

'If you want to go and commiserate,' the nurse suggested, 'you'll find him in Romanov's, just out the front entrance and left.'

'I know it.' Nixon had gone there with Declan Brady, hours after Seppi had wandered into A and E. That was a barely a week ago, but it felt like a year, or more.

A phone began ringing at the duty station. The nurse turned away to answer it. 'I'm sure he'd appreciate the company.'

'The guy called me a stupid Irish bastard and I lost it, gave him a couple of smacks.' Brady gesticulated over the remains of his all-day breakfast. 'I was knackered. My blood sugar was too low. I hadn't eaten anything for more than six hours.'

The doctor was tense, jittery. He knows he fucked up, Nixon thought, big-time. She noted several red marks on his face. 'Looks like you took a few blows yourself.'

'I held my own.' The doctor took a slurp of coffee. 'It wasn't a big deal. The family wasn't happy with the treatment their dad was getting – which was first class, by the way – and things got a bit heated. Happens pretty regularly. Then this one bloke – dunno precisely who he was – started giving me grief and it all kicked off.'

'Who threw the first punch?'

Brady's eyes narrowed. 'Are you questioning me, Officer?'

'I'm trying to work out how much trouble you're in.'

'More than enough.'

'Maybe it'll blow over,' Nixon said hopefully. 'Maybe the family won't make a complaint.'

'Are you serious?' The doctor pushed away his empty plate. 'People complain all the time – if you haven't had a shave or changed your shirt, or the fact Grandpa – who's ninety-two and has no quality of life anyway – can't have the latest wonder drug they've read about on the internet. The fact that it hasn't been licensed for use yet, or that it costs a million quid a dose, is irrelevant. They've paid their taxes – or not – and they're *entitled*.'

You sound like a burnout victim, Nixon thought. Maybe walking away is for the best.

'In a case like this, the family'll pile in, looking for compo. The guy I hit was already talking about needing X-rays. I'd be surprised if he isn't demanding a bed in intensive care by now.'

'Did you hurt him?'

'It was a bit of handbags, no more. If it happened on a football pitch, you'd get a yellow card, at worst.' Brady scratched his head. 'Maybe a red, if the ref was a total wanker. But, even then, you'd only get a three-match ban. Probably.'

'But you were racially abused.'

'It's always the one who retaliates who gets punished. PALS must have its pound of flesh.' Brady patted his stomach. 'Although in my case they'll get rather more.'

Nixon realised she hadn't noticed the padding before. She shivered to recall her initial attraction to the guy. Such a lack of judgement was intensely worrying. 'What'll you do now?' she asked.

'Go home and have a long kip. Then I might think about signing up at my local gym.'

Might not be a bad idea. 'What about longer-term?'

'Missionary work? Flipping burgers? There's a broad range of intriguing possibilities.'

'Seriously.'

'Seriously?' Brady's face darkened. 'Well, my doctoring days are over. I might sign up for a creative-writing course – I'll have time to write my book, now – but, beyond that, I don't know.'

Nixon feigned interest.

'Doctors' misery memoirs are all the rage. The world and his wife's lapping up horror stories from the front line of the NHS. And I've got good stories to tell.' Brady jerked a thumb in the general direction of the hospital. 'Even my sacking can be turned into an amusing anecdote.' He gave her the working title: '"Pills, Thrills and Bellyaches" – good name, dontcha think?'

'The Happy Mondays.'

'Chapeau.' He mimed lifting his hat. 'Very good.'

'They were *way* before my time. My dad might have had one of their albums, back in the day.'

'Whether you get the gag or not, it's still a good title – grabs your attention.'

Nixon tried to think back to anything she might have let slip in her previous conversations with the budding scribe. 'Don't you have to sign an NDA in the NHS?'

'They can only sack me the once. Anyway, all names will be changed to protect the guilty.'

'Hm.'

'Enough about me, though, what did you want to talk about?'

'I wondered how things were going.'

'The woman who wandered into A and E in her undies and was nicked by the Immigration Nazis. Whatever happened to her?'

'No idea.' Nixon wasn't going there, not with Brady planning his book. If the tale were told, Monica Seppi would probably get a chapter all to herself. 'We looked but we never found her.'

'Lost in the system, no doubt.' Brady sighed. 'Another hapless victim of this bastard government's Hostile Environment policy.'

Congratulations. You have been awarded a complimentary trip to TERR. Terms and conditions apply.

'Hm.' Carlyle wasn't sure he would feel comfortable surrounded by all those beautiful people. Still, it was nice of Esther Blake to send him a free gym pass. In the email, she had also pasted a link to a newspaper article from the *Vancouver Sun*. Under the headline *Cryptocurrency Guru Caught by Cops*, the story explained how local police had arrested Consensual Acts founder Bradley Smith – 'a.k.a. Bruno Soutine' – on suspicion of fraud, tax evasion and 'various other alleged offences'.

Apparently Brad Smith was the guy's real name. There was no mention of any cash being recovered.

'Hopefully that should wrap things up.' He handed the phone to Karen O'Sullivan, who read the piece carefully.

'Want me to get in touch with our Canadian colleagues?' The inspector handed back the phone.

'Nah. We should let sleeping dogs lie.' Carlyle shivered at the thought of all the extra-territorial paperwork. 'If the Mounties haven't got enough to put Mr Smith behind bars, we certainly don't.'

O'Sullivan looked vaguely disappointed. 'He did steal Bruno Soutine's identity,' she reminded him.

'Which is no great loss to the poor sod,' Carlyle mused, 'given he's dead. And Brad Smith had nothing to do with the murder.' Without revealing his sources, he added, 'Patrick Dalby put Colin Spooner up to it, not that I'd want to have to prove that in court.'

'How do you want me to write up Bruno Soutine's death?' O'Sullivan asked. 'The file's still open.'

'Keep it short and sweet. The coroner can deliver the official verdict.' Carlyle scanned the squad room. 'Where's Nixon?' He had lost the latest copy of the statement he was supposed to sign following the restaurant fracas and needed the sergeant to give him another one.

'She's gone to visit a safe house.' O'Sullivan mentioned one of the International Network Against Human Trafficking's shelters in Mornington Crescent. 'There's a woman who took a pretty bad beating. Laura's trying to get her to make a complaint.'

'Let her know I was looking for her.'

'Will do.' O'Sullivan went back to whatever she was working on. Carlyle headed upstairs. Joaquin, as usual, was nowhere to be seen. The commander wandered into his office to find an unwelcome guest waiting for him.

'An unannounced visit.' Jamie Worby did not get out of his chair. 'I wanted to see what progress you've made in your search for Monica Seppi.'

Carlyle considered the urn, still sitting on his desk. 'Well,' he sighed, 'we're still looking but the woman seems to have vanished.'

'She's wanted for murder. I would have hoped your people might have made more of an effort.'

'I don't want to turn your hopes to ashes,' Carlyle bit his lower lip, 'but I think the trail is pretty dead.'

'Are you telling me you've given up?' Worby seemed genuinely outraged at his lack of zeal.

'I can assure you my officers are making every possible effort,' Carlyle lifted his hands to the heavens, 'but, unfortunately, sometimes . . .'

'Sometimes what?' Worby snapped. 'What're the odds you'll find her?'

Carlyle refused to be drawn. 'I try to be hopeful but realistic.'

Worby's gaze fell on the urn. 'Isn't it a bit morbid having that on your desk?'

'A pet,' Carlyle improvised. 'I need to take it home, but not too soon. Tiddles was a much-loved member of the family and emotions are still a bit raw.'

'Tiddles?' Worby made a face. 'That's not a very original name for a cat, is it?'

'We went for a classic moniker.'

'What did it die of?'

'Erm, cancer. Very sad. The vet did all he could. Cost a fortune.'

'Tell me about it,' Worby harrumphed. 'The amount my wife spends on her bloody dog – makes your eyes water.'

'Still, Tiddles had a good life.' Carlyle just managed to stop short of crossing himself.

'Anyway, that's not why I'm here, to talk about dead cats.' Worby pulled a sheet of paper from his jacket pocket and placed it on Carlyle's desk. 'Sixty-one names. Alleged victims of crime who, it transpires, do not have leave to stay in the UK.'

'Hm.'

'We need to pluck as much of the low-hanging fruit as we can, as quickly as we can. There are quotas to meet, deadlines to hit.'

'I can imagine.'

'Which is why we need the cooperation of all state agencies, including yours. The Home Office is currently waiting for the Metropolitan Police to hand over these sixty-one individuals so they can be processed and deported as quickly as possible. The list excludes Monica Seppi – I left her off to spare your blushes.'

To spare your own blushes, more like. Carlyle remained quiet.

'According to the data, the Met is the English police authority with the biggest number of illegals and the worst record in handing them over to Immigration Enforcement.'

'Doesn't surprise me,' Carlyle grunted.

'I need you to sort it out.'

'I'll certainly try my best.'

Apparently mollified by the commander's words, Worby offered an olive branch. 'We started off on the wrong foot, but I'm not one to bear grudges – I'm a bigger man than that, and I hope you are too. It's important to see the big picture. We must work together. I don't know what you were playing at with the Monica Seppi thing but, in my book, everyone deserves a second chance.' He gestured at the list. 'Get me those illegals, soon, and we can recalibrate our relationship. Do a good job on this and you can become my go-to guy here in London.'

Once the man had gone, Carlyle picked up the sheet and tore it into little pieces. Stalking into Joaquin's still empty office, he shoved the shreds into a waste bin for confidential material. 'Go-to guy, my arse.'

In a gloomy bar off the Edgware Road, a tired-looking Rita Vicedo weighed the envelope in her hand, trying to estimate the value of the cash inside.

'Where did this come from?'

'Think of it as a gift . . .' Carlyle almost said 'from God' but stopped himself just in time. 'You can take it from me, it hasn't been stolen. No one will miss it.'

The nun gave him a suspicious look. 'It's clean?'

He took a mouthful of Jameson's. 'It's money in need of a home.'

'The International Network Against Human Trafficking has clear protocols about accepting donations.' Her tone was bordering on hostile. She placed the envelope on the table. 'We don't take money from just anyone.'

Carlyle took a deep breath. 'You took Karol Lacko's cash,' he pointed out, finishing his drink. 'Or, rather, Monica Seppi's.'

'Zuzana Klek.' Muttering a prayer, the nun crossed herself. 'A poor, tortured soul. May she rest in peace.'

Carlyle said nothing.

Vicedo tapped the envelope with a finger. 'This was her money also?'

'That was the money I was planning to give to her,' Carlyle admitted, 'to make up for the previous donation, which she wasn't too happy about.'

'But where did you get it in the first place?'

Admitting defeat, Carlyle confessed the truth. 'Between you and me,' he whispered, 'it's the proceeds of crime. It was recovered from a raid on a drugs house.'

'It's evidence?'

'There was an administrative mix-up. If we enter the cash

into evidence now, it will only serve to undermine our case and the bad guys will get to walk free.'

Vicedo thought about it. 'You messed up and now you're using me to help cover it up.'

'I see it more as a kind of win-win but, yes, a couple of mistakes were made when it came to maintaining the chain of custody.'

The nun stared at the envelope for several more seconds before slipping it into her pocket. 'The Network thanks you for your donation.'

'For the *anonymous* donation,' Carlyle reminded her. 'If anyone were ever to ask, I trust the Network would protect the identity of a generous benefactor who wished to remain unknown.'

Vicedo confirmed that it would. 'After all,' she said primly, 'protecting the guilty is sometimes part of the job.'

'The urn's still sitting on my desk. What d'you think I should do with the ashes?'

'Huh?' Focusing on a crossword puzzle, Helen made no pretence of having been listening from the other end of the sofa.

'Never mind, I'll sort it out.' Carlyle fiddled with his phone. 'Have you got the money from Vicky Dalby-Cummins's will yet?'

'Not yet.' His wife looked at him over the top of her newly acquired reading glasses. 'Imogen Edelman's on long-term sick leave with stress. They need to find a new executor.'

'How long's that going to take?'

'Dunno. Months? Years? In the meantime, the money sits in a bank account earning zero interest.'

'You seem very philosophical about it.'

'What can I do?' Helen tentatively filled in an answer. 'Anyway, I'm used to people letting me down. When your own husband fails to step up to the plate, why should you expect anybody else to deliver?'

'That's a bit harsh.' Carlyle bridled. 'I didn't let you down.'

'You didn't catch Patrick Dalby.'

'No need.' Carlyle had been informed by the local police that Dalby and his boyfriend, the lawyer Colin Spooner, had been found hacked to death in a Monterrey motel room. 'The case is *closed*.'

'Do you know what happened yet?' Helen asked.

'I'd like to think it was a crime of passion on Spooner's part – he caught up with Dalby and savagely chopped him up into chunks – but the local cops reckon it was a robbery gone wrong.' Dave Holland was as delighted by the news as Carlyle himself. The chief inspector immediately declared the case closed and went on holiday. 'Either way, job done.'

'It's not the same as bringing him to justice,' Helen insisted.

It's better, if you ask me. 'You'd have thought it would be enough to solve Imogen's stress problems.'

'John,' she tutted, 'you are such a total Philistine. Mental health is a serious matter.'

'The woman,' Carlyle intoned, 'should pull herself together. It's over.'

'You're winding me up.'

'No, seriously. You can't be a victim all your life.'

'For a long while, I'd have imagined you can't be an idiot all your life but now I'm beginning to wonder.' Helen chuckled to herself. She pointed towards the kitchen with her pen. 'See if you can go and ever-so-slightly redeem yourself by making me a cup of green tea.'

Energised by the prospect of salvation, he jumped to his feet. 'Sure thing.'

By the time he returned, Helen had given up on the crossword and was watching some reality TV show, a bunch of Barbie lookalikes sitting round a swimming pool in tiny bikinis. He settled in for a spot of gawking just as Helen began channel surfing. 'Another problem's resolved itself.' Taking a sip of her tea, she gave a murmur of approval. 'Chris Sandland's resigned.'

'Better late than never.' Carlyle was pleased the predatory doctor would be one less thing for Helen to worry about.

She named another big charity. 'He's got a job in the Philippines.'

'They took him on?' Carlyle was genuinely shocked. 'Didn't you tell them that Sandland's a sex offender?'

'Nothing was proven,' Helen replied. 'He's already left, so the disciplinary process has lapsed. The investigation was never completed.'

'But you didn't think you should have a quiet word with his new employers?'

'The lawyers told us to play it straight.'

'More like passing the buck.'

'Yeah, well . . .' Alighting on some property programme, Helen placed the remote on the coffee table. 'In the words of Commander J. Carlyle, "Shit happens".'